Critical acclaim for David Baldacci's novels

'Baldacci is the master of American detective stories'
Jeffrey Archer

'One of his finest books. Great character, great story, great portrait of an era'
Bill Clinton

'*One Good Deed* represents David Baldacci's move into historical crime with a new character, ex-jailbird Aloysius Archer . . . Unsurprisingly, the talented Baldacci proves to be as adept in this new venture as he is in his contemporary-set novels'
Financial Times

'A mile-a-minute read that proves once again why David Baldacci has readers the world over flocking for more'
Jane Harper, *New York Times* bestselling author of *The Dry*

'Alternately chilling, poignant, and always heart-poundingly suspenseful'
Scott Turow, *New York Times* bestselling author

'As ever, Baldacci keeps things moving at express-train speed . . . this one will whet appetites for the next appearance of his agent hero'
Daily Express

'A typically twisty plot never flags, and benefits from having the likeably offbeat sleuth (whose gifts include synaesthesia and photographic memory) as its pivot'
The Sunday Times

'Already among the world's bestselling writers, Baldacci hardly needs to prove himself but he's created one of the most intriguing, complex anti-heroes . . . Impossible to put down, especially because of Decker, who weaves a powerful spell'
Daily Mail

'If you're wondering why David Baldacci is considered the best, look no further than *Long Road to Mercy*. It should come as no shock that a thriller writer for the ages has created a character for the ages!'
Gregg Hurwitz, the *New York Times* bestselling author of *Orphan X*

The Edge

David Baldacci is one of the world's bestselling and favourite thriller writers. A former trial lawyer with a keen interest in world politics, he has specialist knowledge in the US political system and intelligence services, and his first book, *Absolute Power,* became an instant international bestseller, with the movie starring Clint Eastwood a major box office hit. He has since written more than fifty bestsellers, featuring, most recently, Travis Devine, Mickey Gibson, Amos Decker and Aloysius Archer. David is also the co-founder, along with his wife, of the Wish You Well Foundation®, a nonprofit organization dedicated to supporting literacy efforts across the US. Still a resident of his native Virginia, he invites you to visit him at DavidBaldacci.com and his foundation at WishYouWellFoundation.org.

KILLER TWISTS. HEROES TO BELIEVE IN.
TRUST BALDACCI.

By David Baldacci

Travis Devine series

(Retired from the Army's most prestigious special ops force, this is a man with a nose for trouble)

The 6:20 Man • The Edge

Amos Decker series

(A damaged but brilliant special agent who possesses an extraordinary set of skills)

Memory Man • The Last Mile • The Fix
The Fallen • Redemption • Walk the Wire
Long Shadows

Aloysius Archer series

(A former soldier and wrongfully convicted ex-prisoner with a strong moral compass)

One Good Deed • A Gambling Man • Dream Town

Atlee Pine series

(A tenacious female FBI special agent assigned to the wilds of the western US)

Long Road to Mercy • A Minute to Midnight
Daylight • Mercy

Will Robie series featuring Jessica Reel

(A highly trained CIA assassin and his deadly fellow agent)

The Innocent • The Hit • The Target

The Guilty • End Game

John Puller series

(A gifted investigator with an unstoppable drive to find out the truth)

Zero Day • The Forgotten • The Escape

No Man's Land • Daylight

King and Maxwell series

(Two disgraced Secret Service agents turn their skills to private investigation)

Split Second • Hour Game • Simple Genius

First Family • The Sixth Man • King and Maxwell

The Camel Club series

(An eccentric group of social outcasts who seek to unearth corruption at the heart of the US government)

The Camel Club • The Collectors • Stone Cold

Divine Justice • Hell's Corner

Shaw series

(A mysterious operative hunting down the world's most notorious criminals)

The Whole Truth • Deliver Us from Evil

Vega Jane series

(The bestselling young adult adventure series)

Vega Jane and the Secrets of Sorcery

Vega Jane and the Maze of Monsters

Vega Jane and the Rebels' Revolt

Vega Jane and the End of Time

Other novels

Absolute Power • Total Control

The Winner • The Simple Truth • Saving Faith

Wish You Well • Last Man Standing

The Christmas Train • True Blue

One Summer • Simply Lies

Short stories

Waiting for Santa • No Time Left • Bullseye

The Final Play (previously published as

The Mighty Johns)

DAVID BALDACCI

The Edge

PAN BOOKS

First published 2023 by Grand Central Publishing, USA

First published in the UK 2023 by Macmillan

This paperback edition first published 2024 by Pan Books
an imprint of Pan Macmillan
The Smithson, 6 Briset Street, London EC1M 5NR
EU representative: Macmillan Publishers Ireland Ltd, 1st Floor,
The Liffey Trust Centre, 117–126 Sheriff Street Upper,
Dublin 1, D01 YC43
Associated companies throughout the world
www.panmacmillan.com

ISBN 978-1-5290-6211-3

1 3 5 7 9 8 6 4 2

A CIP catalogue record for this book is available from the British Library.

Typeset in Bembo by Jouve (UK), Milton Keynes
Printed and bound by CPI Group (UK) Ltd, Croydon, CR0 4YY

To the memory of Lee Calligaro,
a man who taught me a lot,
and the finest trial lawyer I've ever known

The Edge

1

Passenger train travel was not known to be particularly dangerous, especially in Europe where the machines soared like the wind on rigorously sculpted rails that translated to silky smooth rides. There were many departures a day between Geneva and Milan operated by several railway companies; one could travel early in the morning or later at night. The trains ran at a maximum speed of two hundred kilometers per hour, while their passengers napped, worked, binged shows on streaming platforms, or ate and drank in considerable comfort. This particular ride was a bullet-nosed silver Astoro tilt train operated by Trenitalia. None of the hundred-plus passengers was contemplating dying today.

Except for one.

As far as Travis Devine was concerned this ride was fraught with peril of the kind that would not send you to a hospital, but rather a half dozen feet into the cold earth. The source of the danger had nothing to do with the train. It had been ferreted out by his well-honed situational awareness, which had led him to conclude that his life was in imminent jeopardy.

The trip from Geneva to Milan contained beautiful scenery: the soaring, snow-capped Swiss Alps, the lush, verdant valleys, immaculate, aromatic vineyards, two pristine lakes, and the quaint, picturesque villages of Europe ladled in between the two venerable cities. Devine cared nothing about this as he sat in his first-class seat upholstered in brown leather staring at seemingly nothing, while actually taking in everything inside the train car. And there was a lot to observe.

Devine checked his watch. On some trains this trip could take five hours and a quarter, but he was on an express ride that would do it in just under four. He had ninety minutes of that trip left, and maybe that same number of ticks to live. Devine would have preferred a packed train car, but his tight escape from Geneva had not allowed for any latitude on the travel time, and this early in the morning there were only three other passengers in the first-class car. The attendants had already been through checking tickets. Despite this being first class, food was not served at the seat, but there was a dining car between the first- and second-class sections. The attendants were now off somewhere else as the train had settled into the second half of its journey south.

Alpha, Bravo, and Charlie. It was how the former U.S. Army Ranger Devine referred to the three other passengers. Two men, one woman. Not passengers, at least not to him.

Adversaries. Bogies. The enemy.

The men were sitting together in seats facing each

other, forward of Devine's position, near the front of the car. The woman was on the other side of the aisle, two up from him. She looked like a student. Textbooks stacked high, a bulky rucksack in a storage rack behind her; she was drawing something in a sketchbook. But Devine had been fooled by people posing as students before.

The men wore thick overcoats against the climate just outside the slender train windows. Overcoats that could hide a lot.

Devine had gotten up and gone to the bathroom twice now, but only once to relieve himself; the other was solely for recon. He had also gotten some food in the dining car and brought it back to his seat. Each time after returning, Devine had glanced at his gear bag, which was behind him on a luggage rack.

And the third time he saw what he thought he would.

On his phone he brought up his train's journey, saw its exact route, its progression, and most critically its timing. Of particular note was the Simplon Tunnel, which they would enter after passing through the Swiss town of Brig. When they exited the tunnel they would be in Italy. The article he was now reading said that the tunnel was twelve miles long and would take the train eight minutes to pass through. The tunnel had opened in 1906 and had given its name to perhaps the most famous train in the world, the Simplon-Orient-Express.

Devine wasn't interested in the history; he was focused on the tunnel.

He texted a high-priority message to an interested party and then checked his watch.

He had caught Alpha and Bravo staring at him, at different times, but he had made no reaction. These were known, in Devine's world, as *target* glances. Charlie, who was wearing a Real Madrid ballcap, had never looked at him, but she had surreptitiously eyed the two men while getting something from her bag. Her movements were mildly tensed, even robotic, he'd observed. She was trying overly hard to appear normal, which was causing her anxiety. Stress activated the sympathetic nervous system, the flight-fight-or-freeze part of the body that present-day humankind could thank its cavemen ancestors for. Fear did things to a body physiologically. The mind could screw with you in ways you could hardly imagine. In trying to save you, its stressor signals could actually kill you with a heart attack or render you incapable of saving yourself. Or, in his case, blow a plan to kill someone right out of the water, and give the potential victim a chance to survive.

Devine analyzed the situation exactly as he had been trained to do, every contingency, every weak point. The men had never removed their overcoats even though the climate inside was quite comfortable. In fact, Devine had taken his parka off because he had felt warm.

Keeping their hands in their pockets, in particular, was an informed tell of malevolent intent, because hands were a necessary accompaniment to a primary weapon, usually a gun. And they had target-glanced Devine not once but twice. Finally, they had never left their seats as far as he could tell. There were no food or drink containers at their tables. That completed the Rule of Three for Devine. A trio of behavior patterns that were out of the ordinary meant you needed to come up with a plan if you wanted to walk away under your own power.

Well, I've got at least four warning signs here, because of what I saw on my gear bag, so I need to get my shit together.

Devine checked his watch once more and then eyed his bag. After he'd gone to the dining car he'd come back to find that the zipper was three teeth above where he had left it; and, in just the right light, he had seen the whorls of a thumbprint on the pull tab, a thumbprint that was assuredly not his. There was nothing in his bag other than clothes and a toiletry kit; otherwise, he never would have left it unguarded. He was also kicking himself for not bringing a gun with him on this trip, but that would have been problematic for a number of reasons.

At the border station of Domodossola a contingent of the Swiss Guard boarded to do a customs check. Devine was asked if he had anything to declare and how much cash he had on his person, and he had to show his passport. He watched carefully without seeming to as they asked the same of the other three passengers. He couldn't see the passports of the two men, but the woman's appeared to be a post-Brexit UK blue and gold, which mimicked the original colors that had been in place on British passports since 1921.

Later, he eyed the window as the train began slowing.

They pulled into the town of Brig. No one got on in first class, and no one got off, except for the Swiss Guard contingent. For a moment Devine thought about exiting the train, too, or telling them of his concerns with the other passengers. However, he had his plan now and he was sticking to it. And he wasn't trusting anyone right now, not even the Swiss Guard. The opponents he was battling had the resources to buy pretty much anyone and anything.

And these foes of his had great incentive to wish Devine harm. Working on behalf of the United States, Devine had helped foil a ballsy attempt by some powerful if unscrupulous interests to promote global unrest for pure profit, with the added kicker of overthrowing several governments hostile to the players behind this scheme. It seemed as long as people lusted for wealth and power, this crap would just keep happening. And one day they might just succeed in taking over the world, thought Devine.

The train glided away from the station. The two attendants came through, and then, seeing no new passengers, or anything that needed their attention, other than Devine handing one of them the trash from his meal, they left through the opposite end of the train car to do whatever attendants did when their official work was done.

The train speed was posted on a digital screen attached to the bulkhead at the front of the car. Devine watched it rise to 180 kilometers an hour before it started to drop. He did the mile-to-kilometer calculation in his head to arrive at the length of time the train would be in the Simplon Tunnel.

Twelve miles is nineteen kilometers. Doing that in eight minutes would mean a constant speed of . . . right.

He looked at the screen again. One hundred and sixty kilometers . . . one fifty-three . . . one forty-two point . . .

He put on his parka and rose just as the train entered the tunnel; now the only real illumination came from the interior car lights. Devine strode up the aisle to the toilet in the connecting vestibule. As he passed the woman he glanced down at what she was drawing in charcoal.

Okay, that makes sense. And it's nice to have at least partial confirmation.

But the real proof is about to come, and it will be unequivocal.

Devine started to combat-breathe: inhale for a four count, hold for four, exhale for four, and hold for four. Repeat. This would stop his sympathetic nervous system from kicking on, wiping out his peripheral vision, blowing to shit his fine motor skills, and turning him into a big dumb animal just waiting to be killed. He would die one day just like everyone else, but it would never happen like that.

He passed by Alpha and Bravo, neither of whom looked at him. The automatic doors slid open with a hydraulic sigh, and Devine entered the vestibule. The toilet was off to the right, just out of eyeline of the passengers.

A few moments later the toilet door opened and a few moments later it closed.

The big men rose as though tied together by string and headed after Devine.

As they walked they screwed suppressor cans onto the muzzles of overkill German-made machine pistols pulled from their overcoat pockets. They reached the vestibule, where they could hear water running, and someone talking inside the toilet. They took aim and fired right through the flimsy toilet door. The sounds of the suppressed rounds were covered by the enhanced roar of the train going through the tunnel, which was why they had waited until now to do the deed. They shot in tight patterns, high to low and in between, followed by crisscrossed streams; they were fields of fire that left no room for survival in the confined space. With sixty rounds total, death of the target was guaranteed.

While Bravo covered him, Alpha nudged open the wrecked door, just to make sure, since their kill contract required it, along with an iPhone pic of the corpse texted to their employer.

However, all he saw was an empty toilet with the water tap wedged on. And a phone on the floor and leaning against the wall next to the toilet; a podcast was playing on the device.

At that moment the door to the storage closet opposite the toilet swung open and caught Bravo at the right temple.

Having let them empty out their weapons, Devine was now the predator. Where each man stood Devine's goal was to claim that ground. And the only way to do that was to go *through* them.

Devine opened his campaign with twin-thumb eye gouges that blinded Bravo. Devine next formed a V with his hand, the thumb on one side and the four fingers on the other, and slammed the hard groove of the flesh between them against the man's throat, collapsing his trachea. This was followed by twin crushing elbow strikes to the right side of the cervical spine that snapped two of the man's vertebrae, cutting off his brain from the rest of his body. He dropped to the floor out of the fight and also out of life. This continuous, fluid movement had taken all of four seconds.

Devine next trapped a stunned Alpha and his machine pistol against the doorjamb of the toilet as the man tried to slap in a fresh mag. Devine made the gun fall from his hand by wrenching it downward and then to the side past the joint's limits with cartilage-cracking torque. Alpha should have already reloaded and attempted to shoot Devine, but the man's breathing was ragged as his adrenal glands flooded his bloodstream with adrenaline, fouling his mind-body connection. His pupils went from two millimeters to nine in less than a breath; his peripheral vision was completely blown. Devine already knew he was going to win this fight, because none of that was happening to him. His cognitive, and hence his fighting, skills were operating fine.

Alpha awkwardly swung at Devine and caught him a glancing blow on the jaw. It was not hard enough to do any real damage, and the panicked man had forced himself off balance with the move. Two punishing elbow slams to the exposed right kidney dropped Alpha to his knees. Devine grabbed him by the collar and flung him headfirst against the train wall once and then again. The desperate man, perhaps sensing his own imminent death, pulled a knife and spun around, and the blade slashed against Devine's arm. But his aim was shaky and thus off, and Devine's thick parka took most of the damage.

Okay, time to end this. And him.

Devine broke the man's grip on the knife and it clattered to the floor. He then slapped the man's right ear with such force, the eardrum burst. The man seized up, presenting his face directly to Devine, who used a palm strike on his nose, hitting him once and then again with the cup of his hand, releasing all the kinetic energy from his brawny arm, shoulder, broad back, and thrust hip. This streamlined attack delivered massive torque that propelled the nose's brittlely sharp cartilage straight into Alpha's soft brain tissue. He dropped to the floor face first. Just to be certain, Devine reached down and broke the man's neck in the exact way the U.S. Army had taught him.

Devine dragged both dead men and their weapons into the toilet, turned off the water, retrieved his phone, and wedged the shot-riddled door shut.

Fighting wasn't just knowing certain techniques, although that was important; it was mostly an evolved state of mind. Without that, enhanced hand-to-hand combat skills meant squat because you would be too cowed to employ them. And the very concept of *self-defense* was a losing proposition, pretty much conceding the field and making you a victim in waiting. You didn't defend, you attacked. You didn't stop someone from hurting or killing you. *You* hurt or *you* killed. *Them.*

Rubbing his bruised jaw and gingerly touching his cut arm, which he instinctively knew wasn't that serious, he reentered the train car to see Charlie staring at him.

"What happened?" she exclaimed, her eyes agog. "What was that noise?"

All right, thought Devine, *this is where the rubber meets the road.*

As he walked toward her Devine glanced for a moment in the train window, which reflected the interior because they were still in the Simplon Tunnel for at least another few minutes. He saw what he needed to see.

He shrugged. "Two guys. Real mess in the toilet. Going to be quite a cleanup."

"My goodness. Is there anything I can do?"

Her neck muscles were now relaxed, he noted, pupils normal, breathing the same. She was a cut above the deceased goons back there.

Devine stopped next to her, looked down at the drawing, and said, "Yeah, you could explain why you've been sitting here for over two hours working away and you haven't added a damn thing to your sketch."

She half rose and swung the long-bladed knife up from her lap, but Devine had already seen the weapon in the window reflection. He didn't waste any time on a defensive block. He simply clocked her in the jaw, lifting her far smaller body off the floor and knocking her against the wall. She slumped down into unconsciousness from the force of his blow and her collision with the wall. Devine momentarily pondered whether to finish the job. But she was young and might repent of her evil ways. He took the knife, slid her ballcap down, draped her hair around her slender shoulders, and propped her up against her seat as though she were merely napping.

He grabbed his gear bag and walked into the dining car, and then through the second-class carriages until he reached the last car, where he slipped her knife into a trash receptacle. The train cleared the tunnel, and when it slowed and stopped at Stresa, the last station before Milan, Devine got off. The text he had sent earlier paid dividends when the black sedan picked him up. The driver would take Devine the rest of the way to Milan. There he would catch a flight back to the United States, where another mission surely awaited.

As he glanced back at the train, Devine wondered whether he had made a mistake in allowing the woman to live.

The answer wouldn't be long in coming.

2

Sitting in a tacky office in a 1960s-era strip mall in Annandale, Virginia, Emerson Campbell was not a happy man.

He was a retired Army two-star and, like Travis Devine, Ranger tabbed and scrolled, meaning he had graduated from Ranger School and then been accepted into the elite Seventy-Fifth Ranger Regiment, the Army's most prestigious and demanding special ops force. His gunmetal-gray, closely cropped hair and weathered, grim features spoke of a lifetime of discipline and heightened professionalism. And, perhaps most tellingly, all the shit he had seen fighting on behalf of his country through a number of wars and also under-the-radar operations the public would never know about.

Devine sat on the other side of the desk and took in the man who, several months before, had recruited him to serve in the Office of Special Projects under the massive bureaucratic dome of Homeland Security.

Special Projects, thought Devine. *It sounds like we plan office parties and cotillions*.

"It's a shitshow, Devine. The Italian and Swiss governments have filed official complaints. Two dead guys in a shot-up train toilet between their countries. Not a good optic."

"It's a better optic than *one* dead guy, meaning me. IDs on the corpses?"

Campbell shrugged. "Kazakhstan muscle, no more, no less. They've killed at least twenty people. All wired funds upon proof of the kill, no traceable interaction with whoever hired them. No way to dig beyond that, which is the whole point."

"Glad I denied them the twenty-first. And the woman?"

"There was no woman found there," said Campbell. "She must have recovered and high-tailed it out of there."

"CCTV?"

"Working on it, though the Italians and Swiss are not exactly too cooperative right now."

Devine shook his head. *Knew I should have taken her out. But she was unconscious and no threat to me.*

He caught Campbell studying him. "I know it was a hard call, Devine. Don't know what I would have done."

"Well, I gave you a description. Maybe your people can run her down."

"Now, let's focus on your new mission."

"I don't get a couple days off?" said Devine, only half-jokingly.

"You can rest when you're dead."

"Yeah, that's what they told me in the Army, too."

Campbell said, "I emailed you the briefing doc. Pull it up."

Devine opened the attachment to the email on his

phone and gazed at the photo of a lovely woman in her late thirties with smooth, pale skin, blonde hair, and deep-set, intelligent eyes that seemed to shimmer with unsettling intensity in the midst of all the fine pixels.

Campbell said, "That's Jennifer Silkwell. You heard of the Silkwells?"

"No, but I'm sure I'll learn everything about them before this is over."

"Curtis Silkwell was the senior U.S. senator from Maine. His great-great-grandfather made several fortunes, shipping, fishing, real estate, agriculture. All of that wealth is now mostly gone. They have the old homestead in Maine, but that's about it."

"He *was* a senator?"

"He resigned during his third term. Alzheimer's, which has gotten progressively worse. He was treated at Walter Reed before it became clear there was nothing that could be done. He's currently at a private facility in Virginia awaiting the end."

"He was treated at Walter Reed because he was a senator?"

"No, because he was a soldier. He retired from the Marines as a one-star before jumping into politics, getting married, and having a family." Campbell shot Devine a scrutinizing glance. "Full disclosure, Curt is one of my best friends. We fought together in Vietnam. He saved my life twice."

"Okay."

"So this is personal for me, Devine."

"Yes, sir."

"His wife, Clare, divorced him right after he won his last reelection. Between you and me, I think she could see what was coming and decided to bail. So much for 'in sickness and in health.' "

"Where is she now?"

"Already remarried to some rich guy in DC who isn't worthy of polishing Curt's combat boots."

"So, the case?" prompted Devine, wanting to push Campbell off the personal edge and back onto the mission-driven one.

"Go to page five of your briefing. Jennifer is the eldest daughter of Curtis and Clare. She worked for CIA, mostly in field operations, though she once served as a liaison to the White House for Central Intelligence. She was a quick climber and incredibly talented, and she will be sorely missed."

Devine scanned page five. "What happened to her?"

"Someone killed her, four days ago. Up in Maine where she was visiting her old hometown." The man's voice cracked before he finished speaking.

Devine lifted his gaze. Campbell's face was flushed and his bottom lip was trembling.

"I held her in my arms when she was a baby. I was her damn *godfather*." He swiped tears away and, composed, he continued. "Curt got started late on his family. He was nearly forty when Jenny was born. Clare was a lot younger. She was still in college when they got married."

"They have any leads on who might have killed her?"

"None that we know of."

"And our interest?"

"Jenny Silkwell was a valuable asset of this country. She was privy to many of our most precious national secrets. We need to know if her death was connected to that, and whether anyone was able to gain any information that would jeopardize our interests. Her personal laptop has been found at her home, and her government-issued phone was there as well. But her CIA laptop was not found at her office or her home, and neither was her personal phone. The geolocators on the devices have been switched off. That's normally the case for people like Jenny, unless she's in an operational area where orders or logistics require she keep them on. The data is mostly cloud based now, but she might have something on her hard drive or on her phone that is sensitive. And we don't want anyone using her devices to backdoor into our clouds."

"So I'm heading to where she was killed in Maine?"

"Yes. Putnam, Maine. But not yet. I want you to talk to Clare first in DC. She may know something helpful. *Then* you head to Maine. The details of Jenny's death are contained in your briefing book, pages eight through ten."

Devine read quickly, but comprehensively, just as the Army had trained him. In combat, time was not on your side. But neither was skipping over something in a briefing that might prove catastrophic later.

"The shooter didn't police their brass?"

"Right. And, technically, the casing was polymer, not brass."

Devine looked surprised because he was. "A *polymer* casing?"

"Yes. It expands and then contracts in the chamber immediately. Brass just expands, as you well know. Less degradation on the equipment, because the polymer insulates the heat from the chamber."

"And less heat and friction reduces choke rate," said Devine, referring to the hesitation of the weapon in firing due to those factors.

"The Army's been slowly moving away from brass. Hell, they've been wedded to it since before the Spanish-American War, so it's about damn time. And the Marines are testing polymer casings for their .50-cal. M2 machine gun. And the Brits are looking at polymer too, for their 5.56 mm rounds."

"A good thing, too. Brass adds a lot of weight to your gear pack."

"That's why they're making the switch. What with smartphones and handheld computers and more weaponry and optics, the Army carry load is up to about a hundred pounds now for each soldier. Switching from brass to polymer is a cost-effective way of lightening the load. For the Marines, a forty-eight-box pallet of the .50-cal. in polymer weighs nearly seven hundred pounds less than brass. And there's even the possibility of 3D-printing repair parts in the field because the casings are recyclable."

As he'd been speaking Devine had continued to read. He looked up. "It was a .300 Norma mag round."

"Yes," replied Campbell.

"And the head stamp shows it's a U.S. military round."

"Army snipers and special ops guys chamber the Norma in the Barrett MK22 rifle."

Devine nodded. "They switched from the 6.5 Creedmoor round *after* I mustered out. But does the Army already use polymer casings for the .300 Norma?"

"No, Devine. There are tests being run at various Army facilities across the country chambering the Norma and other ordnance with a *polymer* casing, but it has not been officially deployed. You know how that goes. Army needs to shoot a shit ton of it under every conceivable combat environment before it has any chance of getting approved for mass deployment."

"Who's the manufacturer?"

"Warwick Arsenal. A small firm out of Georgia."

"So, the question becomes: How did a still-in-testing .300 Norma polymer round produced by a firm in Georgia end up at a crime scene in Maine?"

Campbell said, "We've spoken with the people at Warwick. They have checked and rechecked their inventory and found nothing amiss. But to me that's meaningless because they've shipped hundreds of thousands of these rounds to Army facilities throughout the country, with hundreds of personnel taking part in the testing. There is no way that every single round can be accounted for. Proverbial needle in a haystack."

"So someone could have pocketed the polymer casing and given it to someone and then it goes through various hands and ends up being used to kill Jenny Silkwell. Was it important she was shot with that particular bullet? Did she have any involvement with its development?"

"None. And I have no idea if the use of that particular bullet is significant or not. That's your job to find out during your investigation. By the way, the local cops are also working the case. You'll have to team with them."

"And why would they team with me?"

Campbell took from his desk drawer what looked like a black leather wallet and slid it across. "Here's why."

Devine opened what turned out to be a cred pack, complete with shiny badge, and examined it. He looked up in surprise. "I'm a special investigator with Homeland Security? Seriously?"

"Your cover is rock-solid."

"Only I'm not a trained investigator."

Campbell gave Devine a drill sergeant death stare. "Don't sell yourself short. You carried on investigations in the Middle East in addition to your combat duties. And you did a pretty damn good job of sleuthing back in New York on the Brad Cowl case. And you've done stellar work with the other assignments I've given you. Now, you are to find out who killed Jenny and why. And determine if any of our national security interests have been compromised. And find her laptop and phone."

"Well, that sounds simple enough," said Devine dryly.

"Rise to the challenge, soldier," retorted Campbell.

"Why don't the feds have a joint op platoon of agents on this? Central Intelligence goes scorched earth when one of its own goes down. And the FBI, too."

"CIA has no jurisdiction on American soil. And if we deploy an army of FBI the press will start to pry and word will get out. Then our enemies could see us as weakened and themselves emboldened. Jenny Silkwell might very well have been killed because of something having absolutely nothing to do with her status with CIA. If so, we want to go in stealth and stay that way if the facts on the ground allow. So right now you, Devine, *are* the 'army.' "

"And if my 'rock-solid' cover gets blown?"

"We never heard of you."

3

A light drizzle was falling as Devine pulled through the open gates of Clare Robards's mansion in Kalorama in northwest DC. It was one of the most expensive areas in the capital city, with the median price of a home well north of seven figures. *Kalorama*, Devine had learned, was Greek for "beautiful view." And it *was* beautiful, if one had the hefty entrance fee.

Embassy Row was on nearby Massachusetts Avenue, and the Dutch and French ambassadors' official residences were in the vicinity, along with thirty foreign embassies. Jeff Bezos also had a home nearby that he had laid out twenty-three million for, and then bought the place next door for another five mil. Billionaires apparently needed a lot of room, or else a healthy buffer from the merely rich, Devine thought.

At that level it's just Monopoly money anyway.

The Robards's mansion was substantial, made of stone and large rustic timbers with small windows and cone-topped metal turrets. The property had wide, sloping lawns, and mature trees and plantings. No money spared and no detail overlooked to create a display of subdued, old money wealth that judiciously managed not to overwhelm with inflated grandiosity.

He had phoned ahead, so the well-dressed professional-looking woman who answered the door led Devine directly down a long marble-floored hall to a set of imposing solid oak doors.

She knocked and a woman's cultured voice from inside the room said authoritatively, "Come in."

And so Devine stepped into, perhaps, the Lioness's Den.

Clare Robards was perched regally on a settee in a room that was lined with shelves, which were, in turn, filled with leatherbound books. Against one wall a small bar was set up. Was it his imagination or did Robards's gaze slide toward it?

The lady's light green dress was exquisitely tailored to her thin, petite frame. She had allowed her shoulder-length hair to turn an elegant white.

She fiddled with a strand of small lustrous pearls and looked everywhere except at Devine. The woman was clearly uncomfortable with his presence here. She wore little makeup, and the dark circles under her reddened eyes spoke of long bouts of crying.

Maybe she thinks if she ignores me, her eldest daughter wouldn't be dead.

"Ms. Robards, I'm Travis Devine with Homeland Security."

"Yes, I know, Mr. Devine," she said in a low voice. "Please sit."

She finally looked at him—resignedly, Devine concluded.

"Would you like something hot to drink? It's quite chilly today."

"No thank you, I'm fine." He settled into a wingchair opposite her. "And I'm very sorry for your loss."

She twitched at his words, and closed her eyes for a moment. "We all thought Jenny was indomitable, a survivor. She had survived . . . much, until this ugly, ugly business."

"She had a stellar career, and a brilliant future in serving her country."

"That goddamned job cost my daughter her life," she barked. Then she quickly let the regal mask slide back down over her features. "I'm sorry," she said in a hushed voice.

"No reason to be." He glanced around. "Is your husband here?"

"Vernon is in Thailand, at least I think so. Business," she added with a touch of bitterness. "Apparently, for some people business and making money trumps all, even the *murder* of one's stepdaughter." She glanced at her lap and let her fingers intertwine as though she suddenly felt the need to hold on to herself. "It's funny, Mr. Devine."

"What is?"

"When I married Curt, he was already a war hero. This big strong marine that no enemy could defeat. And he was gone all the time, too. Not to make money, but to serve his country, like Jenny did. He survived that. And then he got into politics. Worked his way up and eventually ran for the Senate and won. And he was gone all the time, again, not for the money but to serve. And here's the funny thing." She paused and seemed to collect herself, running her fingers delicately along her expensive pearls. "The funny thing is, for the people left behind, the motivation doesn't matter. The result is the same: one is alone."

"I can see that."

She looked around at the tastefully decorated room in the luxurious mansion in the pricey, sought-after neighborhood with beautiful views. "And in case you're wondering, as so many have, no, the grass is not always greener."

"I understand that Jenny was not in full agreement with the divorce?" he said quietly.

"She hated me for it, plain and simple." Robards dropped her hand to her lap. "She and apparently everyone else thought I left Curt because of his illness. The fact was we had agreed to divorce a year before. But these things take time and he had an election coming up, so we made the mutual decision to wait. He won the race and we went our separate ways. Then he was diagnosed shortly thereafter and I became the thoughtless ex-wife."

"I suppose you could have halted the divorce proceedings," noted Devine.

"I'd already met Vernon and was engaged to him. We were waiting for the final decree to announce our impending wedding. And the truth was I had given Curt four decades of my life and three children. He had his twin careers. And me? I hadn't even started to live my life yet. So I decided to move forward and do just that before it was too late. Curt was going to receive the best care regardless." She glanced up. "I suppose you think me heartless, too?"

"While it may be tempting for many, judging others has never been a fascination of mine."

She nodded. "Now, how can I help you?"

"When was the last time you saw or spoke to your daughter?"

"I saw her at an event at the Senate to honor Curt's legacy about six months ago."

"Was that also the last time you spoke to her?"

Her gaze fell to her lap. "No. She actually called me recently. She said she was heading to Putnam. She grew up there, along with our other two children. An ancestor of Curt's, Hiram Silkwell, built the family home there. It's quite Gothic, and I think extraordinarily ugly. Curt kept paying the taxes on it until he became ill. He couldn't part with it, apparently. He was always a very nostalgic person, very much tied to the past in certain respects."

"Did she say why she was going there?"

"She said she had some unfinished business."

"What sort of business?" asked Devine sharply.

"She didn't say, and I didn't ask."

Devine looked skeptically at her.

She caught this look and explained, "Our relationship had changed, Agent Devine. She was a grown woman who no longer needed or wanted my advice or counseling."

"But she called you, even though you two were estranged. Must have been a reason."

"If there was it eluded me."

"Okay, any *guess* as to what she was referring to about the 'unfinished business'?"

"None."

"And your other children?"

"Dak and Alex. They still live in the family home."

"Any idea why they want to live in an ugly, old Gothic house?"

"They apparently like it there. I lived there with the kids while Curt was in Congress. Neither one of us wanted the children to be here, in the limelight."

"What do they do?"

"Alex is the youngest, and an artist. And an incredibly talented one who could make a fine living if she would ever get an agent. I've been told by old friends up there that she also teaches art in the public school on a part-time basis." She paused and smiled, but it was accompanied by a sad, bittersweet expression.

She said, "Jenny was the golden child. Brilliant, enormously driven, lovely, she had it all. But Alex was no slouch, either. She was more beautiful than Jenny, and smart, too. Because of her late birthday she was always the youngest in her class. Then, because of her ability, she skipped an entire grade in elementary school. Not even Jenny managed to do that," she added.

"And your son?"

"Dak has a tattoo parlor and some other business

interests up there. He's very entrepreneurial. I think he wants to make a zillion dollars to show he doesn't need any of us. He was in the Army but got discharged."

"Can I ask why?"

"Dak can tell you, if he wants."

"Could Jenny have been going to see them?"

"It's possible. I've tried to call both of them but they haven't gotten back to me."

"Were your kids close with one another?"

"They used to be. But life changes people, you know?"

"Yes, ma'am. But I guess Dak and Alex get along, if they live together."

"It's a big house," she said simply. "Big enough to feel like one is living alone."

"Where and when will the funeral take place?"

"There won't be one. In her will Jenny stipulated that she wanted to be cremated and her ashes scattered over the ocean. No ceremony, no fuss."

"I guess she was the sort to plan ahead?"

"I just wish she had managed to stay alive until long after I was dead and buried!"

"Well, she had no choice in the matter," he pointed out.

Sniffling, Clare said, "Curt doesn't even know she's gone."

Devine noted, "Maybe that's for the best. When was the last time you saw Alex or Dak?"

"It's been several years, actually. I suppose that qualifies as 'estranged,'" she added, closing her eyes, her features laden with misery.

"Ever since your divorce?"

"I suppose the two are intertwined," she said dully, opening her eyes and gazing off.

He rose. "Well, thank you for seeing me. If you think of anything else, please contact me." He handed her his card, on which the fresh ink seemed to glow.

She reached across, took the card, and then gripped his hand with surprising strength. "Please find out who took her away from me, Mr. Devine. Please."

He looked down at her. "I'll do my best, ma'am. I can promise you that."

4

The next morning Devine walked into a private care facility in northern Virginia with Emerson Campbell to visit Curtis Silkwell.

"Clare still visits him every week here," said Campbell as he held the door for Devine.

"Not so heartless then," replied Devine, drawing a tortured scowl from the other man.

"Heartless enough," Campbell shot back.

A nurse led them to a room in a secure "memory care" unit. The space was small and sparsely furnished and held, at least for Devine, a sense of marching in slow motion, a wait for the inevitability of death.

After the nurse left them, both men turned their attention to the frail figure in the bed. There were no tubes hooked up to him, though there was a machine monitoring his vitals.

"He's comfortable, in no pain, so they tell me. They're going to have to put a feeding tube in soon," said Campbell grimly. His voice carried a level of distress Devine had never heard before. "He's not eating. He doesn't think to when he's awake. Just stares at the offered food and then goes back to sleep. And when they do get some food in him, things get clogged and he has to be aspirated. He has a DNR in place and pretty soon they will wind things down."

They looked down at the shrunken, sleeping patient.

"I remember a six-two, two-hundred-and-twenty-pound wall of a man," added a hollow-voiced Campbell. "Leading his men into one hell after another and coming out victorious on the other side. Won every medal and commendation the Marines offered. He should have had a shoulder full of stars but he refused to play the necessary games."

"Same as you," noted Devine.

"He was more deserving," replied Campbell.

"To my mind, every person who puts on the uniform and picks up a weapon in defense of their country is deserving."

Silkwell stirred under the sheet and his eyes opened. He looked at neither of them, his unfocused gaze playing across the ceiling for a few moments before the eyes closed once more.

"He stopped recognizing me months ago," said Campbell. "The doctors say the progression is accelerating. No chance of recovery. Fucking disease."

Campbell led Devine out and quietly closed the door behind them before facing off with the younger man.

"I brought you here, Devine, because I wanted you to see a true American hero. And he deserves to have his daughter's murderer brought to justice."

"You have no confidence in the police up there?"

"Since it's a two-person department with few resources, no, my confidence level is not high. And if Jenny's death *is* connected to her work at CIA it comes under the feds' umbrella, not the locals'. But you have to snoop around first and find out something we can hang our jurisdictional hat on."

"So I'm to find the killer and ascertain if any secrets have been stolen?"

"If you find the killer we have lots of experts who can help us determine the secrets issue, or whether her death was retribution for something having to do with national security."

"The sister and brother who live up there in the old homestead, I suppose they're suspects? I told you Clare informed me Jenny was going up there to finish some old business."

"Yes, family, friends, strangers, foreigners—everyone is a suspect right now."

"And what if the killer is long gone by now?"

"We'll attack that bridge *if* we come to it."

Outside the facility, Campbell shook the younger man's hand. "I have no higher priority right now. Good luck. Many things tell me you're going to need it."

Campbell was driven off in a government SUV.

Devine stood in the parking lot for a few moments glancing back at the building where a doomed man didn't even know his eldest daughter had not survived him.

He knew this was personal to Campbell. And while Devine had to maintain a professional objectivity, he knew a certain element of this mission was now personal to him as well.

In his book a dying warrior deserved no less.

5

After a short, pinballing flight in high winds, the plane thudded onto the tarmac in Bangor, Maine. After deplaning, Devine grabbed his rental Tahoe and commenced the two-and-a-half-hour drive east to Putnam. The tiny hamlet was located on the rocky Atlantic coast and had fewer souls than the passengers on the United Airlines jumbo jet flight Devine had taken back from Italy.

The leaves had long since turned color and abandoned their respective trees and bushes. Devine's memories of a scorching summer in New York City and a mild fall in Europe had all been extinguished by the bitter cold here. His cable-knit sweater was underwhelming in its warmth factor.

He reached Machias, turned onto Route 1, and kept going north for a while until he turned off onto another road that took him east toward the world's second biggest ocean. He could already smell the briny air and feel the bite of the punishing wind that kept rocking the Tahoe. He looked at a long inlet the ocean had cut into the rocky shore and, despite the mission he was on, the serene view lent Devine some calm.

Before the storm?

Devine glanced at his gear pack. Inside, among other things, was his Glock nine-millimeter, a backup pistol, and extra ammo for both.

As Devine drove he went over in his mind the briefing details.

Jenny Silkwell had been an operations officer at CIA. Her focus for the past few years had been on the Middle East. Before that her area of involvement was the Russian Federation, and before that, South America. A gifted, natural linguist, she spoke fluent Spanish, Portuguese, Russian, and Polish, and through immersion classes she had learned Arabic and Farsi before moving on to the Middle East region. Her job had led her to travel all over the world to meet with the human intel on the ground that she had recruited to work with America.

And maybe that had placed a wicked bullseye on the back of Jenny Silkwell, because the Russians, as well as factions in the Middle East, were not shy about striking back against perceived enemies. The answer to her murder might well lie in Moscow, Tehran, or Damascus rather than Putnam, Maine.

He had read both the national and local accounts of the murder. The national news had sent crews up here and broadcast stories for a few days until they moved on to newer stories that would capture more eyeballs. He supposed if the killer were tracked down and arrested, the big guns would be back up here to report on it.

In contrast, the local news, such that it was, had continued to go full bore with the story. Devine could imagine that the unsolved murder of a CIA officer and daughter of a war hero and former U.S. senator, who was himself a scion of a prominent and formerly wealthy Maine family, would be the most newsworthy thing that had ever happened in Putnam.

Along the way he had passed signs that said he was on the Bold Coast Scenic Byway. And it fit the bill. As his journey brought him closer to the Gulf of Maine's shoreline, Devine, at intervals, saw narrow strips of sandy and pebble beaches as well as towering granite bluffs standing sentry along craggy coves filled with rock-strewn headlands and stout, robust greenery holding purchase on the saltwater-slicked rock wherever it could. There were also vast forests that reached to the horizon, and old orchards of fruitless trees leading right up to rocky cliffs standing firmly next to the water like silent sentries.

Finally, a weathered board on a rotting post announced the legal boundary of Putnam and stated its official population to be a few shy of 250. They must be hardy souls, thought Devine. The rugged topography and raw weather did not look like it was designed for the fainthearted.

He passed a young man in a New England Patriots ski cap riding a rusted bicycle that had no seat. That was followed by two young women astride mud-splattered ATVs puttering along. A battered 1980s-era station wagon slowly passed him going the other way. The driver had heavily wrinkled features and the hanging jowls of a Great Dane, and a head topped by fine snowy hair. He gave Devine a grim-faced once-over before he headed on down the road.

The Putnam Inn was located on the town's narrow main street, the asphalt barely two cars wide. Devine angled into a parking space and tugged out his bags.

He looked across the street to where a small harbor nearly encircled by chiseled granite bluffs was situated, with a slender outlet to the Gulf of Maine's slice of the ocean. There was also what looked to be a man-made breakwater to give added protection from storms. A number of boats were docked in slips weathered by the unforgiving elements, while others were moored out on the smooth, glassy water of the harbor. Men in heavy work clothing and calf-high waterproof boots were laboring on the docks and also on the boats, tying up ropes, lifting heavy boxes and metal cages, and scrubbing the grime and barnacles off raised hulls. It was a bustle of activity that was probably replicated up and down the coast here.

The smiling woman behind the front desk told Devine she was Patricia Kingman, the inn's owner.

"Welcome to Putnam. I'll apologize in advance if our service is not up to snuff. We're understaffed, it's why I'm manning the front desk. Nobody wants to work anymore. They blame it on COVID. I say it's just being lazy. The X, Y, and Z generations, or whatever they call themselves? No work ethic."

Devine, who was a member in good standing of the millennials, stayed silent as he signed in and produced his driver's license and credit card. He received his room key, one of the old-fashioned kind with a one-pound slug of lead attached.

"You can leave that weapon here when you go out," she quipped, eyeing the key with amusement. "Unless you want to do arm curls."

"I think I'll keep it with me, thanks," replied Devine, who would never leave such an open and easy invitation into his private space lying around.

Kingman's amused expression vanished as she first looked startled and then suspicious.

"What are you in town for, Mr. Devine? Can't be pleasure unless you like the inside of a freezer."

"A little business." He eyed her steadily. "I understand you had some trouble recently?"

"I guess you can call the murder of a poor young woman trouble, yes."

"What was her name again?"

"Jenny Silkwell."

"Wait, wasn't there a senator by that name from up here?"

"Curtis Silkwell. Jenny was his daughter. He got sick and had to resign. I knew Jenny since she was in pigtails and knee socks. Smart as a whip, pretty and nice as can be. She worked in Washington, DC." She glanced carefully around, as though there might be someone listening. "Some folks say she was a spy or some such for us."

"Do these 'folks' believe she was killed because of that?"

A stony expression slid down over the woman's features.

"Well, I can't see anyone from around here hurting one hair on Jenny's head. Everyone loved her."

Well, at least one person didn't, thought Devine. "So she grew up here?"

She nodded. "At the Silkwells' ancestral home, Jocelyn Point. Named after Hiram Silkwell's wife. He made money hand over fist well over a century ago, and built that place."

"Any Silkwells left here?"

"Alex, Jenny's younger sister, and her brother, Dak. They live at Jocelyn Point."

"I suppose Jenny came up to visit with them when she was killed?"

Kingman folded her arms over her chest and took a symbolic step back. "My, my, I can't imagine why I've been gabbing so much about the Silkwells to a complete stranger. You have a nice visit here, Mr. Devine. And just so you know, outsiders aren't usually welcome here."

"But I would imagine your entire business model depends on the exact opposite of that sentiment."

She twisted her mouth in displeasure. "Your place is right behind here, first cottage on the right."

She walked through a blue curtain set behind the front counter.

Devine grabbed his bags and off he went, a stranger in a place that didn't particularly care for them.

Story of my life.

6

The cottage was comfortably furnished, with a big four-poster bed being its chief feature with a duvet and matching canopy done in seascapes and lobsters. A blackened-faced wood-burning fireplace with a small stack of cedar logs and kindling set next to it in a wrought iron holder took up much of another wall.

He put his things away and laid out several telltale traps in case anyone breached his room while he was away. He then sat at a small desk set up by the window and looked over the briefing book on his phone.

Jenny Silkwell could have certainly made enemies in her line of work. But if a foreign government wasn't behind her death, who else would have the motive?

Well, that's what you're here to find out. So let's get to it.

He slipped his Glock into a belt holster, locked his door, deposited the one-pound lead slug key in his pocket, climbed into his Tahoe, and set off.

He drove slowly past the harbor and marveled at the beauty of nature's rock carvings. He saw a few boats puttering back in, the men on them looking bleary-eyed and exhausted, and smoking cigarettes and gulping bottled water, even in the cold.

Tough way to make a buck. Hope they scored big on whatever they were going out for.

He drove to Jocelyn Point along the winding coast road. As dusk set in, the equal parts grim and picturesque landscape assumed patches of pulsing darkness shouldered with sections still lit by the fading sun. Devine pulled out his military-grade optics and took a look.

Set far off the road on an otherwise deserted stretch of land, the home's backdrop was the black rock-strewn craggy coastline that the Atlantic pummeled unceasingly.

Devine had seen pictures of the home, but it hadn't done the place justice. The building itself looked like every haunted house you had seen in movies or on TV. Grim, stark, joyless, it stood like a defiant remembrance of a far more somber and unforgiving era.

Constructed of rough-hewn timbers and rugged dark stone that was probably locally quarried, Jocelyn Point possessed the tall, looming face of a hunk of marble statuary with a wooden-railed widow's walk at its zenith. Multiple turrets, both cone- and square-shaped, all topped by slate roofs fouled by the elements, stuck out here and there from the home's façade like wayward strands of hair. The exterior was covered with nature's makeup—chunks of moss and patches of lichen, which evidently flourished in the damp, briny air.

He saw other buildings dotting the large property. Some looked abandoned, others were falling down, but still others looked reasonably habitable. Maybe these were old servants' quarters, he thought, for when people actually had them on properties like this.

The grounds had been allowed to mostly go to ruin. The hefty wrought iron gates that had once been attached to stout stone pedestals—emblazoned with the letter *J* on one and the letter *P* on the other—were both hanging on to life by a single rusted hinge each.

The place had innumerable windows, all small, gleaming, and mullioned, like the eyes of a spider, with little ability to capture much sunlight but only to reflect it back. The large wooden door that was the main entrance to the place was battered and sullied by weather. Straggly, leafless trees stood next to the house, their bare limbs caressing the crudded walls with every passing breeze.

Devine lowered his optics as the sun fell rapidly into the pocket of the western sky. Darkening clouds scudded overhead as the northeasterly breeze stiffened. As he continued to watch, a light came on in a second-floor window. Devine once more lifted his optics to his eyes. The range and clarity on this piece of surveillance equipment was impressive. For what it had cost the government he knew it should be.

Twenty minutes later, as the darkness deepened, someone appeared at the lighted window, and Devine was quick to focus his device on the person.

Alexandra "Alex" Silkwell had blonde hair piled on top of her head, with a few tendrils slipping down to bookend her elegantly chiseled features. Her eyes were full of intensity, or at least it seemed to him that they were.

Devine noted all of these things secondarily. Chiefly, he was riveted by the fact that she wore no clothes.

Embarrassed, he lowered his optics but kept his unaided gaze on her, though he couldn't make out the finer details now.

Does she know she's being watched?

His was the only car out here. And she could obviously see it and its lights. Was she being defiant, giving the curious a show? Or did she not think anyone would be watching the house with the optics Devine was using?

Yeah, that might be it, thought a shamed Devine. *I'm a peeping Tom with next-gen hardware.*

He waited until the room went dark once more before driving off.

As he headed along the whipsawing coast road he wondered what Alex and Dak thought about the violent end of their older sibling's life.

He also wondered whether one of them had killed her. Or knew who had.

Dak had been in the Army, where he had obviously received extensive weapons instruction. Devine would have to find out why the Army and Dak Silkwell had parted company. The Army didn't give up its recruits easily. They didn't have nearly enough volunteers to fill the ranks, which had caused them to overlook things that in the not-too-distant past would have resulted in outright dismissal.

He stopped and sent off a text to Campbell asking for these details.

As he drove north to his prearranged meeting with the local cops, Devine thought back to the woman at the window of an ancient house that had long outlived its useful life and was aging with little grace; and yet two young people still resided there.

This case might turn out to be even more complicated than he had thought.

He checked his watch, hit the gas, and sped up. Time to go look at the body of a woman who should not be dead.

7

Devine had seen violent death in multiple countries and had caused some of them in his role as a soldier. In certain respects he had grown desensitized to it. Once you'd seen a human being shot up, blown up, or hacked to pieces, what was one more? They all bled and died pretty much the same.

He pulled into the parking lot of a funeral home named Bing and Sons. A police cruiser was parked near the front door. PUTNAM POLICE DEPARTMENT was emblazoned on the cruiser's side door, along with a picture of an eagle. The majestic bird's claws clenched an arrow shaft, its expression one of fierce determination.

The building looked to be originally 1950s construction. It had obviously been remodeled and expanded, Devine noted, with two relatively new wings and what looked to be a crematorium with a long chimney stack housed in a separate building in the rear.

He trudged across the asphalt, feeling the biting wind every step of the way as it pushed against him.

Before he could tug on the door, it opened, revealing a woman in a police officer's uniform and cap, who was standing just inside. No doubt she had been waiting for Devine.

She was in her thirties, shortish and thickly built, and, to Devine's eye, looked like she pumped some serious gym iron. She had on a long-sleeved shirt but no coat or jacket. The brown hair was clipped back. A Smith & Wesson .44 Magnum revolver rested in her holster. He didn't know the police still carried revolvers. But whatever she shot with that bazooka would not be getting back up, ever.

"You Travis Devine with Homeland Security?" she said shortly.

"I am."

"Let me see your ID," she demanded.

He showed her. "And you?" he said.

"Sergeant Wendy Fuss. Chief's with Françoise and the body. This way."

They began walking down the hall.

"Françoise?"

"Dr. Françoise Guillaume. She's the medical examiner for this area. Her grandfather and his brother started this funeral home. Passed it down to their sons. Now her brother, Fred Bing, runs it. But Françoise works here, too, in addition to being the local doctor."

"Busy lady. So did Dr. Guillaume perform the autopsy?"

She stopped and turned to him. "You shitting me?"

"I don't know what you mean."

"The fact is there was a pissing contest between your folks and ours. They brought someone up from DC to do the postmortem over in Augusta at the OCME, the Office of Chief Medical Examiner. Dr. Guillaume assisted because the chief medical examiner for Maine insisted. Jenny was killed here, making it *our* jurisdiction, *not* federal."

"Are the people from DC still here?"

"No, they flew in on a government jet, did the postmortem, and flew right back out. Showed me how my tax dollars are being spent." She looked Devine up and down in a disgusted manner. "And now you're here to do the job we're already doing."

"I was hoping we could collaborate."

"Sure you do. Feds are all the same. Think you're better'n the locals."

"Have you had much experience with the federal government?"

"The IRS. That was enough to last me the rest of my days."

She picked up her pace and Devine followed. He noticed that she was pigeon-toed and her left shoulder hung a bit lower than her right. Her gun belt squeaked as she walked, as did her rubber-soled shoes over the soft linoleum. That could give away your position and get you killed, but Devine did not think Fuss would be receptive to such *federal* criticism right now.

She reached a door down a short hall, pushed it open, and motioned Devine inside.

Fuss put out a blocking hand as he started to cross the threshold. "You seen a dead body before?" she asked in a brusque tone. "Don't want you puking on my shoes or passing out."

"I wouldn't worry about that if I were you," said Devine tightly.

Two people were waiting in an interior room off the one they had entered. They were standing next to a metal gurney with a sheet over the body. The room held the potent smells of death and chemicals.

Devine was introduced to Chief of Police Richard Wayne Harper, who was quick to tell Devine that he went by Richard, not Rich or Dick.

"Or 'Chief' will do just fine," he quipped, though the look he gave Devine held no humor.

He was in his late forties, paunchy, and around five ten. But he seemed light on his feet and moved with the nimbleness of a far younger man. His hair was thick, and the original brown was mixed liberally with gray. He wore no gun, but he did have a metal baton in a holder on his belt. His thick fingers hovered near it at all times. He seemed to exude electrical pulses of confidence with every breath.

Françoise Guillaume was also in her forties, an inch taller than Harper, and athletically lean, with auburn hair pulled back at her nape and secured with a band. Her eyes, active and intelligent, scanned Devine from behind tortoiseshell glasses strung on a synthetic cord. Her white lab coat only partially obscured her dark blue jacket and slacks.

She looked no-nonsense and proved it by saying, "Ready to get to it, Agent Devine?"

"I thought the autopsy was done in Augusta."

"It was. We transported Jenny's remains back here so that you could examine them."

"Okay, let's do it."

She lifted the sheet off Silkwell, former CIA ops officer and now a murder victim.

Devine ran his gaze down the woman's body. He thought for a moment of the woman's sister standing unclothed at the window. There the similarity ended. Alex Silkwell did not have a large exit wound in the back of her head that had removed a chunk of her brain along with her life. The small, blackened, and crusty entry wound dead center of the forehead didn't seem lethal enough to have killed her. Devine had seen far worse mortal injuries, but looking at the remains of the woman affected him more than he thought it would.

He steeled himself to forget about the person and focus on the crime. But it was never easy, not as a soldier and not now.

8

Jenny Silkwell had similar features to her younger sister: a long, slender nose, broad smooth forehead, classic jawline. He couldn't see the color of her eyes because they were closed. In response to Devine's query Guillaume said they were light blue, bordering on gray.

She said, "This was a distant gunshot wound. The abrasion collar was typical, meaning there was no deformity of the bullet before entry into the body. A contact wound would look much different, with triangular-shaped tears in the skin and evidence of searing along with soot deposits. And there was no indication of soot, seared skin, or gunpowder tattooing on the body. You'll usually get soot with close-range wounds of half a foot or less. Now, tattooing of the skin with powder grains is pathognomonic of *intermediate*-range gunshot wounds. It's burned into the skin so it can't be removed. That's why I ruled out an intermediate-range gunshot. There was no bullet wipe on her clothing since the bullet did not pass through any of that." She looked up at Devine. "That's residue from the surface of the bullet itself that ends up on the clothing."

"I understand she was immersed in salt water," commented Devine. "Even if there was bullet wipe it probably would not have survived. Along with any soot."

"But there wouldn't have been soot with a distant gunshot wound, and water would not have impacted any tattooing." Guillaume pointed to Silkwell's forehead. "There you can see what's referred to as the 'comet tail.' It usually shows the direction of the bullet's flight, from left to right. The minimal presence of the tail here demonstrates the entry was pretty much straight-on." She turned Jenny's head to the side to show the exit wound. "People assume the exit wound is always larger than the entry," she said. "But it's a fallacy to determine entry and exit wounds based on the sizes of the holes. And abrasion collars, soot, and tattooing are not associated with exit wounds. As you can see, her abrasion collar clearly shows the entry came in the front. The exit wound is gaping, which speaks to the transfer of energy through the frontal bone of the skull, then passing through the soft brain tissue, and exiting out the occipital bone. Skull fragments were propelled through the wound track, which also widened the exit wound. Her death would have been instantaneous," she added in a less professorial tone. "She would have been dead before she knew it."

Death would have been instantaneous. She would have been dead before she knew it.

Devine had heard those phrases many times, and though he knew the physiology behind it, he had never really believed it. He had come close to death several times, and each time, it was like the brain sped up as though not to miss a second of its imminent demise.

Even for a millisecond or less, I think you know that it's over. That it's the end of you.

He said, "I suppose the tox screens haven't come back yet?"

"Good Lord, no. And they won't for a while, along with the blood workup. I know how fast they do it on TV. Get a tox and DNA report back by the second commercial break. But the real world moves a lot slower. I guess we don't have the budget Hollywood does."

"What else can you tell me?"

"Her stomach was empty and the prelim blood work and examination of her tissue suggested nothing unusual in her system. But the tox screens will be far more definitive. All tox screens in Maine go to a private accredited lab in Pennsylvania for analysis, but I understand these are going to a federal lab for testing. So the turnaround might be faster."

"We also had two MDIs over from the medical examiner's office to help in the investigation," volunteered Harper. "They've gone back to Augusta now."

"MDI?" said Devine.

"Medicolegal Death Investigator," replied Guillaume. "They're part of the OCME. There are only three in the entire state, but this case was important enough to get two of them here."

"But all in all we didn't make much progress," said

Harper. He glanced at Devine, and his look was not friendly. “Guess that’s why they sent you in.”

“I think it’ll take more than one person to solve this,” said Devine diplomatically.

Harper said, “Hell, we have fewer than thirty homicides a year in the whole damn state. And now I got two of ’em in a short period of time.”

“Two?” said Devine.

“Hit-and-run,” interjected Fuss. “Not connected to this.”

“Did you autopsy that one, too?” asked Devine, looking at Guillaume.

“The deputy ME did the actual workup, but I assisted. It was a suspicious death, and Chief Harper immediately reported it to the OCME. There was no question a full autopsy would be done under the circumstances.”

“Don’t they autopsy all of them?” asked Devine.

“Hardly. Around fifteen thousand Mainers die every year. The vast majority by accident. We’re an outdoorsy, independent people, and that comes with risks. Next-highest cause of death is natural, then suicide, undetermined, and homicide is in last place, thank God. But the autopsy rates are going up. Six percent in 2000, eleven percent the next year, and fifteen percent of total deaths last year received the full workup.”

“What’s driving the increase?” asked Devine.

“Drug overdoses,” replied Guillaume immediately.

“Specifically, that fentanyl shit,” growled Harper.

Guillaume nodded. “It’s blowing up the OCME’s

budget. Full autopsy and full tox and blood workups are not cheap. They're building a new OCME facility in Augusta with more capacity, but it'll be a while before it's online. We used to only fully autopsy for those cases necessary for criminal prosecution, or unexpected deaths in people under fifty-five or where there's a public safety concern like an infectious disease. But now, because of the fentanyl crisis, the decision has been made to fully autopsy all decedents under age thirty if there is any question as to cause of death. But with, say, a self-inflicted shotgun wound to the head, we're not going to autopsy. Jenny was otherwise in remarkable physical shape, probably would've lived to be a hundred."

"Time of death?" asked Devine as he watched Harper and Fuss watch him.

"Between nine and eleven p.m. on the night she was found."

"You're comfortable with that window?" asked Devine.

"The deputy ME was, and I concurred. Your ME signed off on it, too. It's not just based on forensics, but also the time window from when she was last seen alive and then found dead."

"I understand a military ammo casing was found at the scene?"

Harper answered. "A 'federal' round. You think one of her own killed her?"

When Devine looked at him, the man's expression was mocking, and Devine had to fight back the urge to voice his *displeasure* at the comment.

"Early days yet," replied Devine. "Can you describe more fully the damage you saw in the wound track?"

"It was substantial," said Guillaume.

"Define *substantial.*"

She looked a bit put out by this query.

"I'm not trying to be a jerk," said Devine. "But a .300 Norma Magnum round is a high-velocity ordnance with a heavy load. It'll drop large game with no problem."

"You doubt the casing we found matches the bullet that hit her?" said Harper.

"Since the actual round was not found, I'm just dotting the *i*'s and crossing the *t*'s." He looked expectantly at Guillaume.

"I would say that a high-velocity round was indeed used. The kinetic energy was substantial, as was the exit wound, where, as I already showed you, there was a large amount of bone and tissue extruded from the wound. The bullet was not a dumdum, because there was no evidence of mushrooming in the wound track. It went pretty much straight through her head and out the rear."

"Then maybe a full metal-jacketed, or ball round, as the military often refers to it?" said Devine.

"It's certainly possible."

"What does that matter?" asked Fuss. She looked genuinely curious.

Devine said, "Most NATO military forces only use FMJ—or full metal-jacketed—ammo because of a Hague Convention international treaty signed well over a century ago. They banned the use of expanding bullets, even though FMJs have a greater risk of hitting unintended targets. Mushrooms tend to stay in the body. That's why cops all around the world use dumdum ammo, because they put the target down with little risk of doing damage to nontargets."

Guillaume interjected, "But the tumbling effect does catastrophic damage to the target."

Devine continued, "The U.S. never ratified the treaty, but they've followed it, mostly. However, the Army now uses hollow points in some of their ammo chains. Sidearms and the like. The Hague treaty only applies to wartime—but let's face it, the landscape of war has changed. It's more like urban and rural street fighting rather than big armies going at each other over far-flung, isolated ground."

Harper looked at Guillaume. "So just to be clear, Jenny was not shot by a dumdum? But by something that would include this .300 Norma round?"

"Correct," said Guillaume. "I believe I already said that."

Harper looked triumphantly at Devine. "Satisfied?"

"For now. Did she see anyone while she was up here? Her sister or brother?"

"We don't know," said Harper. "Leastways about Alex and Dak."

"You haven't spoken to them after all this time?" said Devine. He might not be an experienced investigator, but he knew the importance of collecting statements from persons of interest as quickly as possible because memories rapidly faded or became distorted. Or stories could be made up, practiced, and falsely corroborated.

"They're grieving," replied Fuss. "We'll talk to them at the appropriate time. It's how we do things up here."

Devine glanced at Guillaume, who was staring at him as though awaiting his response to this professional slap.

"Okay, did you manage to talk to anyone else who *wasn't* grieving?" Devine asked, his ire rising and uncomfortably so.

Dial it back, Travis—you have to work with these folks.

"A few people saw her around, nothing more than hello," replied Harper curtly.

"Where was she staying? Jocelyn Point?"

"No," said Harper. "Putnam Inn. Same place as you. Didn't you know that?"

Fuss looked like she might start laughing.

Small town, thought Devine. *Everybody knows everybody else's business. Even the outsider's.*

"So she spoke to the owner?"

"Sure, she's known Pat for years. Nothing of any note though, meaning their conversation. Just 'hi, how you doing.' Nothing about why she was up here."

"Did she say whether Silkwell appeared nervous or out of sorts?"

"No, nothing like that. She visited up here pretty much every year," said Fuss.

"Did you find anything relevant when you searched her room?" he asked.

Fuss said, "We *haven't* searched it." Before Devine could comment on that she added, "We secured it, taped it off, and waited for you to show up, because that's what we were ordered to do from the get-go. By *your* folks."

Harper didn't look happy about this, and Devine could hardly blame him. And now he somewhat understood their unfriendly behavior toward him.

"So any idea why Silkwell was in town?" He was holding back what Clare Silkwell had told him—that Jenny was coming here to settle some unfinished business.

"No idea, yet. But like you said, early days," added Fuss while Guillaume covered the body and then turned away to line up some instruments on a metal table. However, Devine could see from the woman's tensed manner that she was intently listening to every word.

"Tell me about Earl Palmer, the man who found the body."

Fuss and Harper exchanged a quick glance that Devine couldn't readily interpret. And Guillaume's shoulders had stiffened and then immediately relaxed when Palmer's name had been mentioned.

Harper took a moment to clear his throat while Fuss looked away. Clearly she was going to let her boss handle this one. "Earl's lived here his whole life. Retired lobsterman and a damn fine one. His wife, Alberta, died recently. And it rocked him to his core. He's salt of the earth. And his wife was, too."

"Okay. How did he happen to discover the body? She died between nine and eleven at night. But I understand that he called the police at one forty-five in the morning. What was he doing out at that hour?"

"Hell, lobstermen, like dairy farmers, don't really sleep," scoffed Fuss with a forced grin tacked on. "Even retired ones," she hastily added when she saw Devine was about to interject.

"Granted, but how did he find the body? I was told it was in an isolated place."

Harper said, "Earl likes to walk the shoreline. Ever since Bertie—that was what everybody called Alberta—died, he can't sleep. Just drives around or goes out and walks. He likes to hear the ocean. He spent enough of his life on it to where it's in his DNA."

Devine slowly nodded and decided he was going to get no farther on this. "Did Jenny have a rental car?"

"Yep," offered Fuss.

"Was it found near the crime scene? Did she drive it there?"

"No. It's back at the Putnam Inn. White two-door Honda, you might have seen it. New York plates."

Devine *had* seen such a car there. "So, like the room, have you not searched it yet?"

"Those were our instructions," said Harper sharply. "*Federal* instructions."

"Did anyone see her the night she died?" asked Devine. "Dr. Guillaume mentioned a time window."

"Pat Kingman saw her walk out of the inn around seven thirty," said Fuss. "She didn't see which way she went."

"How far from there was she found?"

"Three point two miles. I clocked it in the car," answered Fuss.

"Weather that night?"

"Raining like cats and dogs," answered Fuss.

Devine shifted his focus to Guillaume. "Anything else I should know? Signs of a struggle? Defensive wounds? Skin of an assailant under her nails? Any other forensic evidence at all?"

"No," said Guillaume. "Just the casing."

"Are you still looking for the round?"

Fuss said, "It was heading toward the ocean after it left Jenny's body. Long gone by now, don't you think?"

Devine glanced at her and noted the condescending expression. He had seen that look sometimes on superior officers of his, the ones who had been several degrees removed from the actual conditions on the ground, but thought they knew better. He hadn't liked it then and he didn't like it now.

"Any luck on tracking down the person she was with?"

"Whoa now, who said she was *with* anyone?" exclaimed Harper.

"I doubt she walked over three miles in the pouring rain to where she was killed. And she obviously didn't drive herself."

A wide-eyed Harper said, "Hell, you think she drove over there with someone?"

"Well, it's our job to find that out, right? So let's go to the crime scene."

When Devine looked at Guillaume, she was giving him a tiny smile. He returned it.

I'll take any support I can get right now, thought Devine.

It was like he was back in Afghanistan looking for a friendly face.

And I never found many. Let's hope I do better on American soil.

9

A light drizzle was falling as Devine followed the pair in the muddy cruiser with a bent front ram bar. Devine knew they would learn little at the crime scene in the darkness. But he needed to get a feel for its structures, its parameters and possibilities.

He had been right in telling Campbell that he was not a trained investigator, but the old general had also been correct in informing Devine not to sell himself short in that regard. He had solved the mystery in New York. But he'd had help, and he'd also allowed himself to get shot. With his own gun! That still hurt his pride.

In the Middle East he had done countless battlefield assessments. The Army documented everything. Battle assessment methodologies, collateral damage assessment, munitions effectiveness, reattack recommendation methodologies, post–campaign operations actions. In this regard they were looking for the smallest clues and telltale signs as to why a combat operation had not gone according to plan or why damage was above expectations. Or how an IED had been able to get close enough to kill its intended target. So his mind was trained to see certain things.

Sometimes things went sideways just due to shitty luck, Devine knew. When many people were gathered in close quarters trying their best to kill one another, there wasn't a report or methodology in the world that could cover all the possible contingencies or outcomes. Humans under threat of death were just too unpredictable; some turned into cowards, and others into heroes, and still others into both.

Devine had, on numerous occasions, successfully interrogated people he thought were allies and those he knew to be enemies, and found out vital information in most of those cases. He had not done it with brute force, though on occasion he had wanted to as he stared into smug expressions projecting unearned superiority. They were the hardened countenances of people who would do absolutely nothing to help you and absolutely anything to do the opposite to you. He hoped whatever talent he possessed for this sort of work was enough for this case. Campbell seemed to have faith in him, justified or not.

He looked over, and there stood Jocelyn Point like a lighthouse on the coast, only with very little light to offer. Offshore a collection of blackened clouds was gathering and perhaps pondering whether to come onto land and pummel the puny scattering of humans who dwelled there.

A few minutes later the cruiser pulled off to the side of the road, rubber gripping mud, and stopped. Devine slipped his Tahoe in behind and got out.

So she died not that far from her old homestead.

The wind seemed fiercer at this point. He didn't know if it was due to the approaching storm or some weird topographical feature at this spot. But as he walked up to join the two officers of the law, Devine thought this was a perfectly macabre backdrop for violent death. It was essentially Edgar Allan Poe–esque in its deep sense of potentially sinister intrigue.

He stood there for a few moments and gave a sweeping gaze across the landscape, taking in all points that seemed to him of interest. Fuss held one powerful light, and she produced another from the cruiser and handed it to Devine. He used it to illuminate a stand of scrub pines off to the left. There was also an open field of grass and wild plants that seemed to thrive even in the stark chill. Another stand of deciduous trees was off to the far right, their trunks and naked branches registering as shadows in the dark. Thick, burly bushes were everywhere, with many of them also bereft of leaves.

Devine had been to Maine before on training exercises with the Rangers. He knew it held the highest percentage of wooded land of any state, at nearly ninety percent. And he had become something of an amateur horticulturist, so as to determine the types of trees and bushes for suitable concealment while being shot at or attempting to sneak up on an enemy, as well as what one could safely eat when one's own food ran out. And which bark and herbs and flowers were viable for treating wounds when there was no more medicine at hand. Thus, he knew the Maine state tree was the eastern white pine, several of which he could see here now. The state flower was the white pinecone.

He eyed his two companions, who were staring resolutely at him.

Time to turn from botany to homicide.

"Where was she found?" he asked.

They led him along a broad, rutted path through the trees and kept going until they reached the end of land.

More than a dozen feet below there was nothing except a shelf of blackened and eroded rocks and boulders that acted as a natural sea wall against the pounding surf. It was close to high tide now, and hard spray from the incoming water meeting this immovable boundary of stone nearly reached them where they stood.

Fuss shone her light on one spot and held it.

"Right about there," she said.

"The body had fallen from here to there after Jenny was shot," explained Harper.

Devine looked at where they were all standing and then down at the rocks. "You're sure that's what happened? She was shot and then fell down there?"

"Pretty damn sure, yeah. I mean, what else?" said Harper.

"How was the body facing?"

Harper looked at Fuss, who said, "Best as I can remember, head to land and feet out to the ocean. She could've flipped over on her way down, since she was shot from the front."

"Best as you can remember? Didn't somebody take

pictures? Didn't the feds go over it before the body was moved?"

Fuss barked, "Hell, we couldn't leave her there. Tide was coming in and there was a storm. She would have been washed out to sea if we waited another minute."

"But you have pictures, before she was moved?"

"Look, Devine, you weren't here, okay?" said Fuss. "The water was all over Jenny when we got here. You heard Doc Guillaume. Time of death was between nine and eleven. We didn't get here until after two in the morning. We had to move fast, real fast. And we're not CSI. We got one ambulance and two volunteer EMTs in Putnam. I called in everybody I could, including some men I knew from the county with climbing experience to go down there and help bring her up. Before they got here we put a rope around Jenny to keep her from getting swept out. We all got soaked to the skin, and the water was so cold it damn well burned. We had to use a truck with a winch to bring her up, but we did our best to make sure we did as little damage to the body as possible. We didn't have hours or days to plan this out, we had minutes," she ended with a bark, her posture all defensive and annoyed.

"Okay, okay," said Devine. "I get it. Where was the casing found?"

They led him back to a spot that lined up with where Jenny had been shot and gone over the edge. Devine gauged it to be a little over three hundred or so yards from where Jenny had purportedly been shot. There was a cleft in the tree line here with an unobstructed sight line to the edge of the bluff.

On his voicing this opinion on the distance, Fuss told him, "It's three hundred and twenty-one yards. I measured it myself."

Devine worked the sight line and trajectory in his head. While officers could not become snipers in the Army, Devine had supervised several teams of snipers and spotters. He was intimately familiar with the weapons and ammo used, the physiological processes involved, and the ballistic calculations that went into ending the life of another human being over substantial distances using a long-barreled rifle and scope. And he came away with the conclusion that things were not making sense. "You're sure this is the spot?" he asked.

Fuss said angrily, "I marked it myself! We did have the time to work the scene up here. That was where the casing was found and I'll swear to that in court."

Devine knew they were upset that the feds were looking over their shoulders and controlling the investigation and the processing of the evidence. But was there something *else* behind Fuss's look of vitriol?

"Any evidence of robbery?"

"None. She had two rings and a necklace and a fancy watch, a Breitling," said Fuss, her tone less aggressive now. "We got it all back in the evidence room along with her other things."

"Purse, wallet?"

"I imagine they're back in her room. If you give the okay we can search it *finally*," said Harper.

"Tomorrow morning work for you?" said Devine. "Nine o'clock? I'll bring the coffee. Saw a place close to the inn. Maine Brew. How's that sound?"

"Sure, that works," said Harper in a friendlier tone, acknowledging this olive branch offered by Devine. "We both take it black."

"I suppose with the weather there were no footprints, tire tracks?"

"We looked," said Fuss. "But it was a quagmire by then. Truck we used to winch her up got stuck. Had to get a tow truck to pull it out. We weren't getting any trace from that mess."

Devine looked back at the cliff where Jenny had allegedly gone over. "So, how did Palmer find her body? He would have had to go right up to the edge and then look down."

Harper said, "Earl told me he was out walking late that night. He couldn't sleep."

"Out walking, in the pouring rain?"

Fuss interjected, "Earl Palmer had nothing to do with what happened to Jenny."

Devine kept his gaze on Harper. "Never said he did. I'm just trying to understand the situation. I have superiors I have to report to, and they'll be asking me very pointed questions, like I'm asking you."

Harper and Fuss exchanged a glance, a worried one.

Harper said, "He was a lobsterman. Foul weather

means nothing to him. And I told you he lost his wife. He probably didn't even know what he was doing. Just wandering aimlessly."

"Did he walk from his house, or drive?"

"He walked. And he happened to come over to this spot and just stared out at the ocean. A place he spent most of his life. And then he looked down and saw her. And called 911."

"So it was just a coincidence that he picked this spot out of all the others around here to go and take a look at the water and happen to glance down and find a body?" Each word that came out of Devine's mouth sounded more unbelievable to him than the previous one.

"Coincidences like that *do* happen, Devine," said Fuss.

Maybe in novels, thought Devine. *But not ever in real life*.

They parted company with the agreement to meet up at the inn the following morning.

As Devine drove back into town he stopped and quickly pulled over to the curb.

Dak Silkwell, whom he recognized from the photo in his briefing book, had just walked into a bar called The Hops.

10

Devine had been in countless watering holes in many countries during his military career. They pretty much all looked and functioned the same. Although there had been one in South Korea that had been a little out there. Over their torsos the waitresses had worn crisscrossed ammo belts with orange-flavored tequila shots instead of bullets in the cartridge pouches. And that was pretty much all they had on.

The Hops was far more formulaic in its offerings: a scattering of tables and chairs; a small, scuffed parquet dance floor; a tiny, raised stage for live music, empty now; and a long bar with wooden stools, a big mirror, rows of terraced liquor bottles, and six beers on tap.

A Janis Joplin song was playing on an old-fashioned jukebox and the late singer's one-of-a-kind voice resonated over them like thunder across a flowered meadow. Although the singer had died over two decades before he was born, one of Devine's father's friends had introduced him to rock-and-roll performers from that era. Joplin had quickly become one of his favorite vocalists. He had often listened to her songs during combat deployments overseas, much to the amusement of his fellow soldiers, who were far more into musicians from their own generation.

Oh Lord, won't you buy me a Mercedes-Benz . . .

The bar was mostly full, and Devine could imagine it was probably the only such establishment in town. Set off in a small wing of the building were two pool tables, where men and women were smacking the balls around and performing the flirty, maybe-something-later ritual that such social environments inspired. A well-used Terminator pinball machine was being played by a blonde woman in her mid-thirties dressed in tight jeans and a loose black blouse that enticingly displayed her ample cleavage. Nearby, two young men in their early twenties were enjoying a furious match of foosball, all the while eyeballing the blonde with equal parts lust and youthful hope.

Dak Silkwell was easy to spot, with his height and heft. Devine knew all the man's vitals from viewing his Army file. He was six four and looked to be carrying about two hundred and thirty pounds. He had on jeans, muddy boots, and a leather jacket. Devine watched as he shed the jacket and hung it on a wall peg. Underneath he had on a white muscle shirt that showed off his impressive biceps and delts as well as a sculpted back, his lats and rhomboid muscles heavily chiseled. Both arms were fully tatted, as were the tops of his pecs. The image of an emerald-green snake wrapped around his thick, veined neck.

Dak claimed a stool and lifted a finger at one of the women working behind the bar. The young woman poured out a Yuengling from one of the taps and carried it over to him. Dak waved and nodded to several people, who performed the same gesture back.

A regular, thought Devine.

An old man next to Dak paid his bill, hopped off his stool, threw on his coat, and was gone, his thirst evidently satiated.

Devine sat down on the vacated stool and motioned to the other woman working the bar. She was in her forties, with sandy hair and a wiry physique. In the mirror he could see the edge of her smartphone sticking out of one rear pocket and the top of a purple vape out of the other.

"Yuengling, on draft," he said.

She nodded, poured, and delivered it. "Five bucks."

Devine slipped her a ten and told her to keep it.

Dak sipped his beer, staring straight ahead, but Devine knew this game and had glanced twice in the mirror to see Dak's pupils swivel in his direction. In fact, everyone in the place pretty much had shot looks at the outsider in their midst.

Before Devine had sat down he had seen in the mirror's reflection that Dak had said something to the old man right before he so readily jumped up, leaving the stool empty. If Devine's lip-reading was right, it was something like, *Beat it, Joe. Somebody wants your seat*.

Devine sipped his beer and contemplated his next move. Tactics and strategies rolled through his head like they had during combat on unforgiving terrain with a wily opponent who was doing the same thing.

He finally said, "I'm sure you know who I am. Probably

when Patricia Kingman started making the phone rounds about the stranger in town. And then maybe a heads-up from the local constabulary?"

Dak didn't turn his head, but both men were now eyeing each other in the mirror. Devine watched as the other man's muscles tensed. Devine's muscles did nothing. There was no reason to. Yet. And the other man's respiration had noticeably elevated while Devine's had actually slowed. Dak Silkwell had obviously forgotten some or all of what the Army had painstakingly taught him. Or maybe he'd never taken it seriously in the first place. Perhaps that was why they had parted company. His phone buzzed. He eased it from his pocket and read the text that Campbell had just sent.

PFC Dak Silkwell, OTH.

That was Army-speak for "Other Than Honorable." This meant that Dak had done something bad, but not egregious enough for a punitive consequence such as a court-martial and prison confinement under the Uniform Code of Military Justice. That also meant Dak couldn't rejoin the Army and had forfeited most if not all of his military benefits.

Campbell had not indicated the reason for the OTH, but Devine knew most of them by heart: violence against military personnel or a civilian, adultery, drug or alcohol abuse. And a security violation. Anything more serious and the OTH would not have been possible.

So which one are you, Dak?

The man finally stirred, but only to order another beer.

When it came, Dak broke the silence. "Travis Devine. Homeland Security. And I know why you're here."

Devine said, "I'm sorry for your loss."

Dak turned to him, perhaps to gauge Devine's level of sincerity without the mirrored buffer. "Jenny didn't deserve to go out that way. She was a good person."

"She have enemies that you know of?"

"You'd know that better than me, considering what she did for a living."

"That would require a stranger in town. Anyone see anything like that?"

Dak shook his head, clearly thinking this through. "I haven't. You'd have to ask around."

"Everyone picked up on me really fast. Just thought it would have worked through the grapevine if another outsider had passed through."

Dak shrugged. "Don't know what to tell you."

Literally, or is something else getting played out here?

"You see your sister or talk to her while she was here?"

Dak took longer than was necessary to answer this simple question. "I didn't even know she was in town. It was a shock when we found out she was dead."

"'We' as in you and your sister?" asked Devine.

Dak nodded and sipped his beer.

"Did Jenny see or talk to your sister while she was here?"

"Not that she mentioned. You'd have to ask her."

"I plan to. You know Earl Palmer?"

"Sure, a good man. He found Jenny's body," said Dak.

"I understand he just recently lost his wife. Likes to wander at night."

"Lucky for us. Otherwise, Jenny might have gotten washed out to sea."

"When can I have a more formal interview with you? And your sister, of course."

"Doesn't this count as my formal interview?" Dak wanted to know.

"Afraid not."

"I work six days a week. Ten to eight. My tattoo shop's around the corner. Ink Well. Get it?"

"Yeah, clever. Small town keep you that busy?"

"I've built a rep. Lots of folks from Jonesport, Machias, and Cutler. And I have clients from all over New England. Even Canada."

"Nice," replied Devine.

He ran his gaze over Devine. "You got tats? You look the sort."

"None voluntarily. But I've got a real wicked one around my ankle and calf. Picked it up in the Middle East on the biting end of an IED."

Dak shot him a funny look. "Army or Marine?"

"The former."

"You couldn't have pulled the full ride. You're way too young."

"Decided to do something else with my life."

Dak drained his beer. "Yeah, me too." A pulse throbbed in the man's temple.

He knows that I know about the OTH.

"We can grab some breakfast or late dinner. Your call. And my treat."

"I'm not usually an early riser," said Dak.

"Dinner then."

"I only do organic."

"They got a place here for that?" asked Devine doubtfully.

"Yeah. It's called Only Real Food. I'm an investor. They get customers from all over Maine, Aroostook, Piscataquis, Waldo, Kennebec, York. Canada, too. Just like my tat shop. It's no coincidence. I push all my investments with my clients."

"Congrats. So nine o'clock tomorrow night?"

"I guess," said Dak.

"I'd like a more definitive reply."

"Okay, nine it is. The restaurant is two blocks south of here, take a left on Hiram Silkwell Street."

"Seriously?"

"Named after the man who was born and grew up here and made all that money."

"Less than three hundred people now. What happened?"

"It's always been a toy town. But outside the town line is our version of the burbs, where we have nearly four thousand people."

"And your sister? Where can I see her?"

"She's usually home."

"I need her phone number. I'd like to set something up."

Dak gave it to him but added, "She doesn't usually answer, particularly if she doesn't know who's calling."

He handed Dak a card. "Here's my number. Then you can tell her to answer when I call."

"Alex doesn't follow orders and usually not advice, either."

"I'm persistent. I understand she's quite an artist."

"Says who?" asked Dak.

"So, she's not a good artist?"

"No, she's good. Better than good, actually. But her taste is . . . eclectic. And she only parts with a piece when she really needs the money."

"Big house. You'd think she'd really need the money a lot."

"I do well at the tattoo parlor. And I make good money off my investments. Okay, I'm not in Hiram Silkwell's league. But give me time."

"I saw your father," Devine told him.

Now came the first hint of strong emotion on Dak's expressive face. "He's not doing well," he said.

"You're in the loop on all that?"

Dak nodded. "I've been down to see him. Go as often as I can. He say anything to you?"

"He wasn't really awake."

"They say he doesn't have long."

"A warrior deserves a better exit," said Devine.

Dak tapped his surprisingly delicate fingers against his

empty beer mug. They also looked to have been manicured. Devine looked down at his own ragged ones and frowned.

"Yeah, you'd think so, wouldn't you?" replied Dak.

"You disagree?"

"His military days were pretty much over when I came along. But then he got into politics. He wasn't around much."

Devine decided to go there. "But *you* suited up. Wore the Army green."

Dak eyed him. "Yeah, it was a lotta fun." He dropped some cash for the beers and rose. "I'm beat. Gotta get going."

"You need a lift?"

"Nah. Got my Harley. Love that thing."

Devine watched him every step of the way. He was seriously thinking of following him home when he spotted three large men, pool sticks in hand, staring dead at him.

When Devine left, so did they. The sounds of what might have been Dak's Harley soared off into the night, leaving him alone with his three new Maine besties.

Wonderful way to end a long unproductive day.

11

The body will not go where the mind has not been.

That was why most people were victims, Devine knew. They could not imagine themselves grievously injuring or killing someone else, for any reason, even in order to save their own lives. So they wasted time in attempting to flee or in pleading for mercy to men who had none to give.

Show a picture of someone attacking someone else and ask for a reaction, and 99 percent of the people will say they would be in fear of their life if that happened to them. The other 1 percent, the criminal element, have a different reaction. They will say, "I'd hit them harder." This was because they never saw themselves as the victim, only the predator. Their minds have been there, and so their bodies were ready, willing, and able to go there too.

Yet all humans were built to be predators. Sharp, strong teeth, forward eyes that were far more efficient for hunting, opposable thumbs, and, most of all, the best brain of any animal.

And we all possess a latent primal ability to fight to the death.

Devine walked toward his Tahoe even as he heard the men follow. When he reached it he turned and faced them. They looked angry and puffed up. That was all he needed to know both of their intent and their being afraid of him. The ones Devine always worried about were not the giant red-faced screamers; they were secretly shitting their pants. It was the quiet, stone-faced scrawny guys that would suddenly gut you with a shiv or pop a bullet into your brain and walk, not run, away, disappearing into the night to do it again when someone else was stupid enough to underestimate them.

His senses did the preliminary calculation and ran it through the combat computer under his skull. Walking away from a fight, if you could do so safely, was usually the best answer. Looking at the three men, Devine knew that was not going to be an option. Unless he did something creative. And he didn't want to fight them. Not because he knew he would lose; it was because he was certain he would win, and didn't want to unnecessarily injure them.

And he was also wondering why they had decided to come after him in the first place.

"Can I help you?" he said.

The biggest one said, "Yeah, dude, you can get out of town. That'd be a good start." He looked at his friends and grinned.

"Sorry. I have a job to do and it can't be done remotely."

"Then we got us a problem. Or more to the point, *you* do," said the same man.

Devine glanced up and down the street. Not another living soul. Other than the bar, the storefronts were dark.

The roar of the incoming tide along the harbor was really the only sound, other than the men's collective breathing. They were all big and strong and pumped full of alcohol and who knew what else. Two of them were in short sleeves despite the chilly weather. He looked at the drug tracks on their beefy arms and came up with a plan.

He pointed at the man who had spoken. "I know you, don't I?"

The man, in his late forties and taller than Devine by about three inches and outweighing him by thirty pounds, looked taken aback. "I don't know *you*," he snarled.

"You need to think again," said Devine. He opened his jacket to show his Glock. The men saw it, and the dynamic instantly changed. He took out his cred pack with the badge and held it up for all to see.

"Homeland Security. But you already knew that. You talked to us about a domestic terrorist network operating up here and selling drugs to fund their operations. I never forget a face. We did the briefing over in Bangor so nobody would know."

The man looked apoplectic. "I never talked to no fuckin' feds!"

Devine watched as the other two men glanced suspiciously at their comrade.

"What's your name?" asked Devine.

"I don't need to tell you a damn thing."

"That's okay. It'll be in our files. But from what I remember, you were a big help, so thanks. We nailed some *local* badasses because of you."

The man suddenly realized his friends were staring at him, and not in a good way.

"He's lying. I didn't do any of that shit. You know that. You know *me*."

Devine was not going to give up precious ground. "Well, that's why we recruit people like you. You're on the inside and you know everybody's business."

"You're lying," the man roared.

Devine touched the butt of his gun just as a reminder that it was there and had the means to kill all three of them with hardly any effort on his part. "Now, again, what can I do for you? No, scrap that, I don't have the time. Any of you see Jenny Silkwell before she died?"

The men looked at one another, ostensibly flummoxed by another abrupt change in the direction of the conversation.

"We don't know nothing about that," said the second man, shorter than his friend, but thicker. The drug tracks on his left arm looked like the measles: swollen, nasty, and painful.

"I'm not accusing you of having anything to do with her death. But I need to find out why she was here and who she might have met and spoken with. Did you know her?"

The men seemed reluctant to say one way or another until the third fellow spoke up. He was younger than the other two, late thirties at most.

"I went to high school with her. I played football and she ran track and did gymnastics. And she was smart, too.

Graduated top in the class. She was the . . . what do you call it?"

"Valedictorian."

"Yeah."

"So what was your take on her?" asked Devine.

"She . . . everybody loved Jenny, me included." He glanced at his companions, clearly embarrassed at this frank admission.

"Did you see her when she was last up here?"

He nodded. "Saw her on the street. I waved to her and she waved back. Called me by my name, though I've changed some, gotten fat and lost most of my hair. But she remembered *me*."

This was obviously a point of pride with the man.

"Did she seem . . . okay?"

"Yeah, I mean, I think so. She comes up here from time to time, but that was the first I'd seen her in a few years."

"She comes to visit her brother and sister?"

He wiped his nose. "I guess so. I don't really know. I'm not really tight with the family."

Devine eyed the tats on the other two men. "You guys know Alex, or Dak? Looks like you both got inked by him."

The smaller of them said, "Yeah, dude's an artist. And fair with his prices."

"He ever talk about Jenny?"

The one looked at the other. "No, not really," said the man Devine had accused of being an informant. He scowled and added, "Hear *she* was a fed."

"You know her sister? She's an artist, too."

"Alex is . . . different," said the same man.

"Goes to the beat of her own drummer," said the other. "Gorgeous gal, but . . . Hell, don't know why she's still here. She could go out to LA or somewhere and make a helluva lot of money."

"Or marry some rich dude and fly around in a private jet," said the man Devine had accused. "Not live in some spooky old house in the middle of fuckin' nowhere."

"So why do you think she never did that?" asked Devine.

The man shrugged. "Like I said, she's different. I don't think she cares about money and shit like that."

"When was the last time you saw her?"

"Maybe six months ago, when she rode her bike into town."

"Motorbike?"

"No, a pedal bike."

"You speak to her?"

"No, she don't like to . . . *interact* with folks. Keeps to herself. Don't mess with nobody."

"Okay. What do you know about Earl Palmer? He found the body."

They all looked at one another. Again, the man he'd accused of being an informant answered. "Good man, old-school, but he's hurting bad. Just lost his wife. Then to find Jenny. Shit, man, talk about bad luck."

"Where exactly does he live? I'll just need to get his statement."

The man told him and added, "Little cottage way off

the road. White with green shutters. Can't miss it. Only place around there."

"I understand he was a lobsterman."

"One of the best," said the same man. "And I should know. I'm one, too. Damn hard work for not much money. And the lobsters? They're going AWOL. Say it's climate change, warming water, and they're heading north. All I know is my money got cut in half. Had to get a second job. Most days I come off the boat all tired as hell and go right to work at another gig."

"Then you needed that beer in The Hop," observed Devine.

The man grinned. "Damn sure did."

Devine looked at the other men. "And just so you know, I made up the stuff about him working with the feds."

"Why the hell did you do that?" barked the man he'd accused.

"Because I could sense you three might want to do me physical harm. And I didn't want to pull my gun on you and start shooting, so I used that to defuse the situation. What do you think? Did I make the right call?"

"Yeah, you did." The man now looked sheepish. "We're pretty much just being drunk and stupid."

Devine said, "Any particular reason why you decided to have a beef with me? Other than the drunk-and-stupid part?"

The men looked at one another again. The first man said, "Nope, that's about it."

"Uh-huh," said Devine, who didn't believe this. "Well, I appreciate the help. If you think of anything else." He handed each of them his card with his cell phone number.

Then the man who had gone to school with Jenny said, "I can't think of no reason why somebody'd want to hurt her."

"Well, it's my job to find out. And I'm pretty good at my job."

I hope.

12

Devine headed back to the inn but then decided to take a detour. Following the directions he'd been given, he had no difficulty in finding the turnoff and mailbox with the name PALMER.

He didn't pull up directly to the house, but got out and walked along the winding gravel drive until he reached the cottage, which seemed to sit orphaned from the rest of Putnam. There was a cluster of denuded serviceberry trees next to the small cottage. Devine could see no lights on in the house, but the same ancient station wagon he had seen when first heading into town was parked in front, next to a rugged old Ford F150 with a rear winch.

He tried to recall the details of the man in the vehicle from earlier.

Fine snowy white hair, leathery skin, deep-set eyes, jowly features, and a pained expression mixed with disinterest.

Now that Devine knew of the man's loss, he decided that Palmer had looked like a bereaved person, aimless, disconnected. He could see such a man wandering late at night. But to wander through a forest path all the way over to the exact spot where Jenny Silkwell's body lay? Devine was not buying it. And the police seemed to be going to great pains to throw off any suspicion of Palmer. And Dak and the fellow lobsterman from the bar had sung the man's praises and voiced sympathy for his personal loss without questioning the veracity of the man's account of finding Jenny Silkwell's body.

The two vehicles were unlocked. He saw right away that in the station wagon the gas and brake pedals had been modified to allow them both to be worked via hand controls mounted on the steering column. Why, he didn't know. Then he saw extra hand grips that had been bolted to the car's interior just above the window frame and another one mounted on the dash.

He turned around, walked back to the Tahoe, and drove past Jocelyn Point once more. As he did so, he spotted a Harley with a helmetless Dak astride it pull into the drive and head up to the house.

That was interesting, because Dak should have been home a while ago. Unless he had stopped somewhere first. And maybe his conversation with Devine had prompted that detour?

The questions kept piling up, and Devine hadn't been here even half a day.

He parked in front of the inn and walked into the reception area, where Kingman was tidying up the front counter. She gave him a piercing, unfriendly look. "You should have told me who you were," she admonished.

"You're probably right," he said in a disarming tone. "Now that you know, is there anything you can tell me?"

"I already told Chief Harper all that I know."

"I'd appreciate if you could take a minute and tell me. That way there's no buffer between accounts, and you might remember something else. I'm just trying to find out what happened to Jenny."

She sighed as her frostiness melted away. "Would you like some hot chocolate?"

"I sure would. I'm not used to the cold yet."

She put a hand on her hip and smirked. "Young man, this isn't cold. This is mildly chilly. Come with me."

She led him through the curtain, and Devine found himself in a comfortable apartment setup. While Kingman busied herself with cups, cocoa, and a new-looking electric hot water kettle, he looked around.

Some logs sat unburned in a stone hearth. While the furniture was clearly old, it all looked comfortable. Knickknacks abounded on tables and shelves, and the vast array of photos on one wall seemed to indicate that Kingman had a great many grandchildren.

"Nice-looking crew," he said.

She looked up to see what he was referring to and smiled. "Eight and counting. Oldest one is ten. Wish my Wilbur could be around to see them."

"I didn't know you were a widow."

"Wilbur was a lobsterman. There was an accident out at sea, and the boat went down and took Wilbur with it."

"I'm really sorry."

"Thank you. It was just horribly bad luck."

"Sometimes there is nothing you can do despite the best of intentions. And no one's perfect. Lord knows I'm not."

"You're messing up all my preconceived notions of federal folks."

He smiled. "You met many?"

"Just on TV. Well, there was Jenny, but she was one of us, no matter where she moved to or what she did."

They sat in rocking chairs in front of the fireplace and drank their hot chocolate.

"It really is so sad," said Kingman, suddenly tearing up. "I never thought . . . Jenny would be the last person I thought this would happen to." She pulled a tissue from her pocket and dabbed at her eyes. She stared over at Devine. "She was such a good person."

"Seems to be the consensus of everyone I spoke with."

"Do you think it has to do with the work she was doing?"

"What do you know about that?"

"Just dribs and drabs I heard over the years. And I had a cousin who worked doing something for the Department of Defense. Whenever I asked him what he did he said, 'It's better if you don't know. You'd never sleep again.' Scary."

"In answer to your question, I don't know who killed her or why. Just because she died here does not mean that anybody local had anything to do with it."

"God, I would hope not."

"I understand you saw Jenny on the night she died."

Kingman looked even more depressed. "If I had known what was going to happen, I would have held on to her with both arms."

"Tell me about it. Did she look normal? Anything you can remember."

"She passed by the office and I saw her out the window. This is from the back path, you understand, the one leading to the cottages."

"Right."

"It was about a quarter to eight. I remember glancing at the clock. I thought she might be going to get some dinner. She was dressed in jeans and a big parka. Her hair was in a ponytail, and I remembered thinking I hadn't seen her wear it like that for a long time. She seemed fine, if a little focused, I guess. She never looked around, just kept looking straight ahead. But then she was always focused, even as a little girl."

"And you didn't see her after that? Didn't hear a car come by? Maybe she was getting a ride with someone because her car was left here?"

"I had the TV on, so I don't think I would have heard that. And that was the last time I saw her," she concluded miserably.

Devine absorbed this and said, "I ran into Dak Silkwell tonight. He's a reserved guy but he seemed shaken up by what happened."

"I'm sure he was."

"So they were close, him and Jenny and Alex?"

She took time to sip her drink, set the mug down, placed her hands in her lap, and looked at him. "I suppose you need to know this for your investigation. I read somewhere most murders are committed by people you know, friends and family."

"Unfortunately, yes."

"They were all close growing up. Saw that for myself. Dak was all sports all the time. Big and strong, that boy was. Lettered in everything. Thought he was going to be playing professional football or baseball, but it didn't work out. Guess that's a pipe dream for most. Jenny was the oldest and the golden child. Everything she touched. Smart as all get out. Kind too. Pretty. We all knew she was destined to do something special."

"And Alex?"

"Alex is the youngest and is drop-dead gorgeous, and I don't use that term lightly. Not as smart as Jenny, at least in some ways. She could draw anything, from an early age. I mean really, really talented. The family wanted her to go away to a really great art school, UCLA, Chicago, or Virginia Commonwealth in Richmond. She got accepted at them all."

"But she didn't go?"

"No, she didn't."

"Any idea why?"

Kingman sighed, and in that release Devine sensed a whole bundle of regrets, not for Kingman personally, or the Silkwells either, but maybe for the whole town of Putnam.

"Alex used to be outgoing, prankish, fun, full of ambition, sort of like Jenny in that way. But then it was like the light turned off and she became withdrawn, moody, scared to . . . live."

"What happened?"

She hesitated, seemingly debating within herself. "I don't really know."

"You really don't know what happened to cause that big a change in her?"

"It was many years ago. And whatever it was the family made sure it was all hushed up."

Devine wondered why Clare Silkwell had not mentioned this.

"So she and Dak stayed here, in the old homestead?"

She nodded absently. "Dak was in the Army for a while and then he wasn't. I don't know why. No one ever said." She gave him a curious look, but Devine merely shrugged. "Then he came back here, learned to be a tattoo artist. And it became his passion. Opened his shop and does really well. Then he invested in some other businesses around town. I think he likes to be a big fish in a teeny pond. And we fit that bill."

"I guess he and Alex get along, living together?"

"I don't know how much they actually interact."

"I thought in small towns, gossip moves faster than jets."

She laughed softly. "It does. But not for every single aspect of someone's life."

"Alex ever come into town?" Devine knew what the man outside the bar had told him about Alex riding her bike into town but not interacting. However, he wanted to hear Kingman's perspective.

"Very rarely. And then it's just to get something she needs and then the girl runs back to her hidey-hole."

Hidey-hole? Interesting choice of words. "Seems like a waste of a promising life."

"I agree with you." She settled her attention fully on Devine. "Maybe you can put that on your list to find out. If you do, it'll be a good thing for all of us that you came to Putnam."

Maybe not for everyone, thought Devine as he finished his hot chocolate.

13

After leaving Kingman in her little apartment, Devine passed by the cottage where Jenny Silkwell had been staying. He had already seen her rental car in the front parking area awaiting a thorough processing. Devine hoped to find her laptop and phone in there or her cottage.

The lights in the cottage were off, and there was police tape across the only entrance.

He stood there in the cold air, his hands stuffed in his pockets, and stared at the little building, which seemed to be a duplicate of the one he was staying in. He wondered what Jenny Silkwell had been thinking on her last night on earth, not realizing that it would be so.

Unfinished business? That could mean a lot of different things.

He also wondered whether he should break into the cottage and her car to see if her electronic devices were inside. That would piss off the local cops, but national security would trump all that. Yet, if the items *had* been in there, the enemies of this country, if they had killed Jenny Silkwell, surely would have already retrieved them.

Then he heard a noise. His hand went automatically to his Glock. He moved forward and then around the side of the cottage. He took one hand off the Glock, reached into his coat pocket, and produced a small flashlight with a high-intensity focused beam setting. He clicked it on, held it just above his Glock while keeping both hands on the weapon, and kept moving forward, toward the sounds.

In three more steps he saw the source of the noise.

The woman was perched on her haunches on the ground. And she was sobbing.

"Ma'am, are you okay?"

When his beam found and held on her features, Devine sucked in a quick breath as he recognized her.

"Get that fucking light out of my face," barked Alex Silkwell.

Devine killed the light and simply stood there gaping. His mind was whirring, trying to process all this. He looked around to see if a window on Jenny's cottage had been broken, or any other sign that her sister had intruded into what was potentially a treasure trove of possible evidence in a murder investigation. He saw nothing of the kind.

"Are you all right?" he asked again.

She rose. Alex was tall, about five eight, and lean.

"Who are you exactly?" she asked in a calmer tone.

"Travis Devine."

"Right. The man they sent to find out about Jenny."

"And you're her sister."

"How brilliant you are. They must have been thrilled when you became a detective, or whatever it is you actually do."

Devine pulled his creds and flashed the light on them. “Homeland Security.”

“Right. Anybody can print a card and make a badge. I can make them for you. How many more do you need?”

“What are you doing here?”

Alex Silkwell *was* beautiful, but there was such misery in the woman’s features that her looks became a secondary consideration. With each rapid breath of hers, visible air was propelled into the sky. Devine’s breaths were less rapid, but not by much. She had done to him what the two assassins on the Geneva train and the three drunk idiots back at the bar had failed to do: thrown him off his game.

“My sister,” she began.

“Yes. By everyone’s accounts she was a wonderful person. I’m sorry for your loss.”

“Not everyone’s account, Mr. Devine. You haven’t talked to me yet.”

And with that stunning statement, she pushed past him and strode off.

Devine knew he should have gone after her. But he didn’t. At least not right away. When the paralysis that had gripped him finally receded, he turned and raced back down the path. Once he reached the main street he gazed up and down it. He hadn’t heard a car start up, and then he recalled being told she had a bicycle.

He trudged off to his cottage, where he checked to make sure none of the traps he had laid had been disturbed. They were all still in place. He stripped down to his skivvies and stared into the bathroom mirror. Devine traced the graphic surgical scar along his shoulder where the Glock round had impacted.

He had a similar wound on his other shoulder from a sniper round fired at him in the Middle East that had penetrated a defect in his body armor. The Iraqi could have finished off the immobilized Devine with a head shot, but Devine supposed it had been his lucky day—though he hadn't really felt all that lucky while he'd been airlifted out nearly unconscious and bleeding like a bitch.

He eyed his calf where the IED had said hello by leaving its bomb pattern forevermore on his flesh.

Will the fourth time punch your ticket for good, Devine? Maybe.

He stretched, and then grimaced as his limb ached from the effort. He lay down on yet another strange bed and stared up at the ceiling. He was most definitely a ceiling starer, where he could watch the imagined frames of his life and his myriad mistakes troop by. This was his version of very cheap therapy. Like many military folks he found it difficult to talk to people about anything, much less his inner feelings, whatever the hell those actually were.

The world used to be divided into black and white for Devine. Good guys versus bad guys. This demarcation used to be true and unassailable and easy to differentiate.

Now?

Now Devine relied on himself only. Thus his longstanding grueling early-morning workouts, and the ceiling analysis of his past actions. He needed to make sure that he could survive. Anything. He trusted only his finely honed military instincts that had told him to turn left instead of right, to duck at just the right time. To wait beside a door just a second longer so the shotgun blast could blow through it without killing him.

Two other faces appeared on the ceiling of his thoughts, as they often did.

Captain Kenneth Hawkins, and Lieutenant Roy Blankenship.

He had served with both men, who were also now both dead. Hawkins had murdered Blankenship and made it look like suicide. His motive was as old as time: he coveted Blankenship's pretty wife, with whom he was having an affair.

Army CID had clusterfucked the case, hamstrung by military politics, and Hawkins had gotten away clean. That was until a suspicious Devine, who had previously learned of the affair from Blankenship, had tried his best to get CID to take another look. When he was stonewalled, Devine had resorted to a personal accounting. He had lured Hawkins out into the Afghanistan mountains, and a furious fight had ensued. Devine had not meant to kill the man. But he had died anyway.

And then Emerson Campbell had come along with all the evidence to put Devine away in the Army prison out in Leavenworth, Kansas. But the man had given Devine a choice.

Prison.

Or this.

His therapy session over, he closed his eyes and, like the Army had taught him, fell asleep within a minute.

14

Devine's phone alarm kicked off at five a.m.

He pulled on sweatpants, stout court shoes, and a thick hoodie, then jogged out onto the dark and empty main street and turned left.

He stopped at the harbor for a minute and watched some boats heading out. Men were lifting metal cages and large wooden boxes on the dock, and hefting some of them into boats cleated to slips. He also saw other men in small dinghies motoring or rowing out to the moored boats. The day apparently started early for those who labored on the waters. Under the lights that illuminated the area, he recognized the man who had confronted him outside the bar and Devine had falsely accused of being an informant. He was in the stern of a good-sized boat that was making its way out of the harbor. He looked like he was not yet over his boozing from the previous night.

Devine continued on. He had already noted the square of dormant grass and leafless trees about a quarter mile down where the small main business area ended. He reached it and did a quick twenty-minute HIIT, or high-intensity interval training routine, to get his heart pumping and his blood flowing. This was followed by push-ups, pull-ups on a tree limb, squats, lunges, jacks, and isometric holds, where his body shook from the effort of holding statue-like poses for less than a minute. This was followed by more core work, followed by even more intense lower-body exercises, which every Army grunt knew was where real strength came from.

He did wind sprints forward and then backward, because all-out charges were often followed by the same level of retreats, and you never wanted to fully look away from whoever was shooting at you.

His breathing was always precisely timed and measured to sync with his body and effort.

He finished with Army low crawls on the wet grass that led to high-kickers and then an exhausting set of burpees.

He slowly cooled down, letting his heart rate and breathing normalize before heading back. It was nearly six thirty when he stepped into the shower back at his cottage.

He dried off, changed into a fresh set of clothes, and headed out. The inn served a continental breakfast, but, as he had mentioned to Harper and Fuss, Devine had spotted a breakfast restaurant, Maine Brew, down the street. He wanted some time to think before he met up with the local police. And he wanted to go over again what he had learned, and not learned, so far.

A short walk through windy cold brought him to the blue-painted door of the restaurant. It was pretty full at a little after seven. The place looked like it had been recently renovated; the clusters of tables and chairs in the middle of the sturdy wood composite floor, and the red vinyl booths that ringed the perimeter, looked new. The counter was long and had deli-style refrigerated, glass-fronted cabinets that were filled with all sorts of meats, salads, sandwiches, and other prepared foods.

Two waitresses were working the tables. At the counter a third young woman was taking care of the half dozen customers seated there on bolted-in whirly stools. The place was definitely bustling, Devine observed, but there might not be many places to get breakfast in town, either.

The sign on a metal stand at the entrance said to seat yourself, so Devine did, at a booth at the very end of one wall and farthest from the kitchen.

A young waitress hurried over with a laminated menu that was clipped to a wooden board. "What can I get you to drink?" she asked.

"Coffee, black, and a big glass of water, no ice."

"Coming up."

She hurried off while Devine looked at the menu. There were some healthier selections, like avocado toast and stone-cut oatmeal with fruit, but he decided to opt for an old favorite, with one modification thrown into the mix.

When she brought the coffee, which was piping hot and smelled wonderful, he ordered the Lobsterman's Breakfast, which basically covered all major food groups, with a piece of fried cod—the one modification—thrown in.

She left the menu behind after he gave his order, and he

ran his gaze down it. The owner was Annie . . . Palmer? Devine did a double take at the name. Palmer was a pretty common surname, but in a town with fewer than three hundred people could she be related to Earl?

He took out his phone and Googled the restaurant. On the website he saw a photo of a smiling young woman. He glanced up to see the same woman working the breakfast counter.

Annie Palmer was in her late twenties, with dark hair, brown eyes, and of medium height. The woman didn't seem to be carrying an ounce of fat on her. But with her job he assumed she never stopped moving. There was no mention of any connection to Earl in the online materials, but there wouldn't necessarily be, either.

His breakfast arrived, and it was as good as the coffee. He was surprised how much he liked the combo of fried cod, scrambled eggs with bacon and ham, and thick pieces of buttered toast. He took his time eating and watching everyone around him without seeming to do so. He caught several people staring at him and making no pains to disguise it.

He thought back to his encounters with Dak and, later, his sister. Alex seemed truly brokenhearted about her sibling's death. But then what had her parting comment been about?

Did she mean that not everyone thought Jenny was a good person, maybe including her?

These musings were interrupted by someone coming over and approaching his table.

Annie Palmer tucked a strand of hair back into place behind her ear and slid him a fresh cup of coffee. She had also brought one for herself. Up close, he could see the smattering of freckles over her cheeks and nose. She sat down across from him.

Devine glanced over to see that the counter crowd had mostly dissipated. In fact, the place only had a few tables still occupied. He eyed his watch. He'd been here nearly fifty minutes. It had felt like five seconds.

"Thanks," he said. "Does the boss usually make table calls?"

She smiled and it was warm and genuine, and the woman looked like she was used to doing it. "The boss does everything that she needs to do to keep this place afloat."

"Well, it looks to me like you have fair winds and following seas."

"In Maine, that can change in a heartbeat."

"I suppose. You're young to be running your own business, but then what do I know."

"I'll be thirty in two years, but some days I feel a lot older."

"Don't we all."

Small talk over, she took a sip of her coffee and gave him a serious stare; her freckles seemed to enlarge with the change in demeanor. "Jenny?"

"Yes."

She looked down, but not before Devine could see her lips tremble.

"It was a shock," said Palmer, lifting her chin to look at him.

"I'm sure."

"I guess you're working with Chief Harper and Wendy?"

"I am."

"They're good people, but probably not very experienced in this sort of thing. We . . . we don't have many murders in Putnam, thank God."

"But they know all the local angles, which I'll need to learn, too."

"So you think it was someone from Putnam who killed her?"

The query was blunt, and Devine could sense that Palmer craved a blunt response.

But he could not give it.

"I don't know. I've been here less than twenty-four hours. I haven't even gotten the lay of the land yet."

"I heard you haven't let the grass grow under your feet. Really hit the ground running."

"That's my job. But going fast is not always good. One might jump to conclusions that later turn out to be wrong. I avoid that if I can. I'm Travis Devine, by the way, but you probably already knew that."

"And I'm Annie Palmer, but you obviously already knew that I owned this place."

He held up his phone. "Not much privacy anymore."

"No, there's not." Her face flushed and he wasn't sure why.

"So, any relation to Earl?"

"He's my grandfather."

"And your parents?"

"House fire, fifteen years ago. Neither one of them made it out alive."

"I'm very sorry."

"I was away at summer camp." Palmer put a hand to her mouth and, in spite of obviously trying hard not to, she briefly teared up.

"I'm sorry," said Devine, handing her a napkin from the holder on the table. "I didn't mean for you to recall painful memories."

"It's okay." She wiped her eyes and let out a long, cleansing breath. "Then Bertie, that's my grandmother, died a few weeks ago. Always thought Gramps would go first. He did too, I'm sure."

"That is so incredibly hard. For both *you* and your grandfather." He paused. "I understand that he found Jenny's body?"

She had to know that he knew this, thought Devine, but she still looked troubled by his query. "He just stumbled on it. I mean, what else, right? It was terrible."

Devine assumed his poker face and just nodded. "I suppose he recognized Jenny?"

"Yes, yes he did. I mean, he'd known Jenny her whole life."

Devine thought about the distance from the edge of the bluff down to the rock shelf where Jenny's body lay in the darkness, partially covered in water, and mentally shook his head in disbelief at what she had said. And there was something else.

"When I was by his place, I saw that your grandfather has special pedal controls on his station wagon? And some extra handholds?"

"Yes. He has bad arthritis and some spine issues. He had neck surgery that didn't turn out too well. He can't really use his legs and feet to work the gas and brake, but he can do it with his hands. He's still pretty strong in the upper body. The handholds let him pull himself out of the car. But he doesn't drive much anymore unless he has to, or he's in a stubborn mood. And he can't drive his truck anymore. Too hard to get in and out. Mostly, he just walks . . . slowly."

"So were you friends with the Silkwells?"

"Yes. They were the most famous family here." She attempted a smile. "We didn't move in the same social circles, to the extent Putnam has any. But Alex isn't that much older than I am. We used to hang out some growing up. She's an amazing artist."

"But you didn't see or talk to Jenny on her last trip here?"

"No, I didn't even know she was in town."

"She's been described as a really good person."

Before answering Palmer took a sip of coffee. "Yes, yes she was. Outgoing and friendly."

"Not like her sister, then. You said you know Alex?"

Palmer scrunched up her nose for a moment before

saying, bluntly, "If anyone says they really know Alex, you know what I would say?"

"What?"

"That they're lying to themselves."

That might have been her most honest statement yet, thought Devine. "Interesting. Why do you say that?"

She shrugged. "She never really lets anyone get close."

"And Dak?"

"What about him?"

"Good person?"

"I'm probably not the one to ask." She rose. "Got cleanup duty now. The glamorous life of a small business owner."

"I'd like to chat again, if that's okay."

She looked around at the four walls of the place, and her expression was not exactly one of unbridled joy. "Well, you know where to find me, pretty much every waking moment."

He glanced at her hand and saw no ring there. "Husband? Kids?"

He knew this question was not particularly appropriate, but criminal investigations seldom were.

"Have a good day, Mr. Devine."

Putnam was getting more interesting, and puzzling, by the minute.

15

Devine handed a cup of coffee to Harper and one to Fuss when they arrived to search Jenny Silkwell's cottage. He'd purchased the drinks before he'd left Maine Brew.

They thanked him, and then looked dumbstruck when he told them that he had discovered Alex Silkwell sobbing outside her sister's cottage last night.

"What was she doing here?" asked Fuss.

"She didn't say. I guess she was upset about what had happened to her sister."

Harper took a drink of his coffee and nodded. "I suppose that makes sense."

"She might have also wanted to get into the cottage," offered Devine. He wanted to see how the officers responded to that possibility.

Fuss cocked her head at him. "What, to get a keepsake or something, you mean?"

"Or something," said Devine delicately.

"You mean, attempting to knowingly procure evidence from a homicide victim's last known place of residence *before* it was processed by law enforcement?" said Harper like he was speaking in open court and striving to be absolutely precise with his language.

"Yes" was Devine's simple response.

"It was locked and covered with police tape."

"She wouldn't have known that until she got here," pointed out Devine. "And how did she know this was Jenny's cottage? Had they met here beforehand?"

Harper waved this query off. "Small town, she would have heard from someone. Maybe Pat told her."

"How did she appear, other than the crying?" asked Fuss. "Did you speak to her?"

He gave a shorthand account of their conversation, leaving out Alex's comment about her perhaps not-so-wonderful sister. But he did tell them how she had put him in his place.

"Yeah, that sounds like Alex," proclaimed Fuss.

Harper said, "Shall we get to the search?"

"Do you have the keys to her rental?" asked Devine.

"They were in the cottage. I made a quick check before I secured it," replied Harper.

They did the rental vehicle first. It had a new car smell, and there was not a single thing of Jenny's in it. And they pulled up the liner in the trunk, looked under the car, in the wheel wells and under the floorboards and seats, and even in the engine compartment and tailpipe.

"Let's head inside," said Harper. Devine was grateful to get out of the cold.

The chief cut the police tape and unlocked the door

with the one-pound slug key. Devine asked if the key had been found on Jenny's body.

"No," said Harper. "But Pat gave me this master key. Well, let's get to it."

They found a small carry-on roller next to the bed. It contained only clothes and a pair of sneakers. The bathroom had her toiletry bag with some of the items laid out neatly on the sink. She had been here only the one day, arriving early, so the bed had not been slept in. There was no briefcase. They did find her purse with her wallet in it. But no laptop or phone.

"You have the clothes she was found in?" asked Devine.

"Back in the evidence locker at the station," said Fuss.

"Got a list on you?"

She pulled out her phone and clicked through some screens. She held it out to him.

He read off, "Parka, jeans, sweater, boots, socks, underwear." He looked up. "Personal effects?"

"Just the two rings, necklace, and the Breitling watch I mentioned before. And now that we found her purse and wallet here we can definitely rule out robbery."

"What about a phone? Everyone carries a phone."

"We found no phone on her person," said Fuss.

"So since it's not here presumably someone took it?"

"Or it got washed away when she fell onto the rocks," said Harper. "Like we told you, by the time we got there she was damn near floating."

Devine didn't buy this but didn't comment.

Harper looked around. "Well, there's nothing much here. We'll bag and tag what is."

"You don't want to call in a forensics team?" said Devine.

"The closest one I know of that's any good is at least two hours away," Fuss pointed out. "And this is *not* the crime scene. If we had found something obvious—blood or signs of a struggle, for example—we would call them in. But this isn't the big city, Devine. No CSI here. Resources are limited and police budgets are tiny. We can't snap our fingers and these folks suddenly appear, even for a priority case like this. Everyone's busy, and they already sent extra people out on it."

"That much crime around here?"

"You'd be surprised. It's just spread over a wide area. There are fewer and fewer jobs, fentanyl use is through the roof. People are just fed up with being crapped on and everyone around here has guns, lots of them. Not a good combo."

"Putnam looks like it's doing okay."

"A few nice shops and a new bar and some fancy restaurants do not make for a paradise for everybody," interjected Harper. "Fishing still drives this part of Maine, and the fishing lately has not been all that good and it's only expected to get more challenging."

The two officers proceeded to methodically collect the woman's personal possessions.

Devine watched them for a bit and then walked around the cottage. He was pretending it was part of an enclave of mud shacks outside of Kabul where they'd found a meticulously hidden IED processing operation. Or twenty clicks to the north of Dohuk, where an entire rural village had banded together to hide a top leader of ISIS. A thorough search had rooted him out and a shoot-out had followed, the intensity of which Devine had seldom seen. Every villager, even grandmothers and kids, had produced a variety of weapons, from old Soviet AK-47 assault rifles to Stechkin machine pistols, and opened fire. Devine's team leader had had to call in reinforcements to eventually win the battle. And the ISIS leader had been killed in the ensuing melee, so they got no intel from him. And the confrontation had cost two American soldiers their lives, along with four kids and three elderly women.

Devine had thrown up after seeing the torn-apart bodies of the children and women. And he had not been alone.

He eyed the small desk set against the window, a duplicate of the one in his room. Bright sunlight was streaming in through the glass, and he stood directly in its path to gain some warmth. When he looked down at the desktop he saw it.

A slight dust pattern. The shape sure looked like the size of a laptop.

He ran the possibilities through in his head: Had Jenny taken it with her? Had her killer taken it from her? Or had her killer come here and taken it after she was dead, as he had speculated the previous night?

If they had taken her laptop and phone, he knew the security on each would be pretty much unbeatable.

But if they somehow got the passwords from her before they killed her?

There was up to several hours between Silkwell's last being seen alive and her death occurring. A lot could have happened during that time.

Guillaume didn't mention any traces of torture in the post-mortem, but still. If our enemies now possess what she had on her laptop or phone?

He knew there were strict protocols and procedures for keeping classified information on government devices. And just like the private sector, much of it was stored in the cloud. But he also knew that some government employees took shortcuts, or didn't always adhere strictly to the protocols.

He glanced over to see Fuss eyeing him cagily where he stood in the sunlight.

"What's up?" she asked.

"Just trying to stay warm."

Fuss scoffed. "Try coming here in January." She went back to work.

And Devine stared back down at a dust pattern that was making his gut churn.

16

After parting company with the local police, Devine walked to his cottage, where he composed and sent off a long email to Campbell, filling him in on everything that had happened since they last communicated, including Silkwell's laptop possibly having been taken and there being no sign of her phone. As Devine wrote it all out, he could see that it was a lot to report, in a short period of time. And his instincts were telling him that there was a lot more to come.

He got into the Tahoe and drove along the coast highway. He had the dinner with Dak tonight, but he'd decided he'd first have a follow-up meeting with his sister, though the initial encounter had hardly been a meeting. He checked his watch and noted that Dak would have been at his tattoo shop for a couple of hours.

Devine arrived at Jocelyn Point and headed up the cracked and pitted asphalt driveway, past landscaping that had once been elegant and substantial but now was just a ruinous mass as nature reclaimed its territory. He parked in front of the house and took in the structure.

It was not in as bad a shape as he had expected. Parts of

the exterior, while grungy and ill-used by the elements, looked like they had been power-washed fairly recently. The front entrance foundation's veneer had some new stone and fresh mortar, and the wooden columns holding up the pitched roof over the front door looked new.

The glass in some of the windows seemed to have been replaced. And though the lawn was now dormant, the sod looked to maybe have been put in during the fall. He eyed one of the tall brick chimney stacks and saw smoke curling out of it.

Directly behind the house was a large clapboard structure with a high-pitched cedar shake roof and a large skylight set in each plane of the shakes. There were windows lining the sidewalls and a large exhaust pipe coming out of the rear wall. He peered inside one of the windows and saw that it was set up as an art studio: easels with works in process on them; long worktables with cans of brushes and small bottles of paint lined up, along with sketchpads, jars of drawing pencils and charcoal sticks, and large and small paint-smeared palettes. In one corner was a potting wheel, and in another corner stood a small kiln. There were also large metal tanks next to what looked to be welding equipment, and a large work sink, and a metal tub set on wooden sawhorses.

He tried the door but it was securely locked.

He looked to his left, and far down the property line he could see some of the ancillary buildings he had glimpsed last night.

He walked over to the coastline. He found it was quite

elevated as he looked over the edge to the rocks below, though there was a path down that looked well used. Some of the boulders were nearly as large as an Abrams tank. The surf pounded against them, sending a drenching spray halfway up from where Devine stood.

He knew that Maine had a long coastline, the fourth longest of all the states, longer even than California's, because of all the jagged clusters of coves and inlets. And out of all that shoreline, in the middle of the night in a downpour, Earl Palmer walked through a forest of trees to the exact spot where Jenny Silkwell lay dead on the rocks below? The odds of that happening were enormous. No, they were beyond impossible.

I need to talk to that man, and sooner rather than later.

He turned and walked back around to the front of the main house and knocked.

No answer. He knocked again and then pounded on the wood.

"Go away," called out Alex Silkwell.

"It's Travis Devine. We met last night."

"Then go away *faster*. I have nothing to say to you."

Devine stared at the weathered door and imagined Silkwell standing just on the other side of it, all defiant and ticked off. He needed to talk to her, but he didn't have a warrant and so there was really nothing he could do.

"I'm leaving my card under the doormat."

Silence greeted this statement, and Devine couldn't really imagine any scenario where she would be phoning him voluntarily.

He walked back to his car and drove off. He reached the coast road, turned left, and hit the gas. Once around a bend, he pulled off, parked his car, and hoofed it back to Jocelyn Point.

He took up a surveillance point behind a stand of white pines, which were bracketed by some leafless ash, birch, and maples. Using his optics, he kept an eye on the main house and also the art studio.

Thirty minutes later his patience was rewarded as Alex, carrying a cup of something, hurried out to the studio, unlocked the door, and went inside.

Devine put his optics away and marched over to the studio. He peered in one window and saw Alex slipping off her coat. Underneath she had on jean overalls and a long-sleeved thermal undershirt. Her hair was piled loosely on top of her head and secured there with some pins and braids.

She picked up a large palette, loaded it with fresh paint from a variety of tubes, and headed over to one of the canvases set on an easel.

Devine slipped to the door and tried the knob. It turned easily. For some reason he was more nervous than when he had been about to breach places in the Middle East where he knew men inside were waiting to kill him. But he actually knew why.

I trained long and hard for the latter scenario. Not so much for what I'm about to do.

He opened the door and walked in.

17

He expected her to start screaming, or maybe throw something at him, or fire up the blowtorch on her welding kit and come at him for a personal charcoaling session.

But Alex just stood there in front of her painting, her palette in one hand and a slender brush in the other. "You're persistent."

"My job sort of requires that." He looked around. "So this is where the magic happens?"

"It's not so much magic as just hard work, luck, and a dash of creativity and talent thrown in."

He looked around at paintings in oil, acrylic, and watercolor along with clay sculptures all in various stages of completion. Bronze and other metallic figures bent and curved by heat and pressure into fascinating shapes were arrayed around the perimeter of the space.

"I think it's more than a dash of talent. I can barely draw a straight line. This . . . this is really impressive, Ms. Silkwell."

His frankness seemed to draw down whatever anger she might have been feeling at his intrusion. "I'm Alex. I've never been Miss anything."

"And I'm Travis."

"From Homeland Security keeping us all safe and the American Dream possible? I think you all need to step up your game."

On that she turned back to her work.

He came to stand behind her and took it in.

While some of the works displayed in the studio were portraits of people, landscapes, and animals, this one was clearly more impressionistic. A yellow ball erupting out of an orange flame that, in turn, devolved into a blue wave that was about to descend, seemingly violently, on what he took to be roofs and a jagged church steeple reaching disproportionately far into the sky.

"What's that?" he asked.

"What I see in my head every morning when I wake up," she replied as she added some shadowing to the flame.

"And what does it represent to you?"

She glanced at him. "More importantly, what does it represent to *you*?"

He was taken aback by her swift counterattack. "I . . . I'm not sure. It looks sort of like Armageddon."

"And here I thought I was being subtle."

Devine looked around, and something occurred to him. "You knew I was coming back. You knew I would see you coming in here. And that's why you began working on this painting."

"I have no idea what you're talking about."

But her cheeks flushed and she wouldn't look at him.

"This work looks finished, while you have lots of

others in far earlier stages. So what's so important about this piece that you wanted me to see you working on it? I take it you believe Armageddon is coming to Putnam?"

"What a vivid imagination you have. You might want to consider a career in fiction."

"Okay, what does it mean to you, the painting? And why do you see that scene in your head every morning?"

"That is my business and no concern of yours. And didn't you come here to ask me questions about my sister?"

Her phone buzzed. She put her brush down, slipped it from her pocket, and glanced at the screen. "Give me a minute," she said and started thumbing a response.

Devine took the time to look around some more. That was when he saw the large framed, finished painting. It looked to be a white dress with a large red spot dead on the center. The way it had been painted, it seemed like the red spot was perpetually growing; a neat optical illusion, he thought. Then he saw a brass plate tacked onto the frame that read, HER FIRST PERIOD.

Okay, didn't see that one coming.

In another corner he spotted something that also gave him considerable pause.

He bent down to peer closer.

Damn.

It was a bronze sculpture that looked like a heavily veined, erect penis that was looped with a chain. And down below, around the testicles, were . . . handcuffs.

"Want to buy it? I'll give you a good price. I bet it would look great in your living room."

He turned to see her staring at him as she slipped her phone back into her pocket.

"I can guess at the symbolism," he said.

"Can you now?" She perched on the edge of a worktable and crossed one long leg over the other. "Please share?"

"Without being too graphic, I suppose it's to shackle, or at least push back against a man's . . . baser impulses."

"In that regard life does not imitate art, because there is no way to really do that."

"Some things are changing, hopefully for the better."

"Some would say the change is happening far too slowly. It can be depressing." She looked around her space. "But some of the greatest artists were depressed all the time. They used that to power their creativity."

"I can understand that."

"You can? Really?"

"I served with a guy who drew these big designs in the sand when we were in the Middle East during some pretty heavy fighting. We were losing guys every day, and we were having to kill people every day, and not just soldiers on the other side, because lots of different sorts of people were fighting against us. After every mission, he'd come back, hang up his gear, pull out this wooden paddle he'd whittled, and mark out, well, what I guess you'd call artwork in the sand. They never lasted because a wind storm would come through and they'd be gone. But he kept at it. I could never figure out what his designs meant and he never said, but they were pretty intricate."

"Did you ask him why he did it?"

"Yeah, I did."

"What'd he say?" she asked, with what seemed genuine interest.

"He said it was either do that or blow his brains out."

"I've never killed anyone, but I think I can understand what your friend meant." She slowly returned to her painting and started adding brushstrokes to it.

"I was told that you turned down some great art schools."

She glanced at him in annoyance. "The timing was not right."

"And now?"

"And now I don't need them, do I? I educated myself. We have a wonderful library here in Putnam filled with books about everything I would want to know about from writers all around the world."

"And I guess you didn't need any formal art instruction."

"I actually had an excellent teacher and mentor right here."

"Who was that?" said a surprised Devine.

"You have no reason to know."

"O-okay," he said, wondering why she would have a problem with sharing information like that. "I understand you teach art part-time at the public school."

Her expression instantly brightened. "I do. Twice a week at the very end of the day. That's all they could afford. They barely have books in the school library or computers for the students. When government budgets are tight they always cut education; the students can't vote."

"But they will one day," pointed out Devine.

"The kids were uninterested in art at first. But their enthusiasm grew as they got better." She looked around. "But the odds are stacked against them. Jobs are limited in this part of Maine, along with opportunity. Drugs are rampant, and grandparents are raising their grandkids because of it. Ninety percent of families are on some sort of government assistance. Many of these kids are being dropped into big black holes, never to be seen again."

"But you might find an artist out there who you could lead to another, better future."

"I doubt I have that ability in me."

"Why don't I believe that?"

She put her brush down and stared at him. "Believe what you want."

"Okay, let's talk about your sister."

"I didn't even know she was in town," she said automatically.

Just like her brother told me. And I believe it even less this time around.

"Did she come here often and not tell you?"

"She didn't come here all that often. Once or twice a year."

"When was the last time?"

"During the summer."

"Why not more often?" asked Devine.

"I don't know. You'd have to ask her, and you can't."

"When was the last time you saw or spoke with her?"

Alex let out an extended breath and shook her head. "Saw her briefly when she came here during the summer. Spoke to her last? I can't really remember."

"Ballpark? Months, weeks, days?"

"Over a month," said Alex.

"What'd you talk about?"

"Nothing important."

"You two weren't close?"

"She had her life and I had mine and they didn't really mix well. She was off somewhere around the world while I was stuck right here in Putnam."

"Stuck? By your choice?"

"Bad choice of words. It has everything I want as an artist. Solitude, incredible beauty, haunting images, a place that makes you think. It's very inspiring."

"I spoke with your mother. She thought you should be in New York, or California, or Europe."

"Of course she did."

"You see her much?"

"Not for years," said Alex.

"I saw your father, too."

Her expression grew firmer and seemed to be pulling her inward. "I didn't know that was possible."

"Your brother said he goes to visit him."

"They have that military connection," she said in answer. "I don't."

"I don't think he has long left."

"None of us know how long we have left," she replied.

"So you didn't know Jenny was in town and you hadn't seen or spoken with her in a while?"

"That's right. So I really can't help you." She turned back to her canvas. "And I have a lot of work to do. So . . ."

"Have you started selling your artwork? Your mother didn't think you were."

"I have an agent now. Over the last few years I've been commissioned to do a number of paintings and sculptures. You can tell my mother that my clients include people from New York and California *and* across the pond."

"You should tell her yourself. I'm sure she'll be very happy for you."

"I'm not nearly as sure about that as you appear to be."

"Are you sad that your sister is no longer living?" Devine had decided to ask this provocative question to get something from the woman that didn't sound scripted.

"What the hell kind of question is that?" she said, her face flushing again and her thick eyebrows nearly touching.

"It's just that, a question."

"You found me sobbing my heart out at the inn."

"I just don't know *why* you were sobbing your heart out. You didn't hang around."

"Well, it was because of her. So now you know. Are we done?"

"Then why did you intimate that you would not be describing your sister to me as a person much loved by folks here?"

"I don't remember saying that."

Devine repeated back the account she had given him from the notes he had put in his iPhone.

"Does that jog your memory?"

"No."

"Okay, one last thing."

"What?" she snapped.

"I'd like you to go with me to where your sister's body was found."

"Why would I do that?" she said slowly. "And why would you *want* me to do that?"

"Because you know this area far better than I do. And you clearly possess something that might help me."

"What, pray tell, is that?"

"An artist's insight into the human soul."

"I still don't think I can help you," she said, her tone and voice not nearly as assured.

"Let's go find out." He paused and added, "Please."

18

He retrieved his rental and drove it to Jocelyn Point to pick her up. Then it wasn't that far to the spot where Jenny Silkwell's body had been found. They walked over the same cold, rugged ground that Jenny had presumably trod during her last night on earth.

Devine wanted to see Alex's reaction to being here, because that might actually help him understand her better. And he thought he was going to have to do that in order to figure out what was really going on.

She had put on an overcoat and scarf and a ski cap pulled down low over her ears. The wind had picked up even more, and they watched as dark clouds gathered just off the coast.

"Looks like snow or sleet is coming," said Devine.

"Let's hope not," she said.

"You don't like the white stuff?"

"I teach my art class late this afternoon. I don't want to miss it."

She looked around as they walked across the field toward the forest and the wide path through it to the bluff overlooking the ocean.

And then something happened to Alex. She started to sway and then she cried out and Devine barely caught her before she slumped to the ground.

"Are you all right?" he exclaimed. "Look, I'm sorry for bringing you here. I didn't stop to think about the effect it might have on you."

She looked up at him, her eyes unfocused and her expression woozy. She slowly came around and then managed to stand without his assistance.

"We can go back," he offered.

She looked at the open field and shuddered. "No, I'm here now. Let's get this done."

As they entered the path she seemed normal again, even walking with spirit. He wondered why that was, since they were getting closer to, not farther away from, where her sister's body had been found.

He led her to the edge of the land, and they gazed down at the rocks and the ocean.

"Is this where she was killed?" she said.

"It appears so."

She shot him a perplexed look. "What do you mean 'appears'?"

"I meant it exactly as I said."

She indicated the rocks. "But her body was found down there."

"Yes, *that* is a fact. Everything else is speculation."

"You've lost me."

Devine didn't answer. He was thinking about possibilities

that he would need to parse through if he was going to get to the truth.

Jenny had been shot in the forehead, and the round exited out the back of her skull and apparently vanished into the ocean. That meant she was looking landward. But if you went to the edge here, wouldn't you be looking at the ocean? Since that was the whole point of coming to this spot. The casing had been found more than three hundred yards away from where Jenny had fallen. At night she wouldn't have even been able to see her shooter from that distance. And if she had turned to leave before she was shot squarely in the forehead, would she have been close enough to the edge to topple over it?

"Why did you want me to come here?" she asked, pulling him from these thoughts.

"I need to know if this spot had some special significance for Jenny."

"None that I know of. Do you think she might have come here to think?"

"In the pouring rain late at night? No, I doubt it."

"Then you think she came here with someone? Her killer?"

Devine didn't answer because he was the one doing the questioning, not her. "Did your sister ever talk to you about her work?"

"No. Wasn't it confidential?"

"Did she say it was?"

"No, and I didn't ask. I was used to our father being unable to talk about political stuff."

"Right. He served on the Senate Intelligence Committee."

"I was never interested in any of that. And he and I—"

"—weren't close?"

"Jenny was his favorite. And I was a distant third behind Dak."

"Jenny was interested in politics?"

"Jenny was interested in everything," she said wearily.

"And you? What are you interested in?"

"My art. And now my students."

Devine thought about what Pat Kingman had said, that Alex had changed years ago, going from outgoing and fun to introverted and . . . scared, diving back into her hidey-hole at Jocelyn Point after venturing out for short intervals. But she was teaching at the local school, so maybe she was getting over whatever had caused her to change.

"I'm having dinner with Dak tonight. Would you like to join us? My treat?"

She frowned and looked away. "Thanks, but I think I'll pass."

As they walked back to the Tahoe, Devine said, "Did your sister have any enemies here?"

"Not that I know of. She was adored in Putnam."

"But, again, you intimated that you didn't share the general opinion that Jenny was a wonderful person, regardless of whether you remember saying it or not. You did."

She wheeled around on him, seemingly itching for a fight. "Look, I meant nothing more than the people with those general opinions never had to *live* with her. She was a tough act to follow. That doesn't mean I didn't love her or make me any less sorry that she's dead. So don't try to put words in my mouth."

"I can understand the hard-act-to-follow piece."

"Can you really?" she said skeptically.

"My two older siblings are roaring successes in their chosen and highly compensated fields. Me, not so much."

She gazed at him with a sudden look of empathy. "Oh, well . . . being a federal agent isn't a small accomplishment . . ." Her voice trailed off as they walked.

He drove her back to Jocelyn Point. She got out and then peered back into the Tahoe. "I'm sorry I wasn't more help."

"You might have been more help than you think," he replied.

"Your meeting with my brother?"

"What about it? Changed your mind and want to join?"

"No. But, piece of advice? Don't believe everything you're told."

She slowly walked to her art studio.

19

Hoping to beat the incoming storm, Devine drove straight back to where Jenny's body had been found and walked the area with a soldier's eye for detail.

He stood at the spot where the shell casing had been found. The .300 Norma magnum round was mostly, but not exclusively, used by the military and its snipers. The casing had been next to a stand of bare trees, providing some good cover. He had noted all of that before. He drew a sight line between the ejected casing and the spot where Jenny had been standing before toppling over the edge after being shot.

Or so the story goes.

He lay prone on the ground and pantomimed taking aim at Jenny Silkwell.

He pulled the invisible trigger and counted three beats. The bullet would have hit her in the blink of an eye from this distance, but it would have taken a few beats for her to fall over the edge and hit the rocks below.

He stood and pulled out his phone. He'd had the medical examiner, Françoise Guillaume, email him the preliminary autopsy report. As he read it, the weather system coming in off the coast had raised the temperature enough to where the precipitation that started to fall was rain, and not sleet or snow.

He caught himself smiling. Alex Silkwell would get to teach her art class today.

He hustled back to the Tahoe and reached it before it really started to pour. He sat there staring at a crime scene that had definite shakiness to its outlines, and thus its substance.

He texted Campbell with his theories and waited for a reply.

He got it five minutes later, a testament to how such a busy man, with a dozen missions like Devine's to oversee, was laser-focused on this one. But it was no doubt the only mission under his command that had to do with a man who had saved his life. As a former soldier Devine got that one really well. It forged a bond stronger than just about everything else in life.

Campbell's advice was explicit:

> Follow your gut and keep things close to the vest. Dak Silkwell's military file is sealed. I cannot break through it as yet. And Curt never talked to me about his son's military career, and why he left, and I never asked. Stay tuned. It is critical to find her government laptop and personal phone, Devine. Ulcers are forming in people's guts here.

He knew that if someone had taken those devices, then Devine might be looking at a stranger having killed Jenny in order to get some intel from her. They had checked the secure cloud of her government-issued computer and personal phone and found nothing unusual, nor had there been any attempts to hack into them. And there had been no calls, emails, or texts that would foreshadow her being murdered. If she had communicated with anyone about her trip here, she had not done so electronically on her personal or government devices.

Being an ops officer, she knew the pitfalls of sending anything over the internet. But she could have used a burner phone or prepaid phone card and left no trail. She had no social media accounts at all, not unusual for someone with her occupation.

He sent a brief reply to Campbell, put the Tahoe in gear, and fought the wind and rain to his next destination.

Earl Palmer's house.

20

The rain started to ease some as Devine pulled onto the long gravel drive. In the daylight everything looked different as he wound back through a thick stand of bare woods with cluttered undergrowth. The long limbs swayed, dipped, and creaked in the stiff breeze that had never been absent since Devine had stepped foot in Putnam.

The little cottage appeared to him in the middle of the woods. Coupled with the inclement weather, the place had an ominous sensibility to it, like something out of a Brothers Grimm violent yarn masquerading as a fairy tale. In the light he could see that it was white clapboard with faded green shutters, just as the man who had confronted Devine outside the bar had said it would be. He eyed the ancient station wagon again. And the F150 looked even older. The truck bed was filled with old tools, long metal rods, what looked to be a small concrete mixer, rolls of fish netting and rope, and grimy buoys.

Next to the house, on a small rusty trailer, was a wooden dinghy with a name neatly stenciled on the side.

He got out of the car and drew close enough to see.

BERTIE'S BOAT.

Named after his dead wife.

Behind the house was a small building with curtained windows that he hadn't noticed on his previous night's recon.

He stepped up to the porch and was about to knock when the door opened and he was staring at the business end of an over-and-under shotgun.

Earl Palmer stood there in a red thermal underwear shirt and soiled dungarees, white socks on shoeless feet. He had about an inch in height on Devine and looked ruggedly strong with a barrel chest and long arms that tapered to slender hips and thin, bowed legs. Not bad for a man in his latter seventies, thought Devine. But lobster fishing demanded a lot of physical strength, he reckoned.

Up close he looked like a taller, broader Robert Frost, thought Devine, who had read the man's poetry at West Point. His comrades at the Point had teased him about this, until some pretty local girls they had gone into town to see had told them that they found an interest in poetry incredibly attractive in a man. All the way back to West Point the guys had pestered him for details on some of Frost's best-known lines that they could use for their own pickup efforts.

"'Two roads diverged in the woods and I, I took the one less traveled,'" he had told them. He had learned that the line was often misinterpreted because Frost had regrets in his life and had not actually taken that road. When his buddies asked him what it meant he said, with all sincerity, "We chose a path almost no one else does. We're going to risk our lives to protect our country and way of life. We chose the most honorable journey and also the most dangerous. It's a selfless act of sacrifice in a country that routinely worships individualism over the collective."

None of them had expected that response, he could tell. Hell, he still didn't know exactly from where inside him those words had come. They had ridden the rest of the way back in silence, each man seemingly lost in thought over what Devine had said.

Devine had lost four of his classmates to war, including one in their group from that night, and three more to suicide after tours of duty that had forced them to see and do things that people should not have to ever see or do.

"Who are you?" Palmer said in a steady, calm voice that put Devine more on edge than if the man had been screaming. "I don't know you. What are you doing on my property?"

"Travis Devine. I'm with Homeland Security. I'm here investigating Jenny Silkwell's murder. I wanted to ask you a few questions, if I may."

"Let me see some ID. Slow," Palmer added.

Devine tentatively reached into his coat pocket and produced his identification.

"Hold it up high so I can see it."

Devine did so and Palmer studied it at eye level before reluctantly lowering his weapon.

"What do you want to know?"

"Can we do this inside?" said Devine as the rain started

up again. The porch had no roof, so he was getting the full effect.

Palmer stepped aside and motioned him in with the gun muzzle. Then he closed the door and pointed Devine into the room overlooking the front yard.

It was small and minimally furnished, but as neat and organized as, well, a ship's cabin, concluded Devine. There was a woodstove that was generating considerable and welcome warmth. On a wooden shelf bolted to the wall were pictures of various people. Devine saw a younger Annie and what were probably her parents. And hugging Earl Palmer was, no doubt, his wife, Alberta. They looked about as much in love as a couple could be. And that picture was fairly recent, he could tell.

Palmer broke the breech on his gun and carefully set it on a table by the window. Devine sat in an old, rumpled chair by the woodstove. A stiff-moving Palmer opened the stove door and threw in some more pellets. Then he moved over to a new-looking recliner and picked up a remote. The chair lifted up so that he barely had to bend his knees to sit down. When he did, he hit another button and the chair lowered.

"Nifty," said Devine.

"Damn body's useless. Feel like an infant. Be wearing a diaper before long."

Palmer set the remote aside and clenched the chair's arms with his thick, gnarled hands. His eyes were a soft gray, and his disheveled silky white hair provided a sharp contrast to the reddened weather-beaten face lying just below it. "What do you want to know? I found her, that's it. I don't know any more than that."

"Can you walk me through the time you left your house that night and when you found the body?"

"Why?"

"Because it might make you remember something new. Please," he added. "Anything to help me find out who killed her."

"I thought the chief and Wendy—"

Devine said, "Jenny Silkwell worked for the federal government. That makes it our concern. I'm sure you can understand. But I *am* working with the local police on the case."

Palmer slowly nodded. "There always was scuttlebutt about what Jenny did. Top-secret stuff, I guess. Why you're here, ain't it?"

"Let's assume that's the case, yes."

Palmer sat back and worried at his mouth with his long index finger. He never looked down, but kept his gaze rigidly straight ahead.

"I . . . went for a walk that night. I do that a lot now."

"I understand you recently lost your wife. I'm very sorry."

The thick white-tufted eyebrows rose and fell, like a heartbeat. "Bertie is . . . was built to go the long voyage, you understand. Strong as a bear, good health, sharp mind. I would've gone long before her, that's for sure, if nature had any say about it. Both her parents lived well into their nineties."

"What happened, if you don't mind my asking?"

Palmer pressed his hands against his bony knees, as though bracing himself for whatever he was about to reveal.

"What *happened* was somebody hit her with their car while she was out walking, knocked her into a washed-out gully behind some scrub bushes, and kept right on going. Left her to die, right there. No one could see her. But they say she . . . she dragged herself along that gully trying to get . . . help. Help that never came. And . . . she died. They killed my wife."

Palmer eased his eyes closed for a moment, and his fingers gripped his thighs as though he were riding out some turbulence high in the sky.

That must be the other homicide that Harper mentioned he was handling, thought Devine. "So they never caught the person?" he asked, though he knew the answer.

Palmer opened his eyes. His hands retreated and he placed them back on the arms of his chair. "No, they never did. Some stranger passing through, most like. Putnam folk would've stopped and helped her. She'd still be alive. Wouldn't have suffered like she did."

"I'm so sorry."

"Yep, that's what people say, I guess. All they *can* say," he added.

"I spoke with your granddaughter earlier, at her café."

He nodded and said, "Annie makes real good coffee. Gives it to me free. Has a nice business going, and that ain't easy to do here. Or anywhere, I guess."

"So the night you went out walking?"

"Hell, gets so I can't seem to breathe in this house no more. I grew up here. I see things and it takes me back, to other . . . memories. Better ones."

"I can see that, sure."

"Just head to the road and sometimes turn left and sometimes right. That night I turned left. Carry a flashlight with me. I got one of them reflective jackets. Annie bought it for me."

"So you were walking?"

"I headed towards Jocelyn Point. I figured I'd get to it and then turn around and head home, try and get some sleep though it don't come easy now. With Bertie next to me, I'd be lights out in ten seconds."

"I'm sure. Did you even know Jenny was in town?"

"I'd seen her coming in that very day. I was driving through town. Do that sometimes, just to"—he looked around the space—"get outta here. She pulled into the inn. Supposed she was staying there."

"And not at the family home?" Devine asked.

"Don't think it's the family home no more. Think it's Dak and Alex's place now."

"And Jenny wouldn't be welcome there?" Devine paused again.

Palmer's head turned mechanically from side to side as the pellets popped and glowed behind the glass of the woodstove. "Don't know about that. Have to ask them, don't ya?"

"Okay, go on."

"Every once in a while I'd head to the coast, stand there, look out. Nice bluffs along there. Can see nearly to Nova Scotia, least it seems like. Lived most of my life on the water, you see. Like looking at it. Calms me so."

"You were a lobsterman?"

He perked up at that. "Over fifty years out there. Rough seas and fair. Never got rich but made a decent living. Ain't so easy now. Lobsters moving farther out and heading north. Feel sorry for the folks coming up. It's a lot harder now. Ain't many other ways to make a decent dollar round here."

"So you went to the coastline and looked out?"

"Yes, sir. Did it once more. And then . . ." His lips trembled and his long fingers flew up to settle them down.

"You walked to the coastline at *that* point?"

He removed his fingers and nodded. "Cold that night. And rainy. Had my long waterproof on and my hat. Water don't bother me much, ocean or from the sky. That trail through the woods, I've been there many a time. Nice views from there. You can see the entrance to Putnam Harbor to the south, though I couldn't really at night. But I know right where it is. Went in and outta that place more times than I can remember. Takes me back, you see. Looked out at the clouds over the Atlantic. Beautiful thing to watch, to listen to the rain falling. No lightning, mind you, or I would've skedaddled. Don't much care for lightning."

"And then what happened?"

"I . . . looked down," he said simply, if hesitantly. "I

looked down," he said again, as though he was afraid Devine had not heard him. "And I saw Jenny."

"Wait, you knew it was her from where you were standing?"

When Devine had gone back to the spot he had more accurately gauged the distance at over fifteen feet from witness to corpse. And the body had been sprawled on black rocks and partially submerged.

Palmer seemed confused for a moment. "No, I . . . I mean, I learned afterward it was her. I just saw *a* body at that point. I had my phone with me and I called the police. I waited till they got there. They rushed to pull her up. Young man went down there on a rope. The tide was coming in fast. They got a truck with a winch. She was half-covered with water. Much longer and she'd have been out to sea. But they got her out all right. Or her body at least. Jenny was long gone."

"So it was just a coincidence that you happened upon that spot and looked down?"

"Yes, sir, it was. But I wish it hadn't happened to me. Lost my son and daughter-in-law to a damn fire years back, then Bertie. Seen enough death. Just . . . seen enough . . ."

His voice trailed off and he swiveled his head and stared at the fire behind the glass.

Devine watched him for a few moments, trying to take in the true, full measure of the man. "Once you learned it was Jenny, what did you think?"

"I didn't think nothing, really. I mean, I couldn't believe it. Who'd want to hurt her?"

"That was my next question to you."

"Must've been a stranger, like who killed Bertie."

Devine thought Palmer very much wanted to believe that. "So anything else you can tell me that might help?"

"Nothing I can think of, son. Sure hope you figure all this out."

"Well, that's why I'm here," he said.

Devine left him with his card and a request to call if Palmer remembered anything else helpful. He did not expect the man to ever take him up on that offer.

As he reached the doorway Palmer stirred.

"I know it don't seem like much to you, son, but Putnam is all I got. It's my home. Only one. Bertie's buried here. So's my son. I can't never leave this place. Not ever."

"Yes, sir," said Devine.

Palmer swiveled his head back around and returned his attention to the fiery pellets locked behind glass. To Devine it seemed that the man was also in a prison of sorts, not of his own making, but just how the life cards had been dealt for him.

Devine veered around the house to the small building with the curtains. The door was locked, and the window coverings made it impossible to see inside. He could go back in and ask the man directly what was in there, but something in his gut said not to. At least right now.

He drove off, firmly convinced that most if not all of what Palmer had told him regarding finding Jenny's body was a lie.

Now the question became why.

21

Devine drove back to the inn and hurried through the rain to his cottage. He checked his little booby traps and they were, once again, undisturbed. He sat down at the small desk by the window, clicked on the lamp, which had been set off to one side to provide some illumination against the gloomy day, and opened up his laptop.

He needed to dig deeper into Jenny's CIA career. Devine had attained top-secret clearances in the military, then reupped those and supplemented them with SCI-level security clearances after joining Campbell at the Office of Special Projects.

Since his time in New York while working at the investment firm Cowl and Comely, Devine, in his new role with Campbell's outfit, had traveled to five countries on three separate missions over the course of several months. In China he had used his business analytical skills to help bring down a shadowy cryptocurrency trader whose ties to the communist government had alerted U.S. intelligence services. Devine had learned a little about crypto while laboring on Wall Street. Now he felt as though he were a full-fledged expert.

His next mission, in the Middle East, had involved an Arab state that was doing its level best to crash the U.S. economy. It was forcing its fellow petrochemical-producing states to agree on a three-million-barrel-a-day pullback in oil production. That would have sent oil prices soaring, crippled the U.S. and other Western countries dependent on oil, and added hundreds of billions of dollars in wealth to the rogue oil producer, while inducing misery across the globe in the form of higher energy prices. It wasn't simply to make money, Devine and his colleagues had discovered; it was to promote unrest in western democracies, as citizens there protested against higher prices. The weaponization of everything seemed to be in vogue these days.

Devine had worked with a team of intelligence and financial specialists to counter that effort, including using denial of access to international lending facilities and wire rooms, along with walling them off from banking support and multinational monetary commissions. This would have made the rogue player a pariah in the global financial community. And even with the trillions of dollars in petrochemical dollars it commanded, such status would have been devastating to the country's future business well-being. They had backed down as a result.

In Geneva, Devine had set his financial background aside and picked up his gun. The result had been another victory for his country, and a target on his back during the train ride to Milan.

Devine read slowly and methodically over Silkwell's

CIA career, making more notes as he did. Then he pulled up and read through a psych eval of Silkwell that had been done about two months before.

The blunt conclusions on the eval were not personally flattering: controlling, manipulative, secretive to the point of mild paranoia, with an all-encompassing drive for mission success regardless of who or what got in the way. But for an ops officer, it was the perfect formula. She had leapfrogged over several of her colleagues, mainly due to the results derived from her bevy of recruited spies and intel leveraged from those relationships. Being a White House liaison for Central Intelligence hadn't hurt, he knew. And he wondered if her father being a war hero and beloved senator had helped with that assignment.

Of course it did. That's how DC operates, at least in the shadows.

He turned off his computer and sat back. The weather did not appear to be getting any better. He might have to start doing his early morning workout in the dry and warmer environs of the cottage.

He made sure the damper was open and laid some of the stacked wood in the fireplace. He got it to draw using some strips of paper provided by the inn for this purpose. He knelt in front of the opening and let the warmth embrace him. He had been trained to withstand the rigors of intense heat and cold, but he'd always been able to handle the heat better than the cold. And that was despite having grown up with bitter Connecticut winters.

He drew his desk chair up to the flames and sat down,

letting his mind go over each conversation he'd had about the case so far, starting with Emerson Campbell, then Clare Robards, and ending on his talk with Earl Palmer.

He next envisioned the crime scene, the shooter prone on the ground, firing at the standing Jenny Silkwell, the Norma round blowing a hole through her head fore and aft, the bullet lost to the Atlantic.

Then there was the angle of entry of the bullet as calculated by the medical examiner during the postmortem; that was the most troublesome of all in some ways.

Ninety-three degrees.

And it had come out of her head at a descending angle of 102 degrees, probably due to the impact with the skull.

The only problem with all of that was a shooter aiming from a prone position could never have fired a round that would have entered Silkwell's brain at that angle. It would have defied the laws of physics. Forty degrees, maybe forty-five. But a bullet couldn't bend itself downward *before* entering its target, not even with gravity.

At long distances the rotation of the earth's axis would impact the flight of the bullet. This was known as the Coriolis effect, and it differed depending on what hemisphere you were operating in. Snipers in the northern hemisphere would see their bullets drift to the left, and those in the southern hemisphere to the right. And at such distances one had to also account for the vertical tilt of the earth's axis. The calculations for such shooting used to be done manually; now they were done by ballistic apps. All one had to do was enter the requisite data and the algorithm would dial up the proper shooting coordinates. And sniper teams deployed spotters as well who fed data and observations to the actual shooters. In fact, the spotter was usually more experienced than the one holding the gun because spotting was, in certain important respects, more difficult than pulling the trigger.

The bottom line was her killer had not shot Silkwell from a distance of slightly over three hundred yards with a sniper rifle. She might have been shot with such a rifle, although other weapons would chamber the Norma round, but the shooter had definitely been standing and not lying prone. And he would have been far closer to Silkwell to achieve pretty much a level shot into her brain. The entry angle also told Devine that her killer was taller than she was, which accounted for the slightly descending entry into her head. A taller person would obviously aim down when shooting a shorter one.

Had the killer marched her to the edge of the bluff, made Silkwell turn around, and shot her? *Like a firing squad?* That seemed highly unlikely.

But Jenny *had* been found on the boulders at the spot indicated. Many people had helped get her up from that spot. They could not all have been in on some grand conspiracy.

So it seemed reasonable to conclude that Silkwell had been killed elsewhere, and her body had been transported and then placed on the rocks where Palmer found her.

The Norma casing could easily have been dropped where it was found to give off the appearance of a long-range sniper shot. Which would have also bolstered the argument that Silkwell's death was tied to her career at CIA and not the act of a local person from Putnam.

But what if she had been killed by someone here and it had been made to look like something else? Who had the motive? And the resources to pull it off?

Unfinished business. That was what Clare Robards had said her daughter had told her was the reason for Jenny visiting her old hometown.

So what was the unfinished business, Jenny? And did it get you killed?

Devine moved his chair back over to the desk and looked out the window right as the rain stopped and sun broke through the clouds and shone down on Maine once more.

The light played over the metal roof of the inn and sparkled off the windows.

It made for a good feeling, he thought, like when you saw a hummingbird hovering over a flower. Some warmth and sun always buoyed the human spirit.

As he glanced farther down the path he saw what looked to be a starburst resting just above a bush, a flash of light as the sunbeams encountered a reflective surface. It was fairly dazzling, to those of the casual observer variety, of which Travis Devine was not a member and never would be.

He dove sideways a split second before the window glass of his cottage exploded as the bullet powered through it, lodging into the far wall instead of Devine's head.

He pulled his gun and edged next to the shattered window. He heard what sounded like footsteps running away. He got to the door and did a turkey peek, and when he saw no one he jumped out, did a roll, and came up in a kneeling firing position. He heard a vehicle start up. By the time he got to the street, he could see nothing or no one in either direction. He hurried back to the spot where he'd seen the flash of light coming off the rifle scope. He stooped and ran his fingers through the grass. They stopped when he felt it. He saw the special marking on the head stamp of the casing.

It isn't a .300 Norma. It's a NATO round.

What the hell is going on?

22

"You say you didn't see *anyone*?" asked Chief Harper.

He and Devine were outside the latter's cottage looking at the large hole in the center of the window.

"No, just the reflection off the scope," said Devine. "If I hadn't looked out the window and the sun hadn't just come out, we would not be having this conversation, and your ME would be cutting me up to get the bullet out."

"Glad it didn't come to that," said Harper as he held up the bagged shell casing.

Devine pointed to it. "It has a cross-in-a-circle stamping. That means it meets NATO specs. But the caliber was also stamped on it, which means it's a civilian and not a military round."

"Okay, that narrows things, but only a little."

"I heard someone running. And then a vehicle started up. By the time I got to the street, it was gone."

A breathless Fuss hurried up to them. "Did a quick canvass of the area. Nobody saw anybody with a gun, but Joe Martin was coming out of the hardware store and saw a van getting out of here right quick, about the time Devine said the shot was fired."

"Did he get the plate?" asked Devine.

Fuss shook her head. "No, I mean he had no reason to. He didn't know anything had happened."

Devine sighed and looked around. *Someone takes a shot at me in broad daylight and no one sees anything?*

Fuss seemed to be reading his mind. "Pat Kingman was out running errands and you're the only cottage rented. This is not the high season. And this time of day the downtown area is pretty dead."

Like I almost was, thought Devine.

"Well, let's get the bullet out of the wall. Hopefully we'll find the rifle to match it to."

"Even though it's a different caliber, you think it might be from the same weapon that killed Jenny?" asked Harper.

"The rounds chamber different pressure settings and though they look identical, the thickness of the brass and the head space are different. Some might disagree, but I wouldn't fire a .300 or .308 round in a rifle chambered for NATO ordnance unless it was specifically chambered for both. It might blow up in your face, or the ejector might jam because the casing stretched too much."

"Okay, but who would want to kill you?" asked Fuss.

"Someone who doesn't want me to find out who murdered Jenny Silkwell would be my first and only guess."

"But *we're* investigating her death, too," pointed out Fuss.

"Then I'd watch your back if I were you," said Devine before walking off.

He headed to Maine Brew, where he found Annie Palmer cleaning the front counter.

"Want a cup of coffee on the house?" she said.

"Thanks."

He took a seat on one of the counter stools and watched as she poured out two cups from a full pot. She set one down in front of him and said, "Just made it, should be extra fresh."

"Did you hear anything about a half hour ago?" he asked after taking a sip.

She leaned against the counter, fingering her cup. "Hear anything? Like what?"

"A bang, like a firecracker going off?"

"No, but I was in the kitchen for the last hour doing inventory with my AirPods in. I wouldn't have heard much except Rihanna. Why?"

"Just something I was checking out." He put his cup down and decided to plunge in. "I went by to see your grandfather this morning."

He saw her neck tense as she took a slow sip of her drink. "Really? Why? Because he found Jenny's body?"

"Yes."

"What did he tell you?" There was an anxiety in her voice that bothered him.

"He said he was out walking late at night like he often does. He stopped and looked out at the ocean at various places along the coast. The last place he stopped, he looked down and there she was. Then he called the cops."

"That's what he told me, too. Guess if he hadn't, Jenny

would've been carried out to sea. Then nobody would have known what happened to her."

"You didn't mention that your grandmother was out walking and got hit by a driver who then drove off."

She looked down into her coffee cup. "I didn't think to. Why would you have cared what happened to her?"

"I'm just sorry it happened."

"Yeah," she said brusquely. "Everybody's sorry except for the fuckwad who did it." Her cheeks flamed and she cleared her throat. "Sorry, I don't usually use language like that."

"I was in the Army; I've heard far worse."

"Did Gramps tell you that she dragged herself looking for help before she died?"

"Yes, he did."

"Living in a small town has its good points, but sometimes the isolation isn't a positive."

"No, it's not."

"You any closer to finding out who killed Jenny?"

"Just really starting. Interviewing people, taking statements, going over the crime scene, checking the forensics. Not very exciting but all very necessary."

Says the fake investigator from Homeland Security.

"I also met with Alex Silkwell. You mentioned before that no one really knows her?"

Palmer dabbed at a spot on the counter with her cleaning rag. "Yeah, well, I shouldn't have said that. What business is it of mine? So what'd she have to say?"

"Nothing too remarkable. I went inside her studio. She's quite an artist."

"She should be. My grandmother mentored her."

"Bertie taught Alex?"

"Yes. When Alex was in high school. You wouldn't know that, of course. Bertie was incredibly talented. She could have really been something if she had pursued it. When she was young she was even offered a spot at an art school in Paris."

"Damn. So what happened?"

Palmer shrugged. "She loved Gramps. They were high school sweethearts. They decided to stay here and raise a family. But she continued with her artwork. And taught folks like Alex."

"The building behind the house? Was that her art studio?"

"Yes."

"Alex seems to have followed her example of staying put. She had offers, too."

"Yeah, I know," Palmer said absently, with a frown. "If I had been Alex, I would've been gone in two seconds flat."

"Not into small towns?"

"I could always come back to visit." She looked around the café. "And this may come as a shock, but serving food and coffee in the town where I was born and grew up was not a significant element of my youthful dreams. In fact, it had no place whatsoever," she added with a sad smile.

"I went away to college and didn't think I'd be coming back. But here I am."

"You're still young. You can still dream and then do something about it."

"Far easier said than done."

"I think that's why they call them dreams."

"You want another cup?"

"No, I think I've hit my caffeine allotment for today. By the way, I'm having dinner with Dak Silkwell tonight."

"Really? You two becoming best buds?" she said jokingly.

"He's just someone I need to talk to."

"Well, I need to get back to work. Hope you and Dak have a great time. But don't let him get you drunk. You won't like yourself in the morning. Trust me."

She walked off, leaving him to wonder about what she had meant by that.

23

By the time Devine got back to the inn Harper and Fuss were gone. He stood at the spot where he had seen the scope flash and then eyed the window of his cottage.

Not a difficult shot. Cover was good. The shooter had chosen their position well. The grass had been too soaked to hold any footprints.

"I can't believe this happened."

He turned to see Pat Kingman standing there.

"Yeah, I wasn't too thrilled, either."

"I can put you in another cottage."

"No, that's okay. I'll just tape the hole up until you can get it repaired. It wasn't too big. The hole it would have put in me would have been a little bigger."

She looked like she might be sick, so Devine said hurriedly, "I'm okay, Ms. Kingman, and I'm sure they'll find out who did it and that will be that."

"Well, I certainly hope so. You let me know if you need anything."

"I will."

She turned and hurried back to the inn.

Devine drove out to Jocelyn Point. He had some more questions for Alex.

When he got there, she was heading out astride a turquoise-colored bike with a big basket. There was a cool hand-painted slash of lightning along the frame. In the basket was a large waterproof knapsack.

She had on wool pants and a thick white sweater with a tweed blazer over that, and her hands were gloved. Her hair was in a ponytail and she had on earmuffs. Her expression was excited.

"Where you headed?" he asked.

"My art class, remember?" she said.

"Oh, right. Little nippy to be riding a bike."

"It's only a few miles."

"How about I give you a lift? We can talk on the way and then I can wait and drive you back here."

"You don't have to do that."

"I don't mind, really."

"Well, it would save me some time, and this heavy knapsack makes turning a chore."

She parked her bike on the porch, while he stowed her knapsack in the back seat.

She directed him to the public school, which was set in a block of empty warehouses, boarded-up business parks, and vacant, weed-filled lots.

As he pulled into the school she said, "This was all starting to go downhill when I was a little girl. Then all the businesses closed, jobs went overseas, and there was no backstop. Rural Maine has lost a lot of population.

Mainers rely a lot on tourism, but the pandemic blasted a big hole in that, and we still haven't recovered."

"I'm sure."

"Compared to Boston and New York the cost of living is lower, but it's not all that cheap to live here, either, when you factor in food and fuel, and a lot of the jobs don't pay a living wage." She looked out the window. "And the weather can be . . . challenging. We're actually projected to lose population for the next twenty years. Leaders need to step up. Invest in the state, in the people, or the picture is not going to miraculously get better. Mainers deserve that. Hell, everybody in this country does."

"You're very well informed."

"It's my home and my country," she said. "I *need* to be informed. Where do you live?"

"Right now, it's a moving target. Did you get your interest in all that from your father?"

She looked at him warily. "I am *not* a politician. I have no interest in that at all."

"You don't have to be a politician to help your community."

"Right now, I just want to help the kids in my class." She opened the car door. "Are you coming in or staying out here?"

"*Can* I come in?"

"You have to sign in at the front desk and I have to vouch for you." She eyed his waist. "I don't know about the gun."

"Do they have a security person here?"

"They used to, until they couldn't afford the position anymore."

"I think my federal creds will carry the day."

And they did.

For the next hour and twenty minutes Devine watched from a corner as Alex taught two classes of sixth graders in a makeshift classroom with no windows, high ceilings, and not much heat. And yet the kids loved it. He could see that from their enthusiasm and their questions and how seriously they took Alex's comments as she went around the room to view each student's efforts. She was unfailingly positive and detailed, and her suggestions were delivered with genuineness, humor, self-deprecation, and delicacy.

And she smiled—often, he saw, which he had never really seen her do in the limited time he had known her. At the beginning of the class she had passed out granola bars and juice boxes, which, she had told Devine, she paid for with her own money. That was why the knapsack had been so heavy.

Later, as they walked back to the Tahoe, she said, "The entire school is 130 percenters."

"What does that mean?"

"The government pays for lunches for students whose family income is at or below 130 percent of the federal poverty line. That's about thirty-six thousand a year for a family of four."

"That seems ridiculously low for a family to live on. I don't have kids but I remember how much I ate. I would think it would be damn hard to make ends meet on double that."

"It is, but that's the law. And the extra federal funds doled out during the pandemic have dried up. With those dollars, the income level was waived and all kids could eat for free. Not anymore. And a hungry kid has a difficult time learning. That's why I give them something before the class. Near the end of the school day they start to run out of gas. I wish they let me teach the class earlier, but art is sort of an afterthought. I guess I'm lucky they offer it at all."

He opened the passenger door for her, took her knapsack, and put it in the back seat.

"It's a really good thing that you're doing, Alex."

"Most days it doesn't seem like much," she said. "Throwing a pebble at a tidal wave."

"Every little bit helps. And you connected with those kids."

"Do you really think so?"

"I know so. I saw it for myself. Hell, if you'd been my art teacher I would have been a lot more interested in painting. And it's not just because you're so . . . What I mean to say is . . . I . . ."

Shit.

She put a hand on his arm as he put the SUV in gear. "Thank you," she said simply.

On the drive back, Devine said, "Not to unduly alarm you, but someone took a shot at me earlier today."

"What! Where?" She ran her gaze frantically over his person. "Are you . . . did it . . . ?"

"No, it missed, but it was a little closer than I would have wanted."

"Please tell me they got whoever did it!"

"No, they didn't."

"First Jenny and now you? This sort of stuff does not happen in Putnam."

"Violent things can happen anywhere, Alex. Even in Putnam. Look at Alberta Palmer. Her death was very violent. And the person got away."

He looked at her to gauge her reaction to this.

She was sitting there staring straight out the windshield, her body trembling and spasming like she had been doused with ice water.

"I heard that Alberta taught you art?"

Alex stopped trembling, closed her eyes, and drew a long, composing breath as she said some words that Devine tried to lip-read or hear but couldn't. She opened her eyes and seemed back to normal. "She was a wonderful artist in her own right. And the kindest person I ever met."

"You must have been devastated when she was killed."

"I'm not sure that's a strong enough word, actually. I'm embarrassed to say that my sister's death didn't affect me as much as Bertie's did." She glanced at him. "I guess you think I'm an awful person for saying that."

"Your feelings are your feelings. And there's no law that says you have to love your family above all others. Everyone has their own experiences in that regard."

Alex nodded appreciatively and said, "She was actually the reason I started teaching at the school. Bertie had done it for decades. But then her eyesight started to fail and her fingers weren't as nimble and she . . . It was just time for her to let someone else do it. And that someone else was me."

"I'm sure she was pleased."

"She was, very much so. Which made me incredibly happy."

They drove on in silence for a few moments.

"Last chance on joining us for dinner tonight," said Devine.

She hesitated but then shook her head. "I have some work to catch up on, and then I think I'll go to bed early. But thanks."

He dropped Alex off and watched her walk into her home. Then he turned the car around. He had some things to do before meeting Dak tonight.

But in light of recent events, his primary objective right now was to stay alive.

24

He stopped by a hardware store and bought some duct tape. When he got to his room at the inn, he checked his booby traps, then he duct-taped over the hole in the window and closed the curtains. He eyed the opposite wall where the round had embedded itself, and he wondered if the locals had made any progress on finding out who had fired it.

Devine then emailed Campbell with his report, recounting everything he had learned since his last communication to his boss.

A minute later his phone buzzed. It was Campbell.

"You've clearly stirred the hornet's nest," he said.

"Seems like it."

"We have been monitoring chatter from the regions where Jenny operated."

"And?"

"It's an interesting silence," replied Campbell. "We would have expected more after an event like that."

"As in trying too hard not to say something?"

"Exactly."

"So are we leaning toward her murder being related to her job?"

"Not yet. The silence may be genuine."

"Well, the crime scene was staged."

"Explain."

Devine went over the points and concluded with, "I think she was brought there after she was shot and her body was dumped on the rocks. The bullet entry angle alone blows up the official theory."

"I agree with you."

"The casing could have just been dropped at that spot easily enough. But whoever put that scheme together didn't take into account the entry angle, or the fact that the shooter would be lying prone on the ground."

Campbell said, "So no spot there where he could have rested the stock on a tree limb and fired pretty much at eye level? Or maybe a full-size tripod that would make for the same angle?"

"All the limbs on the trees around there were well off the ground. And a full-size tripod and a shot from three hundred yards away to make it a level entry into her head? What would have been the point? Why not just fire from a prone position? You're still going to hit the target."

"Okay, she was killed elsewhere and dumped where she was found, and the scene was doctored to suggest otherwise. Why?"

"Obviously to cover up where she was really killed, and by whom. The time-of-death window allowed plenty of wiggle room on alibis, so I don't think that will help us."

"The environmental elements did a number on the body, I was told."

"But her body had to be transported there, probably in a vehicle. If we could find it, there might be some trace of her still there. And now we come to the man who found her. Everyone up here seems to think it's just a coincidence that Earl Palmer happened upon that stretch of coast and looked down and saw her. Me? I think it's the same odds as winning the lottery."

"Well, people *do* win the lottery, Devine."

"Yeah, but millions of people play the lottery. He was the only one playing this game."

"You think he was told to lie, then?"

"I think a lot of odd things are occurring in a town filled with odd people. But I don't know what it all means. Yet. Did you find out anything on Dak Silkwell's OTH?"

"It's buried deep. I really sense the hand of his father on this one, Devine. As I told you before, Curt never talked about his son's service, other than to tell me that he joined up. So what's your preliminary assessment? Local or global source for her murder?"

"But for one thing I'd say global."

"What's that?"

"She told her mother that she had unfinished business up here."

The call ended a few moments later, and Devine set the phone down. Then he heard a knock on his door.

His hand on the Glock, Devine peered around the

corner to see a bespectacled man in his fifties with a gray beard standing there.

"Yeah?" said Devine, from a distance.

The man seemed startled and looked around. "Mr. Devine? Harvey Watkins, I'm a local reporter. I'd like to ask you a few questions if I could."

Devine opened the door.

Watkins held up his ID showing him to be a reporter with the *Putnam Press*.

"What sort of questions?"

Watkins gave him a condescending expression. "Jenny Silkwell's murder? And you're here to investigate it."

"If so, you look seasoned enough to know that I can't comment on an ongoing investigation."

"I've already interviewed Chief Harper and Sergeant Fuss."

"Then you have your story."

"But our readers would like to hear from you."

"I'm surprised a town this small even has a newspaper."

"Well, it's only published digitally, but local news is making a comeback and it's about time. I only work there part-time. I also work at the hardware store. Someone pointed you out when you were there buying duct tape." Watkins looked over at the window. "Understand someone took a shot at you."

"If you were told that, I won't deny it."

"Any idea who did it?"

"If I knew that they'd be in custody."

"So, the investigation?" asked Watkins.

"I'm working in cooperation with the local police, who have been professional and helpful. We hope to make progress and find out the truth."

"You sound like a PR person now," said Watkins, smiling.

"Good, then I hit my mark."

"Can't you give me anything? I used to be a reporter full-time over in Bangor. Never had a story like this on my doorstep. And I'm not getting any younger."

He held up his phone with the record function showing and a pleading look on his face.

Devine leaned against the doorjamb. "All right, turn on your recorder." He waited for Watkins to do so. "Okay, someone did take a shot at me. You and your readers can ask yourselves why. And the answer that occurs most likely at least to me is that our investigations are getting closer to the truth and someone is obviously not happy about that." He wasn't going to mention the different types of bullets used.

"Do you think the person is local?" Watkins asked.

"Don't know. But we can't rule anything out at this point."

"We all know that Jenny was engaged in some, well, confidential matters for the federal government. Could that be the reason she was killed?"

"Again, we can rule nothing out. But any new information will be given out to the local press at the appropriate time. We like to be transparent, but we can't jeopardize the investigation. I'm sure your readers will understand."

Watkins turned off his recorder and smiled. "Thanks for that."

"Now can I ask you something?"

"Sure."

"Did you know Jenny?"

"I knew all the Silkwells, including the senator. I came here from Bangor over thirty years ago. My wife has family in the area, and a job had opened up on the daily paper here that was better than what I had in Bangor. Of course, over the years, things change and that job went away. But we liked it here and stayed."

"So you knew Jenny as a child?"

"Sure did. Precocious and curious about everything."

"I've heard that from other people."

"We all knew she was destined for bigger and better things, and she was. What we didn't know was that she was also destined for a premature death."

"Did you know her parents well?"

"Oh, sure. Covered all of Curt's campaigns. War hero turned maverick politician. The people of Maine loved him. And he did right by them. Maine has gone through some tough times. But we're hardy folks and we keep plugging away. Curt was one of us. He was tough and kept plugging, too. Sure sad to hear how sick he is now."

"What did you think of Clare?"

"She was a good partner to Curt, and I mean as a wife, mother, and political spouse. Those are three distinct roles, and most people fall down on at least one of them. Not Clare."

"And the kids?"

"Nice, polite, all talented in their own way."

"I understand that years ago Alex sort of had a personality transformation. You know anything about that? Because the people I talked to had nothing specific to tell me."

Watkins looked around nervously. "You can't quote me or anything."

Devine straightened and his expression sharpened. "Anything you tell me is confidential. You want to come inside?"

Watkins nodded and stepped across the threshold.

Devine sat on the bed while Watkins perched on the edge of the desk chair.

"It was during the summer. She was a rising junior in high school."

"What happened?" asked Devine.

"Alex was assaulted and ended up in the hospital. I believe she almost died."

Devine was stunned. "Did they catch the person?"

"No, they never did."

"So Alex didn't know who it was? Or why she was attacked?"

"No. It was either a stranger, or Alex couldn't identify the person for some reason. The whole thing was hushed up, if you want the truth. Curt was running for the Senate for the first time back then. Most people in Putnam probably don't know what really happened. I only know what I told you because I was a reporter. And I have to say that back then my boss put the kibosh on digging into it or me really talking about it."

"So she became . . . reclusive?"

"Changed her whole life, really. She just became a shadow of what she had been. It was really very sad."

"You'd think it would have made her want to move away from here."

Watkins took off his glasses and cleaned them on the sleeve of his coat. "I think it just made her afraid, Mr. Devine. Afraid of the old *and* the new. She at least was familiar with this place. But other locations just became too big a potential nightmare for her. And as the years passed, I think whatever walls she built solidified. She has the old house, and now her studio, the kids she teaches, and that's about it. At least that's my two cents' worth of psychology."

"Did she get counseling?"

"I would imagine she did."

"Did her family support her?"

"Jenny was working in DC at the time. She came straight home and spent every day at the hospital. And after her sister was released, she was with her all the time. Probably calming her, reassuring her, supporting her. That was Jenny."

"And Dak?"

"He was away in the Army at the time."

Devine nodded, his mind going back to a naked Alex standing defiantly in that window. *Does she feel safe there? Invulnerable? Am I overthinking this?*

"Mr. Devine, you okay?"

Devine came out of his thoughts to find the man staring worriedly at him.

"What a terrible thing to have happen," he said. And then Devine thought how lame that must sound.

"Happens to far too many women," noted Watkins. "Although one is one too many. But we live in a troubled society and things are not always what they appear to be, people included. Had a neighbor back in Bangor. Nicest guy, help you whenever you needed it. The year we left Bangor to move here he was arrested for possession of child pornography. You think you know someone, and then, hell, you realize maybe you don't know a damn thing."

After Watkins left, Devine sat there thinking that the reporter's last words were some of the truest he had ever heard.

25

Devine drove over to the Bing and Sons Funeral Home and parked next to the front door. A long black hearse stood with its rear doors open next to the side entrance. A young woman at the front desk, upon seeing Devine's credentials, made a call and then led him back to a small office where Françoise Guillaume was sitting behind her desk.

"Haven't gone back to Augusta yet?" he asked.

"I actually live here," she said, rising to shake his hand. "I just keep a condo in Augusta. I'm one of thirty-five medical examiners appointed by the chief medical examiner, whose office is under the attorney general's department. It's a volunteer job. I'm assigned to this part of the state. But I have a medical practice in town. And I also work here with my brother, Fred. We both have degrees in mortuary science, and are licensed embalmers. My brother also has a degree in funeral services. Plus we're certified in cremation services, which is the route more people are choosing."

"You're a very busy woman, Ms. Guillaume."

"I'm used to juggling lots of balls in the air. Keeps me energized and engaged."

She sat down and pointed to a chair, which Devine took. "What can I do for you?"

"Angle of bullet entry on Jenny Silkwell?"

Guillaume's cheek bulged as she clenched her jaw. "What about it?"

He just stared at her until the woman dropped her gaze and started to fiddle with a pen on her desk blotter.

"I suppose you're referring specifically to the path the bullet traveled through the deceased's head."

"I know quite a bit about guns and shooting them. There are basically four ways to do it: prone, sitting, kneeling, and standing. The latter, for a long-range shot, is by far the worst because it's the most inaccurate. The best is the first method. It takes away most of the physiological wobbles that can mar the shot. And while three hundred yards away at night, with rain and wind, is not the most difficult shot an accomplished sniper has to make, it's not easy, either. And you're not making it by standing."

"Really?" she said, not looking convinced at all.

"Yes, really. If you're holding your weapon under your own power, you do not have a stable foundation to prevent body shakes. A sniper rifle feels like a barbell. I don't care how strong you are, or whether you use the sling for support to create tension between the rifle and your arm, the so-called Hasty Sling, you're going to get some movement. Some hunters use the kneeling position in knee-high grass, placing the elbow on the lower quad muscle, not the bone of the knee because bone on bone is not stable. Same with the sitting position. None of that matters very much over a short distance, but it's critical at long ones. And the only way the angle of entry makes sense in *this* case is if the shooter was *standing*, probably less than ten feet from Jenny, not over three hundred yards away lying on his belly."

He had taken a risk telling her this, since she could run to Harper and reveal to him all that Devine had just said. But he remembered the smile she had given him at the end of their first meeting. He thought she could possibly be an ally. Well, he would find out if he was right or not.

"I see that you've thought this through."

"I try to do so in all important matters."

"Did *your* ME come to this conclusion?"

"It wasn't that hard, was it?"

Guillaume steepled her fingers and sat forward, her elbows pressed into her desktop so rigidly that her own fingers were now shaking.

"The fact of the matter is, I made no *official* finding on anything that you just spoke to. I accurately measured the angle of entry and exit. I did not address where the casing was found or make an opinion or finding as regards the exact distance between the shooter and the victim or the firing position the shooter was using."

"Spoken like a prepared witness in court."

"*I* try to be accurate."

"So do I. The thing is, Harper and Fuss have never raised that point with me. As far as I can tell, their official position is the shot came from where the casing was found."

"I'm not sure I know what to tell you."

He decided on the direct route. "Is it just me or does this town have secrets?"

"Every place has secrets," she countered.

"I think Putnam hits above its weight on that score."

"Maybe it does," she conceded.

"My only goal is to find out who killed Jenny Silkwell."

"I know," she said in a bare whisper.

He sensed a shifting dynamic between them right now.

"I'd appreciate any insights you can provide," he said.

She looked up, her expression pained. "This is my hometown, too, Mr. Devine."

"Meaning?"

"Meaning I might be the wrong person to ask."

"I thought medical examiners just wanted to get to the truth, by letting the dead speak to them? Every victim of violence deserves that, don't they?"

"They . . . do."

"Did you know Jenny?"

"I was a few years older than she was, but, yes, I knew her."

So come on and tell me what you know.

However, before she could say anything the door opened and a man leaned in. He was tall and looked to be in his late thirties; his features neatly copied Guillaume's.

Devine said, "You must be Fred Bing?"

"I am. Do we know each other?"

The two men shook hands after Devine introduced himself.

Bing wore his brown hair on the longish side. About

six three, he had a clean-shaven face, a long, fit runner's build, and penetrating grayish eyes. His white dress shirtsleeves were rolled up, revealing pale muscular forearms. He looked tired.

"What do you need?" asked his sister.

He held up some papers. "Your signature." He looked at Devine. "We're refinancing our working capital loan. The documents one has to read to do so will cure any insomnia."

Devine smiled. "I'm sure."

"I would like to talk to you about some of the terms, sis," said Bing. "Get your advice before we actually sign off."

She glanced at Devine. "Sure, we were just finishing up, weren't we, Mr. Devine?" The woman's look was more pleading than triumphant.

Devine rose and handed her his card. "If you remember anything else helpful," he said.

"Yes, of course," she said, hastily pocketing the card.

"I heard you're here about Jenny?" said Bing. "Awful, just awful."

"You knew her?"

"Oh yes. Jenny and I were in the same high school class. I went to college and got my teaching certificate, and went back and taught science at the high school for a while. Then I got the necessary degrees before coming to work here. Jenny was the cream of the crop. We all knew she was destined for bigger and better things."

"Yeah, so I keep hearing. Did you see her during her last visit?"

"No. I had no idea she was here."

Right, just like everybody else in this town. "Okay, well, thanks." Devine started to take his leave but then turned back. " 'And Sons'?"

"What?" said Guillaume.

"The sign out front says 'Bing and Sons.' I was just wondering who the other sons were."

Bing said, "Oh, our uncle, John, and our father, Ted Bing. Our grandfather Frederic—I'm his namesake—founded the business. Our father and uncle worked for him until he passed, and they ran the business until they retired. That's when we took it over." He looked at his sister. "Françoise and me. We should probably change the sign to 'Bing and Associates.' "

"Or 'Bing and Guillaume,' " suggested Devine. "I guess that's your married name?"

"It is, but I'm not married any longer."

"So it's just the two of you left?"

"Yes," said Guillaume before her brother could answer.

Devine glanced at Bing, who was looking confusedly at his sister. "Great, thanks."

Devine walked out. He had collected a lot of data, and very little that made any sense. But somehow he needed to make meaning of it, all while someone was gunning for him.

Why do I suddenly miss being deployed to Iraq? At least there I was pretty sure of who I was fighting against. Here, not so much.

26

Only Real Food was a hopping place, Devine discovered as he turned the corner onto Hiram Silkwell Boulevard after walking from the Putnam Inn. Cars lined both sides of the street, and there were some folks milling about the entrance. The brick building occupied about a half block and looked to have once been some sort of warehouse or industrial space. The sign for the restaurant was formed from chunky welded metal, with the letters done in calligraphy. Two gas flames encased in glass lanterns flickered on either side of the double wooden door.

Inside, the floor plan was wide open, with wrought iron pipes and other metal fittings ornately bent into enormous light fixtures dominating the walls and the ceiling, the latter of which was open to the rafters. There were about thirty tables of varying sizes, most of them full of hungry customers and the accompanying noises of conversation and clatter of glasses and utensils. The kitchen was visible through large windows, and the professionally clad cooks and staff could be seen working behind large stoves and in front of commercial ovens, with huge pans and skillets and dishes in use, and orders digitally flying across computer screens.

Waitstaff emerged through double doors with large platters of food or armloads of drinks. Piped-in music wafted over the clientele, and a small bar set up along one wall was doing a healthy business.

In a town of fewer than three hundred people, thought Devine. *But then Dak Silkwell told me about the thousands who live in the surrounding area*.

But still, what made Putnam such a happening place?

As he looked around the room trying to find Silkwell, he noted two large paintings that were mounted on one wall. He walked over and eyeballed them. One was of a fisherman with a large net filled with . . . yes, it was mermaids, he concluded. The other painting depicted a storm blowing in off the coast and in the foreground a large home with a widow's walk, where he could see the image of a woman looking anxiously out to sea.

The house, he easily noted, was Jocelyn Point. He looked down at the signatures at the bottom of both paintings.

The initials ADS. Alexandra Silkwell? With the D being her middle name, probably. The style was definitely hers. He could see that even though he'd only viewed a few of her pieces.

"Hey."

He turned to see Dak striding toward him. The man had exchanged his muscle shirt and jeans for a tailored two-piece dark suit with an open-collared white shirt.

His hair was slicked back and wound up in a ponytail. He looked like a totally different person, Devine noted. And maybe that was the man's intent.

"You like them?" Dak asked, pointing at the paintings.

"Yes. Your sister's work, right?"

"How the hell did you know that?"

"I saw some of Alex's work when I spoke to her at her studio. But these are different. The mermaids I don't really see her doing. I mean, catching them in a net like—"

"—fish? Yeah. She didn't want to do it, actually. It was the owner's idea, and the money they were willing to pay was too good."

"And the house? That's your place."

"Yes."

"And the lady looking out to the ocean with the storm coming?"

"Typical New England scene. We probably had ancestors who did that very thing. Alex has a great imagination, but for her paying customers she sticks to more traditional themes."

Dak led Devine over to an empty table with a RESERVED sign on it. They sat down, and a waitress immediately came over with water and menus.

"Evening, Mr. Silkwell," she said.

"Beth, this is Travis Devine. A friend of mine, so let's treat him real good, okay?"

"Yes, sir."

Big fish in a teeny pond, thought Devine. This also probably explained the suit.

Silkwell ordered a glass of cabernet, while Devine opted for an IPA on draft.

"Busy place," said Devine.

"Oh yeah, they do a great business."

Devine looked at the menu and noted the prices.

"No offense, but for a sleepy little town with the kids getting free school lunches, how does the place charge these prices and sell out?"

"You've been talking to my sister about that, right? The 130 percenters?"

"Yes. She didn't paint a really rosy picture of the economic climate here."

"She's always been a Debbie Downer. The fact is, COVID changed everything. We got nearly a thousand families who moved to the area from Boston, New York, Miami, Seattle, Chicago, LA, San Francisco, and other metro areas where the cost of living is through the roof. They can work remotely, still pull in an income that is many times what most Mainers make, and build or buy homes for peanuts. Cheapest oceanfront in the country, or at least that's what one Realtor told me."

"I didn't see much construction going on along the coast here."

"It started about a mile down but it'll get here, and some of it is inland, too." He looked around. "Most of the customers in here tonight are the 'remoters,' as I like to call them. State used federal dollars to bring superfast broadband here. That was key to getting these highly educated and highly compensated folks to come.

And they're putting down roots. And all of the people working at this restaurant are locals. But Real Food pays a living wage, and the employees get health insurance and a 401(k)."

"That's great. And the weather?"

"Hell, you think Chicago, Boston, and New York don't get cold? And you want to be in Miami, Phoenix, or Houston in the summer? Sure, it gets warm here, but nothing like that, and the proximity to the ocean actually keeps the winters bearable. And if folks can save a ton of money? It's not rocket science. And there are developers coming in who want to build an oceanfront hotel, a spa resort, and new residential communities. If that happens, this place is going to boom, and the people who bought here before that are going to make a fortune. And instead of eroding sand, we have sturdy, rocky shorelines, so houses aren't going to topple into the sea as the water levels rise, at least not for a long time. So you get ocean views without that worry for rock-bottom prices. And there's plans to build new elementary and high schools. And businesses are starting up all the time, and I invest in the ones that I believe in, like this place. I've already made back ten times what I put in. Only good thing that came out of COVID, as far as I'm concerned."

"Was Jenny involved in any of this?"

"No. I talked to her about it, but she was government. And some of the monies coming our way are tied to federal dollars. She couldn't risk the conflict."

"Okay, I can understand that."

"And that oceanfront hotel? Guess where they're thinking of building it?"

"Jocelyn Point?"

Dak nodded with a self-satisfied smile. "I've had preliminary talks with them. The house is a knockdown but we have tons of acreage right on the water, plenty of room to put in a nice facility and amenities. Hell, it could accommodate a residential development and retail businesses, too. And the dollars they're talking? Well, I might leave old Hiram Silkwell in the dust."

"Congrats. So with Jenny gone I guess it'll just be you and Alex splitting the fortune?"

Dak looked at him sharply. "What the hell are you implying?"

"I'm implying nothing. Just trying to thoroughly understand the situation."

Dak said, "Well, *understand* this. Jenny's share of the sale, if it happens, will go into a trust to promote conservation and protect endangered species in Maine."

"Why is that?"

"Because I know that's what she would have wanted. So don't go thinking that I knocked off my sister for money. That deal alone will give us all more money than we would ever need."

"Thanks for the clarification. When did you hear about Jenny's death?"

"I was in Boston that night. Had a meeting with a business I'm trying to get to open a location in Putnam. It's one of those gym franchises. Healthy people make for a healthy community. I got a call from Chief Harper. I was asleep in my hotel room when my phone rang. Scared the shit out of me. It was like three in the morning." Dak looked down at his drink. "At first I thought it was folks calling about Dad. I'd prepared myself for that for a while now."

"Yeah, I guess so," said Devine quietly.

He shook his head. "But not Jenny. I couldn't believe it. I thought he was out of his fucking mind. I didn't even know Jenny was in town. I'll admit we weren't as close as we were when we were kids, but she usually let us know when she was coming up."

"So any ideas on why she didn't this time?"

Dak shook his head. "I've been letting that rattle around in my head ever since I got that call. The thing is, she doesn't usually come up this time of year. There's not that much to do. Sometimes she'd go sailing right off the coast. And she liked deep-sea fishing. But you don't do that now. Or she'd just walk or bike around, go for hikes. Again, that stuff is better left to the summers or fall. And Jenny *was* here during the summer. We met up a few times, talked about Dad and the old days. She seemed really good."

"She didn't mention anything out of the ordinary, any unfinished business up here?"

"Unfinished business? Like what?"

"I don't know. It's why I'm asking."

"No, nothing like that. She seemed, well, like the old Jenny."

"What about Alex? Where was she when Jenny died?"

Devine had forgotten to ask the woman, but he could do so later and compare it to what Dak told him.

"At that time of night she'd have been at the house asleep."

"So you two didn't talk about that?"

"If you want the truth, Alex and I don't really talk all that much."

"What happened to her?"

Dak shot him a troubled look. "What do you mean?"

"I was told that she was assaulted many years ago. And the person who did it got away. But that it changed her."

"Who did you hear that from?"

"Is it not true?"

Dak finished off his drink. "Yes, it's true. But she wasn't just assaulted. She was *raped*, beaten, and left for dead."

Devine flinched. Harvey Watkins hadn't told him Alex had been *raped*. But maybe he didn't know. Watkins had said it had all been hushed up.

"Alex couldn't ID her attacker?"

"No, she couldn't for some reason. I was never clear on why."

"You didn't ask?"

"I was pulling a deployment in Germany. With the different time zones it was hard to keep up with life back here. I heard snatches of what happened. I tried to get leave to come home, but apparently your sister getting raped wasn't a big enough deal for the Army to allow that. When I finally got back no one was talking about it. Everybody was actually walking around on eggshells."

"But she was different?"

"Yeah, she sure as hell was. If I ever catch the son of a bitch that did it—"

"So no leads or anything?"

"Apparently not. The cops concluded it was some stranger."

Devine decided to shift gears. "Do you know Annie Palmer?"

Dak looked at him suspiciously. "Why do you ask?"

"Just trying to understand as much as I can about this place and its dynamics."

"I know her. In fact, we dated off and on a few years ago."

"Didn't work out?"

"Hell, Devine, we weren't looking to get married, just have some fun."

"And did you?"

"Yeah, she was cool. Nice girl. Why, did she say different?"

"No, I didn't even talk to her about you," said Devine.

"I've dated lots of women. And we all had good times. Up here, that's important. Otherwise you could go stir-crazy."

"But you have all your business interests."

"Business is business, pleasure is something else."

Devine decided to change gears. "So what's your criteria for investing? Free cash flow in what time period?

ROI minimums? Growth prospects? Do you have a typical exit strategy or do you just reexamine every so often? And what's your stop loss plan? And do you invest solo or with a fund or a syndicate?"

"You sound like you know your way around a balance sheet and P and L statement."

"I have my MBA. Worked on Wall Street for a time."

"Why the hell did you leave? You make it there you had to be pulling in serious bucks."

"Just wasn't for me."

"Okay," Dak said incredulously. "I have some financial backers for my investments. That was another reason why I was in Boston, to meet with them. I've got a proven track record, so they trust me. We like to be cash flow positive within eighteen months, but there's wiggle room there on a case-by-case basis. Exit within five years unless there's a compelling reason to get out earlier or stay in longer. Flexibility is the key. ROI expectation is high. A hundred percent is the minimum. We shoot for the moon."

"Do you insist on board representation?"

"We always take at least one board seat and more depending on our investment piece. But keep in mind this is not Apple or Google, these are start-ups. They actually need our business expertise. I usually like to have my hand in, and we just closed our twentieth deal last month. And the other nineteen? I think we're going to hit home runs in all but two."

"That's a much higher percentage than the Wall Street boys have."

"I get to really dig into the business plans and meet the people before the dollars go in. And then I'm right here watching my investment and jumping in or pulling the plug if I have to."

"You ever think of going somewhere else?"

"Every second of every day. But I've got time on my side and a plan, a big one."

"The new Silkwell empire?"

"The new Dak empire."

The two men ate their meal and then went their separate ways.

As Devine was walking back to the inn, he looked to the sky, which was growing cloudy. The wind was picking up. He could feel the barometric pressure dropping as the storm system moved in. He was halfway back to the inn when he was confronted by three men who stepped out from the darkness in a particularly lonely area of Putnam. And these men were not drunk and stupid local yokels like the ones who had followed him out of the bar. They got Devine's immediate attention primarily for one reason.

They look like me right before I go into battle. Calm, focused, and lethal.

27

Three guns to his one made it a quick end to a fight that never materialized. Devine was disarmed and pulled into an alley, where his hands were zip-tied behind him, and then he was taken to an SUV with blacked-out windows that was parked there. No hood was put over his head and he wasn't blindfolded.

They aren't worried about me knowing where I'm going because they know I won't be coming back.

He studied the three men. One driving and one on either side of him. They hadn't uttered a word; they had let their weapons and hand signals do the messaging.

He guessed two of the men's ethnicity to be Middle Eastern, and the third was clearly Asian. This was business to them and they deployed the ideal skill set to get the job done. They were all around six feet, lean and wiry, without the big flashy muscles that most people believed signified great strength and fighting ability.

Nothing could be further from the truth, Devine knew. Being strong was great for one's health and longevity, but he had seen six-foot-five dudes with six-packs and bulging biceps and quads taken down by short, skinny guys who understood precisely how to wreck a person without an ounce of remorse; that made them unpredictably dangerous and, crucially, a millisecond faster. And that was the whole ballgame when you were fighting for your life.

None of the men looked at him, not because they were afraid he could identify them but because they were probably bored. This was business, and the hard part—the abduction—had gone seamlessly. Now there was just the execution phase to come, which would be the easiest element of the job. Then it was on to the next assignment. They were as different from the Alpha and Bravo from the Geneva train as it was possible to be. That pair had relied on their guns. When that failed them, they were roadkill to anyone like Devine, who actually knew what they were doing.

The drive took them out of town, along the coast and due south, Devine gauged. After about twenty minutes they turned off the road, and the SUV trundled over a bumpy, unpaved street. Another turnoff there, and about five hundred feet later over crunching gravel they came to a stop.

Devine was bundled into a small wooden house that was closer to falling down than remaining standing. He could feel tendrils of cold air coming in through cracks in the exterior walls. He was hurried up a narrow, enclosed set of stairs, down a hall, and into a room that was bare except for a chair in the middle. He was pushed into the chair and duct-taped to it. With his hands still zip-tied behind him, he appeared to be securely immobilized.

He had swept the room doing a KIM recon, or Keep In Mind. You looked at as many different details as possible in a short amount of time, with the ability to recall them later, as needed. This told him there was one window where the curtains were flapping because the window was either open or the glass was missing. The floor was made of wooden planks. The only door was the one they had entered. The walls looked to be solid plaster. There was a nail sticking out of the plaster where a picture had probably hung. The chair was an ordinary wooden one, with spindly arms. It might have already been in the house, or they had bought it at some junk shop to use as his execution perch. It felt fragile under his 220 pounds.

Not much to work with, but he probably wasn't going to have that option anyway. Looking at the men he was reminded of a Mark Twain quote one of his instructors at West Point had taught them: *Of all the animals man is the only one that is cruel. He is the only one that inflicts pain for the pleasure of doing it.*

He didn't know if these men took any pleasure in their work, but he did know they took pleasure in the payment they would receive for ending his life.

He knew the hit rate for a moving target was less than 4 percent and the kill rate was under one in a hundred. Only he was stationary. He calculated the kill rate on him at damn near perfect.

When engaged in his ceiling staring process, Devine had sometimes gone through this scenario in his mind. No way out. The last full measure. The end. As it came to all of us, just not so violently. He already knew he was not going to beg for his life, because he refused to waste his last few remaining breaths on useless things.

He had almost died twice while in uniform, and once in civilian clothes. In each case, as his life seemed to trickle from him, Devine recalled being in the moment. He was certainly feeling the pain, and he was experiencing the sense of impending doom that anyone dying suddenly felt, because your brain was releasing all sorts of chemicals into your bloodstream to try to stave off the end of its existence, and yours. And, when all hope was gone, the brain would begin methodically shutting down all the body's organs in an orderly procession, turning the lights out at the very end. This would normally take moments, not minutes.

Devine had felt all of those things, three times now, and, with that experience behind him reinforcing his psyche, he prepared for what he knew was coming.

What had Dr. Guillaume said? That Jenny's death was instantaneous. That she was dead before her brain even realized it was over.

But that hadn't really been the way it had gone down. Jenny had been staring at the shooter, her killer, much like Devine was now looking at the three hardened men in front of him. She knew what was coming. Your brain knew, which meant *you* knew, that the end of you was imminent. Devine wondered what she had thought about. Had she panicked, pleaded for her life? Sobbed uncontrollably?

No, he didn't believe she had done any of those things. Everything she had done in her life up to that point spoke of a person in control. She would have stood there staring back at the person about to kill her, with a calm, even defiant detachment, maybe even daring them to pull the trigger before they wanted to. To assume, for one final time, the upper hand over someone, a measure of control, even if that person was going to be the instrument of her demise.

Devine stared back at the men with a calm detachment. He wasn't going to give the fuckers the satisfaction that what they were about to do had rattled him in the least.

You go out like an Army Ranger, tabbed and scrolled.

But they did not pull their weapons and shoot him dead. They left him there.

He counted three sets of footsteps passing down the hall and then down the stairs.

They had made their first mistake tonight, after an otherwise flawlessly executed mission.

But to Devine's mind it was a big one.

They had left him alone.

And alive.

28

Most people bound in duct tape would expend all of their energy pulling and tugging at their bonds, which only made the bindings that much tighter, like a fly struggling in a spider's web. But duct tape, like many such things, had one weak spot.

Focused, immediate torque.

With that in mind Devine leaned back in his chair as far as he could and then threw his torso forward with as much force as he could muster.

The duct tape sheared off at multiple weak points. He didn't wait to hear if any sound he had made doing this had reached downstairs. That was just wasted time better spent elsewhere.

He stood, turned to the side, and got free of the remaining dregs of the tape.

He then sat on the floor. Devine, despite his size and musculature, was quite limber and flexible. This was not all genetic or by happenstance; he had worked at it.

He brought his hands under his butt and then passed them along his hamstrings, down his calves, and under his feet until his hands were now in front of him. He held his arms up in front of him and examined the zip ties. They were black and police grade, meaning they were thicker than what one normally associated with such devices.

They also were susceptible to torque, but you had to line up the weak point.

He used his teeth to pull the end part of the ties so it was directly in the middle of his wrists. Then he once more used his teeth to make sure the ties were as tight as possible. He sat in the chair, lifted his arms straight up over his head, and then brought them down with every ounce of adrenaline-fueled force he could. His arms passed on either side of his torso. The zip ties, incapable of surviving this sort of torque directed right at their weakest point, snapped in two at the site of the locking mechanism.

Devine didn't take even a second to rejoice over his twin victories. He went straight to the window and looked out. The lower window had been removed for some reason, though the upper part was still there. But he wasn't focused on that.

Brand-new-looking bars had been screwed into the exterior walls, turning his room into a cell. Since he was not escaping via that route, he would have to get out of here the hard way.

He turned, raced back to the duct tape, tore off some strips, used considerable strength to pull the long nail out of the wall, and rushed back to the window. The storm was starting in earnest and a bolt of lightning struck nearby. He waited, his elbow poised near the window.

As soon as the deafening thunderclap sounded, he hit the glass with his elbow. The glass shattered, and he used the duct tape to pull out a long, pointed shard. He wound the duct tape around the top of it so he could grip it there without cutting his hand.

He placed the nail between his fingers and let the business end stick out the top.

He slowly opened the door, inch by inch, because it had creaked before. He had already seen another partially open door along the hallway when they had brought him up. He closed the door behind him and slid on his hands and knees down the hall to the other door. He pushed it open a little more so he could slide through before easing it back to its original position.

He peered out through the gap. Perfect sight line of anyone coming up the stairs, and when they turned to the room where he had just been, their backs would be to him.

He heard another vehicle pull up outside. The room he was in now had no window. But he could hear feet running through the rain and then the front door opened. He heard voices, some in English, some in other languages. He had a conversational knowledge of Farsi and Arabic, but those linguistic skills had withered from nonuse. It didn't matter; the people were speaking fast and in low voices.

He relaxed and did his combat breathing when he heard footsteps on the stairs. Two sets, two men.

Through the gap he could see the countenances of the

Asian in the lead and one of the Middle Easterners right behind. They reached the top of the stairs and turned right, their backs to Devine, just as he'd planned.

He was on full autopilot now. It was known as unconscious competence because he had practiced both the analysis and actions based on that analysis so many times, and carried it out for real countless more times, that his mental and muscle memory was near absolute.

Devine knew that there were around seventy-five areas of the body that could trigger incapacitating reflex injury. Now his task was to ID a few of those locations in this situation and inflict just such an injury. And do it with speed, surprise, and overwhelming aggression.

There was a reason why a lion always went for the throat.

He'd wanted to do this completely silently, but with two adversaries that was problematic. There were at least two more downstairs, the third man and whoever had come in just now.

He stepped out in such a way as to give the Middle Easterner a sight of him in his peripheral. That would expose the target Devine was aiming for.

When the man turned the glass knife slashed his throat, severing the windpipe so the man would not cry out. The thrust had also split the carotid sheath in two. The blood geyser painted the opposite wall a dripping red and splattered all over Devine as well.

The lead man was pulling out his gun when Devine struck, and the nail hit the man's windpipe. He recoiled and dropped his weapon, gasping for air, unable to call out. Devine next pulled the glass knife free from the first man's throat, pivoted, and severed the second man's carotid with it. Devine caught the man and gently laid him down on the floor, even as he gave a last, rattling gasp and joined his partner in death.

The sounds of the attack and the men falling were fortunately mostly covered up by the sounds of the raging storm.

Devine searched both men and found his phone and his gun.

He quickly sent a text to Harper and Fuss telling them what had happened and approximately where he was, but that they could also track his phone. He was just about to send a message to Campbell when a voice called up, speaking in Farsi.

Devine answered back in a low voice in Farsi, saying basically, "Be right down."

As soon as the other Middle Easterner poked his head up the staircase, Devine put two bullets in it. The dead man slumped to the floor, the wall behind him painted with his blood.

There was a scream—a woman's, Devine thought—and then he jumped to the side as the muzzle of an MP5 entered the stairwell and on full auto sprayed the area with a wall of bullets.

Next, Devine heard people running away, and he got to his feet.

He made his way cautiously down the stairs and then

poked his head around the corner. He ducked down as more gunfire erupted. When he then heard a vehicle start he ran to the front door and jumped out onto the porch in time to see the taillights of the SUV fleeing down the road as the storm continued to roar overhead.

He ran back to the dead man at the bottom of the stairs, because he had been the one driving before. He snagged the vehicle keys from his pocket and ran back outside. He got into the SUV, fired it up, and started to back out. However, the truck wobbled badly and he slammed it in park and hopped out.

He went around the vehicle, his fury accelerating as he did so.

They had shot out all four tires on their way to escaping. That was the gunfire he had heard.

He slumped against the SUV's fender and let the rain wash over him.

Despite their escape Devine had one thing to be happy about.

I'm alive.

29

Devine sat on the front steps of a place where three men lay dead inside.

He was listening to the sounds of someone vomiting into the scraggly bushes on the right side of the old shack.

Sergeant Wendy Fuss came into view, wiping at her mouth and looking wretched.

"Jesus, Devine," she said, spitting onto the ground and looking at his clothes that were soaked with the blood of other men.

Harper came out of the front door, snapped off his nitrile gloves, and glowered down at Devine.

"How in the hell did you get outta *that*?"

"You can thank the United States Army."

Harper glanced at the house. "I think I need to call in the county and state police on this. It's out of my jurisdiction."

"Feel free."

"And you gonna contact your folks?" he added. "I mean, those bodies, they sort of look . . . well, *federal*."

"Already done and they're on their way."

"So we should just seal this thing off then and wait for folks to show up?"

"That's what I would do," said Devine. "And I need a ride back to town."

"We'll need your statement," said Fuss, wrinkling her nose as she rubbed her belly.

"I can do it back in town."

Harper said quickly, "I'll run you back. Wendy, you stay here on guard till the people show up."

Fuss looked like that was the last thing on earth she wanted to do, but the woman gamely nodded and said, "Sure, okay, Chief."

"I'll radio the county and state folks right now and let them know what's what," said Harper as he hurried over to his cruiser.

Fuss moved closer to Devine and looked up at him. "Did you *really* kill all those men?"

"If I hadn't, I wouldn't be standing here talking to you."

"It was a damn miracle."

"No, it wasn't. It was slow training, deep practice, and fast execution."

"Well, you sure as hell *executed* them."

Devine really wasn't listening now. He was thinking ahead, leaping from one possibility to the next: *Is this related to my investigation of Jenny Silkwell? Is whoever fired at me through the window also involved in this?*

Or does it have nothing to do with Silkwell? And everything to do with me?

★

Back in Putnam he gave his statement to Harper. Afterward, he went to his cottage and showered, scrubbing extra hard, then changed into clean clothes and phoned Campbell to give him a fuller report. It was late but he could always leave a message. However, the man picked up on the second ring.

"Okay, this is getting weirder every minute," noted the retired general after Devine had made his report.

"The question is, is it connected to the Silkwell case, or something else, meaning me?"

"The group in Geneva, you mean?"

"They were speaking Farsi and I heard a woman's voice."

"You thinking the woman on the train?"

"It's possible."

"How would they have tracked you down so fast?"

"There's only one way, sir."

Campbell said, "Wait, you think we have a *mole* in *our* organization?"

"We wouldn't be the first."

"I can't believe—"

Devine cut him off, because, one, he was tired, and two, he was pissed. "What I know to be true is that two Middle Easterners and one Asian guy knew exactly where I was and almost punched my ticket for good. I want to know why. So should you."

Campbell was a fine leader, which is why he simply said, "You're right. On it. Stay tuned and watch yourself."

Devine put his phone away and looked around his room. *Right. Watch myself. But who's watching me?*

Best-case scenario: He had seriously reduced their manpower resources and they would have to pull back and regroup, which would give him time. They would also probably know that the feds would be all over this, another reason to lie low for a while.

Worst-case scenario: They would redouble their efforts and try to finish the job tonight because he wouldn't be expecting it.

And worst-case scenario is what you always prepped for.

He walked out to his rental, grabbed his go bag, and walked back to his cottage. He waited ten minutes and then turned the lights out. The rain had stopped and the sky had cleared. It was actually warmer than it had been.

He constantly checked the door and the windows, looking for anyone watching him. An hour passed. He opened the window in the bathroom, and knelt there for five minutes, watching, listening, and using his sense of smell to detect anything that might do him harm.

Satisfied, he clambered out and closed the window. He paralleled the main road for a quarter mile, then turned toward it and picked up his pace. His Army jog was designed to set a pace, not too fast and not too slow, that he could maintain pretty much forever with a sixty-pound pack on his back.

He reached Jocelyn Point and jogged up the main drive. He had taken great pains and used all his skills to make sure he was not being followed either by vehicle or on foot. He had even scanned the skies for drones. He saw

Dak's Harley with a customized rain cover over it. Alex's bike was still parked on the covered porch.

He walked over to the art studio and tried the door. It was locked. He took a pick gun from his go bag, and twenty seconds later he opened the door and slipped inside.

He looked around the dark space, took in the smells of the paints and the charcoal pencils, and the peculiar aroma of drying clay. And he could also sense the woman's shampoo and the body wash, which he had earlier imprinted in his brain in case it became important later.

That also meant it had not been so long ago that Alex had left her studio.

He checked his watch. After three in the morning.

But what did they say about artists: When the creative bell sounded you needed to answer the call no matter the time. He used his phone light to look around at her works in process and he marveled at both the woman's obvious skill and imagination. He didn't know which one he admired more.

Then he came to a sketch he had not seen before, because it hadn't existed when he had been here previously.

She had gotten the jawline right, and the eyes, too. Deep-set and brooding, looking angry even when the person wasn't. The neck was a bit thicker than he had thought, at least in perspective to the head, but everyone had their interpretation.

But for having not spent much time with the person, Alex had done quite a good likeness.

Of me.

30

"What the hell are you doing here?"

Devine woke and sat up straight to see the morning sunlight shafting into the skylight.

He scrambled to his feet from his sleeping berth on the floor and faced off with Alex Silkwell, who was not looking as angry as her words might have implied, but more curious.

And perhaps a bit amused.

She had on the same clothes as the last time he'd seen her in the studio. Her hair hung wet and limp around her face. He actually liked it that way better than piled on top. The latter was too theatrical, he supposed was the word. The former just seemed more . . . *truthful*?

And why are you even thinking about that?

"Well?" said Alex, giving him a raised-eyebrow look.

"I had a spot of trouble in town and decided my cottage at the inn might be compromised."

"So you picked *my* studio to be compromised instead?"

"I had few options. But I made sure I wasn't followed."

"Okay, but you were sleeping so hard I could have taken my time and killed you."

Devine didn't say anything to this, because he knew she was probably right.

She perched on a worktable. "What sort of trouble?"

"Just some guys who wanted me to do something I didn't want to do."

"Like what?"

Like die, he thought. But said, "Nothing important."

"Why don't I believe you?"

"I'm not sure, but I'm willing to listen."

She scowled at his flippancy. "You don't look like the sort that anyone could make do anything."

"You never know. So that's why I came here."

"The door was locked. I *always* lock it."

He took out his pick gun. "Then you should strongly consider a stronger lock."

Her scowl deepened. "Should I call the police? Isn't breaking and entering illegal?"

"I swear I broke nothing."

She seemed to think of something and glanced at the sketch of him on the easel.

Her face flushed. "I . . . you're probably thinking . . ." She gave up.

"I think you're an artist who sees creative opportunities in everything you see and everyone you meet."

Her flush vanished, and so did her scowl *and* reserved manner. Her smile lit the room stronger than the sunlight, at least to Devine.

"You look like you could use some coffee. And food."

"I could, yes," he said.

"Come on. I'll make you breakfast."

"You don't have to—"

"It's the least I can do for someone who entered but didn't break, and who thought my studio would be as much of a safe haven for him as it is for . . . me."

Her smile retreated with these words, and that bothered Devine far more than he had thought possible. He barely knew the woman, but he wanted to make her happy, to make her whole again.

They left her studio and she led him into the main house through a rear entrance that opened into a cathedral-sized kitchen.

"Damn," said Devine. "How do you not get lost going from the fridge to the stove?"

"It comes with directions," she quipped. "Seriously, the place was set up for a home with a dozen servants."

"And how many do you have now?"

"You're looking at her. I've got some eggs, fresh berries, ham, avocados, and home-baked sourdough."

"All of that sounds great."

She pointed to a cupboard. "Plates, utensils, and cups over there. How do you like your eggs?"

"Any way you care to make them."

She brewed a fresh pot of coffee, and he helped her get the items out of the fridge.

"That looks new," said Devine, staring at the Sub-Zero double wide.

"Courtesy of my dear, entrepreneurial brother. He's been slowly fixing up the place."

They decided on an omelet. He did the chopping and slicing of the onions, peppers, tomatoes, and mushrooms while she split and spooned out the avocado, put the fruit into a bowl, and put two slices of her sourdough in the toaster. She mixed the eggs and other items and cooked it in a stovetop pan.

Later, she sat across from him in the breakfast nook, sipped her coffee, and watched him chow down.

"You *were* hungry," she observed.

He checked his watch. It was after ten. *Shit*.

"I usually eat before now. Where's Dak?"

"Probably already at work."

"You don't know for sure?"

"It's a big house. He lives in one wing and I live in another."

"And it all works?"

"So far." She rapped on the tabletop. "So what happened last night? You said you had trouble with some guys? What kind of trouble?"

"Trouble enough."

"Then you can stay here as long as you need."

"Thank you," said Devine, who was surprised by the offer, but also humbled by it.

"Are they after you?" she asked.

"Three of them aren't."

"So you, what, arrested them or something?"

"Or something, yeah."

"So you're not going to tell me what happened?'

"I thought I just did."

She sat back and took him in, it seemed to Devine, line by line, crevice by crevice.

Artist as observer, he concluded. And it was a little intimidating, as though she could see through the flesh and bone and home right in on the thoughts right now hovering in his mind.

"You know what I really love about creating art?"

"No, what?" asked Devine.

"It's all about perspective. Of both the artist and the viewer."

He finished his coffee and rose to pour another cup and took her empty cup to refill. "How so?"

"You looked at my sculpture of the big penis roped and the testicles cuffed and concluded it was meant to symbolize women pushing back against a man's baser instincts."

He sat back down after handing Alex a full cup. "And it wasn't?"

"From your perspective it clearly was, which is why you voiced that opinion."

"And from *your* perspective?"

"You looked at it from a male's point of view. As the artist I look at it differently."

"You mean from a *woman's* point of view?"

"I mean from a neutral observer's perspective."

"I didn't know there was such a thing," said Devine half-jokingly.

"There can be, if one tries," she said, her voice low, modulated, and serious.

"So, as a neutral observer?" he said, losing his amused expression.

She slid her finger along the top of the table. "Life can be unfair for anyone, those with a penis and those without."

"Then why—"

"A man can be trapped by his own masculinity, or what is perceived as masculinity. Dick chained, balls cuffed. They feel they have to act in a certain way because that is what society as a whole expects. For some men it's no problem. It's who they are anyway. Rambo or whatever. But that's not most men. So most men end up living a life that is not really . . . theirs. It's dictated by societal expectation."

"And women?"

"Women have a whole other set of problems and challenges and expectations that are impossibly unattainable. So you have people getting rich off selling crap to women to put on their faces, or lips or eyes, devices to suck in their gut and ass, or encouraging them to go under the knife to get bigger boobs or bigger butts or fewer wrinkles, or smaller boobs, or lesser butts, as the tastes of the money-grubbing influencers change. Or become skeletons so they can squeeze into latex miniskirts and cleavage-baring tops, without the benefit of personal chefs and trainers, all in the name of female empowerment. Which is one of the biggest hypocrisies I can think of, while others applaud, idolize, and enrich these people for telling females, particularly young and impressionable ones, that not rigidly adhering to *their* definition of physical attractiveness will doom them to be considered ugly by society. As though beauty and confidence and empowerment can't exist in any shape, size, or color. But it's all about the almighty dollar and it makes people do awful things to each other, but they rationalize it as actually helping those who are not perfect become *perfect*. So you see, it really is all about perspective."

Devine laid down his fork. "Okay, men's dilemma covered, neutral observer's side taken care of, women's challenges done. Now let's hear *your* side."

"Who says I have one?"

"All of what I saw in your studio says you do. Am I wrong?"

She rose. "Yes, you're wrong. You done? I need to get back to work. You can stay here until your place is no longer *compromised*. And you can think about the fact that I asked you a simple question about what happened to you last night. And you had so little respect for me that you couldn't think of anything other than to bullshit me. There, you finally got *my* side. Feel better?"

She walked out, leaving Devine sitting there thinking, first, that she was absolutely right in what she had said, and he felt like crap for doing that to her. And, second, that the more time he spent with the woman, the less he understood her.

And that had never happened to him before.

So am I losing my talent at evaluating people? Or have I just met my match in Alex Silkwell?

31

Alex was in her studio when he left. Devine didn't say goodbye. He just saw her through the window, but she didn't see him because the woman was totally absorbed in her work. He did note that she had taken down the sketch of him from the easel. It was probably in the trash. He thought about telling her what had really happened to him last night, particularly after she had guilt-tripped him, and rightly so. But his loyalty to the mission prevented him from doing that. He didn't yet know whom to trust in this town. Not even the woman who had given him sanctuary and made him a delicious breakfast. And whom he wanted, for some reason not yet clear to him, to help heal.

He jogged back to the inn, where he found Harper waiting for him out front.

The man was upset. "Where the hell have you been? I've been calling and texting."

"Sorry, I had my phone turned off," Devine lied. He'd just not felt like talking to the lawman. "What's up?"

The police chief's ticked-off features hardened to a bristling scowl. "What's up is your folks showed up to that hellhole with all the dead people inside and cut off access to everyone, even the state police."

"Did they say why?"

"They didn't say anything. Just flashed their fed creds and told us to back the hell off. They took the bodies and they have armed guards encircling the place while they do God knows what in there. The state police are pissed, I can tell you that. This might go all the way up to the governor's office."

"I'll make a call and see what I can find out."

Harper did not look mollified in the least by this offer. "Nothing against you, Devine, I know you're just doing your job. But I sure as hell wish you'd never shown up in Putnam."

Yeah, well, I'm feeling the same way, thought Devine.

He left Harper and walked to his cottage. Which was occupied.

Two men who screamed National Security were waiting for him. Plain suits, plain shoes, plain ties, uniform haircuts, unreadable expressions. One was tall and basketball player lean, the other medium height with some iron-pumping heft to his frame.

"Agent Mann," said the shorter fellow, indicating himself. "And Agent Saxon," he added, with a nod to his colleague.

They showed their creds. They were members of a little-known agency that was right at the heart of the country's most stalwart defenses against enemies, both foreign and domestic, and their very presence made Devine tense.

"We need a detailed statement from you," said Mann.

"Can I ask one thing first?"

"Sure, what?"

"How'd you access my room?"

Mann looked at Saxon and then turned back to Devine. "Our badges prompted the landlady to open sesame with her master key."

"Thanks, I'll keep that in mind."

"We're on the same team," said Saxon in a voice that was as drawn out as his frame.

"So everyone keeps telling me. But at the end of the day I think we're all engaged in an individual sport."

"Take it up with a government shrink to get your head on straight," snapped Mann. "Your statement?"

"Have you looped in Campbell?"

"We're actually here at his behest. Your boss carries a lot of horsepower in our world."

"I'm sure."

He spent the next five minutes recounting everything from the moment of his abduction to his running out of the house only to find the tires shot out on the SUV. He did not tell them about spending the night at Alex Silkwell's art studio.

"So where have you been since then?" asked Saxon, apparently reading Devine's mind. "We checked here hours ago. You didn't sleep in this room."

"No. It didn't appear to be a safe place."

"So where did you go?"

"Somewhere else. And why does that matter to you? I'm alive, right, to tell you what happened. So why don't you reciprocate by telling me who it was who snatched me?"

Mann looked at Saxon, who shrugged. He said, "We don't know."

"Bullshit," said Devine.

"We got the bodies, sure. We have printed them and nothing came up on any database we put them into. We got their DNA and we're running that, too, on priority, but so far, squat."

Saxon said, "Not so surprising, Devine. They appear to be international muscle for hire. They might never have been arrested, at least in this country, or in any other country that reports to the international-bad-guy clouds we use. We're circulating pictures in various places hoping for a hit."

"No ID on them?"

"None."

"They had to get into the country somehow," Devine pointed out.

Saxon said, "They could have done it under aliases and then dumped the fake IDs. They clearly took into account that their mission could go sideways and brought nothing that we could use to trace them when they snatched you. We're checking camera feeds at all major points of entry, but it's slow going."

"The SUV?"

"Rented under a shell company with a fake ID and stolen credit card that our tech people tell us was of the very first order."

Mann fixed him with a pointed stare that had much behind it, Devine could tell.

"So the question becomes: Why target you?" Mann said.

"Have you talked to Campbell about that?"

"No, but we're talking to you right now. We know about Jenny Silkwell. I actually worked on a joint task force with her back in the day."

"Any leads on her murder?" interjected Saxon.

"I've only been working this case a short while."

"You didn't answer my question."

"No leads."

"You think these people were here to stop you investigating the Silkwell case?"

"Maybe, maybe not."

"What other reason?" asked Mann.

"Take it up with Campbell. It's not for me to say."

"We will."

"There was another vehicle, and I heard a woman's voice. Anything on that?"

Saxon shrugged. "Not yet. We have BOLOs out but not much to go on. I would imagine they're long gone by now."

"Or hiding in plain sight," noted Devine.

"In this Podunk place?" said Mann.

"This Podunk place has a lot of newcomers from all over."

"What's the attraction?" Saxon wanted to know.

"Lower cost of living for those who can work remotely and wanted to get out from being around millions of people."

Saxon nodded thoughtfully. "COVID changed a lot."

"In some ways it changed everything," replied Devine.

He stood and Saxon said, "Where are you going?"

"Back to work."

"With people gunning for you?"

"Assuming a fetal position is not an option. And when you're in combat the mission comes before personal safety, at least they taught me that in the Army."

"Four-one-one, Devine: You're not in combat anymore," growled Saxon.

"Could've fucking fooled me," replied Devine as he walked out.

32

Devine drove to a place he'd already been, twice. And this time he was not leaving without answers, truthful ones.

Earl Palmer answered the door. He looked pale and ill, thought Devine. His white sweater was stained and his pants drooped off his skinny hips and shriveled glutes.

"You okay, Mr. Palmer?" asked Devine, genuinely concerned about him.

"Yeah, yeah, just a twelve-hour bug. I'm getting over it. What do you want?"

"To ask you some more questions."

His expression lapsed into a scowl. "Look, son, I've told you all I know."

"Never hurts to go over it again. And I'd like you to go somewhere with me if you feel up to it."

"Where?" said Palmer guardedly.

"To where you found the body."

Palmer shook his head. "I don't want to go back there. Almost had a heart attack."

"Please, Mr. Palmer, it won't take long. I'll drive you and bring you right back here."

"What else can—"

"I'm sure you believe that Jenny deserves justice."

The old man stared at him, his white tufts of eyebrows twitching like he'd been mildly shocked. "Let me get my coat and stick."

After Earl had been helped into the SUV, they drove in silence until Devine said, "I understand that your wife taught Alex Silkwell to be an artist?"

"Bertie taught lots of folks. But with Alex, she said it was different."

"How so?" asked Devine. He wasn't just making small talk, he wanted to know if only to help him better understand the youngest Silkwell.

"Bertie said some folks are born to do what they do. Write, draw—hell, fish for lobster, whatever. She said Alex would've been an artist with or without her. Bertie just happened to be there to help the girl along."

"She has a studio out back like your wife did at your house."

Palmer stared out at a sky that didn't seem to be able to make up its mind: remain calm or turn stormy.

"Way back used to be my gear shed," said Palmer. "But I fixed it up for Bertie about twenty years ago as her art place. Should've done it long before, but I didn't and Bertie never complained, not once and . . ." He seemed to run out of energy.

"You miss fishing for lobster?" asked Devine after a few moments of quiet.

Palmer wiped at his mouth. "I was a stern man." He smiled weakly. "Doesn't refer to my personality, that's just the part of the boat I worked. Stern man does the grunt work, but we shared the duties, more or less. Me and the captain on a thirty-foot Beal boat built in 1969. Damn fine vessel. Could handle any weather, any seas, really. Every morning, crack of dawn, we'd row out to the boat with our thermoses of coffee and our lunch pails. Get out of the harbor and onto the open seas. Big rolling swells out there. Make you puke if you had motion sickness. I never did. Even in a fog when you couldn't see the horizon, and the smell of fish guts and diesel fuel was coming at you from all compass points."

"I really don't know anything about fishing for lobster, but I do like eating them."

Palmer's mouth eased into a broad grin that reached his eyes and held there. "When I was a kid I had my rec license, five lobster traps. As proud of them as I was of anything I ever owned. Then I got my student license and moved up to ten traps. Then I got to working for others. Eight-hundred-trap license with commercial fishermen."

"That's a lot of lobsters."

"Oh yeah, money was good back then. We did a rotation of the traps every day. Collect the lobsters, rebait with herring, you put 'em in mesh bags and either tie it off or stick it on a metal shaft in the trap. Get to about two hundred or so traps a day. Each buoy marks two traps attached together by a rope called a trailer. I'd pull one and the captain the other. Now, them traps alone weigh about fifty pounds. Then you add in the ballast, which is about a half dozen cement bricks plus the weight of the lobster, and the water you're pulling it through, it's a backbreaker all right. Builds you up, though. I was strong, real strong. Leastways, I used to be," he added, his voice diminishing with each word spoken.

"I bet. How do you know which trap is yours?"

"Buoys have distinctive colors, and every trap has to have a tag that matches your license, which you got to display on your buoys. And you gotta replace the tags every year. You pick your colors, can't be same as anybody else's, of course. Have to carry a buoy with those colors in plain sight on the deck, too. So's we pulled the traps up and collected the lobsters from them. Then I put them in a sectioned-off box."

"Why is that?"

"Bugs are vicious. Attack and eat each other give 'em half a chance."

"Bugs?"

"What we call the lobsters. Now once we're done with the rotation we head on back. That's cleaning time for the stern man. Back at the mooring in the harbor we unload the lobster from the drained holding tank and put them into crates that float right behind the boat. When we get a big enough load, we take 'em to sell. That's about it, son. Doesn't sound like something you'd spend most of your life doing, but I did. And I don't have no regrets."

His face screwed up and he looked away from Devine. "They say right now the Gulf of Maine is warming faster than just about any other body of ocean water on earth. That ain't good for folks do what I did. Already pretty much wiped out the cod and shrimp populations around here. Lobster and oysters don't like warm water either. They'll keep trekking north till they run out of planet, I guess. Canadians will be smiling for a while, I suppose, till the bugs abandon them, too." He smiled and paired it with a bittersweet expression. "We been catching and eating those crustaceans for centuries. Guess they got the last laugh on old mankind."

"But there're still lobsters out there," said Devine. "I see boats coming and going."

"Oh, yeah, just not what it was. That's why a lot of restaurants don't have it on the menu no more—can't get it. And when they do, who wants to pay eighty bucks for a dang lobster? And Lord, they got regulations you got to jump through. We got different fishing zones in Maine. In our zone we got large tides, mor'n fifteen feet and strong bottom currents, so the ropes we use with the traps move. They said endangered whales were getting stuck in the vertical lines and such, so you got to use different gear and change how you lay it so a passing whale can snap it. If they do, there goes your gear. And the ropes get snagged on rock and such down there. Lose the rope, the traps, the whole shebang with that as well. Now, some lobstermen won't fish in certain areas because of that. They go to muddy or sandy bottom so their ropes don't get snagged. But the thing is lobster like the hard bottom, so you're not going to trap as many. Catch-22, that is."

"I can see that," said Devine. "We had some Catch-22s in the military as well. And lots of early mornings, too."

"Best time of the day to be out there, though. You wake up before the sun, see a new day unfold right in front of you on the water. Ain't none of us guaranteed another hour of living, don't care who you are or how much you got. Might as well get up early and enjoy what time you got left, I say."

He looked out the SUV's window, and it wasn't hard for Devine to deduce that the older man was thinking about his wife and the car that had killed her and then driven off.

"Yes, sir, you're right about that," said Devine, now thinking about how close the previous night had come to being his last night on earth. "And I appreciate you helping me find out who hurt Jenny," he added, trying to draw the old man back to the task at hand.

But Palmer didn't respond to this. He just kept staring out the window.

They reached the spot and he helped ease Palmer from his seat. Devine walked slowly because Palmer was not moving steadily or swiftly over the distance, even with the sturdy walking stick he had brought along.

"Knees and hips," he said in response to Devine's look. "Need to get 'em all replaced, but I ain't got the money for that. Even with Medicare, which pays a big chunk of it. I ain't got no supplemental, see? The deductible and copayments were just too much for my Social Security, which is all I got. Might be able to get one hip and maybe a knee done, but then who's going to help me with the rehab? Local hospital shut down a decade ago, and the closest place is forty miles from here. And nobody comes to the home no more, not out here."

"Then where do people go for their health issues?"

"Doc Guillaume does all she can. She tried to help me with the insurance stuff and all. A while back she helped me get a surgery I needed done. She comes by to check on me, and Bertie when she was alive. Did the same for others. Very kind woman. Knew her mom and dad and her uncle. Hell, knew their parents, too. The Bings started the funeral business a long time ago."

"How about your granddaughter? Could she help?"

"Annie's got her own life and a business to run. She doesn't need to be cooking my meals and changing my damn diaper."

They slowly walked to the edge and both men looked out at the ocean.

"Prettier than any gal I ever seen, 'cept Bertie," said Palmer.

Devine looked down to the rocks where Jenny's body had fallen.

Or been placed.

Devine noticed that Palmer never once looked down. He kept his gaze on the horizon.

Maybe this is his safe space, like every ceiling I look at.

"So you came to this spot and looked down and there she was?"

"Yes, that's right," replied Palmer, still not looking down, which was odd because most people, with the words Devine had used, *would* look down.

"Is this spot special to you?"

Palmer swiveled his head to the right and eyed him cagily. "Every inch of coastline is special to me. Just happened to be this one I walked to that night. But not the only one. This was my third that night."

"You didn't mention that before."

"Well, *now* I am," Palmer said, more fiercely than Devine's comment really merited.

Devine stared pointedly at the man, specifically at his neck.

"You find it hard to wander around like that at night with your hips and knees the way they are?"

"People are meant to move. Actually helps me. You sit all day you get stiff as a board. Walking lubes the old joints. Least it does mine."

Okay, that was neatly done, thought Devine.

Palmer stared out to the water again. "Penobscot Bay has the best lobster bottom on the East Coast, but it was pretty good in our neck of the woods." He looked up, but only slightly. "Read the sky and the tide like the back of my hand, the depths out there, the temperatures. Used to know every ledge and crag out there. Crags are where the bugs love to hide. Got to lay your traps as close as you can, hope they bite on the herring." He turned stiffly to give Devine a sideways glance. "Communing and competing with Mother Nature every day."

"Right," said Devine, who was not really paying attention to the man's words but was instead focused on

Palmer's stiff movements. He looked down at his feet and had an idea.

"What's that next to your right foot, Mr. Palmer? Did you drop something?"

Palmer didn't look down. Instead, he slowly backed up a few steps.

"What is it? Can you see?"

Devine said, "Never mind, it's nothing, my mistake. So did you remain here when they came to take Jenny's body away?"

Palmer hesitated. "I . . . yes, but after they brought her up I left. The weather was turning bad."

"I thought it had been raining hard since early evening."

"Lightning and all," said Palmer. "They drove me back to my place. Took a hot shower and just sat there, couldn't sleep."

"So you knew it was Jenny by then?"

"I . . . yes, yes I did."

"Who told you?"

"One of the boys that went down there to get her. He knew her. We all knew Jenny."

"Okay. Anything else you can think of?"

Palmer slowly shook his head. "No, not one damn thing, young man."

At least that you're willing to tell me, thought Devine.

33

Devine drove Palmer back home and headed straight to Bing and Sons after checking something on his phone. He found Françoise Guillaume coming out of her office.

"I'm sorry, I really don't have time to talk. I have a body to embalm," she added brusquely.

"I only had one question."

"What?"

"How could Earl have seen the body on the rocks below if he's totally incapable of moving his head to look down?"

She froze and then placed one hand against the wall seemingly to steady herself. "I don't . . . what are you talking about?"

"Earl mentioned that you helped him get a surgery he needed some time back. Why do I think it was cervical spinal surgery? The sort of work he did all those decades would certainly cause some problems there. I had a buddy in the Army who suffered a malfunction on his parachute. He lived but he had to have several spinal fusions, one of which caused *limited* range of motion in his neck. But he was young and strong, so he was able to bounce almost all the way back. So, I'll ask again, how did Earl see a body over twenty feet below his eye level when he can't even look down at his shoes?"

"Can we . . . can we go to my office?"

"Sure, if you'll answer my question."

He sat down across from her in her office and let her take her time.

"Earl had an accident out on a lobster boat once and was badly injured. He underwent cervical spinal fusion surgery by a specialist that I thought was a good one. However, the surgery went poorly and there were complications. Foremost was Earl having a lot of built-up scar tissue and arthritis from the work that he did. A follow-up surgery not only didn't correct the problem, it made it worse. He had to retire because of it. And Earl has, over the years, lost more of his range of motion."

"I'm sorry to hear that. But then how could he see the body?"

"I don't know. Maybe he got down on his knees, which would have him facing down."

"Why would he have gotten down on his knees? How could he have managed it? And then how would he get back up?"

"I don't know. Did you ask him?"

"By the time I do, why do I think a story will have been prepared?"

She looked both offended and flustered. "A story? Prepared by whom?"

"What is going on in this town, Dr. Guillaume?"

"I have no idea what you're talking about!"

"I think you know far more than you're telling me."

"I thought your job was to find out who killed Jenny," she said.

"To do that I have to get the facts right. Lies do not help me."

"Who do you think is lying to you?"

"Pretty much everybody," replied Devine.

She rose. "I have to get to work."

He stood. "I do too. And let me just be straight with you. I will get to the truth. I don't care how many obstacles are thrown in the way."

She looked at him with a mixture of sadness and defiance. "I wish you luck."

Devine ran into Fred Bing as he left. He looked busy and preoccupied, but he stopped and said, "Mr. Devine, did you need something?"

"I already spoke to your sister."

"Was she helpful?"

"Not particularly."

Bing did not look surprised by the response, which intrigued Devine.

"Can *I* help?" asked Bing.

"Do you know Earl Palmer?"

"Earl, oh yes. Everyone knows Earl. I heard he found Jenny's body."

Maybe or maybe not, thought Devine. "You said before you didn't know she was in town this time. So when was the last time you saw Jenny?"

Bing thought for a few moments, running his hand through his hair. "Maybe last year, or the year before. I assumed she was busy with whatever she was doing."

"And what do you think she was doing?"

"Serving her country in some capacity. The actual details of what she did have made for some lively discussions at the local watering holes up here, I can tell you that."

"Dak said that the remote workers have really turned the prospects of the town around."

"They've certainly helped." He grinned wryly. "Although most of the recent influx are too young to have much need of my services. Yet."

"Do you have any thoughts on who might have killed her?"

Bing leaned against the wall and crossed his arms over his slender chest. "I think I just assumed that it had something to do with her work. I mean, why would anyone up here want to kill her? She wasn't really part of our lives anymore. The only real connection was her brother and sister and all that property."

"Property that some may want to develop. And pay a pretty penny for it."

Bing looked surprised. "Really? Who told you that?"

"Does it matter?"

"I guess not," said Bing, looking confused and, to Devine's mind, nervous.

"I assume you handled Mrs. Palmer's funeral arrangements?"

"Yes, yes we did. It was terrible. Bertie's death stunned all of us. And the fact that no one was held accountable? It just makes it even more horrible."

"And I understand her son and daughter-in-law died in a house fire?"

"Yes. That was about, let me think, fifteen years ago now."

"What happened?"

"No one really knows for sure. Steve was a smoker, so that's what we all thought had happened. At least initially. It was early summer but we had a cold snap and turns out they'd been having trouble with their furnace. So they were using one of those old portable heaters without any safety or cutoff features, you know the kind that if they tip over and catch something on fire your whole house can go up in about a minute? So maybe it wasn't his smoking. I wasn't working at the funeral home then, but my uncle told me that it was a challenge making them viewable. Ended up being a closed casket. No one wanted to remember them that way. Their daughter, I think, was away or something." He paused. "But why are you asking about that?"

"Because it has loose ends. Like the person who hit Mrs. Palmer and fled the scene."

"But those two events were fifteen years apart. And one was a tragic accident and one was a hit-and-run."

"And now Jenny."

"Again, I don't see the connection."

"Well, I don't either, to tell you the truth. Maybe there is none."

"I wouldn't think so. I mean, stuff like that does happen."

"Yeah, but this little town has had more than its share of 'stuff,' don't you think?"

Bing just shrugged. "Well, good luck with your investigation. If there's anything I can do to help, please let me know."

"I will."

Devine left, got into his SUV, and drove back to the inn. And all along the way he was wondering why Earl Palmer had been offered up as the one to find Jenny's body when he could not have possibly seen it. Whoever was behind this had not thought that one through. But then again, until Devine had come along, everyone had just accepted what the old man had said at face value.

Maybe I am *good at this. Or maybe no one else really wants to find out the truth.*

34

Harper and Fuss were waiting for him when he returned to the inn. The two cops didn't look happy, and he felt sure he was about to find out why.

Harper said, "Heard you went to see Earl Palmer today."

"News travels fast."

"Can I ask why?"

"He was the one who found Jenny's body. I had follow-up questions."

"Like what?" asked Fuss, giving him a look that Devine didn't really care for.

"Just the standard stuff."

"Learn anything new?" asked Harper, his hand resting on top of his baton.

"I don't know. I have to think about it."

"You were over at the funeral home earlier, too," said Fuss.

"Minutes ago and you already know. You guys need to apply to work for CIA."

"Cut the crap, Devine. What are you trying to get at?" demanded Harper.

"Same as you, the truth. We all just have our own methods of getting there, apparently."

"You seem to doubt that Earl found the body," said Fuss.

"Well, if you mean do I think it odd that he looked down to see the body, only the guy can't look down? Then yeah, I have some doubts. You should too."

Harper eyed Fuss and said, "What do you mean, he 'can't look down'?"

The man seemed to be sincere, thought Devine, or else he was an excellent liar. "A couple of cervical spinal fusions that went bad. He has severely restricted range of motion. Thought Guillaume would have told you. You obviously saw her at the funeral home and she told you that we had met."

"You're wrong. We didn't talk to her," said Fuss. "We saw both your cars in the parking lot when we passed by on our way here."

"Okay."

"Now what about Earl?" asked Harper.

"I gave him a little test at the spot where he claimed to have seen Jenny's body." He filled them in on what he had done to discover the man's inability to look downward.

"Are you sure?" asked Harper.

"Test him yourself," suggested Devine. "And the guy has a hard time walking. No, he doesn't really walk, he shuffles. So he was out in a monsoon shuffling miles, including through the mud, to the edge of that bluff?"

"If what you're suggesting is true, it opens up a can of worms," said Harper.

"It actually changes everything," replied Devine.

"What do you mean by that?" asked Harper.

"If he didn't look down and see her, how was she actually found? Did she really fall on the rocks after being shot, or was she killed elsewhere and moved there later?"

"Hold on, hold on," protested Fuss. "You're getting way over your skis the way I see it."

"I don't think so. It's a fact that when Earl called 911 there was a body at the spot mentioned?"

"Yes," said Harper. "I told you that. The night dispatcher called me and I called Wendy. We went out there straightaway."

"And Earl was there?"

"Sure was, right over at the edge. He pointed to where she was."

"Did he look down when he pointed?"

"I don't remember," snapped Harper. "I had other things to think about."

"But if he didn't find her, what was he really doing there?" asked Devine.

"*You're* the one saying that, not us."

"Then *test* him."

"We do that, it's as good as saying we don't believe him."

Devine retorted, "I thought our job was to find the facts, not worry about hurt feelings."

"We don't need you to tell us how to do our job,"

interjected Fuss heatedly. "In fact, you made our job harder by preventing us from searching Jenny's room and car right away."

"I had nothing to do with that."

"It was still *your* people," pointed out Fuss.

"This is getting us nowhere," said Devine. "Are you going to speak to Earl?"

Harper hitched up his pants. "I'll let you know. In the meantime, what can you tell us about those three people you killed? Your boys turn up anything?"

"Not that they've shared with me."

"Well, as soon as you do hear anything, be sure to let us know."

"I'd appreciate the same," replied Devine.

They walked off without acknowledging this request.

As soon as they left, Alex came riding up on her bicycle, stopping in front of him.

"Can we talk?" she said.

"Sure. About what?"

"About . . . me. And Jenny."

35

She curled and uncurled her fingers around the coffee cup at Maine Brew.

Devine watched those long, lively fingers and judged them to be as artistic in design and function as the mind of the woman who owned them.

"What about you and your sister?" said Devine in a gently prompting manner.

Alex looked up at him, considerable pain in her expression. She fiddled with the colorful scarf tied around her neck. "I . . . I heard about what happened to you. That you almost died last night. That was why you came to my studio, wasn't it?"

"Who told you that?"

"Wendy Fuss. She said that you killed three men who had kidnapped you."

He nodded slowly. "Yes. But we didn't come here to talk about that, did we?" He took a sip of coffee and glanced out the window as a chilly rain started to fall. When she didn't say anything he looked back at her. "I heard something about you."

"What?" she said quickly.

"That you were attacked when you were in high school. And that the person who attacked you got away."

"I . . . I . . ." She looked so distressed that he put his hand out and gripped hers firmly.

"If you don't want to talk about it, then don't. It's up to you. No worries. I shouldn't have brought it up. I'm sorry. It was a stupid thing to do."

He let go of her hand, sat back, and waited.

She took a sip of coffee and then set the cup down and plunged in. "The doctors said that in addition to having physical injuries, I . . . I suffered a traumatic shock. And that shock caused something called localized or situation-specific dissociative amnesia. Back then I had no idea what that meant, but I've come to learn that it means I can't remember certain specific memories. In my case I can remember what I was doing before it happened, but nothing after that."

"So you don't remember *any* details of the assault?"

She shook her head. "I wouldn't have even known that it happened at all except I woke up in a hospital with a skull fracture and . . . the police were there." She touched her scalp in the middle of her head. "They had to shave my head right there to fix it. They also told me I had been—"

"Yes, I know," said Devine quickly. "Will you ever get the memories back?"

"They don't know. Apparently, most of the time they do come back, at least to some degree. But . . . it hasn't happened with me, and it's been over fifteen years now."

"Is there anything they can do to help you get them back?"

"I've been to psychotherapy, but it didn't help. They told me that your mind blocks out something if it's too painful to . . . confront. And there's something called creative therapy that I actually do every day and would have done regardless of whether this had happened to me or not."

"Your artwork, you mean?"

She smiled, sadly, and nodded. "Yes. It's my cocoon. My safe space. When I'm doing it, all is right with the world, at least *my* world."

"Who found you after you were attacked, do you know?"

"If they told me, I don't remember. I was . . . just in shock when they told me what had happened. And my head hurt so badly."

"So the police had nothing to go on? No one else saw anything?"

"No."

"Where did the attack happen?"

Alex shook her head. "I . . . I don't remember."

"I am so very sorry that happened to you, Alex."

She looked down at the table and nodded, and then wiped at her eyes.

"But you didn't come here to tell me this, since I was the one who brought it up."

She looked at him. "I came here to tell you that Jenny *did* come by to see me when she was here." She stopped and looked at him. "Aren't you mad that I didn't tell you before?"

"No. I'll just assume you had your reasons."

Her expression relaxed. "You keep surprising me, Travis. I think I have you figured out and you throw me a curve."

"Not to worry. I was thinking the very same thing about you."

She picked at one of her paint-covered fingers. "It was in the afternoon before she was killed."

"What did she want?"

"She wanted to know if I had remembered anything from when I was attacked."

"And what did you tell her?"

"The same thing I just told you. That I hadn't."

"Why would she be bringing that up now, after all these years? Or did she regularly check in with you about it?"

"No, she had never mentioned it before, aside from when she came home to help me right after it happened. She never left my side for a long while. And she would talk to me about it, trying to get me to recall what had happened. I think she might have tried too hard because it never worked. I remember she got angry with me sometimes about it."

"Why? Like you said, these things happen to people who have experienced what you did."

"Because Jenny would have been strong enough to overcome that, remember every detail, and nail the bastard. Or so she told me when *I* couldn't do that."

"A tough older sister."

"An impossibly perfect older sister." She hesitated. "But she did . . . care about me, Travis. I know she did. Through her actions, if not always through her words."

"But not so easy to love. Your earlier remark about Jenny is making more sense."

"I *did* love her, despite all that," Alex said so quietly Devine almost didn't hear her.

"Is that when Bertie Palmer started to mentor you?"

"Yes. Jenny had to go back to Washington for work. And Mom and Dad were . . . well, they had a lot going on."

"They must have been terribly upset about what happened to you."

"I don't think they knew how to deal with it. Dad went around angry all the time. I believe he blamed himself for not protecting me. And Mom alternated between going into a shell and then coming out of it to smother me." She looked out the window at the rain falling from a gray sky, but her expression brightened in spite of the gloomy weather.

"Bertie was a godsend. A truly wonderful, giving person. She didn't just teach me about art. I mean, I had a natural talent, but my fundamentals were all over the place, especially my line work. She taught me about life, too. About who I was, or could become."

"I heard you had been accepted at some great art schools. I know you have to present a portfolio of your work to be considered for admission."

"Bertie helped me do all that, Travis. She was the

reason I had the courage to apply to those schools in the first place *and* have artwork worthy enough to show them. It was therapy for what I was going through. She urged me to get it out on the drawings, the canvas, whatever I was working on. And it helped, it really did."

"But then you didn't go to any of the schools. Why?"

Alex stared out at the rain, which was starting to fall harder. And, mirroring what the weather was doing, tears started to slide from her eyes and curlicue down her trembling cheeks.

And as Devine watched this, it was like he had forgotten how to breathe. He reached out and gripped her hand once more, not only to reassure her, but to also do so for himself.

"Would you think it unbelievable if I told you I didn't know why?" she said in a hushed voice.

"No, I wouldn't. But there is a big world out there to explore. And capture in your art."

She shifted her gaze to him. "I know," she said in a low voice. But Devine knew the woman had no faith or belief in her own response. At this point, they were just words, expected ones, what she thought he wanted to hear.

He withdrew his hand. "So you stayed in the old homestead, where you grew up?"

"It was a happy time for us. Mostly. At least I remember it that way." She glanced at him. "Did you have a happy place?"

He nodded. "It was called the United States Army."

"So why aren't you still in uniform?"

"Because life came at me fast and I didn't duck in time. So now, here I am."

"Here we both are," she amended. "I . . . I better go."

When she rose he said, "Whether those memories come back or not, Alex, they won't define you if you don't let them."

"I used to think that."

"You still can."

"I used to think that, too, Travis."

He watched her walk off because he could think of nothing to make her stay.

But he did have one thought.

If I find whoever took Alex's life from her I will make them pay.

36

The next morning, after his workout and partaking of the inn's continental breakfast, Devine drove to the police station, where he found Harper and Fuss in the chief's small office. He eyed the pictures on the wall of tough-looking men in uniform.

Harper noted this and said, "Former chiefs of police here. Way back we had six full-time officers, if you can believe it. But then our population fell off a cliff."

"It's going back up, according to Dak Silkwell."

"It is," conceded Harper. "The 'remoters,' he calls them. They *are* coming here in droves. I don't know if it will last, but we'll take it. Only good thing to come out of COVID, for us."

"Any news on Jenny's phone or laptop?"

"We don't know that she had a laptop with her," said Fuss.

Devine pulled out his phone and showed a picture he'd taken. "Dust pattern on her desk at the inn. What else could that be?"

"When did you notice that?" asked Harper.

"When we searched the place."

"And you're just now telling us?" he barked.

"I thought you had noted it."

This seemed to make Harper even madder, and he was clearly struggling to keep his temper in check. "How about your folks? Have they traced any of that electronically?"

Devine shook his head. "No, but I got another question."

"Okay," said Harper, seeming to brace himself.

"Where was Alex Silkwell attacked all those years ago?"

Harper looked at Fuss, who was now looking at the scuffed wooden floor.

"I was a sergeant back then," said Harper. "Like Wendy is now. But we had other officers, like I said."

"Okay. Were you one of the responders? And who called it in? I understand that Alex didn't. She woke up in the hospital."

"Why are you asking about that?" said Fuss, now looking at him.

"Because Jenny asked Alex if she had remembered anything about the attack."

"What?" bellowed Harper. "You mean *this* time? Who told you that?"

"Alex did."

"She never told us," retorted Harper.

"Well, she told me and I'm telling you. So I'd like to know where Alex was found, since it now seems Jenny came up here to look into what happened to her sister."

"Why, after all this time?" said Fuss.

"I don't know, but I'd like to find out. So the place?"

"Before my time," said Fuss quickly.

Devine shifted his focus to Harper, who would not meet his eye. "Chief?"

"It was . . . actually, it was right around where Jenny's body was found, as a matter of fact. But in the open field before you get to the trees and through the trail there to the bluff by the water."

Devine's expression slowly hardened. "And you never put two and two together?"

"No, I didn't. Hell, I hadn't even thought about what happened to Alex in years. Your question just now made me think about it."

"Come on, you really think they're connected?" interjected Fuss. "What about the military round found out there? And the person who took a shot at you? And the ones who kidnapped you? They were all foreign folks. They weren't around when that happened to Alex."

"I don't know what to make of all that, yet," conceded Devine. "But the location being the same for Alex *and* Jenny? It might mean something. We have to follow it up."

"You can, if you want," said Harper. "I have better things to do with my time."

"Okay. Did you confirm that the round fired at me was a NATO round? I'm asking because even though I found the casing, this case is so screwy when it comes to ballistics I want to make sure the casing matches the round fired."

"We confirmed it, yes. Told the other feds, Saxon and Mann."

"Did you check Dak's alibi for the time Jenny was killed?"

Harper exclaimed, "Why in the world would Dak want to kill his own sister?"

"Oldest motivation of all—money."

"What money?"

"Dak told me some developers want to buy Jocelyn Point. It would be worth millions. Now that Jenny's gone, the value of Dak's share went way up."

Harper eyed Devine. "Okay, we'll check it out. Thanks for the info."

"You're welcome."

37

Later that day, after spending time in his room going over the case notes and his briefing book, and pondering how all of this tied together with what he had found out so far, Devine drove through the wind and rain to the spot where Jenny's body had been found, *and* where Alex had also been attacked. As he stared out over the rugged terrain, Devine concluded that the events had to be connected in some way, which meant that the killer of Jenny Silkwell might have also attacked Alex, or at least knew something about it.

But what explained the men who had abducted him? And the woman he had heard? Fuss was right. They were foreigners, most likely, and while they might have reason to kill Jenny because of her ties to CIA, they almost certainly could not have been involved in what happened to Alex fifteen years ago.

He instinctively looked over his shoulder to see if anyone was trying to get a bead on him. That had been a way of life in the Middle East, because there someone was always trying to sneak up and kill you.

This case really came down to one linchpin.

Earl Palmer. He was lying about finding the body, of that Devine was convinced. And the police seemed to have no interest in following that up. Were they being loyal to a local, just equal parts incompetent or stupid, or were they complicit in whatever cover-up was going on?

But the thing was, Palmer didn't strike Devine as a liar. He seemed just like everyone described him: salt of the earth, nursing perhaps the most painful loss any person can endure.

So why lie under those circumstances?

Is someone making you lie, Earl?

He drove off while the rain continued to pour down, and then abruptly transformed to sleet. And then, just as swiftly, it all stopped and the skies began to clear. The weather really was crazy up here, thought Devine.

He turned onto the main road as his phone buzzed.

It was Campbell. Devine hit the speaker function.

"First things first, Agents Saxon and Mann have made a partial trace of the men who kidnapped you."

"What did they find out?"

"They arrived in the country the same day they came after you. Flew in from London. Before that we traced them to Brussels. They are a known quantity, killers for hire."

"Like the guys on the Geneva train?"

"Yes, but at a higher level. You did well to survive, Devine."

"Any idea who hired them?"

"Not yet. The organization you went after in Geneva

has many resources. And while we hit them with a debilitating shot, we obviously didn't knock them out. Now we're doing a deep internal security audit here, trying to compartmentalize who knew about your assignment in Maine."

"Must be a fairly short list."

"It is, Devine, but we need proof. If we have a mole we'll find the person and deal with them accordingly."

"I hope I'm around to see it," replied Devine. "Anything on the woman on the train? She might have been the one in the house that night."

"Apparently a woman of many identities, a number of which we are currently running down. It seems most likely that she was engaged by the Geneva folks to deal with you after what you did to them."

"So she's a freelancer, then?"

"That's the prelim at least, but it has not been confirmed. There's been talk of a new talent out in the mercenary field, but we don't know if it's her or not. Now, what's new on your end?"

Devine went over his suspicions about Earl Palmer and the possible connection of Jenny Silkwell's murder to the assault on her sister years earlier.

"My God. Curt never mentioned anything like that happening to Alex."

"They apparently hushed it all up. Why, I don't know."

"Then what's your take on the Norma casing being found at Jenny's crime scene, but a NATO round being the one that nearly killed you?" asked Campbell.

"I don't really have a take, sir. Yet. It could be someone from the military, or a civilian trying to throw suspicion that way. And we don't know for sure Jenny was killed with the Norma round, since it was never found."

"You have anyone that's giving you certain vibes?"

"Dak Silkwell is an aspiring mini-mogul who will make even more millions off the sale of the old homestead now that Jenny is gone. He says he was in Boston at the time, but he could have paid someone to do it. That much money is a prime motive."

"That's the other thing I meant to share with you. I spoke today with the Silkwell estate lawyers about the trust that left the house and property to the children," said Campbell. "So it might be Dak had even more motive than you thought."

"How do you mean?"

"According to the trust terms there has to be a *unanimous* vote to sell the property. So if Jenny didn't want to sell, Dak was not getting his millions. And if *Alex* doesn't want to sell, Dak has the same problem that he might have had with Jenny."

"I gotta go." Devine ended the call and punched the gas.

38

Devine pounded on the front door at Jocelyn Point, to no avail. Alex's bike was there. But Dak's Harley was not. At this time of day the man was at work inking people's skin.

He tried the door but it was locked. He ran around to the studio, but a quick look in the window revealed it was empty. He hustled back to the house and found the back door unlocked.

"Alex?" he cried out. "You here. We need to talk. Alex?"

He searched the first floor, then the second. He found Dak's bedroom, which was a pigsty; on the other side of the house was Alex's, which was tidy and organized.

Walls built around her to keep the bogeyman away.

He opened a third door and looked in. There were dust cloths on the furniture, but he could tell the space was clearly another bedroom.

On the wall he saw a number of grainy old newspaper articles that had been framed. He walked over to them. The local paper had written stories about Jenny Silkwell's academic and athletic accomplishments, which were many and impressive. And on a shelf were trophies and certificates and other memorabilia that further proclaimed the outstanding youthful achievements of the room's former occupant.

He shook his head and wondered what it would have been like to be Jenny Silkwell's sibling. *Not easy. Not easy at all.*

He closed the door and spied another staircase that headed up.

He took it. The staircase was full of mildew and decay. He saw that it opened out onto the widow's walk that served as a topper to the home.

The weather hit him as soon as he stepped outside, but now it was just wind. The precipitation had carried well off the coast.

The air seemed finer and purer up here, he immediately noted.

He took in the area, with his gaze finally settling on the Atlantic. The wind had churned it, and the whitecaps roiled the surface in a slow-moving motion that struck him as frenetic still. There were a few boats in his sight line, but that was all. The day was beginning to wind down and the setting sun was behind him, casting all he was seeing in a stream of colors that was building as slowly as the waves.

When his gaze dropped to the dark rocks along the coast his throat seized and his heart felt stiff and flimsy. He cried out in his anxiety and ran pell-mell back down the stairs to the first floor and out the back door. He ran flat-out toward the ocean, his heart in his throat as he mumbled every prayer he could think of.

He looked down on the boulders where the tide was just beginning to come in.

Alex was sprawled out on one of them.

He hurried down the rough path leading to the rocks and skipped over them to reach her.

Don't be dead, don't be dead.

He pulled his phone to call 911.

He got to her and knelt down to check the woman's pulse.

She screamed and sat up so abruptly, Devine fell back on his ass on one of the rocks.

"What are you doing?" she demanded.

He was so relieved that he had interpreted the scene incorrectly that he didn't answer. He just laughed, uncontrollably, for a few seconds in a spasm of relief, and then lapsed into an embarrassed silence, his chest heaving with all he was feeling at the moment.

As she stared at him with obvious concern he said, "I saw you lying sprawled on the rocks from the widow's walk. I . . . I thought . . ." He couldn't finish the statement, but he didn't need to.

"Omigod, I'm so sorry," said Alex. She reached out and gripped his hand. "I guess it looked . . . I was like . . . Jenny."

He nodded and then looked off to the encroaching ocean. He closed his eyes and tried to will away that image of a dead Alex. It did not work.

"I come out here a few times a week and lay out on this flat rock before the tide comes in. It's part of my therapy. I was going to bag it today what with the rain, but it stopped, so . . ."

"I didn't know you were still in therapy."

"It's self-imposed. I learned a lot from others and now I practice it. Breathing exercises, meditation, using certain calming phrases, being in the moment, trying to knock as much cortisol out of my system as I can and replacing it with dopamine." She ran her gaze over him. "You should try it; you look very stressed. I can teach you a few things."

"Thanks, maybe I'll take you up on that. But I have some questions first."

"Okay? What?"

"Did you know your brother is negotiating to sell Jocelyn Point? And do you agree with that? And do you know whether your sister did and whether she approved of a potential sale?"

Alex now looked out to sea and didn't answer for a long moment while Devine tensely watched her.

"Dak told me about it. I don't know if Jenny wanted to sell or not. I don't know if she even knew about it."

"She didn't talk about it when she came up here last?"

"No, she never mentioned it. She just wanted to talk about . . . if I had recalled anything from when I was attacked."

"So, are you okay with him selling all this?"

"We haven't really talked about how I feel. And I haven't really thought about it."

"Under the trust document you both have to agree for a sale to go through. When Jenny was alive she would have had to agree, too."

She slowly turned to look at him. "You're not suggesting . . . ?"

"I have to look at every angle, Alex. Dak is negotiating to sell this place, like I said. So how is he doing that if you haven't agreed to the deal?"

"I don't know. I'll have to talk to him about it."

He drew closer. "Alex, do you want to leave here?"

"You told me there's a big world out there for me to capture."

"I know I did, and I meant it. But you can travel to other places without selling this place. Without selling your home."

"In case you hadn't noticed, I'm not exactly rolling in cash. Yeah, I've sold some artwork here and there, but I don't get Picasso-level money in return."

"I thought that Dak does well financially."

"I'm not Dak. But if he weren't paying the taxes on this property we would have already lost it."

"So you're saying you might not have a choice in the matter?"

"If Dak stops paying the taxes there's no way I can keep the house."

"Well, you'll be very rich. Dak said it would be worth millions."

He watched her closely to see how she reacted to this.

Alex just stared off. "My dad probably won't live to see the new year, will he?"

Devine was startled by the segue. "No, it's doubtful that he will. Have you spoken to your mother about it?"

"I know everyone hates her because they think she abandoned Dad, but I don't think that."

"What *do* you think?"

"How about some hot tea? And I can light a fire in my dad's old study. I'm chilled to the bone now, and not just with the weather."

"Sounds good. I can help."

They entered through the back door, where Alex stopped and said, "You mentioned you were on the widow's walk?"

He looked embarrassed. "I was worried about you. I saw your bike and when you didn't answer—the door was unlocked."

"I get it, Travis."

As he watched her in the kitchen prepare the tea he was struck by her vulnerability and, more important, how she was dealing with it. The woman had personal courage that was admirable. He imagined she took each day as it came, not attempting to go any further than that. And one day at a time was probably difficult enough for her.

He carried the tray while she opened the door to the study. Devine looked around at the worm-eaten walnut floorboards and darkened ceiling beams. In the middle of the room was an old partner's desk with a well-worn green leatherback chair and a small wooden holder with a large fountain pen in it, and another stand that held two old smoking pipes. Bookshelves lined two walls. On the third wall was a large window looking out to the water. On the fourth was a brick-faced fireplace with a wooden mantel that held framed pictures. There was an old red leather couch and a couple of armchairs set around an industrial-style coffee table constructed of chunky, weathered wood with metal straps across the top and rusty metal wheels. He set the tray down on the coffee table.

"This place looks full of memories."

Alex smiled as she poured out the teas and set some banana bread out on plates. "Good ones. At least for me."

Devine handled the kindling and stacked the wood in a particular way in the fireplace. He thinned out an old page of newspaper, lit it, and held it up near the flue opening to draw the flames.

"You look like you've done that before," she commented.

"Army and the Boy Scouts. Some of the training is the same."

As the fire picked up they drew closer to it. Devine took a bite of the banana bread and exclaimed, "Damn, that is good."

"I make it myself. It was a recipe Bertie shared."

"A woman of many talents."

"Yes, Bertie was."

"I wasn't talking about Bertie," he said.

They stared awkwardly at one another before Devine broke off his gaze.

She said in a halting voice, "I loved coming in here as a child. This was originally Hiram Silkwell's study, and all the Silkwell men have used it as their inner sanctum over the generations. Those pipes belonged to my grandfather, Tobias Silkwell. My father would be at the desk writing with the fat fountain pen that's still in the holder over there. He had monogrammed stationery and his penmanship was perfect. I always tried to form my letters like he did. He wrote his own speeches and he liked to do it in here. He would read them to Jenny and she would critique them. He usually agreed with her comments. At least that's what she told me."

"One of yours?" said Devine, pointing at the painting hanging next to the window. It depicted four people in a sailboat.

"Yes. That was us, Dad and the three kids. Mom didn't like to sail. She got seasick. But Jenny would race her little boat out on the gulf all the time. She was fearless."

The way she said it made Devine a bit sad. Jenny had clearly intimidated her younger sister, but it seemed her death had also left a void in Alex's life.

She rose and plucked a framed photo off the mantel and held it out to him. "I used this as the model for the painting."

He looked at the picture and saw a sleek blue-and-white sailboat with twin sails and a cabin below. At the helm was Curtis Silkwell with a far younger Jenny next to him, one of her hands on the wheel next to her father's. Off to the side were Alex and Dak.

"Someone took the picture from shore and gave it to us."

"He obviously liked the painting, if it's hanging in here."

"I did that two years after . . . it happened. It was therapy."

"I'm sure it was. It took you back to a safe time and a safe place."

She smiled. "My dad was a daredevil sailor, too, even more than Jenny."

Devine smiled. "How'd you all handle it?"

"Jenny pretended not to be scared. Dak was terrified and screamed bloody murder the first few times we went out, especially if the seas were rough, but then he got the hang of it."

"And you?"

"I trusted my dad," she said simply. She looked up at Devine as she handed him a cup of tea. "I knew he would never do anything to hurt us. And he was always in control even when he seemed not to be. He could do anything."

"Sounds like you really love him," said Devine.

"I knew he was this brave war hero from way back. But I never saw that side of him. He never had any of that stuff here. No medals or anything, and he never talked about it, even when we asked him. Well, Jenny and Dak did. I wasn't interested."

"It's been my experience that the people who did the

most in war talked about it the least, and the reverse is also true."

She nodded and looked out the window, where the wind had intensified. It pushed against the glass with the firm pressure of a leviathan's hand. Then there was a loud smack as possibly a tree limb hit the house; Devine felt his hand dart to his gun.

Get a grip, you idiot.

Alex said, "He was a good congressman and senator. He worked a lot with the state's governors, especially Angus King, who is now a senator, too, and John Baldacci when he was the governor. My dad really cared about the people who live here."

"Will you go down to see him?" he asked. "And your mother? She said she tried to call and got no answer. And she hasn't seen or talked to you since the divorce."

"It's complicated, Travis," she said, her expression tightening. "I'm a different person than I used to be. I don't want to be different. I want to be happy and I am, sometimes. But sometimes things hit me and wipe the smile right off my face. My anxiety goes through the roof. I can barely breathe. The world feels like it's closing in on me. It's not Mom, really, it's . . . me. And I don't want her to see me . . . like that."

She seemed to grip the teacup harder, and glanced at the fire. He could see her taking deep, moderating breaths and saying something under her breath. A calming phrase or chant, like she had mentioned.

"You're safe with me, Alex. I won't let anyone hurt you."

She gave him a sad smile. "But one day you won't be here, and I will."

Of course, and what a stupid thing for me to say.

He stared at the flames, and couldn't think of any suitable reply to her honest from-the-gut words.

39

He left her there by the fire.

Devine looked back at the house as he sat in the SUV, his spirits as bleak as the weather.

The case had its difficulties, but so did every other challenge he'd confronted. No, it wasn't the case that bothered him so much. It was knowing that no matter what he did he could not make people who were not whole, whole. Not Alex. Not Curtis Silkwell. Not his ex-wife. Not Earl or Annie Palmer. Not anyone whose life had been touched by Jenny Silkwell.

Including me, and I never even knew the woman.

He drove to the police station and found that neither Fuss nor Harper was there. But there was a woman he had been introduced to before. Her name was Mildred James, and she handled the dispatch and all the admin work for the department.

"I'm not sure when they'll be back," said James. "Can I do anything for you?"

He sat down across from her. "You lived here long?"

"I was born here fifty-nine years ago next week."

"Happy early birthday, then. So you know the Silkwells?"

"Oh sure. Wonderful family. It's so awful what happened to Jenny. I'm sure her parents are very upset. Well, I heard Senator Silkwell is not well, so he may not . . . be aware."

"You like working here?"

"If I didn't, I wouldn't. There's never too much to do, I mean nothing that you'd call exciting. And that's not a bad thing, don't get me wrong. But with more people moving into the area, we are getting more calls and such. There's even talk of hiring another officer or two."

"Were you working here when Alex was assaulted?"

"Oh, yes. I've been working here over twenty years. Thank God whoever attacked her didn't kill her."

I think they killed part of her, Devine thought.

"What can you tell me about the incident?" he asked.

"Well, I was on duty and got the call that a woman had been attacked. I took the information and dispatched the response."

"Wait a minute, who called it in?"

"The people who found her."

"How *did* they find her?"

"Let me think. Yes, they said they were driving past a spot along the coast and they happened to look out and see something lying there. The husband got out to see what it was while the wife waited in the car. He recognized that it was Alex. He ran back to the car and told his wife to call the police, which she did."

"And then Alex was taken to a hospital where she awoke but couldn't remember anything?"

"That's right. That hospital has since closed, it was only ten minutes from here, thank God, or Alex might not have made it. Now, she couldn't give a statement or help in any way. She was clearly in shock and she had a skull fracture. Her life was in danger until they got things under control. The officers searched the area where she was found, but didn't find any evidence worth anything. And they canvassed for witnesses, but no one saw anything."

"Were her parents in town when it happened?"

"Mrs. Silkwell was, and she rushed right over to the hospital when we notified her. Stayed there all through the night. Jenny came up from Washington to help, too."

"And Dak was out of the country in the Army?"

"I believe that's right."

"And Senator Silkwell?"

"He flew up straightaway on a chartered plane a friend of his arranged. I actually picked him up at the airport and drove him to the hospital. He was beside himself with rage, guilt, you name it and that man was feeling it."

"I understand she had been raped?" Devine said in a low voice.

James assumed a pained expression. "Yes. I'm not sure Alex remembered that part or any part. The mind is funny like that. But her examination clearly showed that she had been raped. We still have the rape kit after all this time, but we never had a suspect to match it to. We ran it through the usual databases and such but never got a hit.

We were all hoping that Alex would regain her memory and identify her attacker if she knew him, or at least give a description, but she never did. Now it's a very cold case."

"Could I look at the file and the evidence?"

"Why? Do you think it might be connected to what happened to Jenny?"

"Well, Jenny had come up here on some unfinished business and she had talked to Alex about the attack. And I understand that Jenny's body was found near where Alex was assaulted."

James frowned. "Yes, I thought that was awfully strange. Well, I can't see how it would hurt to have another pair of eyes on it."

She led him to a locked room at the back of the small building and showed him where the files and evidence were located. She had him sign a logbook.

"There's a little room with a table just through that door you can use. Just let me know when you're done."

He thanked her and she left him there.

Devine gathered up the box of evidence and the related files and carried them to the room, where he set everything out. He first unsealed the evidence bags and took pictures of the items inside with his phone. They consisted of Alex's clothing and underclothing, which was torn and dirty, some hair samples, a pair of women's sneakers, and the contents of a small bag. They were mostly art-related: a couple of tubes of paint, a brush, a pencil, and a small sketchpad.

He opened the latter and saw some pencil drawings that

she had done. They were all of the coastline or else looking out to sea. They were quite good and demonstrated the natural talent that the woman had exhibited while still in her teens.

What he didn't find was the rape kit. He checked the log that was in the box and it showed a rape kit, but he didn't see anything that looked like it. He was familiar with them because he had worked with Army CID overseas when some soldiers in his company had been accused of raping a local woman. Two of them had been found innocent, one had not. He was currently serving time in a military prison at Fort Leavenworth for his crime.

He sealed the evidence bags and put them back in the box. He glanced out the window and saw that the rain had started up again. You would be just as wet walking down the street as you would be jumping in the ocean, he figured.

He went methodically through the files and official statements. Alex had told the investigators that she remembered riding her bicycle along that section of the coast. She was on her way to Jocelyn Point after seeing some friends in town. It was later than she had realized and she was hurrying to get home before it got completely dark. That was the last thing she remembered until she woke up in the hospital. There was semen, hair, and other trace on her person from her attacker, but the police never had anyone to match it to. There were no witnesses. Then he got to the part about the couple who had found Alex.

Their names jumped off the page and seemed to scream at Devine.

Steve and Valerie Palmer had been the ones to find Alex and call the police.

Devine checked the date, and then Googled something on his phone.

The story popped up on his screen.

Three days after finding Alex's body, Steve and Valerie Palmer had died in the house fire. The story said that it had been accidental and due to a portable heater being knocked over, probably by the couple's cat, which had also perished in the fire. It seemed the drapes had caught on fire and the room had been engulfed in flames while the doomed couple had slept. They had apparently been overcome by smoke inhalation because their badly charred bodies had been found in the bed.

Devine went and asked James about the rape kit. She looked through the box and then through the entire evidence room.

"My God, it's not here," she said.

Devine looked at the log to see who had last accessed the evidence. The date was from over ten years ago, and while the ink had faded some, Devine could still make out the name and signature.

Sergeant Richard Wayne Harper.

40

Devine drove straight to Maine Brew to find that Annie Palmer was just leaving. Devine checked his watch. It was after eight. Long, long day for the woman. She had her motorcycle helmet in hand, a rain slicker on, and was climbing onto her scooter as he pulled to the curb.

"Do you have time to talk?" he asked after rolling his window down.

She looked flustered. "I was going to check on my grandfather before heading home."

"It won't take long. Just a few questions."

She hesitated. "Okay, where?"

"In here. Out of the storm."

They sat in the SUV while the rain clattered against the vehicle's roof.

"So, what questions?" she asked, tucking a wet strand of hair behind her ear.

"It's bringing things up in the past, things that will be painful to you."

"I . . . I don't understand," she said, a sense of panic rising in her eyes.

"It has to do with your parents."

"What about them?"

"They were the ones to find Alex after she was attacked."

She stared at him blankly for a moment. "What are you talking about?"

"You didn't know that?"

"No!"

"Your parents didn't tell you?"

"I was at camp when they died in the fire. I'd been there all week. The police brought me home when it happened. It was awful." She punched the dashboard. "I should have been there. I could have saved them."

"You can't blame yourself for that, Annie. For all you know, if you had been there you would have died, too."

"Well, at least we would have died together."

"I don't believe that's what your parents would have wanted."

She looked out the window. "My grandparents took me in and finished raising me. But I never knew about my parents finding Alex. My grandparents never told me. I don't even know if they knew."

"So you knew about her being assaulted?"

"There were rumors, and I heard things from time to time."

"She was also raped."

Palmer's eyes filled with fresh tears. "I didn't know *that*."

"And no one else in town told you about your parents finding her?"

"No. Who else knew?" she asked.

"Well, the police did, surely."

"I can't believe this shit." She paused and studied him. "But what does that matter now? Whether I knew or not?"

"Alex got attacked and your parents found her. And from the timeline I looked at they found her pretty much *immediately* after she was attacked. Then, three days later they die in a house fire?"

"I must be very stupid, but I don't see what you're getting at."

"I think they might have *seen* whoever raped Alex. They could have passed the man on the road, maybe he was running or driving away. The point is, it's a lonely area. It was getting dark. There might not have been anyone else around."

"But if they saw the rapist, why didn't they tell the police?"

"That I haven't figured out yet. I just found out they were the ones who discovered Alex and reported it."

"So are you saying that my parents were, what? Murdered?"

"It's possible."

Palmer shook her head stubbornly. "I just don't see how that could have happened. My parents were friends with the Silkwells. They would have told the police if they had seen a man running or driving away like that. And if they had, what would be the point of killing them to keep them quiet about what they had seen? The police would have arrested the person or at least talked to them."

Devine knew she was probably right about that.

"The police report says the fire was started when a portable heater turned over and caught the drapes on fire."

She nodded. "That's what they told me, too. I remember that old heater. It wasn't safe. Mom was always telling Dad to buy a new one. But . . ."

"But what?"

"Well, to tell the truth, my parents were going through some tough times financially. My dad had put all their savings into a business that went belly-up. And my mom had been recently laid off from her job. I heard them talking about maybe losing the house. I think they sent me off to camp before I started asking too many questions. But later I found out the check they'd paid my camp fee with bounced."

"What happened afterward?"

"The bank foreclosed on the house. Luckily I could go and live with my grandparents. Turned out my dad had debts no one knew about. It was a real mess. I was left with nothing."

"If you don't mind my asking, then how did you open a business? You had to have some capital to do that. And I don't think your grandparents had that sort of money lying around."

Palmer now looked embarrassed. "I . . . Dak invested the money for me to open Maine Brew. We had been seeing each other and . . ."

"And he liked you and also thought you were a crackerjack entrepreneur?"

She snorted. "Yeah, something like that, I guess."

"You also warned me not to let him get me drunk, that I might regret it?"

"I shouldn't have said. If he ever found out—"

"He will *never* find out from me," said Devine.

The panic in her expression eased as she looked at him.

"So why the warning?" he asked.

"We went out one night. I had too much to drink. And I woke up five weeks later and found out I was pregnant."

"Did he rape you?"

"No, he didn't," she said firmly. "Dak . . . is not like that. But his not using protection wasn't what I had in mind. But I was too effed up to think clearly."

"And the baby?"

"I . . . went to a place . . ."

"Did Dak pay for that?"

She nodded.

"I was told that the Silkwell wealth had dried up generations ago. So where did Dak get the money to help you, pay for an abortion, and invest in all these other businesses? He said he had some financial backers in Boston. Do you know who they are?"

"He never told me. But he's doing really well. He fixed up Jocelyn Point some and built that art studio for Alex."

"He *built* it for her?" exclaimed Devine.

"Yeah, about two years ago. You didn't know?"

He shook his head. "She never mentioned that."

"Well, I told you that anyone who thinks they know Alex is lying. Same goes for Dak. He looks like a tatted muscle-head badass, but he's actually quite sensitive."

"And Jenny? Did anyone here really know *her*?"

"She was about ten years older than me, but I knew her. I can't say I knew her all that well, but I was surprised."

"Surprised? By what?"

"Well, the rumor is she was some sort of spy. You know, hiding things, poker face, pretending to be something she's not. Well, with Jenny, she wore it all on her sleeve. I think she was the most open one of the bunch. So I don't know how she made such a good spy."

Devine offered to drive her to Earl Palmer's house because the rain was still pouring down, and she accepted.

"You can just drop me off back here and I'll take my scooter home," Palmer told him.

A bit later he pulled up to Earl's cottage and they ran through the rain up to the porch. She had a key and let them in. They searched the entire house but Earl wasn't there.

"Do you think he went for a walk?" asked Devine.

She looked over at the front door. "His walking stick is against the wall. He never goes out without it." She pointed to a peg on the wall. "And there's his coat, and the reflective vest I bought him. He wouldn't go out without those."

"Where else could he be?" Devine looked out the window at the small studio. "Hey, I think I see a light from behind the curtains."

"What? Really?" She sounded relieved. "He must be in there. Maybe he's going through some of Bertie's artwork. I told him it would help with the grieving process."

They hurried out to the studio.

Palmer opened the unlocked door. "Gramps, it's me. I'm so glad that you—"

She screamed.

Devine pushed past her, his gun out and making wide arcs in front of him.

But then he stopped and lowered his weapon as he stared up at a clearly deceased Earl Palmer hanging from one of the rafters.

41

While Harper and Fuss went about their work with the aid of a crew of volunteer EMTs, and Françoise Guillaume readied her instruments for the preliminary processing of the body, Devine stared up at Palmer, still hanging there.

The image of Sara Ewes came back to him. He had dated her back in New York when he had worked for the investment firm of Cowl and Comely. She had been found hanging in one of the firm's storage closets. The initial cause of death had been deemed suicide. It had soon turned to a verdict of murder.

What about you, Earl? Did you do this, or did someone else do it to you?

With everyone's help they managed to release Earl Palmer from the noose and lowered the body, where it was initially examined by the two officers.

Next, a nitrile-gloved Harper stood on a ladder and cut down the rope that had been used, careful to keep the knots intact.

Devine edged over to where Guillaume was kneeling next to the body, which was lying on a synthetic tarp designed to capture all trace evidence. She used a digital thermometer to test the ambient air temp and then employed a rectal probe to check Palmer's body core temperature.

"How long, Doc?" Devine asked.

"The ambient temp in here is thirty-seven degrees. He has warm clothes on, which would counteract the ambient some. The body loses roughly one point four degrees Fahrenheit of heat per hour after death up to twelve hours and about point seven per hour after that." She looked at the rectal thermometer. "Based on all that, this reading indicates he died between one and three this morning."

Devine looked at the ligature marks on Palmer's neck. "Those look gravity-induced," he said. "As opposed to straight-line, which would show strangulation."

"You know about such matters?"

"I have a little experience with them, yes."

She held Palmer's large head in her gloved hands. "No obvious signs of bleeding or blunt force trauma."

"So he wasn't knocked out and then strung up?"

"Why in the hell would you think that?"

Devine glanced over to see Harper staring angrily at him. He swiveled his glance around to Fuss to see what she looked like. She was staring at her boss—anxiously, it seemed to Devine.

"I'm saying that it might not be a suicide."

"His beloved wife was killed horribly," said Harper, walking forward as he spoke, crossing the footprint of the small building until he was looking up at the taller Devine. "The man is out of his mind with grief. He walks alone in the middle of the night looking for . . . fuck, I don't know what. Maybe a little peace. And then he finds the body of another person he knew." He pointed at the rafter from which Earl Palmer had been hanging. "And now we get this. Seems pretty linear and obvious to me. A person can only take so much."

"So you're convinced he took his own life?" said Devine.

"I'm not convinced of anything until the doc over there gives her verdict. But why would someone want to kill Earl?"

"That's our job—to find out."

Harper stabbed a finger into Devine's left pec. "I've got one murder to solve, Devine, I don't need you going around trying to add to that number with all this bullcrap."

As Devine looked at Harper all he could see was the man's signature on the log list, and the missing rape kit. He was certain that Mildred James had told Harper about Devine's checking out Alex's evidence file. And the man was obviously not happy about it.

"Well, you actually already have *two* murders. Alberta Palmer? Earl would make it three. And like you said, *Chief*, let's wait until we get the verdict from Dr. Guillaume." He looked at the woman. "I'm sure it'll be a top priority for you, right, Doc?"

"Yes, yes of course," she said, looking and sounding agitated. "I'll do it first thing in the morning." She looked at the EMTs. "Load the body in the van and bring it to the funeral home. I can do the post there once I get approval from Augusta. I know they have a backlog right now, and I don't want to get lost in a long queue. But I also want to be fresh when I do the post."

"We'll need the place to be secure," said Devine.

"I'll call the county and have them send a deputy over to watch the place all night," said Harper, taking a step back and seeming to lose all emotion and with it all his vitriol.

"Good," said Devine as he started to walk out.

"Where are you going?" asked Fuss.

"To take Annie home. You got our statements. Anything else can wait until tomorrow."

He left and got into the Tahoe. Palmer was sitting there, staring out the window at the cottage where her grandparents had raised her after a fire had taken her parents away. Then her grandmother had been killed. And now . . . this.

"I'm so sorry," said Devine, and not for the first time.

When they discovered the body, Palmer had rushed forward and grabbed her grandfather's legs, screaming at Devine to help her get him down, to perform CPR, to save him.

But Devine had seen many dead bodies, and he knew he was seeing a long-dead one at the moment. It had taken all his strength to pull her away from him, lead her out to his vehicle, and get her inside. Then he'd called the police. He'd sat with her while he waited for them. He tried to soothe her, come up with words that would make the pain of such a traumatic discovery go away. Until he recalled that those words did not exist.

So he had just held her, let the woman cry into his shoulder, told her it would be okay when he knew it wouldn't. He got her to cup her hands and breathe into them when she sobbed so hard she hyperventilated and couldn't catch her breath. The flood of CO_2 calmed her twitching lungs.

"Is there someone you can stay with tonight? I don't think you should be alone." When she didn't respond he repeated his question. Halfway through she said, "Jocelyn Point. Dak and Alex."

This surprised Devine, especially after she had told him about Dak, but he nodded, and they drove away from the place where a dead man lay on a cold floor.

42

Alex answered the door. Devine quickly explained the situation, and it was gratifying to see Alex put her arm around the woman's shoulders and usher her into the house.

"You can sleep in Jenny's old room," she told Palmer. "You know where it is. I'll be right up to help settle you in."

As Palmer headed up the stairs, Alex turned back to Devine. She had on a pair of men's pajama bottoms and a turquoise sweater and pink socks. Her hair fell around her shoulders, and she had a smudge of charcoal between her thumb and forefinger.

"What happened, exactly?" she said, her voice weary, but her expression anxious.

He recounted the events in a few sentences and Alex's look grew more and more anguished as he did so.

"My God, when is enough going to be enough? Annie's now lost everyone."

"Well, she wanted to come here, so she has you."

"She can stay here as long as she wants. We can get some things from her apartment in the morning."

"I can load her scooter in the back of the SUV and bring it over in the morning."

"Thanks. Do you want some coffee or tea?"

"No, you and Annie need to get some rest, and I've got some things to do."

She furrowed her brow at this statement. "Things to do? Do you know what time it is?"

"My job's like yours; it's not nine-to-five."

She smiled and that lifted his spirits a little. "Okay, but please be careful."

"Thanks for helping, Alex, I know Annie appreciates it."

"That's what we do here, we help each other because each other is all we've really got."

"Where's Dak? I didn't see his Harley?"

"I am not my brother's keeper."

They gazed at each other. Devine didn't really want the moment to end, but . . .

"Good night," she said.

She closed the door, and he hurried back to the Tahoe and drove off.

He could feel things escalating now and he needed information, a lot of it.

As he drove he hit a number on his phone. Campbell picked up on the second ring.

Devine went over finding Earl Palmer's body, and then the fact of the missing rape kit and Chief Harper's having been the last one to check it out.

"And Annie Palmer's parents found Alex right after the

event happened. And three days later they were dead in a house fire."

"And you believe they saw who did it, but didn't report it for some reason, then they were murdered by the man who raped Alex to ensure their permanent silence?"

"It's a plausible theory."

"But you have to get proof."

"The puzzling question is, if I'm right, why *didn't* they report it?"

"Putnam is a small town."

"Meaning they might have known the person who did it and didn't want to expose them for some reason?"

"That's also a plausible theory," noted Campbell. "Now, let's focus on Earl Palmer's death."

"If he was murdered, and there's no proof of that yet, one reason could be he was paid off or forced by someone to pretend he found Jenny's body."

"So the murderer silenced him in case he had a change of heart and decided to tell all?"

"Yes."

"Why involve him in the first place?" asked Campbell.

"I don't believe Jenny was killed where she was found. I think she was taken there. And it wasn't just any location. It was near the spot where Alex was found after she was raped."

"So you think the attack on Alex and the murder of her sister are connected even though they took place fifteen years apart?"

"I'm beginning to. Otherwise, the locations are just too

much of a coincidence, particularly if the place where she was found was staged. That means the killer intentionally picked it."

"Wouldn't most people up there know that was the spot where Alex was found?"

"No, I don't think so. It was apparently hushed up. But I may still have a town full of suspects. Now, Jenny told her mother that she had *unfinished business* up here. And then I found out that she visited Alex and asked her if she remembered anything about that night. To my mind that means the unfinished business has to do with Alex's rape."

"Do you think Jenny had found out something?"

"Yes, I do. And maybe you could check with her colleagues at CIA to see if she said or did something there that might help us."

Campbell said, "You know, it's possible that she could have used some of her government resources to do some sleuthing on her own."

"From the sounds of it the lady was tenacious as hell."

"You're describing yourself, too."

"It's what the Army taught me, as you know. Speaking of, any luck on breaking through the seal on Dak's military record?"

"Yes. He was found in bed with the wife of his CO."

Devine said, "Okay, I can see why he got the OTH rather than a DD. The Army didn't want everyone to know about a cuckolded superior officer."

"But I don't see how that helps you."

"It tells me that Dak will take a big risk if the reward is large enough."

"But it also shows a degree of recklessness," noted Campbell.

"Which makes him unpredictable and more dangerous."

"Exactly."

"The mole?" asked Devine.

"We're ninety percent through our audit."

"Let me know when you finish, with or without an answer."

"What are you going to do now?" Campbell asked.

"Take a nighttime tour of Putnam, Maine."

"In the hopes of finding what?" asked Campbell.

"I'll know it when I see it."

43

Devine drove to the spot where one sister had been raped and the other one found murdered. He got out and walked around, while at the same time in his mind moving through the details he knew about Jenny's murder. And speculating on what had happened to Alex here.

He thought about Jenny with a rifle aimed at her head. And of Alex when she realized what was about to happen to her. The twin images rocked him to his core, when Devine didn't believe anything could anymore. He walked to the edge, and looked down at the rocks and then out at the ocean, which was rumbling and tumbling.

He had seen more violence and depravity in his life than most others had. To a degree it desensitized you to the stunning cruelty of which human beings were capable. Yet in other ways Devine found he was more empathetic than most. It might be because he had comforted, as best he could, colleagues and friends and family members who had lost loved ones. That didn't just include fellow Americans, but soldiers from other countries, and civilians who had lost everything and everyone they cared about to war.

Death was always unsettling, even when it was expected. But violent, unexpected death? It had a horror, a grotesqueness that most humans simply couldn't wrap their minds around. That's because there was nothing logical or understandable about it.

He looked in the direction of Jocelyn Point, where two vulnerable women were hunkering down. Perhaps they were managing to get by together when they might have failed alone. At least he hoped so.

As Devine looked back out to the water he saw the lights of a boat that was very near the shore, and north of his position. He looked at his watch and wondered who it might be out there at this hour of the night.

He hopped into his SUV and drove toward where the boat seemed to be heading. He continually glanced out at the water to follow the vessel's journey. And then the light vanished, which deepened his suspicions. He slowed the SUV, pulled over, and stopped. He slid his optics from his bag, got out, and looked through them over the vehicle's roof. He swept the horizon for a glimpse of the vessel. But it was like the boat had disappeared into the night.

He got back in and was about to pull back on the road when a car passed him, going fast. He glanced quickly enough to see that it was Dr. Guillaume in a gray BMW sedan. He pulled in behind her and followed at a discreet distance. By now she had to have finished at Palmer's place or squared things away at the funeral home before she did the post in the morning. She might be heading home, wherever that was. She had told him she lived here, but also kept a place in Augusta.

He lowered the window a crack because he was feeling warm and a little claustrophobic. The briny smell from the Atlantic flooded the interior and brought back memories of West Point and sailing on the brackish Hudson River.

Officially known as the United States Military Academy, West Point had been identified by George Washington as the most strategic location in the American Revolutionary War. Originally named Fort Clinton, it was the oldest continuously maintained military outpost in the country. It was on the west bank of the Hudson, hence the name. A branch of the U.S. Mint was located there. It was pretty safe, Devine thought, being on a military installation loaded with weapons and people who knew how to use them.

Four of the best years of his life had been spent at the Point. He had made friendships he expected to last the rest of his life. For his comrades who had been killed in battle those lifetime bonds would not happen. But that was something they had signed up for. Collectively, they were all supposed to make the world better, or freer, or safer. The jury was still out on that.

But regardless, we did our duty and did our best.

He slowed down when the Bimmer did. Then it turned onto a paved driveway on a stretch of coast road that was unfamiliar to Devine. The wrought iron gates opened, the Bimmer passed through, and the gates closed behind the car.

He pulled off and watched Guillaume drive up to the side of what could only be termed a mansion. Then the house swallowed the car as she pulled into a side-load garage bay.

He squared up the SUV and pointed the lights at the gate. Coming together, the twin metal gates formed a large *B*.

B for *Bing?*

He'd thought Jocelyn Point was impressive, or at least it had been back in the day. This place looked to be no more than a decade old and was even larger. He wondered if she lived there alone or with around fifty people. It was more hotel than house.

He drove off, his mind tumbling through a number of scenarios. Who would have thought such a little town would have such big secrets? And problems.

He slept deeply, got up early, and did his workout especially hard, as though punishing himself for his lack of progress. With every diamond push-up he chastised himself. Every sprint he dug deeper because he'd been such a failure thus far. He made every burpee hurt a little more as penance for his ineptitude.

He walked back to the inn, showered and changed, and then picked up Annie Palmer's scooter and drove with it in the SUV to Jocelyn Point. It was seven thirty sharp when he knocked on the door. He noticed that the Harley still wasn't there. Dak had left early for work or else had not come home.

Alex answered the door dressed in jeans and a long sweatshirt. She led him into the kitchen and made him a cup of coffee. They sat at a table in the small sunroom.

"How's Annie?"

"She's still sleeping," said Alex. "I didn't want to wake her."

"Her scooter will be waiting for her out front."

"It was nice of you to do that."

"No trouble. She's going through a lot."

"How did you happen to be with her last night?"

Devine looked uncomfortable with the question. Part of him wondered why she wanted to know. But then he concluded it was actually a perfectly reasonable query. He said, "I just wanted to ask her some questions, and I drove her over to Earl's because she wanted to check on him. It was raining hard, and it made no sense for her to go there on her scooter. That's when we found him."

"I still can't believe that Earl would kill himself."

Devine didn't bother to tell her his theory about Earl Palmer being murdered. He had no proof to offer, only speculation. But there was something else he wanted to tell her.

"I don't believe Jenny was killed at the spot where she was found. Based on the angle of shot entry, I think she was killed elsewhere and her body was placed on the rocks at that particular spot. For what it's worth, the local ME agrees with my theory on the shot entry angle."

Alex asked, in a forced calm tone, "Why would they pick that particular location to place my sister's body?"

"It was where you were attacked."

"What?" she said sharply. "There?"

"I think that was why you had that sort of 'event' when I took you to the spot. It had nothing to do with Jenny's death. You got woozy in the open field where you were found. Once you got in the trees, you were fine. So even though you don't consciously remember anything about that night, I think your subconscious does."

Her eyes now brimmed with tears. "The same place. So you're saying whoever attacked me also killed Jenny?"

"I'm saying it's a possibility, that's all. But you told me that Jenny came up here to ask you about it. And she told your mom that she had unfinished business. What else might she have meant by that?"

"I don't know, Travis, I don't fucking know, okay?"

She hurried from the room.

He sighed, finished his coffee, rinsed out the cup, put it in the dishwasher, and left.

You've got to get to the truth, Devine. For a lot of reasons.

44

Devine drove to the police station to find Harper out but Fuss in her office.

She eyed him inscrutably as he sat down across from the woman. "I spoke with Mildred. Understand you came by."

"I did," said Devine evenly.

"I also understand that some evidence went missing."

"Evidence *does* go missing," said Devine, looking at her. "For various reasons."

"Let's cut the shit, Devine. I saw the logbook and so did you."

"Never said otherwise."

"There is no way Chief Harper took that rape kit back then."

"Again, I never said he did." Before she could respond he said, "What about the fire that killed Steve and Valerie Palmer?"

Fuss's eyebrows nearly folded over each other. "What?"

"The Palmer fire."

"Yes, I know about it, though I wasn't on the force then. But I remember it was an accident."

"You mean that was the official finding?"

"That was what *happened*," barked Fuss.

"Look, I'm just thinking things through. Hear me out. They find Alex right after she was raped, and then the Palmers die three days later. Quite a coincidence."

"Apples and oranges. If I recall correctly, it was a faulty portable heater. Happened all the time back then. My cousin is a volunteer firefighter. He said they're still one of the leading causes of fire in the winter."

"I'm sure."

"No, I'm not sure you *are* sure," she exclaimed.

"Heard from the ME on the post yet?" he asked, deciding to change the subject.

"That's where the chief is, attending it."

Devine rose, looking angry. "And I wasn't invited why?"

"Because it's a probable suicide unrelated to the case you're up here investigating."

She sounded like she was reading from a script, thought Devine.

"That's bullshit. He found the body of the murder victim I'm up here investigating. Are they still doing the post at the funeral home?"

"Yes, but—"

He was out the door before she could finish the sentence.

Minutes later Devine hurried into the funeral home, grabbed someone who worked there, flashed his creds at them, and fast-walked to the room set at the back of the building where he had viewed Jenny's body. He didn't bother to knock but just burst in.

Guillaume looked up from what she was doing, which was cutting open Earl Palmer's chest, while Chief Harper stood across from her looking slightly nauseous.

"Can anyone join the party or is it exclusive?" asked Devine with a bite to his words.

Guillaume glanced curiously at Harper. "I thought you knew," she said.

Harper groused, "I thought I asked Wendy to let you know, but maybe I forgot."

"She was actually under the impression that I had no reason to attend," retorted Devine.

"Well, you're here now, so let's get on with it, not that it *has* anything to do with why *you're* here," snapped Harper. He looked at Guillaume and nodded.

For the next hour Guillaume worked over the body, dictating notes into her iPhone, which was on a magnetized stand next to her. Both Devine and Harper asked questions of her throughout the procedure.

"He wasn't strangled and then hanged," said Guillaume in answer to one of Devine's queries. "As you noted before, the ligature mark is gravity-based, with no straight-line ligature marks under it. His stomach had no undigested food in it, which makes sense if he was killed early in the morning, but there were some other substances in his belly."

"Was he on medication?" asked Devine.

She nodded. "I was his PCP. So I know he was on

statins and high blood pressure meds and also some painkillers for his arthritis and other pain issues. Most people his age are on lots of meds, unfortunately."

"But those meds didn't kill him, right?" said Harper.

"I wouldn't think so unless he overdosed on them. And then he would not have been able to hang himself. And there was nothing in the tissue samples that would indicate any toxins in his body."

"There was a chair on its side right under the body," said Harper. "He obviously put the noose up there, climbed onto the chair, and kicked it away, end of story."

Devine didn't believe this, but he wasn't going to say it in front of Harper.

"But you'll run blood work and tox screens?" he said.

Guillaume looked at Harper, who said, "All that costs money, Devine. A lot of it. And for what? The man killed himself. How else could it have happened?"

"I agree. My cause of death will be suicide," said Guillaume.

"Good," said Harper. "Don't get me wrong. I liked Earl. But I also don't need another murder in Putnam. Thanks, Doc." He nodded curtly at Devine and left.

Devine looked down at the cut-up body as Guillaume bagged the organs in thick plastic viscera bags and placed them in the chest cavity. She had already slid Palmer's facial skin and scalp back into place after having pulled it down to saw through the skull and remove the man's brain. She now started to stitch up the Y-incision she had earlier made along the sternum.

"So nothing out of the ordinary then?" asked Devine.

"As you saw, I took one-inch tissue samples of his organs. Didn't see anything unexpected, as I already said. He had heart disease, but I knew that. Although for his age it wasn't that bad."

"When I was with him he had a really hard time walking—he just shuffled, really."

"You know about the spinal fusion surgery. That really limited his range of motion, as I told you before. And he had severe arthritis in both knees and hips, which caused him to have trouble walking."

"So with all those physical limitations, you think he could have hanged himself?"

"A sudden pop of adrenaline can allow you to accomplish many things that you ordinarily would not be able to do. If Earl really wanted to kill himself, he could do it. Anyone could, really. And while he had limitations, Earl was still a big, strong man whose lifelong work had built his upper body to a remarkable degree."

Devine nodded but remained unconvinced. He didn't think *adrenaline* was the answer to this. "By the way, I saw you last night."

She looked up at him, confused. "I know, at Earl's."

"No, I meant later. You were driving home and I was behind you. Wow, that is some place you have."

"It's not really mine," she said quickly, looking down at her stitch work again.

"Oh, really?"

"My father built it about ten years ago."

"Didn't know there was that much money in funerals," Devine said.

"Oh, there's not, believe me. But have you heard of Warren Buffett?"

"Of course."

"Way back when, my grandfather subscribed to his investment newsletter. Whatever Buffett invested in, so did my grandfather, every spare penny he had, and he was notoriously frugal in his personal spending. Over the decades the returns have been quite large—well, enormous, really, far more than any of us knew. When my grandfather died, my father and uncle inherited everything. My uncle retired and went off to Florida, but my father stayed here for a time and built that place. My mother was still alive back then and she was really the force behind it. You have to understand she spent most of her married life in a cramped two-bedroom rancher. When my brother and I came along, things got really tight but my father refused to buy a new house."

"Two bedrooms? What did you and your brother do as you got older?"

"He slept in the den. I kept the bedroom. I was the oldest." She smiled. "Anyway, that house was my mother's revenge, as it were. She lived in it for exactly two years before she got cancer and died."

"I'm sorry."

"No, it's fine. She really enjoyed those two years, let me tell you. After that my father moved to Florida to be near my uncle. My brother and I got to live in the house. And we both have trust funds set up."

"So you really don't have to work anymore, then?"

She sighed. "Well, that's the catch."

"What?"

"My grandfather set up trusts for his sons, and my father did the same thing with the house and his inheritance for me and my brother."

"Did the same thing? I'm not following."

"In order to inherit all that wealth my father and uncle had to work at the funeral home until age sixty-five. My father made a similar arrangement for my brother and me, although we *only* have to work there until age sixty. Until then we get a little money from the trust and we get to live in the house, but we have to work at the business to earn money, and I have my medical practice, of course, which, quite frankly, doesn't generate a lot of income. And it's not like there's a lot of money left over. That house is expensive to keep up."

"What happens if you leave before then?"

"The child who stays with the business until they turn sixty inherits it all. If we both leave before that then we lose the trust funds, and we can't live in the house or get the proceeds from selling it. It would all go to charity. If we both stay, we split it."

"You going for the duration so you can cash in?"

She looked pensive, and conflicted. "I'm not sure I can hang in there. I never had kids. And I've actually been thinking about relocating. To Charlotte, North Carolina.

I'm tired of the cold. And that house is far too big for two people. And I don't like the idea of my life decisions being dictated by the sole thought of gaining wealth that I had no hand in creating."

"And your brother?"

"I think Fred actually likes running the business. So it's not so much of a hardship for him. And in his leisure time he's quite the outdoorsman. He likes to hike and rock-climb. And New England has a lot of places to do that. He kayaks and bikes, too."

"He never married?"

"I think he saw my experience and swore it off."

"That bad?"

"My ex stole all my money, left me with all his debts, and ran off with someone who I thought was my best friend."

"Damn, I'm sorry."

"It was a long time ago. I dream of running into him one day and . . . well, I guess I better not elaborate, considering you're a federal agent. But it is a great deal of money at stake. So for now, I'll continue to live in a house that is far too big, with my little brother."

"Sort of like Jocelyn Point and Dak and Alex."

"I never really thought of that, but you're right. By the way, Senator Silkwell was very close friends with our family. My grandfather and father supported all of his campaigns, and the Bing name means something in Maine. I had relatives in state government, and one of my great-uncles was a long-serving congressman."

Devine thought of something. "Was it your family that chartered a jet to bring the senator back from Washington when Alex was attacked fifteen years ago?"

"Yes. I believe it was my uncle or grandfather. How did you know about that?"

He shrugged. "Just putting two and two together."

"We couldn't believe that someone would attack Alex."

"Were you here when it happened?"

"No, I was still doing my medical residency out of state."

"Okay. Can you email me your report on Earl, with a set of pictures of the body?"

"Of course. You'll have it straightaway."

"I hear Charlotte is really nice. Might be worth it to give up the bucks and live your life on your own terms and not someone else's."

"Yes," she said dully. "It certainly might."

He left her there staring down at a dead body.

45

On the way out he bumped into Fred Bing, who was looking upset.

When Devine commented on this, Bing said, "Small business ownership is not all it's cracked up to be. I had two people call in sick and a delivery I really needed did not come in."

"Your sister told me about the unusual trust arrangement with your father."

Bing sighed and leaned against the wall. "It actually wasn't unusual for him. It was a simple power play all the way. He didn't really care about keeping this place going. He did it for his inheritance. And he made sure that my sister and I have to do the same."

"It sounds like a shitty thing to do to your kids."

"On the plus side, I actually enjoy what I do. I mean, despite the day-to-day hiccups."

"And you like the outdoors, your sister told me."

Bing's face lighted up. "I spend my workdays in the dark with dead bodies and grieving families. So I like to spend my free time in the sunshine with nature. Strikes a nice balance."

"She also told me about her disastrous marriage."

Bing's smile faded. "Stuart Guillaume was the world's biggest jerk. I could have killed him for what he did to my sister." He blanched. "I mean . . . I didn't mean that I would . . ."

"Relax, Fred, there's no law against thinking about killing someone. And if he'd done that to my sister, *I'd* be *thinking* the same thing."

Bing's expression turned somber. "I heard about Earl."

"Your sister and Chief Harper believe he killed himself."

"Suicide? Earl? Look, I'm not trying to tell you how to do your job, but I will tell you this: Earl Palmer would have been the last person in the world I thought would take his own life."

"Then you know what the alternative is."

Bing nodded and looked deeply troubled. He drew closer. "This town is small and isolated. But every place, no matter how big or small, has secrets, Agent Devine. Secrets that some folks would rather keep hidden."

"Can you be more specific?"

"I wish I could, but that's all I know. Just a weird feeling."

"Do you think Jenny was killed because she might have known specifics?"

"I don't gamble, Agent Devine. Never saw the logic in it. But if I were a betting man I would lay down money that that was why she was killed. I mean, to my knowledge, she never came up here at this time of year before. There had to be a reason."

"I appreciate your frankness. So you're going to hang on here for the full ride?"

"I think so."

"Your sister may cut out early."

"She should. But I've told her that it won't matter as far as the money goes."

"What do you mean?" said Devine, startled.

"If she leaves the business and loses out, when I inherit, I'm giving her half. I mean, it's plenty of money for us both, even if I eventually marry and have a family, which looks less and less likely every day. But you never know."

"You told her that? I mean, about the inheritance?"

"Oh yes. In fact, I had it put in writing, just so there could be no misunderstanding in case I did get married and something happened to me. Now, if you'll excuse me, I've got a couple of fires to put out."

He rushed off, leaving Devine wondering what the hell was going on in this town.

Again.

Later, Devine pulled in front of Ink Well, Dak Silkwell's tat parlor. It was not as big or elaborate as he had thought it would be, based on what he had heard about the man's ambitions and achievements.

But when he looked at the samples of tattoos exhibited on the front plate glass, he came away impressed with Dak's creative ability. He tried to walk in but the door was locked. He rang the buzzer next to the door and a woman's voice said, "Yes?"

"Travis Devine to see Dak Silkwell."

"Just a minute."

Twenty seconds later the door buzzed open and Devine walked in.

Dak met him and shook his hand.

Devine looked around and saw four people in specially designed chairs. Two tattoo artists were seeing to them.

"You came to get a tat, right?" said Dak with a smile. "Just couldn't stay away, could you?" Despite the cold outside he had on a yellow tank top and lightweight cargo pants.

"Not right now, maybe later. You have time to talk?"

"Got a shop full of customers and a long list of others coming in today."

"Looks like the ones here now are being attended to."

"Yeah, but I oversee each one. Give me ten minutes. I can meet you at the Brew."

"It's not open."

"Why not?"

"I guess you didn't hear. Earl Palmer's dead. I actually took Annie to stay at your house last night. I thought you knew."

Dak looked stunned by the news. "I . . . I didn't go home last night. I stayed in town. At a friend's place," he added hastily. "What the hell happened? Did he have a heart attack or something?"

"Annie and I found him hanging in his wife's art studio."

Dak looked like he might be sick. "Hanging? He killed himself? Earl?"

The customers and the other tattoo artists were staring now, so Dak motioned Devine to follow him into a small office at the back of the shop. Dak closed the door and sat behind the desk, while Devine took a seat across from him.

"We're not sure yet what happened," said Devine. "Still investigating."

"What is going on around here? First Jenny, now Earl?"

"When was the last time you saw Earl?"

"I'm not sure. Maybe a week ago, just seen him driving through town. He didn't come around much, not after Bertie died." He looked up at Devine with an expression of hope, which Devine could partly understand. "Maybe that's why he did it, because of losing Bertie?"

"It's possible, certainly."

Dak shook his head. "So what did you want to ask me?"

"You said you had investors from Boston backing you."

"That's right."

"Who are they?"

"Why does it matter to you?" asked Dak sharply, evidently not pleased at all about this change in the conversation.

"Knowing more is better than knowing less."

"My business is *private*."

"If that's how you want to play it. So how goes the negotiation on selling Jocelyn Point?"

"It's going well, actually."

"And Alex is all on board?"

"When the time comes she will be."

"You sound confident."

"You may think you know my baby sister after meeting her a few times, but you don't. She wants out of this place even more than I do."

"Really? I thought she saw it as her safe space. And she likes teaching the kids."

"She can teach kids anywhere. Putnam is where someone raped and nearly killed her. Do you really think she wants to be reminded of that every damn day?"

"Interesting choice of words, since she doesn't *remember* the attack."

"But people have told her what happened. Every time she passes by that spot she probably has all that horror rushing back to her, even if she can't technically 'remember' it."

"She didn't know where it happened, until *very* recently. And now that spot will also always be the place where Jenny's body was found. Don't you find that curious? All the possible locations to leave Jenny's body, and they chose *that* one?"

"I don't know what to think about that. It *does* seem weird, but hell, life is weird."

"I need something more definite than that."

Dak rose. "Well, good luck on that. I've got to get back to making money."

Outside, Devine found Harper and Fuss waiting next

to his SUV. Their expressions were tight, focused, and grim, none of which he cared for, not a single one.

"What's up?" he asked, half expecting them to say that someone else was dead.

Harper nodded at Fuss, who slowly took out her cuffs and said, "Travis Devine, you're under arrest. You have the right to remain silent."

"What?" said a startled Devine, who took a step back.

"Anything you say can and may be used in evidence against you in a court of law."

Devine took another step back. "What the hell is going on here?"

Harper said, "Do not resist, Devine, it'll only make it worse."

"What am I being arrested for, exactly?"

"On suspicion of theft of police evidence," replied Harper.

"What evidence?"

"Alex Silkwell's rape kit."

"Bullshit!"

Harper put his hand on top of his baton. "Do not be stupid. I do not want to hurt you."

Devine almost laughed at that one.

Fuss seemed to read his mind and said nervously, "Look, I know you could kill both of us with just your pinkie, but we're only doing our job."

Devine glared at Harper as he slowly put his hands behind his back. Fuss cuffed him while she finished the

Miranda warning. "You're making a big mistake," Devine said to Harper.

"Just doing my job."

"And I'll do mine," retorted Devine. "And then maybe you'll be the one with the cuffs on."

46

The two men stared at each other over the width of a table in the small interview room of the police station. A Bell and Howell surveillance camera that looked to be from the 1980s hung in the corner like a deflated party balloon.

Harper looked both cagey and pensive as he turned on a recorder and stated the date, time, and the identities of the two parties in the room.

Devine said, "Why are you doing this?"

"Are you having a relationship with Alex Silkwell?"

"What does that even mean?"

"I understand that you slept at her place one night, the night you were attacked."

"Who told you that?"

"Is it true?" demanded Harper.

"I stayed in her art studio that night. I thought it would be safer than my place since someone has tried to kill me twice, including once there!"

"You stayed there with her permission?" said Harper impassively.

"She found out about it afterward."

"So you broke in?"

Devine slammed his fist down on the table. "Are you really going down *that* road?"

"Breaking and entering is a crime, Devine," Harper said calmly.

Devine struggled to get his temper under control, but the smug look on Harper's face made it easier. And he'd been grilled by the best of Army CID agents.

"She approved of what I did after the fact, so I don't see what the problem is. And I thought you were trying to nail me on stealing her rape kit?"

"Why does it have to be just one crime?"

"I've committed no crime."

"Why did you want to look at that evidence file?"

"Because I think whoever killed Jenny also attacked Alex fifteen years ago. I already suggested that theory to you."

"I don't agree."

"You don't have to. But you didn't have to drag me in here on some trumped-up charge."

"The rape kit is missing."

"Yeah, I know. It was missing when I opened the box. Mildred James knows that, too."

"No, she looked at the box *after* you told her it was missing."

"Why would I take it?"

"I don't know. Why don't you tell me?"

"Why did *you* look at the box ten years ago? You were the last one to sign it out before I came along."

"*I'm* asking the questions here, not you!"

Now Harper was struggling to get his temper under control while Devine gazed at him placidly.

"Answer my question," demanded Harper.

"I already did. I didn't take it, so I can't have a reason why I did. But I am puzzled."

"About what?"

"Did you have doubts about the case? Did you wonder why it was never solved? Did you wonder why there was never a suspect to match the forensics to?"

"You're not listening, Devine."

"Did *you* take the rape kit?"

"No, I didn't," huffed Harper.

"Good, neither did I. I think we can call it a day."

Harper pointed a finger at him. "You were the last person to access that box."

"After you did, a long time ago. When you were still a sergeant."

Harper shifted in his seat and shrugged. "Okay, you're right. It was unsolved. I wanted to see if something clicked. It was part of my job."

"Did anything click?"

"No."

Something occurred to Devine. "Was the rape kit there when *you* accessed the box?"

Harper didn't answer right away. "Y-yes."

"Would you swear to that on the witness stand?" asked a clearly incredulous Devine.

"I'm not on a fucking witness stand," roared Harper.

"You might be one day," Devine shot back. "If you push this."

Harper sat there for a few moments before ending the interview and turning off the recorder. "Get out of here."

"You read me my rights. Am I being formally charged?"

"We didn't process you yet, and you haven't been officially booked or arraigned. But we can pick you up anytime. So much as a parking ticket."

Devine rose. "I'm not the enemy here."

"The enemy is who I say it is."

Devine walked out. In the lobby he saw Mildred James. She looked up at him guiltily. In a low voice she said, "I am so sorry about all this." Her gaze darted toward the hall where the interview room was. "I know you didn't take that rape kit. The rear doors are alarmed. You would have had to pass me with it, and you didn't. It's not like you could have hidden the dang thing in your pants. I told the chief that."

"I appreciate that. Well, at least I'm free to go, for now. Where is Sergeant Fuss?"

"She got called out on something."

He nodded and glanced through the glass partition into Harper's office. He eyed the line of photos on the wall of former police chiefs he had seen before. As he looked more closely, the picture of the man next to Harper seemed familiar for some reason.

He pointed at it. "Who's that man? The one who was chief before Harper?"

James glanced at it. "Oh, that's Benjamin Bing."

Devine's jaw dropped. "Bing like in Bing and Sons?"

"Yes, he was the third brother. The other two followed their father and uncle into the funeral business, but Ben became a police officer. Worked his way up to chief. A little too overbearing and full of himself for my tastes. He would grind you up if you made him look bad."

"What happened to him?"

"He retired and moved to Florida to be with his brothers."

"Where in Florida?"

"Naples. I saw a picture of the house once. Right on the beach. It was breathtaking."

"Interesting. Is he still alive?"

"Probably. He's still young, maybe a year or so older than me. Françoise or her brother might know for sure. Or the chief. He probably keeps in touch. They were tight."

"Yeah, I bet," said Devine, who now had a whole new angle to explore.

47

Devine called Campbell and filled him in on his arrest, the missing rape kit, the fact that Benjamin Bing was the police chief when Alex was attacked, and his strong opinion that Françoise Guillaume was lying to him.

"She's thinking of moving to Charlotte and fed me a bullshit story about losing the money, when her brother was giving her half regardless."

"So do you think Benjamin Bing took the rape kit? Or Harper?"

"Why leave it there all those years in case it incriminates someone you know? I think Harper was going to look at it for the reasons he said, found the kit missing, and either kept his mouth shut or did speak to Bing and probably got his ass handed to him. We need to find out if Bing is still alive. Jenny came up here to take on some unfinished business and the attacker obviously didn't like that."

"And you said you believe Steve and Valerie Palmer saw who the attacker was or at least suspected, and thus they had to die?"

"Yes," said Devine.

"But why didn't they report it immediately? You didn't have an answer to that."

"The Palmers were going through tough times financially," Devine said. "After their deaths their house was actually foreclosed on."

"Why is that significant?"

"You have to understand I have no proof of this, but one possibility is they might have known the rapist and decided to *blackmail* him to get needed money. But instead of paying, the rapist struck back, hard."

"And Earl Palmer? I understand why he had to die. If he was forced to lie about finding Jenny's body, he's a loose thread. But how did the person get him to pretend to find Jenny's body in the first place? From all accounts he was an honest man."

"Maybe they had some dirt on him. If they did, I need to find out what it was."

"I found something out about Jenny's activities that might help you," said Campbell.

"What?"

"She *did* use her CIA resources to investigate the attack on Alex."

"How?" exclaimed Devine.

"Satellite surveillance imagery for the night in question."

"How did that come to be?"

"As you know, we have satellites that sweep the globe around the clock. That particular part of the country is pretty important. The Canadian border is nearby.

There are planes coming in from overseas nonstop along that route, and that sector is right along a principal trajectory path for both in- and outbound nuclear missiles. So there were pictures of Putnam, Maine, in the database."

"How come no one thought of that before?" said Devine.

"I have no idea, but I confess, I didn't."

"But why did Jenny wait all this time before checking that angle?"

"I think I know the answer to that. It was only three months ago that she was elevated to a position at CIA where she would have unfettered access to intel like this. Knowing her, she probably tried before, and was rebuffed. But we have the digital trail of her requesting and accessing this data about three weeks ago, from sat pictures taken on the very night Alex was attacked fifteen years ago."

"They keep that stuff from back then?"

"They keep a lot of stuff forever, Devine. Sometimes it's patterns people are looking for and then changes to those patterns. And for that you need the context that only *time* delivers. The U.S. government is the world's biggest data hoarder when it comes to that."

"Did the satellite record the actual attack on Alex?"

"No, we weren't that lucky. It wasn't positioned in a spot that would show that."

"What, then?"

"It shows a vehicle traveling away from that location at

the time in question. And before you ask, no, there was no license plate shown. Again, it couldn't be that easy, right?"

"That doesn't help us much."

"Ah, but that's not all it showed. The vehicle passed a car coming the other way. It was around a curve so both vehicles had to slow. The way the other vehicle was positioned it blocked the other car for the most part from the satellite's cameras. Remember it doesn't remain static. It keeps roaming."

"And?" Devine said expectantly.

"And that satellite *did* capture the plate on the other car."

"Let me guess—it belonged to Steve and Valerie Palmer."

"Bingo," replied Campbell. "And now the blackmail theory you just articulated seems far more plausible."

"And that means they *recognized* whoever it was. Which means the attacker was probably *local*."

"And still in Putnam if he's the same person who killed Jenny," noted Campbell.

"Was there anything on the imagery that can help us identify the other vehicle?"

"Not much, no."

"Can you send me the imagery?" said Devine.

"Yes. Now one thing puzzled me and I know it puzzles you," said Campbell.

"What's that?"

"Jenny and her mother were estranged. So why would Jenny tell Clare what she was planning? About the unfinished business?"

"I can call Clare and ask her," said Devine.

"I think it better to confront her personally."

"I can fly down and—"

Campbell interrupted. "You've got your hands full up there. It would be counterproductive to pull you away. *I'll* meet with her."

"You sure that's smart, sir? I know this is personal with you."

"It *is* personal, Devine. And it's also my job. I'll report back what I find out."

48

"It's been a long time, Emerson," said Clare Robards.

It was evening and she and Campbell were sitting in front of a roaring fire, which eased the chill from the old general's bones.

"Yes, it has been," he agreed. He studied her for a moment, his thickly tufted eyebrows edging up and down. "Look, people have their opinions, Clare. But it's your life to lead and no one else's."

His words did nothing to lighten the mood of the room. Indeed, Clare's features grew even more unfriendly.

He noted this and said, "Um, I know that you visit him regularly. That's good of you."

She leveled a rigid gaze on him and said in a querulous tone, "*Good of me?* We were married for a long time, and we had three children together. Do you really think I would simply abandon him, Emerson? Although I guess that's what people do think. Including *you*. But Curt also wanted the divorce. We had gone our separate ways. We only stayed married because of his upcoming election."

"I know," said Campbell curtly, looking down.

She pressed on. "But you don't want to believe it, do

you? It's easier to think poorly of me and never bring *perfect* Curt into the equation. But he was seeing someone, too, did you know that?"

Campbell stiffened and eyed her cautiously. "No, I didn't."

"Now she *did* clear out at the first sign of his declining health. I was already engaged to Vernon by then. I suppose you didn't know that, either. Or didn't *want* to know it."

Campbell cleared his throat and said, "Well, you have put me in my place by simply asserting the facts, Clare. I'm . . . I'm sorry. I really am."

"Thank you," she said, her cheeks flushing with emotion. It seemed that Campbell's last words had finally mollified her. "Now, how can I help you?"

"Agent Devine reported that you told him that Jenny had informed you about her trip to Maine. And that it was for some unfinished business."

"Yes, that's right. I . . . I told him that she called me. But . . . she actually came in person to visit me here. We sat in this room together." Her gaze swept across the library and the pain associated with the loss of her eldest child became starkly etched in the woman's features. "I had no idea it would be the last time I would see . . . Jenny."

"I apologize if my questions are causing you pain."

"They can cause me any level of pain so long as whoever killed Jenny is arrested and punished," Robards cried out.

Campbell waited a few moments before continuing. "I

knew that you and Jenny were estranged. So it was curious that she—"

Robards put up a hand. "That she would bother to come here and tell me of her plans?"

"Yes."

Robards dropped her hand to her lap and studied the fire. "I suppose Jenny wanted me to know that she had never stopped trying to find out who had attacked Alex."

"Why would that be important to her? Making sure *you* knew?"

The anguish in the woman's features became starker. "Because she was of the opinion that Curt and I never did enough to pursue the matter. She even accused me of being derelict in my duties. She said the same of Curt. Only she couldn't say it to his face, not now anyway."

"Why would she think that?" asked Campbell.

"Because in some ways it's true. Don't be mistaken, what happened to Alex tore us apart. Curt would have killed the man if he could be found. But . . . Alex survived and recovered, and the police had no leads and . . . it was probably not good optics for Curt's political career."

"No one could blame him or you for what happened," Campbell pointed out.

"Politics is an ugly business, Emerson. It was back then and it's even dirtier today. People would blame Curt for not protecting his daughter. For allowing a teenage girl to wander around by herself at night. *Looking for trouble?* Count on it."

"I never thought of it that way."

"That's because you're a soldier and an honorable one." She fidgeted in her seat, playing with the hem of her dress. "And then I suppose for those reasons we . . . we moved on from what happened to Alex, even though no one was ever held accountable. For Jenny that was an outright betrayal, I suppose. But, we did just move on with our lives and never really talked about it."

Tears trickled down her cheeks as she spoke these last words. Then she composed herself. "God, it sounds so callous, so heartless, when I say it like that. Particularly since Alex *didn't* recover. Not fully. She's still trapped up in that damn town, in that goddamn house because she's still afraid to . . . to move on with her life. She keeps looking over her shoulder, terrified because he's still out there."

"You'd think she'd want to get as far away from there as possible."

"There is nothing logical about fear, Emerson. The mind can play incredibly cruel tricks on you. It can make you do or not do what you couldn't have imagined yourself ever doing, or not doing."

"You sound like you speak from experience."

"Do you really think being married to Curt for all those years was a walk in the park?"

"No one who knew the man would say that. But what more could you have done? That's the police's job," noted Campbell.

"Oh, dear Emerson, there is always more that could have been done. To Jenny, her father walked on water. If Curtis Silkwell wanted it done, it would be done." She paused. "All I can tell you is that after it happened, he was never the same man again. He had failed his sweet, innocent child. For him, there was no greater crime."

"So Jenny basically came here to throw all that in your face and state that she was going up there to finally see the truth come out?"

"Something like that, yes."

"Did you tell anyone what Jenny was going to do? Anyone at all?"

"No, Emerson, I swear. Not a soul." She added, "But if we had done our duty back then she never would have had to deal with it. She would still be alive. This is our fault, Emerson, Curt's and mine." She put a shaky hand to her face to wipe the tears away.

He reached across and gripped her arm. "What happened to Jenny is the responsibility of one person and one person only. And I promise you that we will find him."

She calmed and nodded. "You must have great confidence in your Mr. Devine."

"I do. More than perhaps even *he* knows."

49

Devine was in his cottage the next day studying the satellite images that he'd received on his laptop from Campbell. He'd enlarged the pictures as much as possible on his computer.

Frustratingly, there was no detail of the other vehicle that stood out, and there was no image of the person driving it because the Palmers' car was blocking it. Campbell had confirmed that this was the only picture of the two vehicles passing each other that the sat had captured. It had spun on to other sectors and left a mystery down on Earth.

But wait a minute.

As he looked more closely he could just make out what looked like a small dark pyramid on the door panel of the other car.

A pyramid? What could that be?

The Palmers' vehicle was a Jeep, the shot of the license plate as it passed by was head-on, but there was nothing on the other car once it had cleared the Jeep because the satellite then spun and pointed in the direction the Palmers were heading, and its tracking path was narrow. If only the satellite had swiveled its electronic eyes a bit the plate of the other car might have been visible. Detection, like football, was indeed a game of the most minimal of distances, and the most slender margins of error.

The images of the man and woman in the Jeep were also relatively clear before it passed by. Facial recognition had been performed and had confirmed they were Steve and Valerie Palmer.

Devine peered as close as he could at their faces. They seemed to be looking at the car as they passed. Were their expressions surprised? Yes, they seemed to be. But they had found Alex *after* this interaction with the car. Only then would their suspicions have been aroused. But had something in the other driver's expression given away what he had just done?

Devine was also convinced that the Palmers had known who the man was. If it had been a stranger, someone from outside of Putnam who had attacked Alex, they would surely have reported seeing the man in the vehicle fleeing the scene of a crime they were just about to discover. But they hadn't. Had they tried to blackmail the man, as he had theorized? And gotten their house burned down with them in it as their *reward*?

He was heading to his SUV when he ran into Pat Kingman in the front of the inn. She looked upset.

"You okay?" he said.

"I heard about Earl."

"It was a real tragedy."

"I wish he had talked to me. I would have helped him, considering what he did for me."

"What do you mean, did for you?" asked Devine curiously.

"You remember I told you about my husband's boat going down in an accident a number of years back?"

"Yeah, I do."

"Well, Earl worked on that boat. Had for decades. As good a stern man as there ever was. Earl tried to save Wilbur, but he drowned. Rocked the whole town, I can tell you that. They recovered his body, and we had the funeral and all. And they held a ceremony out at sea for Wilbur, to honor him. I cried my eyes out for six months, it seemed like. And so did Earl. Poor thing. He was hanging on to some debris for hours in that cold water. Almost died. Hurt his neck and back. He couldn't work after that. Now, I didn't think I could get by without my Wilbur. But I used his life insurance proceeds to buy this place and fix it up. I mean, you have to go on living, right?"

"Yes, you do," said Devine. "And I'm sure Wilbur would have wanted that."

"Well, Earl and I really became close after that. I even gave him some of the insurance money, though he fought me tooth and nail over that. Now, Bertie and I had been friends for decades. We'd sit and clean barnacles off the cages before the new season started, put the new tags on, check the runners, repaint the buoys, and repair the hog rings. But after that I was friends with Earl, too. He was a real hero for what he tried to do, but he never talked about it. Just said he was lucky to be alive and that it should have been Wilbur who'd made it, not him."

"I understand that," said Devine, thinking about how the same philosophy worked in the military.

She said, "You'd think a man like that would be able to find some peace, that the Lord would grant him some solace. But instead he loses his son and daughter-in-law, and then his wife. And now this."

"Life rarely works out the way we expect it to."

"Though I was raised Catholic, I'm not a churchgoer. But I'm heading there today to say a prayer for his soul. See, taking your own life is a mortal sin. You're not supposed to get into heaven with that hanging over your head. Or be buried in consecrated ground, or at least it used to be that way. My thinking is God should cut Earl some slack." She gave Devine a raised eyebrow as she said, "I mean, we're only human after all."

"Yes, we are," replied Devine.

50

“What are you doing here?” asked Alex as she opened the door to her studio. There were paint smudges on her hands and a broad charcoal stroke on her nose.

Devine looked down at her. “Thought I’d check up on my favorite local artist.”

She grinned and then looked skeptical. “Why don’t I believe that?”

“Can I come in? Pretty cold out here.”

“You’ll have to watch me work. I’ve got a tight deadline.”

“My pleasure.”

He looked at the easel with a four-by-four-foot canvas on it.

“Coffee’s fresh,” she said, pointing to the pot on an electric plate and some cups next to it.

He poured himself a cup and leaned against a table to watch as she went back to work.

“Seems pretty sedate for you,” he noted as he looked over the painting of a lake’s surface with colorful water lilies floating on top. “No male genitalia or anything.”

She laughed. “The client loves Monet but can’t afford

that sort of artwork, not that you can just go buy an original Monet these days. They're either in museums or owned by billionaires. But I'm a good chameleon. I can imitate lots of styles."

"But you prefer your own style?"

"Every artist does, but you have to pay the bills, too."

"Did you mention to anyone that I slept here that night?"

She shot him a glance. "No, why?"

"Harper knew about it. He arrested me for breaking and entering—at least that was one of the charges."

She lowered her palette and brush. "You've got to be joking."

"I wish I were. He let me out but he could pick me up anytime."

"I'll talk to him and tell him it was fine that you were here."

"But, like I said, those weren't the only charges."

"What else? Urinating in public? From what I've seen you could get half the male population up here on that one," she said jokingly.

He debated whether to say. "It actually involved a piece of evidence from . . . your case."

She looked startled. "*My* case?"

"He accused me of stealing it."

"Why would you do that?"

"I wouldn't. And didn't. But the evidence *is* missing. Someone took it."

She set her palette and brush down and came over to him. "What was it?"

He glanced at her before answering. She seemed equal parts angry and . . . frightened? "It was your rape kit."

Alex looked down, her facial features tight, her body rigid where it had been relaxed and loose while painting. "Why would anyone take that?" she asked, her gaze still averted from him.

"I don't know. But it would make it impossible to compare anyone's DNA to it, so there is that." He waited for her to say something but when she didn't, he added, "Your sister came up here because I think she had figured out who had attacked you."

"How . . . how could she possibly have done that? And after all this time?"

"She used some of her resources at CIA to work the case."

"What?!"

"She told your mother that she came up here for unfinished business. And she asked you about the attack."

Alex started to crumple. "But . . . but she never told me that . . . that she . . . knew who—"

Seeing how she was being affected by this revelation he said quickly, "I'm not saying she knew for certain. But I think Jenny might have suspected."

She looked up at him in a way that made his skin tingle. She seemed wobbly and dazed, and Devine felt like an insensitive idiot for having brought all of this up.

"I just meant that if she really knew who it was and

had proof of that, she would have just contacted the authorities. I don't know what the statute of limitations up here is, but I doubt it goes back fifteen years for what happened to you."

Alex did not appear to be listening. Then, while Devine was preparing what he would say next, she slumped to the floor.

"Alex!" he cried out, kneeling down next to her. Her eyelids were fluttering and her breathing was erratic. It was like when he had unwittingly brought her to the place where she'd been attacked, only this time was worse.

Devine gripped her hand. "Breathe in and out, nice and slow, in and out. Come on, you can do it."

Instead, the woman went completely rigid and her eyelids stopped fluttering and closed.

"Get off me," she screamed.

He let go of her and sprang back, stunned. "Alex, I'm just trying to—"

"Stop it, stop it! Let me go. Let me go. You're hurting me. I . . . I don't want to do this! Stop!" she shrieked.

She started writhing on the ground, punching with her arms and kicking with her legs.

"Alex, I'm not touching you. I'm over—"

"I will kill you. Let me go . . . stop it, don't, don't! Stop . . . Please!" She screamed again. And then fell silent, her body now still. And then she started to weep, softly, agonizingly, her whole body shuddering with the effort.

"Alex, I'm . . ." Devine stopped and looked helplessly down at her.

She grew still and the cries stopped. She opened her eyes and looked around in a daze.

When she saw him she said quietly, "What happened?" She looked around and noticed that she was on the floor. She slowly got to her feet, putting a hand on a table to help lever herself up on shaky legs while Devine just stood there, stunned. "Why was I on the floor? I remember talking to you and then . . . nothing."

He looked at her closely. "You just sort of passed out, Alex. Do you not feel well? Are you dehydrated?"

"No, I mean I've been drinking water and coffee. But I haven't been feeling all that well lately. And I do get anxious. Maybe fainting is my self-defense mechanism."

"Do you feel all right now?"

"Yes, I feel fine now."

Devine didn't want to upset her unduly, which was why he had not told Alex what she had said while she had been on the floor. He didn't think she was dehydrated or had fainted from anxiety. She seemed to be reliving what had happened to her when she had been attacked.

Something occurred to Devine as he connected one thing to another. "Alex, has this ever happened to you before? You . . . you sort of faint and then don't remember anything?"

"What? No. I mean, not that I remember . . . But wait, okay, one time I was at Bertie's studio. I was working on a sketch that I was later going to turn into a painting. She was helping me to get my three-point perspective and vanishing points just right. I was doing a building with people walking in front, but there was tricky trajectory to work out and my 3D boxing skills on the people weren't all that stellar, especially getting the middle point right. I hadn't really done something that complicated before."

"I won't even pretend to understand what you just said."

She smiled. "There's more math in art than most people think. But the world is three-dimensional and art has to be as well. There are skills of the trade to get that effect, and having a grasp of geometry and other disciplines helps. Anyway, I was sketching it and Bertie asked me something."

"What did she ask you?"

"As a matter of fact, I don't really remember. She said I had just collapsed."

"Do you recall when that was?"

"It was a long time ago. My senior year of high school, I do remember that. The painting was going into a school competition."

"Is that the only other time this happened to you besides with me just now?"

She frowned. "No, come to think, the same thing happened here. Bertie was with me again. She was over helping me on a sculpture I was doing. The piece was just physically hard to maneuver and she was very strong. Boom, I just collapsed, and the next thing I knew she was kneeling next to me shaking me."

"Were you talking to her about anything before you fainted?"

She thought for a moment. "Bertie was asking me if I was ever going to leave Putnam. Look, it was probably all the paint fumes I was breathing." When Devine looked worried she added, "Don't worry. I've been to a doctor and gotten checked out. No brain issues or anything like that. And I had my air-filtration and ventilator systems here upgraded. You have to be careful with all the fumes and such. It can be toxic."

"What doctor did you see?"

"Françoise Guillaume. She checked me out thoroughly. I'm fit as a fiddle."

"Okay, so when did the last episode happen with Bertie?"

Alex let out a protracted sigh and her expression darkened. "It was the last time I saw her, actually. She was killed by the hit-and-run driver two days later."

51

Devine drove back to the inn. His phone buzzed as he opened the door to his cottage.

It was Campbell. He told Devine about his visit to Clare Robards the previous evening.

"So Jenny thought her parents hadn't done enough to find whoever had attacked Alex?"

"Yes. And she wanted to make that point clear to her mother, and also let her know that she *was* going to solve the crime. By the way, Clare blames herself for Jenny's death. She said if she and Curt had pushed harder Jenny wouldn't have had to do what she did, and sacrifice her life in the process."

Devine said, "That's a lot of guilt to carry around. In addition to people feeling Clare abandoned her former husband during his hour of need."

"She told me some things I didn't know about that," said Campbell quietly, a distinct level of chagrin in his voice.

"So are you second-guessing your opinion of Clare Robards, sir?"

"She devoted most of her life to him, Devine. Carried

and raised three children. Fought every political battle with him side by side." The former general paused. "I guess I don't have the right to judge her, because I've never been in her circumstances. The bottom line is she's a good person who did right by Curt for a long time. And he was not easy to get along with. Now, that is something I can opine on, having known him all those decades. He was as loyal a friend as you would ever want, but if you got on his bad side it was a battle to the death. And as a politician he was ruthlessly ambitious. Sometimes to an extent that it clouded his judgment. And the higher up he went in the political food chain, the more he was apparently willing to do in order to stay there. He and I had sharp words on the subject, but still maintained our friendship."

"Sounds like the marine who never could take losing on the battlefield carried that same standard to running for office," opined Devine.

"Yes. But if one compromises one's principles in the bargain? You have victory without honor, at least in my opinion."

"Yes sir."

"So anything new to report?" asked Campbell.

"I met with Alex. I told her about Jenny using her government resources to find out who had raped her."

"What did she say to that?" Campbell wanted to know.

"It's not so much what she said as what she did."

"I'm not following. What did she do?"

Devine explained about her collapsing. "At first I

thought she had passed out. But when I went to help her she started screaming at me to leave her alone, to get off her. Then she started punching and kicking."

"My God, was she having some sort of seizure? Did you make her understand that you were not attacking her?"

"The thing is, I don't believe she was addressing *me*."

"Who then?" asked a clearly confused Campbell.

"I think what I told her prompted her to have some sort of an unconscious memory episode. That's the only way I can think of to describe it," said Devine.

"Wait, do you mean your discussing the attack again made her, what, relive it?"

"Yes. I think she was defending herself against her attacker. When she finally came around she had no memory of any of it. I didn't tell her what she said or did. I'm not a psychiatrist. I didn't want to mess her up even more."

"No, you did the right thing. Now, Devine, did she mention a name or give you any clue as to who it might have been?"

"No, nothing like that."

"And you're certain that whoever killed Jenny attacked Alex?" asked Campbell.

"Not only am I sure of that, but also, based on something else Alex told me, I'm pretty sure the person who attacked Alex and killed Jenny also murdered Alberta Palmer."

Campbell blurted out, "How do you figure that?"

"Alex had an episode like she did with me today, with Bertie, two days before she was killed. Only I think Bertie got lucky where I didn't."

"You mean Alex *named* the person who attacked her?" said Campbell.

"Or at least gave enough information that allowed Bertie to figure it out."

"You think she confronted the person?"

"I do. And if I'm right, we saw the person's homicidal reaction," noted Devine.

"Two murders tied to Alex's rape. Which means *you* could be a target," added Campbell.

"I've been a target ever since I stepped foot in this place. Okay, since you brought that up, anything new on the mole? Or the woman from Geneva?"

"Yes and no." Campbell paused. "I blame myself."

"What do you mean?" said Devine sharply.

"My admin assistant has vanished."

"What's her name and what happened?" asked Devine.

"Dawn Schuman. And we don't know what happened to her. She didn't show up for work yesterday. We called and then sent a team to her house. Her car was missing and it seems as though she had packed a bag. We have alerts out on her everywhere but so far nothing."

"And why do you blame yourself?"

"Because I knew something was off and I did nothing about it. She'd gotten divorced and there was a custody dispute over her kids. And she was struggling financially. She had confided in me some of these personal issues. I should have followed up with our security folks to keep an eye on her but I didn't."

"Because her personal issues could have compromised her?"

"Yes, and now with her disappearance, I think she might well have been compromised."

"And she knew about my movements?" said Devine.

"She arranged your travel while you were overseas, and also your itinerary for Maine."

"But why run now?" asked Devine.

"They might have asked for something she was unwilling to give. Or she felt guilty, or scared that we would find out once we began our internal security audit. Ironically, her fleeing was what made us look at her."

"They might have grabbed her and made it look like she left voluntarily."

"Trust me, Devine, I had thought of that possibility. Should I send you reinforcements?"

"No. That'll just spook our killer and then the guy goes even deeper underground."

"Well, be careful."

"I'm not sure that's going to get it done, sir," replied Devine before clicking off.

52

Devine could not sleep that night. The rain beating down on the roof, normally a soothing white noise, simply served to pound relentlessly into his head, and also into his thoughts.

A mole in Campbell's organization had likely helped put a bullseye on his back. There were forces up here who wanted him dead. And he had a murderer that hopefully he was closing in on. And while he had fought battles on two fronts before, it had never been quite like this.

He gave up the attempt at sleep, got dressed, grabbed his gun, and headed out, running to his SUV through the rain and cranking up the heat once he got inside. The trip he was about to take was not all about his insomnia. He needed to follow up on a possible lead that he had failed to do before.

He headed through the darkened streets. He didn't know if he would again see what he had glimpsed once before, but he had his fingers crossed that he would. It might not be connected to Jenny's death, but he couldn't rule it out until he knew a lot more. And it was intriguingly odd; that alone deserved scrutiny.

Devine approached the spot where he'd been when he'd lost sight of the boat he'd seen before. That time he'd become distracted by seeing Françoise Guillaume drive by and following her to the mansion where she lived with her brother.

No distractions tonight, at least I hope not.

He parked off the road, killed his lights, and waited. An hour later he had just about given up hope and was getting ready to head back to the inn when he saw it.

The light was quite a ways out on the water, but as he watched, Devine judged that it was definitely heading toward shore.

He started the SUV and, driving without his lights on, he moved slowly down the road in the direction of where he had roughly calculated the landing spot to be.

It was a long ride at a slow speed while his focus was on the light out at sea. A few minutes later the rising winds cleared the dense cloud coverage and the light, which Devine had lost sight of for about a minute, reappeared farther down the coast. He pointed his ride that way, and soon the light became more and more vivid, like a star fallen into the ocean.

He finally pulled to a stop along an isolated stretch of coastline. He figured he was about six miles north of Putnam at this juncture.

Directly east, across the Gulf of Maine, lay Nova Scotia. Directly north was New Brunswick, which Devine knew was separated from Nova Scotia by the Bay of Fundy.

His gaze fixed steadily on the approaching boat light,

Devine got out of the Tahoe, hurried toward the rocky shore, and took up position behind a stand of white pines that had been battered and deformed by the stiff ocean wind. He placed a hand against one of the lean, bristly trunks.

He thought, *If this is just a fishing boat and I've wasted time and sleep for nothing?*

Devine tensed as the boat drew ever closer to shore. He wondered how they were going to manage it, because the coastline here was every bit as rocky as the one back in Putnam, and the breakers were not going to be easy to navigate.

He once more drew out his military-grade optics. They were the latest generation of surveillance technology, cost a fortune, and were worth every dime.

He squared up on the boat. The vessel didn't appear to be a lobster boat, at least not like the ones he'd seen at the harbor in Putnam. It was larger and sleeker and had sophisticated sat-nav tower modules mounted on the pilothouse roof. He didn't see anyone on deck and the pilothouse glass was darkened. He scanned the portside of the boat for ID markers but saw none. The boat had been powering along all this time, but as it grew closer it suddenly slowed and then stopped so abruptly a stiff stern wake jostled it.

As he watched, a smaller boat was lowered from the port side, and he saw three figures board it. And then several crates were passed down to the people on the smaller boat. One of them sat in the rear and operated the outboard motor and tiller. The small boat headed directly to shore.

Devine took out his phone and filmed this through his optics so it was as magnified as possible. He looked to the spot on land where the boat was headed and thought he saw movement there. He looked through his optics and confirmed at least one person standing at a spot near the shore. The person was moving a light up and down, clearly signaling to the boat.

Right as the vessel reached the breakers Devine heard something behind him. Coming from the south on the road were twin lights as a vehicle raced through the dark. He used his optics and saw that it was a black Cadillac Escalade, the same type of vehicle in which he'd been kidnapped.

Shit.

Devine hoofed it to his SUV, jumped in, and fired it up. He saw in his rearview that the Escalade was bearing down on him now. He pulled onto the road and punched the gas, making his tires squeal against the pavement as they strained to gain purchase. The Escalade countered this move by speeding up.

His ride was lighter and nimbler than the Escalade, but had nowhere near the horsepower. He knew this to be true because, despite his pressing the accelerator to the floor, the Escalade closed the gap with authority and rammed him from behind.

Devine fought to keep control of the Tahoe, but it was difficult on the rain-slicked road. And then a sudden gust of wind sent dead leaves and other debris barreling across the road, nearly blinding him. That was troubling but manageable. Far more problematic were the shots fired through his back glass, shattering it. The bullets passed uncomfortably close to him on either side before exiting out the windshield, leaving three small holes and one larger one, and an accompanying long crack in the glass as grim evidence of their passage.

Devine slipped out his gun, rolled down his window, pointed his Glock behind him, and fired six shots left-handed and blindly at the Caddy.

It did absolutely no good. A crescendo of shots pinged all over the interior of his SUV, forcing him to duck while still trying to see to drive. His vehicle went off the road before veering back on as Devine tried desperately to get out of the way of the shooter's sight line.

As he got the Tahoe back under control, the Escalade sped forward and came up next to him. His window was now parallel with the front passenger-side window of the Escalade.

The window on the other vehicle slid down and Devine saw a man sitting there wearing a black ski mask. He didn't focus long on the man but turned his attention to the biting end of the side-by-side shotgun, which was pointing right at Devine's head.

Devine slammed on the brakes a split second before the shotgun roared, and the buckshot load passed harmlessly in front of his windshield.

Devine put the Tahoe in reverse, punched the gas,

and hurtled backward for about fifty yards. He next performed a J-turn by tapping the gas and brake at precisely the right moments, and spun the steering wheel just as he'd been taught in the military during evasive maneuvers training. He'd done it back then in a three-ton armored Humvee the size of a hippo. By comparison, the Tahoe was not much of a challenge. He drove off going south, back toward Putnam.

However, the Escalade driver performed the exact same maneuver and impressively did it even more tightly than Devine had managed. In his rearview Devine saw the rear driver's side window come down, and the muzzle of an MP5 poked out as the Escalade soared after him.

Devine wasn't sure what he was going to do about this development, only that he wasn't going to sit there and go down quietly. He dropped back and was about to ram the larger vehicle as it came up beside him when a series of shots rang out. Only the shots weren't coming from the Escalade.

The big SUV immediately swerved and went off the road in a swirl of mud and flying leaves. Devine checked his rearview again; the Escalade appeared to be out of the chase.

He floored it and drove straight back to Putnam. When he got to his room he texted Campbell. He didn't expect an answer but he got one a minute later.

Glad you're all right. Hunker down for the night.

Devine texted back a reply and then started to wonder who had fired the shots that had saved his life.

And then a moment later he realized he had forgotten all about the boat coming to shore.

He slumped back on the bed and groaned.

And then his phone rang. The retired general must have thought of something else.

Only it wasn't Campbell.

And Devine wasn't going to be hunkering down.

53

Annie Palmer sounded stressed.

"Travis, can you come over?" she said. "I know it's late. But I really need you."

"Okay. Where do you live?"

"Not my place. I'm still at Alex's. She asked me to stay."

"What's wrong? Is she okay?"

"That's why I'm calling. She's . . . I don't know what to call it. But she's not in a good place."

"Should you call 911?" snapped Devine.

"She's not sick or injured or anything. She's just . . . mentally, something is going on. Please, can you come?"

"I'm leaving right now. Where's Dak?"

"I have no idea. I checked, he's not asleep in his room. And his bike isn't here. He's probably out getting drunk and screwing somebody. Please hurry!" she implored.

He drove his SUV as fast as he could while still maintaining control. It was freezing inside with the back window shot out, and the crack in the windshield was spreading. He cranked the heat up high and tried to ignore the chill.

He slid to a stop in front of Jocelyn Point, jumped out, and double-timed it to the front door.

Palmer was waiting for him there.

"Where is she?" said Devine.

"In her room."

She led him up the stairs and tried to open the door but it wouldn't budge. She looked fearfully at Devine. "I left it unlocked."

Devine pushed past her and rapped on the wood. "Hey, Alex, it's Travis. You in there? You okay?"

There was no answer but Devine could hear an odd sound coming from inside the room.

"I just want to talk, okay? I've got some things to tell you. Stuff I found out. Open the door, okay?"

There was no response.

Devine put his ear to the door and listened for a few moments, while Palmer stood there frozen, her eyes filling with tears.

"Alex!" barked Devine.

"Do . . . do you think . . ." began Palmer, but Devine wasn't listening.

He stepped back a few feet and then charged forward, throwing his bulk against the door. It burst open and he was inside the room. He scanned every inch and saw that the window was open and the drapes were flapping in the wind. That must have been the sound he'd heard. He raced to the window and looked down, his heartbeat thumping in his ears.

Please, God, no. No.

She wasn't down there. He breathed a sigh of relief and then looked at Palmer, who was standing next to him.

"Was she here when you came down to answer the door?"

"Yes, she was lying all curled up in the bed."

"Her bathroom?"

"Down this way."

They rushed out into the hall when they both heard a noise. Overhead.

"What is that?" asked Palmer in a hushed tone.

Devine looked up at the ceiling. And then it dawned on him.

"Oh my God!"

"What? What's wrong?" cried out Palmer as Devine rushed to the stairs and ran pell-mell up them. "Where are you going?" she called out, running after him.

Devine burst through the door leading outside and then pulled up abruptly.

Palmer ran into him and bounced off Devine like she'd hit a wall.

Devine didn't even notice the impact with the woman. His attention was in front of him.

"Hey, Alex."

She was standing there in a white nightgown that swirled around her long, pale legs with the rush of the wind. She didn't turn or acknowledge him. Palmer came to stand next to Devine.

"Oh, Lord," she whispered in a fearful tone.

Her fright was understandable.

Unlike them, Alex was standing on the *outside* of the widow's walk, right near the edge of the roof. It was at least a forty-foot drop to the ground.

"Hey, Alex, it's me, Travis. Can we talk?"

She still didn't look at him, but her head turned just a bit, as though she had heard him over the wind.

He took a few steps forward. "I've got some things to tell you. About your sister. I think you'll be happy. I'm making progress. I really am. But I could use your help."

Palmer gripped his sleeve as Alex took a step toward the edge.

Devine had been in Kandahar when a young woman had walked up to him, he thought, with a request for food and/or water. All the locals assumed American soldiers had plenty of food and water. And he had some extra provisions that he carried for that very reason.

He had reached into his pocket and when he looked back up she was holding a detonator in her shaky hand. All she had to do was push the button and they were both dead.

He could have done many things in that situation. Tried to shoot or knife or grab her before she blew the bomb pack, plead for his life, which was out of the question for him. Call for backup and hope that it arrived in time. Or do what he ended up doing.

He had held out several packages of food and two bottles of water and added a smile on top of it, as though his initial assumption was actually the correct one, and that she was not going to C4 them both to an early grave.

In her native language he said, "For you and your family. God be with you."

And she had taken the water and the food, and Devine and the woman had lived to see another day.

In a calm voice he now said, "Alex, I know you don't know this about me. But a woman I really cared for was found hanging in an office where I used to work."

He saw her bare shoulders tense and knew he had her attention now.

Next to him he heard Palmer gasp.

"But we later found out that she didn't kill herself. Someone killed her." He glanced at Palmer. "Like someone did Earl Palmer."

Annie Palmer's mouth dropped open with that statement, and Alex turned a bit so she could see him and he could see her, especially her eyes.

"W-what?" Alex said. "Earl?"

"I know how incredibly frustrating it must be not to remember something, Alex. I have memories from the Middle East that I've tried for years to forget. And I just can't. I may never be able to." He tapped his head. "But to have something that you know is up there and you can't find it?" He shook his head. "It's not fair."

She started to rock back and forth. "I . . . if I could have remembered, Jenny w-wouldn't be d-dead . . . If I . . . m-my fault . . ."

He took a step toward her. "You were the victim, Alex, not the cause of anything. You were attacked and left for dead. And then your mind played tricks on you to try to get you through the mental trauma in one piece. But in doing so it might have made things worse."

Fat tears formed under Alex's closed eyes. As they slid down her cheeks she shook her head. "Jenny shouldn't be dead. She was so . . . perfect."

She turned and took another deliberate step toward the edge. There was nowhere else to go now. Except down.

Palmer moaned and clutched his arm in fright.

Devine said, "She loved you, Alex. She loved you so much that she refused to stop trying to find the truth, even after all these years. She risked her life to help you. You . . . you can't answer that love, that devotion by . . . voluntarily taking your own life, when Jenny's was *stolen* from her. I know you know that, in your heart."

As Alex hovered near the edge she opened her eyes fully and looked down as the gusts of wind, stronger up here than at ground level, swirled and throbbed around her slim, fragile figure.

"You just can't, Alex," repeated Devine. "You know that. Jenny was a fighter. And so are you. I know you are. I believe in you. I believe in *you*."

A long moment passed during which both Devine and Palmer were holding their breaths.

Then Alex slowly took a symbolic step away from the edge. A moment later she turned toward them. Devine hopped over the railing of the widow's walk, rushed to her side, slipped one arm around her waist, and gripped her hand with his free one.

"Come on," he said. "You must be exhausted. And freezing."

Devine led her off the roof and down to the second floor, where he and Palmer got her into bed.

At the doorway Devine said to Palmer, "Do you know what triggered this?"

Palmer looked unsure. "I heard her call out, so I went to see if she needed anything. I don't think she was awake. I mean, she was lying in bed, but she was moving around sort of jerkily and saying stuff."

"What kind of stuff?" Devine said quickly.

"I don't know. I mean, it seemed like she was having a nightmare, but where it seems so real you're punching and kicking in bed? You know what I'm talking about?"

He glanced at the now-sleeping Alex. "Yeah, I know." He looked back at Palmer. "Anything you can remember her saying? It's important."

An agitated Palmer thought for a few moments. "I remember her saying something like, 'Why are you doing this to me? I thought we were friends.'"

In his anxiety Devine gripped Palmer's shoulders. "She said that, you're sure? *Friends?*"

"Yes. Why?" she exclaimed, looking both confused and uncomfortable.

Devine didn't answer her. He just turned and stared over at Alex.

A friend who tried to kill you.

54

Devine awoke with a start and looked around at the somewhat familiar surroundings. He was in Jenny's old room, where he had fallen asleep—he checked his watch—a mere four hours ago.

He yawned and slowly stood, pressing down his rumpled clothes. He hadn't bothered to disrobe because he had been too tired and the room was too cold.

He washed his face in the bathroom down the hall, tried and failed to smooth down his hair, and slowly opened the door to Alex's bedroom after knocking quietly and not getting an answer. She looked to still be asleep. He leaned in close enough to make sure he could see the steady rise and fall of her chest.

He glanced over at a chaise against one wall, where Annie Palmer lay fast asleep under a heavy blanket. She had insisted on staying in Alex's room, and Devine had decided to sleep on the premises, just in case something else happened.

He quietly closed the door and headed down to the kitchen. He didn't see Dak. He made himself coffee and drank it while staring out at the ocean through a rear-facing window. The tide was coming in and breakers were exploding against the rocky shore.

"You're up early."

He turned to see Alex standing there, barefoot and in the same white nightgown. Her hair was sleep tousled, and her eyes and face were puffy.

"Just woke up and couldn't go back to sleep." He held up the coffee. "Want a cup?"

She shook her head and walked over to stand next to him. She gazed out the window, her features troubled; her eyes seemed to be searching for . . . something out there.

"Thank you," she said.

"For what?"

"For not letting me do . . ."

"I don't think you would have, regardless of whether I was there or not."

Alex looked up at him. "Why? Why do you say that?"

"Because you're stronger than you think. Because you reached a tipping point, but didn't go over the edge."

"Why do you believe that was?"

"Because you have a lot more you want to accomplish in life."

The look she gave him was soul-breaking, even for the hardened seen-all-the-bad-in-life former soldier.

"I'm really, really . . . screwed up, Travis." Tears slid down her cheeks. "And I don't know if I can ever get back to . . . where I started."

He put down his cup, turned to her, and gently took

ahold of her shoulders. "For the record, and I'm not just saying this, we are all screwed up, Alex. All of us, including me. It's only a matter of degrees. What happened to you was horrifying and traumatizing and unfair as hell. None of it had anything to do with you and everything to do with the person who did it. So with that said, I'll answer your question: Can you ever get back to where you started? The answer is no."

She shivered and started to say something, but he put a finger to her lips.

"You will be *better*. You will be stronger. You will be able to take on far more than you ever thought possible. That's the thing with life, Alex. It tests us, all the time. It wants to see how much we can take, before we crack."

"You sound like you speak from experience," she said in a hollow voice.

"The Army's fundamental concept is based on breaking down every soldier to nothing, absolutely nothing. And then rebuilding that soldier in the version of the human fighting machine they want and need to do the job. I'm not saying it's perfect or right or anything. I'm just saying that's the deal. Only I *volunteered* to be put through that transformation. What happened to you took place without your consent. But the end result can be similar. You come out of it changed. But you come out of it tougher, because you took the worst shit life can throw at you, and you're still standing."

"I don't feel very tough right now."

"You do your art, you teach kids, you get out of bed

every day and go about life. You're a caring and compassionate person with a huge heart when you have every reason not to be any of that. That's an enormous victory, Alex, don't let anyone ever tell you it's not."

She looked unsure, but gripped his arm, and said, "I think I'm starting to remember some things . . . about that night."

"I think you are, too," he said softly.

"But it's still not there yet. I can't . . . I don't know . . . who . . ." She looked at him miserably.

"There's no rush on this, Alex, none at all. You take your time and just let it happen naturally, or as naturally as it can be." He drew closer. "But look, one thing you can't do is tell anyone that you're starting to remember things, okay?"

She looked up at him, and he could tell Alex knew exactly what he was leaving unsaid, because Devine felt to say it out loud now might do damage to her, real damage. But he didn't want anyone stopping her from fully remembering either. It was a tricky balance, and Devine was not confident in his ability to get it right.

"What did you remember?" He knew what she was going to say, because Annie Palmer had told him. But Devine wanted to hear Alex say it, if she remembered.

"That it was a *friend*. That it was someone I knew who . . . hurt me." She kneaded a finger into the side of her head. "It's right up here, Travis. The name. I know it is. If I could only make it come out."

"Sometimes the harder you try to make something

happen, particularly with your mind, the tougher it becomes to actually get to where you want to go. You will remember who it was, Alex. And when you do, you tell me, and then that person will be held accountable."

"Do you really think he was the one who hurt Jenny?"

He hesitated, but he couldn't bring himself to lie to the woman. Not now. Not in the precarious state she was in. "I think he was, yes."

"When it happened, I was stunned. I couldn't believe it. Believe that someone, anyone, could do that to . . . Jenny. She was so strong, so . . ."

". . . invincible?" suggested Devine.

She looked up at him with her big, sad eyes. "Yes."

"The thing is, Alex, none of us are invincible, not a single one of us. And that includes the person who hurt you and killed your sister. And when we find him, he will come to realize that clear as day. I give you my word on that."

"I've never met anyone quite like you," she said, a smile breaking through the gloom in her expression.

"I can say the same about you."

She slowly wrapped her arms around him and leaned her head against his chest. "Thank you, Travis."

And Devine held the woman as tightly as he could because he knew better than most that either of them could be gone tomorrow, which was promised to no one.

55

"My God, Devine, you are a one-man trouble magnet," exclaimed Fuss as she examined Devine's shot-up car outside the police station. "Did you get a good look at them?"

"The shooter I saw had on a ski mask. I already told you about the vehicle. I didn't get the plate because there were no plates. They had at least one shotgun and one MP5."

"How in the hell did you get away, again?"

He didn't want to tell her about the unexpected aid from quarters unknown. "Outdrove them."

"But this happened last night and you didn't call us," she said. "Why?"

"I didn't want you guys walking into a trap where you were outmanned and outgunned. I did pass it along to my superiors. They're following it up."

"Same people as the other time, you figure?"

"Probably, with a fresh crew," noted Devine. "Where's the closest airport?"

"The closest major airport is in Bar Harbor. They have twin asphalt runways, and commercial and private jets can land there."

"Then my people can check the flight data there for the last couple of days and see if something pops."

"What are you going to do for wheels? You'll freeze to death in that thing. And the windshield crack's gotten so big I'd have to ticket you. And there's no rental place around."

"I made other arrangements."

As he finished speaking, Annie Palmer drove up in her grandfather's old pickup truck. Her scooter was tied down in the truck bed.

She rolled down the window. "It's not fancy but it does run and the heater works. And it has one of those old track tape player things and a box of tapes. My granddad was a big fan of some guy named Hendrix and a band called . . . the Doors?"

Devine cracked a grin. "Jimi Hendrix and Jim Morrison, what more does one need? I'll drive you back to the Brew and offload your scooter."

"Thanks."

Devine turned to Fuss. "I'll let you know what we find out."

"Thanks. And don't get *this* truck shot up, okay?" warned Fuss.

Palmer looked surprised and then noted the shattered condition of Devine's Tahoe, with particular focus on the small holes in the windshield.

"Wait, are those—"

Devine opened the driver's side door. "Slide over. You

have hungry customers also craving caffeine and I'm one of them."

As they drove off she said, "What did you mean last night when you said someone killed my grandfather?"

"I'll explain all that later, I promise. But I need to think it through and then dig up some more facts, okay?"

"Okay," she said, though she didn't look or sound happy about it.

He dropped Palmer and her scooter off at Maine Brew, had some breakfast, and got back into the truck.

He saw Earl's box of tapes, which was on the floorboard. "Damn," he said to himself as he looked at the array of works by iconic musicians.

A master sergeant he'd served with overseas had taught him about sixties rock-and-roll and it was now Devine's favorite genre of music. A minute later he was listening to Hendrix bang out "The Star Spangled Banner" like no one else ever could, even with the left-handed Hendrix playing the right-handed guitar upside down. And the Kinks, the Who, and the Grateful Dead were all up on deck.

He tapped the steering wheel in rhythm with the music while he drove to the location where he'd seen the light on the shore. He pulled onto the shoulder, got out, and walked in that direction. And then he understood why this spot had been chosen. Amid the rock there was a short stretch of sandy beach. He didn't think anyone would want to wade through waist-high icy water to get to shore once the rocks kept the smaller boat from proceeding any further. But here they could have run right up on the beach, dropped off whatever, and the boat would have returned to the larger vessel out in the Gulf of Maine. He walked around to see if he could find any evidence of the people who had been here the previous night, like a cigarette butt or a footprint, but there was nothing. They had come and gone without leaving a trace. Devine figured this was not their first rodeo doing whatever they were doing.

He got back into the truck and drove the short distance to where the Escalade had rammed the Tahoe and started firing at him. He saw lots of shiny glass shards from his back window and the windshield, and the part of the Tahoe's rear bumper that had been torn off with the impact between the two trucks. He found some shell casings and pocketed them. He doubted he would ever find a gun to match them to, but one never knew.

Devine then walked to the spot where the Escalade had spun off the road. The ground was all chewed up here but he could see the tire tracks clearly. He also noted where the SUV had gone back on the road. So it had not been disabled, but merely knocked out of the chase by the anonymous shots.

He stood off to the side of the road and tried to re-create the scene in his mind.

Devine had performed a J-turn and was heading in the opposite direction. The Escalade had mimicked this maneuver and was speeding after him when the shots had struck the larger SUV.

He looked in front of him and then behind, trying to configure a rough trajectory of the third party's shooting lanes in his head.

Devine walked along the side of the road about a hundred yards and stopped, then looked up and down the road. It was all open field except for this spot where a towering multilimbed evergreen sat.

He walked over to it and looked all around. A nice spot to do some decent sniping and not be seen, he concluded. But not a single shell casing could he find, so they had policed their brass, or maybe their *polymer*. But how had they gotten here? He'd seen or heard no other vehicle. And surely he would have under the darkened, isolated conditions. And they couldn't have been simply waiting here, guns ready, for Devine and a chase car to just happen by.

There was clearly more here than met the eye. And then a thought occurred to him.

He called Campbell. "Is there a reason you didn't mention you sent backup to cover my rear flank?"

"You had enough on your plate."

"But I saw or heard nothing. And the only possible sniper position had no trace."

"It wasn't a person."

"Come again?"

"It was an armed drone employing AI to fire a machine gun on a target, Devine."

"Seriously?" said Devine.

"Yes."

"Then real soldiers will be obsolete before long. Did you catch the guys, then?"

"Agents Saxon and Mann were close, but they found nothing."

"Couldn't the drone follow them, or shoot out the tires?"

"It would have, but it suffered a mechanical failure and had to be recalled. It might have been shot for all I know, and those things are not cheap, let me tell you. They're examining it as we speak. We also checked the film footage from the drone's camera, but there was nothing helpful. Nifty piece of driving on your part, by the way."

"They might have flown into Bar Harbor airport. That's the closest for jets."

"We're already checking the flight logs. Got anything new to report?"

Devine told him about Alex starting to remember details from that night. "It was a friend, someone she knew."

"Think they're still in town?"

"I believe Earl Palmer would say they are, if he could."

"But again, we come back to how would someone leverage Palmer to pretend to find Jenny's body? Does the man have skeletons in his closet?"

"By all accounts he's a stand-up guy."

"Everybody has some shit that stinks, Devine. Everybody. So find his, and maybe that leads you to where you need to go. Oh, and about saving your ass last night? You're welcome. But don't take that to mean you're special or anything. I just don't have time to train a new one."

Campbell clicked off.

56

Devine later drove to Putnam Harbor and looked around. The air was a little warmer today and the skies clear. The salt air smells filled his lungs as he watched men work on the few boats still docked here. And another man was taking a dinghy stacked with lobster traps out to one of the moored vessels.

He looked over when someone called out to him. It was the same man that Devine had falsely accused of being a government informant his first night here.

"Hey, dude, how's it going?" said the man, walking over. "Name's Phil Cooper, by the way, folks call me Coop."

"Okay, Coop, I'm Travis. I saw you on a lobster boat leaving out of here a few mornings back."

"You must've been up real early then," said Cooper with a grin.

"I thought you would have been out to sea today," noted Devine.

Cooper's grin faded. "Damn motor on the boat burned out. I told the owner he needed to get the thing overhauled. He said that costs money. Well, so does having your boat sitting over there and not being able to catch lobster."

"Can you get on with another boat while his is down?"

"Probably can, tomorrow at least. Thin crews these days. Not many guys want to take up the trade. Some captains go out by themselves now. Backbreaking work, and the money ain't what it used to be."

"Earl Palmer was telling me that, too."

"Damn shame about Earl. Heard he hung himself. Shit. I mean, I know he was depressed about Bertie. But still, he had Annie. He had friends. Now I wish I had spent more time with him. Gone by to see him, shoot the shit about the old days. Drink some beers with him."

"We all have regrets like that, Coop. Hey, got a question."

"Okay, Travis, fire away."

"That night outside the bar? Dak left before I did, and he passed you and your friends. I'd seen him give a high sign to an old guy to leave his stool so I could sit down. Did Dak by any chance give you boys the sign to come after me?"

This query wiped the smile right off Coop's face. "Look, I don't want to get in no trouble with a fed."

"You won't, because you just answered my question. Now I've got another one."

"Okay," said Cooper warily.

"What would a boat be doing out in the middle of the night with a smaller boat lowered off that, and heading to shore where it could beach and then offload something?"

"Where the hell did you see that?" asked a startled Cooper.

Devine told him the general location. The other man slowly shook his head. "I don't know. Nothing to do with lobster fishing or oyster farming, I can tell you that. Maybe it was the government. Coast Guard?"

"I thought about that and looked it up. There's a Coast Guard station at Boothbay Harbor, but they have a thousand-square-mile area of responsibility along the coast that ends far to the south of here."

Cooper scratched his head. "Yeah, that's right."

"There's another Coast Guard station in South Portland. It's part of Sector Northern New England. It covers multiple states, works with Homeland Security, performs search and rescues, and helps keep the maritime lanes running smooth. My people can check in with them to see if they had an op in the area, but it really didn't look like that to me."

Cooper glanced out to the water. "You think somebody might be smuggling stuff in?"

"I don't know. I guess it's possible." Devine looked out at the water, too, and a question occurred to him. "What can you tell me about Wilbur Kingman's boat going down?"

"Really tragic. Hell, come to think, *Earl* was on that boat when it sank. He and Wilbur worked together for decades."

"I know. How exactly did it happen?"

Cooper sat down on a bench and said, "It was a real

foggy morning. Couldn't see a foot in front of you. Most boats didn't even head out, but Wilbur knew these waters like nobody else. At least we thought he did."

"What do you mean by that?"

"There are rocky outcrops everywhere along the coast here, and some are farther out than you would think, just a quirk of Maine's oceanic topography." He grinned. "Didn't expect those high-falutin' words to come out my mouth, did you? Anyway, we all have sonar and depth finders and whatnot on our boats, so we don't run into stuff we shouldn't, including other boats. Well, apparently somehow Wilbur's boat hit one of those rocks out there, hard enough to cave in the hull. Most commercial lobster boats range from around twenty-two feet on up to over forty. Wilbur's boat, *The Kingman*, was a thirty-foot closed stern Beal, a nice size, and it handled real well on the water. But it didn't have a hydraulic hauler, so they brought the traps up the old-fashioned way, with muscle."

"How do you know it handled well in the water?"

"Whenever Earl was sick or couldn't go out, I'd be the stern man for Wilbur. He ran a good operation, real safe."

"Until he didn't," noted Devine.

"Right. Anyway, the thing was apparently loaded with lobsters in holding tanks full of water. It went down fast. Didn't even get a distress signal or anything from them."

"Weren't they wearing life jackets?"

Cooper said, "You're supposed to, sure. But you're pulling up heavy traps all damn day, last thing you want is something restrictive like that on you. I just wear my orange overalls and heavy gloves. But all boats carry life-saving gear. It's required."

"What did Earl say happened then?"

"He didn't say much, which is very much like Earl. But he did say that in the collision he got thrown overboard and Wilbur got knocked out cold. He said he swam back to the boat and tried to get a life jacket on Wilbur, but the damn boat was sinking so fast, and stuff was sliding all around so much that he couldn't. And Wilbur was a big man—hard to corral dead weight like that when you're in the water. Earl barely had time to grab a floatable himself before it all went under and Wilbur was gone."

"But with Wilbur knowing the waters so well, and all the nav gear you carry, how did he hit the rocks?"

Cooper shrugged. "Shouldn't have happened, but it does. You lose focus, you don't look at your screen consistently enough. Fog rolls in, you don't know where the hell you are or what's around you. It's like that condition a pilot can get up in the air on a cloudy night, don't know up from down and won't believe his own instruments."

"It's called spatial disorientation," said Devine. "It's what probably caused the deaths of JFK Jr. and his wife and sister-in-law in the plane he was piloting."

"Well, I think Wilbur got distracted and the fog didn't help none, or his nav gear malfunctioned and bam, he hit the rock at speed. Hell, he really shouldn't have gone out that morning, and he shouldn't have been going that fast. But humans aren't perfect. We make mistakes, particularly in situations like that. It's not easy navigating in deep waters in the fog even with all the whiz-bang nav stuff they got. I've been on boats in real bad weather where I wasn't sure the captain knew where the hell he was. And we've had some close calls. But we never wrecked. Just bad luck for Wilbur. Real bad."

"How was Earl rescued?"

"Fog lifted and boats started going out. They saw him and picked him up. Poor man was in the water for hours. He's lucky hypothermia didn't get him. He was in shock, traumatized beyond all get out. They said he was still trying to find Wilbur. Didn't want to get out of the water till he found his captain. Fought the folks trying to help him into the boat. Finally had to hog-tie the poor guy to save him. They recovered Wilbur's body and he got a proper burial. Bing and Sons went all out for it, best of everything, and didn't charge Ms. Kingman a dime for it."

"That was good of them," said Devine.

"Big loss for the town, for sure. But goes to show that no matter how much you think you know about what's out there, the ocean always has surprises in store for you."

Just like this damn town, thought Devine.

57

"A guy named Phil Cooper spoke with me about the accident involving your husband."

Devine was standing across from Pat Kingman at the front desk of the inn. She was on the other side, sorting some papers.

She looked up and slipped off her glasses, her expression pensive and faraway. "I've been thinking that it wasn't just Bertie's death eating Earl up. It was what happened with Wilbur. Even after all these years."

"You said he did everything he could to save him."

"But you didn't really know Earl. He was as loyal as they come. He told me many times over the years that he wished he could have done more to save Wilbur. I told him he'd done all that was humanly possible. But I could tell he didn't believe me. And then when Bertie died? It was too much."

"So you think that's why he killed himself?"

"Well, I can't think of any other reason, can you?"

"Did he have any enemies?"

"Earl?! You must be joking. Everybody loved Earl. And Bertie."

"So no grudges with anyone? How about any strangers that might have come into town?"

"Why in the world are you asking these questions? Earl killed himself. Nobody murdered him, if that's what you're implying."

"Just the investigator in me, trying to cover all the angles."

She frowned. "Well, you can stop, at least with Earl. Poor man. Let him rest in peace."

"Getting back to the accident with your husband's boat, seems the theory is he got disoriented out there, or his nav system failed, or both. What do you think happened?"

She leaned on the front desk and shook her head. "If you want the God's honest truth, I think Wilbur had a heart attack or a stroke while he was at the wheel. Maybe he fell on the throttle and slammed *The Kingman* at speed right into those damn rocks. His hull paint was found on them, clear as day. That boat was sturdy as a brick wall. The hull would not have failed with just a light impact."

"Did he have health problems?"

"He was overweight, smoked and drank too much. Had high blood pressure and suffered from angina. I told him a million times to go get checked out, but he never would. Said doctors just wanted to find something wrong with you so they could make money. I think that attitude cost him his life."

"Was an autopsy performed?"

"No. Everybody knew he drowned. And if he had a

heart attack beforehand, what did it matter? He was still dead."

"You'd think they'd want to know the cause of the accident."

"Well, as far as I know, they spoke with Earl and he told them what happened. I guess if Earl hadn't survived they would have done autopsies on both of them if they recovered the bodies. But he *did* survive," she added emphatically.

"Did Earl see him having a health episode or slump over?"

"No. He was in the stern cleaning the deck. Had his back to the pilothouse. Next thing he knew he was in the water—the impact knocked him overboard. Earl hurt his neck when that happened. Had to have surgery afterward. I think it also messed up his back and knees, too—he hit the side of the boat as he went over."

Devine left her and drove to the police station. Thankfully, Harper and Fuss were out.

Mildred James greeted him with a smile, and he asked her if he could look at the file for Steve and Valerie Palmer.

"Can I ask what for?" she said warily.

He leaned forward and spoke in a low voice. "What with Earl's death and Bertie's recently before that, it's gotten my suspicions up."

"But Earl killed himself."

"Did you know Earl?"

"Sure did. All my life."

Devine knew he was taking a risk with his next question, but he had few options. He needed to see that file. "Do you think Earl, with all his physical ailments, could have climbed up on a chair, stood there stable while he put up a noose, wrapped it around his neck, and then kicked the chair away?"

"Is that how it happened?"

"You didn't know?"

"I didn't know the exact details, no."

"So what do you think?"

"Earl had one of those lift chairs put in his house."

"Right, I was there once when he used it."

"And he couldn't do the stairs anymore, so he slept in what used to be the dining room on the first floor. And he had those special gadgets put in his car. So, no, Agent Devine, I don't see him doing that at all." Her eyes widened appreciably. "You don't think . . . you think someone might have killed him?"

"I just need to rule it out, or not. And four unnatural deaths in the same family? That's a little much, don't you think?"

James nodded. "Yes, now that you put it that way, it is. I'll get the files for you."

She settled him in the same room as before and then left him to it.

Devine went methodically through the postmortem report. Smoke inhalation was the cause of death, the report concluded. There were no other indications of violence on the bodies, though they had both been badly burned. Even the hardened Devine was repulsed by the graphic photos of the couple's remains. The official conclusion had been accidental death.

Then he came to the official signature of the medical examiner at the end of the report and his suspicions spiked to a whole new level.

Françoise Bing.

58

Devine walked into the funeral home, spoke to a woman at the front desk, and was directed back to Guillaume's office.

She was just rising from her desk. "I have an embalming to perform."

"This can't wait."

Guillaume studied him for a moment, oscillating back and forth on her feet as she did so. "Then follow me." She led him down a hall and through a door that she used a passkey to open.

Inside was a long metal table with equipment on a rolling rack next to it. Under a sheet on the table was the body—to be embalmed, Devine assumed.

"I hope that's not another suicide or homicide," he said.

"No. A ninety-year-old who died peacefully in his sleep. We should all be so lucky." She readied the equipment and some instruments. "I hope you don't have much to ask unless you really want to see this procedure take place. I've never met a layperson who did."

In answer Devine pulled out a copy of the postmortem report on the Palmers. He held up the signature page.

"You told me you were still in medical residency out of state fifteen years ago. So why is your signature on Steve and Valerie Palmer's autopsy report? This was obviously before you were married, since you used your maiden name on the form."

She stared at the page for a few moments. He could almost see the inner machinery of her brain in high gear as it processed all this.

"Oh, now I remember. I was home on vacation. The state had no one available to do the job. They asked me and I said yes. I wasn't certified yet, and hadn't taken the oath of office, but I was a licensed MD in the state of Maine. The chief medical examiner can make temporary appointments when the need arises, and it did in the Palmer case. Besides, it was a fairly straightforward matter, no evidence of foul play, but under the circumstances a postmortem of sorts was legally required."

"A 'postmortem of sorts'? What does that mean?"

"A *full* autopsy wasn't required. I determined the cause of death. Smoke inhalation, if I remember correctly. They were dead before the flames reached them. Lucky for the Palmers."

"I wouldn't call that lucky," replied Devine. "Who suggested you for the job?"

"I don't remember."

"Maybe your uncle, Benjamin Bing? He was police chief back then, right?"

"Okay, yes, I guess that makes sense. Uncle Ben would have done that. In fact, I recall now that he *did* contact me and told me the situation. He knew I was home, so that worked out all right." She smiled tightly. "Forgive me for not remembering right off. It was a long time ago."

"Only you didn't do a tox report or any blood work."

"Like I said, a full autopsy was not conducted. There was no need, Agent Devine. They weren't poisoned."

"Since you didn't do the necessary workup, we don't really know that for sure, do we?"

Her neutral expression devolved to a scowl. "I really don't like what you're implying."

"Just stating facts. I'll leave the implications for another time."

"I need to get to work, so if you'll excuse me?" She pulled back the sheet, revealing the body of an aged man.

However, Devine wasn't finished. "So if you were in town then, were you also in Putnam when Alex was attacked? Probably, since that event and the Palmers' deaths were only three days apart."

"What, are you going to accuse me of sexually assaulting Alex now? Do I need an alibi? But I guess the statute of limitations has long passed."

"Oh, so you looked that up?"

"Okay, get out. Now."

Devine turned and left but before he shut the door he looked back at Guillaume, who was looking down at the body she had to embalm. To Devine, at the moment, it didn't look like the woman even realized it was in front of her.

He saw Fred Bing at the front desk talking with the

person there. He was dressed all in black except for his white shirt. His black tie was neatly done and his hair was slicked back.

"Funeral?" said Devine.

Bing looked over and smiled sadly. "Yes. She was in hospice. But she lived a good long life. She doesn't have much family left in the area, so it will be a small affair, but we will do her proud."

"I heard about your handling of Wilbur Kingman's funeral."

"That was so sad. Wilbur was a fine man. He and my father used to go deep-sea fishing together before my dad retired to Florida. Pat really had no money at the time for an elaborate funeral, but we made the decision to cover the costs. It was the right thing to do."

" 'We'?"

"My sister and I. And my father called from Florida and voiced the same opinion. He actually came up for the service." Bing looked chagrined. "Only time he's ever been back. I guess visiting his own children isn't a high priority." He glanced in embarrassment at the woman at the front desk and motioned Devine over to a corner of the hall for privacy.

"What brings you here?" he asked in a hushed tone.

"I had some questions for your sister."

"Was she helpful?" asked Bing.

"More than she probably knows. I have a question for you."

"Okay."

"Benjamin Bing? What can you tell me about him?"

"Ah, the lawman of the family," he said with a grin. "Uncle Ben liked guns, liked to tell people what to do, and liked to wield power over others. He rose quickly to chief and stayed there until his retirement."

"Which I understand he's doing in Florida?"

"Yes."

"Is he still alive?" asked Devine.

Bing blinked. "Um, yes. Well, as far as I know. I mean no one has told me otherwise."

"Would they necessarily?"

"The fact is our family is not particularly close."

"Could you make a call to your father and confirm one way or another?"

"Well, certainly, if it will help. I can't guarantee when I might hear back. The last time I called my dad it was around a month before he *texted* back."

"Whatever you can do, I would appreciate it."

"Of course," said Bing.

"Now, I understand that your uncle Ben has quite a nice house in Naples. And he only had the policeman's salary I'm assuming. Your grandfather's trust didn't extend to him?"

Bing looked uncertain. "I suppose not. I guess I've never really thought about that."

"So I was just wondering how he could afford a Naples beach house."

"Yes, I suppose you are. I could ask my father."

"The simplest answer would be that his two brothers gave him money to buy it."

Bing shook his head. "My father and Uncle John are many things, Agent Devine. But generous is not one of them. And, frankly, I don't think the two of them really like Uncle Ben. He made it clear that he thought what they did for a living was at best a joke and at worst revolting, and that he had taken a far higher road in life. He would even ticket them for illegally parking during funeral services."

"So, he was kind of an . . . asshole?"

Bing laughed. "More than kind of." His expression turned serious. "Why are you asking about all of this? I mean, if you can tell me."

"Not right now, I can't. So if they didn't get along, why did he move down there with them?"

"Another good question to which I don't have a good answer. Maybe they reconciled."

"Okay, did your uncle Ben know the Silkwells?"

"Oh, sure. He and Senator Silkwell were good friends. Uncle Ben locked up the police vote for him. He was very involved in police union politics in Maine."

"Did your uncle know the children well?"

"I believe Dak interviewed for a job with the police here when he got out of the military. It didn't work out. I don't think Dak likes to take orders," he added with a grin.

"And the sisters?" asked Devine.

"I know he wrote a recommendation letter for Jenny

when she was applying to college. And then I think he did another one when she wanted to work for the federal government."

"And Alex?"

Now Bing looked uncomfortable. "Again, any particular reason you're asking all this?"

"There is a reason. I just can't share it right now."

Bing blew air out of his mouth and rubbed at his neat hair, mussing it a bit. "Well, I'm sure they knew each other."

"That's it? No personal contact like he had with her siblings?"

Bing looked even more conflicted. But he finally said, "No, none that I can think of."

Devine stared at him for so long that the other man finally dropped his gaze to his highly polished shoes.

"Let me know when you hear back from your father."

"Yes, yes, absolutely," said Bing hastily.

Devine left the man there.

A numb-looking Fred Bing turned and slowly walked back down the hall.

59

Devine drove to Jocelyn Point. When Alex answered his knock he said, "You have time to help me with something?"

"Sure, what?"

"I'll show you. It's right down the road."

They drove to Earl Palmer's house while Alex looked anxiously out the window. They didn't go to the house, but rather into Bertie's old studio.

"Is this where it happened?" she said, looking around and nervously tugging on the yellow and gray scarf around her neck.

"Yes."

"This place represented so many happy memories for me. And now? Bertie would be so sad that Earl . . ."

She wandered around and took the cover off an easel set in the corner.

"My God, I can't believe she kept this."

"What is it?" said Devine, walking over to join her.

"The first painting I did under Bertie's tutelage."

Devine took a look at it. The image was clear enough. He shot her a glance.

"It's you. You started out with a self-portrait?"

She nodded. "Only it was Bertie's idea."

"What was the reasoning behind that?" asked Devine curiously.

Alex leaned against the wall, put her hands in her pockets, and stared at the painting.

"It wasn't that long after . . . I was attacked. Bertie wanted me to know that I was still there. That I had meaning and value. That the person who did that to me could never take that away. Ever. That Alex Silkwell was alive and would thrive."

"In addition to being an artist, Bertie sounded like she would have made a great counselor."

"She helped me more than all the fancy shrinks ever did. But it was more or less what you told me, too, when I was on the roof. So are you a great counselor, as well?"

"Depends on who I'm counseling."

Alex stepped forward, put her hand out to the painting, and gently traced her jawline, and next the curve of her right eye.

"I had just turned sixteen when I painted this. I'm twice as old as that now."

"Still a young woman with most of her life ahead of her."

"I'm a very different person now, Travis."

"Experience changes all of us, no matter whether we want it to or not. And like I said before, you're stronger and better than your younger version."

"And like you said, I guess the fact that I'm still standing is a victory of sorts."

"In the Army it was the only one that counted."

"You never told me why you left the military."

"Some days I don't even know," he lied.

She seemed to sense this and looked away. "You expect truthfulness from everyone except yourself?" she said coldly.

Devine sighed and nodded. "You're right. I'm being a hypocrite. The truth is I left the Army because I had to. Officially, it was my decision, but I really had no other pathway."

"Why?"

"Someone committed a wrong, a horrible wrong, against a fellow colleague of ours, and was never held accountable for it. I tried to work through the proper channels to right that wrong. And I was stonewalled. So I took matters into my own hands. But by righting a wrong I committed one of my own. After that I felt I didn't have the right to wear the uniform. The honorable thing to do was leave, and so I did. My penance was giving up the thing I loved the most."

She stared at him for an uncomfortably long time before saying, "I'm sorry that happened to you. But thank you for being honest with me."

"You deserve it."

She looked around and said, "Why did you bring me here?"

"I want you to see if you notice anything different from when you were here last working with Bertie."

"Why?"

"Just bear with me and I'll explain later. Go ahead. Use your artist's eye for detail."

She shrugged and walked around looking at everything. Then she stopped and pointed toward the ceiling rafter. "That wasn't there before."

He looked where she was motioning. A blackened pulley had been screwed into a roof joist directly above where Earl had been found hanging. It was the same color as the board it was attached to and thus blended right in. Devine wasn't certain he had even noticed it before.

"You're sure it wasn't there?"

"Very sure. We could have actually used something like that to lift up a few of the heavy sculpture pieces Bertie and I did here."

Lift up?

She eyed the pulley and then glanced at him. "On the widow's walk, you mentioned that someone might have killed Earl?"

"Yes."

"Why?"

"I'm not sure. Yet."

Devine quickly formulated a rough trajectory that carried him back to a large bolt that was screwed into the wall over the top of a wooden workbench set there.

He bent down and examined the bolt more closely

with his phone light. Was that a rope fiber on top of the workbench?

Things were starting to make sense. Still, there were unanswered questions. Lots of them.

"Was that helpful?" she said, drawing Devine from his reverie.

He looked at her. "Oh, Alex, you don't know how much. Thank you."

60

Devine and Alex next drove to the police station, where Mildred James greeted them.

"Alex?" she said in surprise. "I haven't seen you in some time."

Alex looked down at her boots. "Yes, I've . . . been pretty busy."

"I'm sure. And I am so sorry about your sister, hon. Jenny was so—"

"—perfect?" said Alex, looking up with a sad expression. "I know everyone says that, but she really was, you know." She glanced nervously at Devine. "At least she was to me. She looked after me and supported me, when others were . . . *preoccupied*."

James looked a bit confused by all this, and Devine hastened to move things along.

"The evidence file for Earl Palmer? Can I take a look at it?"

"Certainly."

She led them back, warned Devine that he couldn't let Alex touch anything, and then left them. He figured she would have been far more hesitant to let the two of them have access to this evidence if Palmer's death had not been officially ruled a suicide, despite her agreeing with Devine's theory as to it possibly having been a murder.

"What are we looking for?" asked Alex.

Devine proceeded to tell her about his theory of the case with Earl's death having been a homicide because of the man's physical limitations. "And your seeing the pulley bolsters that."

"That all makes sense, Travis. You would think Chief Harper could see that, too."

"When he was *Sergeant* Harper he accessed your evidence file."

"Why?"

"I guess he wanted to see if he could solve it, but your rape kit was missing, as I told you before."

"Who would take it?"

"Whoever didn't want your attacker to be found."

"Do you have any idea who it is, Travis?" she asked in a trembling voice.

"I'm getting closer, I can feel it."

He looked over the evidence that had been gathered from the Palmers' studio and focused on the noose.

He took pictures of it with his camera.

"God, that is a gruesome-looking thing," said Alex.

"Between World War II and 1961 the U.S. military executed 160 soldiers for various offenses. They were all hanged, and the Army was responsible for 157 of them."

"An eye for an eye?"

"Not really. Fourteen offenses are punishable by death

during times of war or peace. Every soldier knows what they are, or should. So long as he or she avoids them, they have no problem." He didn't tell her that one of them was for rape.

"And for times of war only?" she said.

"Four, including desertion and willfully disobeying or assaulting a superior officer."

"I suppose you never willfully disobeyed or assaulted a superior officer?"

"Not a *superior* officer, no," said Devine, thinking of Kenneth Hawkins, who had, like Devine, also held the rank of captain.

He drove Alex back to Jocelyn Point. She got out of the truck and then poked her head back in. "I heard about your rental. Annie said it was shot full of holes."

"It was. But I'm not."

She visibly shuddered at his flippant remark. "Do you know why they're trying to kill you? Is it connected to what happened to Jenny?"

"I don't know, honestly. It could be connected to something totally unrelated. Old enemies," he added.

"Please be careful."

"I always am, Alex. It's why I'm still here."

Devine watched her walk inside, then started back down the drive. But as he was doing so he noted for the first time that the drive also had a branch off to the right, heading toward some of the other buildings he had seen on his first night here. He hung a quick right and drove off.

The first three buildings he reached were abandoned or falling down, and otherwise uninhabitable. The fourth one was not.

He parked in front and looked back at the main house. It was not visible from here because the trees and large bushes neatly blocked this building from both the house's view and from the coast road.

He got out and approached the door. The walls were stone while the door was wood. It was locked. The windows were blacked out and seemed to be painted shut. He tried his lock gun, but the lock was superior to his skill and equipment. He walked around the building and quickly found that was the only door.

He studied the path to the building's entrance. Well-worn, so well used. And recently. He stood at the window and took a quick inhale. He had done this in the Middle East. Munitions and explosives all had distinct odors. He wasn't smelling anything like that. Yet there was some scent in there that he couldn't readily identify. And there was also a humming. Was it insects, bees? Was there infestation in there?

He waited, listened. No, it was too consistent, same sounds, same rhythm.

Mechanical, not natural, he concluded.

He took out his phone and Googled something. It took a few minutes of searching before he found what he was looking for.

Closest place was twenty miles from here.

He jumped into the truck and sped off.

Nearly two hours later Devine was back with what he needed. He returned to Jocelyn Point but stopped short of the entry driveway.

He made the rest of the trip on foot as darkening clouds gathered above him.

He slipped in and out of tree lines, and waited behind bushes to make sure there was no one about. It felt like he was back in the Afghan mountains hunting the Taliban and its iterations, all while they hunted him.

He reached the building, found a good spot, and set up what he had purchased.

The surveillance camera was motion operated so it wouldn't be on continuous feed and was capable of being synced with his phone, which would alert him if there was any activity. He performed all the necessary tasks, including securing the tiny camera to the trunk of a tree with a direct sight line to the door.

Now he just had to wait for his trap to be sprung. But while he was waiting for that he had things to do. He drove off.

However, he was just about to run into an obstacle.

61

Harper and Fuss passed him going the other way in their patrol car.

The cruiser whipped around, the roof lights cranked on, and the siren ruptured an otherwise quiet day in Putnam, Maine.

An exasperated Devine slammed a fist against the dashboard and barked, "I don't have time for this shit!"

He steered the truck over to the shoulder, cut the engine, and waited for them to pull in behind. He didn't get out. Devine decided to let them come to him.

And they did.

"Step out of the truck, Devine," said Harper, his hand once more on the head of his baton.

Devine poked his head outside the truck window. "Are you arresting me . . . again? What was wrong with the first time?"

"Out, now!"

Devine climbed out just as it began to rain.

"Come back to the cruiser and get in," ordered Harper. "Before we all catch pneumonia."

Devine sat in the back seat, with Harper next to him. Fuss leaned over the front seat to face them.

"What's up?" Devine asked.

"What's up is why do you think it's your job to go around riling people up?"

"Not sure what you're talking about."

"Then let me give you an example. You basically accused Françoise Guillaume of dereliction of duty if not outright conspiracy."

"I never said that and—"

"And I heard that Alex Silkwell nearly killed herself because you were throwing around wild accusations about her sister and the attack on Alex all those years ago."

"Who the hell told you about—"

Harper continued to talk right over him. "And you've pretty much convinced Mildred that Earl Palmer was murdered when there is no evidence, nada, of that being the case."

Devine flicked his phone screen and tapped an icon. Then he held up the phone. On it was the picture he'd taken of the noose. "Eight coils plus a round turn and two half hitches."

"What?"

"The noose. Eight coils. And then it was secured to the rafter with a round turn and two half hitches. It's typically used to secure a rope to a stationary object."

"So? Earl was a lobsterman. He probably knew every damn knot there was."

"I took Alex to Bertie's studio. She remembered

everything that was in it while she worked there with Bertie, which was mere days before she was killed. The only thing she saw there that she had never seen before was a pulley bolted into another rafter directly above where Earl was hanging from. It had been painted black to match the color of the wood so as to blend in. I didn't even remember seeing it. And then there's an iron bolt set into the wall over the workbench. Under the iron bolt was a fiber, looked to be a rope fiber."

"What are you saying, Devine?" demanded Fuss.

"I'm saying someone strung Earl up using that pulley."

"Who the hell would have done that?" barked Harper.

"Whoever got Earl to lie about finding Jenny's body. That made him a loose end."

"Oh, okay, here we go again with your bullshit theory," said an exasperated Harper.

"Even if you think a crippled Earl could climb up on that chair, set the noose, and then kick the chair away, how did he do the eight coils on the noose and the round turn and two half hitches?"

"He was a *lobsterman*. He's been tying knots since he came out of the womb," barked Harper.

"Not lately he hasn't. Have you seen the size of his fingers? How bent and stiff they are? They're full of arthritis. When I was walking with him he could barely hold on to the head of his cane. And he can't even look down, which you're going to have to do to make these knots." He pointed at the picture of the complicated knots. "It requires dexterity he no longer had. And why hang himself in the first place? He had a shotgun. Why not just pull the trigger on that, which he could have done even with those fingers? Why go to all that trouble? I'll tell you why. Faking a death by suicide using a shotgun is a whole lot more difficult than doing it by hanging. You've got possible forensic trace in the former that you really don't have in the latter."

Fuss eyed her boss nervously. "Maybe worth checking out, Chief."

Devine added, "And the knot used to secure the noose?"

"What about it?" demanded a still irate Harper.

"It was chosen for a reason, because the first part of the knot, the round turn, would keep the load in place until the two half hitches could be secured."

"You mean if the killer used the pulley he'd have to secure Earl up there somehow until he finished off the knot?" said Fuss.

"Yes. He obviously couldn't leave it strung through the pulley, otherwise we'd know it was probably murder. If Earl had used the pulley to kill himself there would have been no need to secure the noose to the rafters. The pulley and bolt would have worked just fine. In fact, if they had just used the pulley and left Earl hanging from it I wouldn't have been nearly as suspicious. But they overthought it." He paused. "I actually picture two people. One on a ladder next to Earl, whose head is in the noose after being hoisted there using the pulley, and his feet on the chair. The end of the rope is secured to the bolt.

Then the second person cuts the rope but holds on to the end with all his weight, while the first man holds on to Earl, who would have gone slack with the rope cut. The two killers then work together to wrap the rope around the rafter and manage to complete the round turn. I'm not saying it would be easy, but it is doable. And if they strung him up with one rope, put another noose around his neck, and then cut away the first rope, the subterfuge would have been discovered during the autopsy, with the misaligned ligature markings and such. They must have known that, which means they might have some specialized knowledge in forensics. Then they can complete the two half hitches and let go of Earl completely, kick out the chair, and the man goes swinging."

"You're overlooking one obvious problem," said Harper. "How did they get Earl there in the first place? No signs of forced entry. No defensive wounds. No signs of a struggle. Earl might have been crippled, like you said, but he was still a big man. He wouldn't have gone quietly into the night."

"He would if he'd been drugged."

"Françoise found nothing like that," said Harper dismissively.

"She didn't *check* for any of that," retorted Devine. "She ruled it a suicide by hanging."

Harper started to say something and then stopped. He eyed Fuss, who was looking concerned, very concerned. He glanced back at Devine. "How do you know so much about knot tying?"

"The Rangers train in high altitudes because we have missions in those types of environments. We climb and rappel and do all sorts of things that require intimate familiarity with ropes and knots, belays, climbing stop descenders, carabiners, and the like."

Harper sighed. "Okay, let's get over to the funeral home and we'll have Françoise run those tests. Okay?"

"Thank you, Chief," said Devine quite sincerely.

"But if it's all negative, will you stop with all this murder talk?"

"Yes. You have my word."

"Okay, we'll leave your truck here. You can ride with us."

At the funeral home, they found Fred Bing and asked where his sister was.

"She's just finishing something up. Should be done in a few minutes. I'll let her know you're here."

"Thanks," said Harper.

Five minutes later Guillaume appeared. She was wearing a full leather apron and was taking off a pair of sturdy gloves.

"What's up, Chief?" she said after giving Devine a glare.

"I want you to run some tests on Earl's remains."

"Tests? On Earl?" she said, looking stunned.

"Yeah, blood and tox. We want to check to see if he was maybe drugged or something. Devine has a theory." He added, "Probably won't amount to much."

"I'm sorry. I can't run those tests," she said quickly.

Devine stepped forward. "If you won't, we'll find someone else who will."

"You don't understand, no one can run those tests now," she persisted.

"Why the hell not?" demanded a confused Fuss.

"Because Earl's remains have been cremated. I just finished doing it."

62

Annie Palmer looked traumatized. She was sitting in a booth at Maine Brew with Devine next to her and Harper and Fuss across from her. They had previously taken Devine back to retrieve his truck and then followed him here.

"I signed the papers for them to cremate Gramps. It's what he wanted. Bertie was cremated and her ashes spread over the harbor. I was planning to do the same with his. Dr. Guillaume called and had me come in. She said everything was done and it was time to take care of the body. I was happy that he wanted to be cremated. I mean, I don't have the money for a casket and burial plot and all. I was planning on having a celebration of his life here at the café, for his friends." She paused. "I'm the only family left; my mom and dad had no siblings."

Harper sighed and looked at Devine. "Just unfortunate, way I see it. But nothing out of the ordinary, either. They're running a business. And they'd jumped through all the hoops. We knew the tests hadn't been done, and I didn't order any. Buck stops with me. We were a day late and a dollar short."

Devine rubbed his brow, looking and feeling immensely frustrated.

"I'm sorry if I messed up," said Palmer.

Fuss took her hand with a gentleness that surprised Devine. She said, "You did nothing wrong, hon. You did what your granddad wanted."

They left Palmer there and walked out. On the pavement Harper studied his muddy shoes before looking up at Devine. "So what now?"

"I don't know," Devine said frankly. "I need to think some things through."

Devine got into the truck and drove off. He popped in a tape and started listening to CCR. He eyed the sky where the sun was long gone and the darkness was coming for them all. He sang along with the lyrics on the tape: *"Well, don't go 'round tonight / It's bound to take your life / There's a bad moon on the rise."*

He pressed the gas and went faster.

His phone buzzed.

"Agent Devine, it's Fred Bing. I wanted to let you know that I heard back from my father. A lot quicker than I had imagined."

"What did he say?"

"That he hasn't seen or spoken to my uncle in over two weeks."

"Is it unusual for your father not to have heard from him?"

"They're not close, but they do live near each other. And they were scheduled to play golf together the other day, but my uncle sent a text saying he couldn't make it."

"Does your father know how long his brother has been away?"

"I don't think he has a firm date, other than the two weeks not having heard from him until he sent the text about golf."

"How old a man is Benjamin Bing?"

"He's the youngest brother. By a lot. So, sixty maybe? My father is seventy-two but he's the oldest, and there was a wide gap between kids."

"Describe your uncle physically."

"Big man. As tall as me but a lot broader. Strong as a horse. They used to joke in my family that he could be all six pallbearers in one."

"You got a recent picture of him?"

"It was taken a few years ago. I can text it to you."

"Thanks."

"I understand there was some misunderstanding about Earl Palmer's cremation?"

"Yeah, you could say that."

"Well, I was surprised, too, if you want the truth," said Bing.

"What do you mean?"

"I usually call the family and arrange things. And then I do the cremation."

"But not with Earl?"

"No."

"Why?" asked Devine.

"My sister wanted to handle it."

"Do you know why?"

"No, I mean, I didn't ask her. I was just happy to get it off my plate. We have four funerals coming up. I'm barely keeping my head above water."

Devine wasn't really listening. "Remember to send me the pic of your uncle. Thanks."

He clicked off and kept driving, his mind littered with possibilities.

He called Alex. She answered on the second ring.

"You hungry?" he said.

"Actually, very. And I don't feel like cooking."

"I'll pick you up in ten minutes if that works."

"It does."

Along the way his phone dinged and he opened it, his eyes going back and forth from the road to the phone screen.

Benjamin Bing had memorable features: strong chin and jaw, thick, graying hair, what Devine referred to as buzzard eyes—the sort that immediately made you uncomfortable—and slender lips just beneath a nose as sharp as a Ka-Bar blade.

Damn if he doesn't look like a soldier.

Alex was waiting for him in front of the house. The wind slightly lifted the hem of her knee-length skirt. Long boots covered her calves. Her parka looked warm and comfortable.

She slid into the truck and said, "How are you doing?"

"I was about to ask you that."

"I got a lot of work done today, so that's good."

"And everything else?" he said.

She eyed him pensively. "I had no thoughts of jumping off the top of the house, if that's what you mean."

"I didn't mean that . . . necessarily."

"Do you know why I went up there?"

"Tell me."

"It's the place where I can see the farthest. I don't mean out on the ocean. I mean in my head."

"But you were very close to the edge. I was afraid . . . that you might . . ."

"I can't say that the thought has never entered my mind. But after what happened to Jenny . . ." She frowned, shook her head, and adopted a look of intense focus. "It was exactly like you said. If I did something like that, it would be as though what Jenny did was worthless. She sacrificed her life to find out the truth about what happened to me. I . . . could never do that to her. To her memory. I just couldn't."

She faced away from him but he could see, in her reflection in the window, the tears sliding down the woman's face.

"You know, you're pretty much the most honest person I've ever met," said Devine. "And . . . I find I can't be anything other than frank with you, even when I don't want to be."

"Is that a good thing?" she asked, now looking at him.

"I think it is, yes. If a little unnerving."

They drove on.

63

She directed him to a little hole-in-the-wall Greek restaurant that was as far removed from the organic bulk of Only Real Food as it was possible to be. The interior was comprised of four tables and one waitress. She greeted Alex with a warm smile and a lingering hug and cast Devine an intrigued glance.

"Travis Devine, this is Chloe Samaras," said Alex.

The three other tables were occupied, and Samaras directed them to the fourth and most private table, well away from the others and along the back wall. She deposited the menus in front of them, took their drink orders—Mythos beer for Devine and a glass of Prosecco for Alex—and left.

"I didn't think you came into town much," he said.

"When I do, I usually come here to eat."

"Why's that?"

"Chloe and I went to high school together. She's really nice. Her uncle Tony is the chef. He taught me how to cook some really cool Greek dishes."

Their drinks came. After Alex took a sip of her Prosecco she said, "So why dinner? Do you have more questions?"

"Yes, but I also wanted to see you. Make sure you were okay."

She fingered the stem of her glass and sank back in her chair. It started to rain, the drops pattering against the restaurant's plate glass window.

"When I was little my dad and I would go up to the widow's walk and watch the storms roll in and out. Not if it was lightning, of course. And we would talk about stuff. It was really nice. Like when I would sit in his office and watch him write while I drew things in my sketchpad."

"Did you ever draw him?"

She smiled. "All the time, with varying degrees of success."

"Ever think you finally captured the true essence of the man?"

Alex's smile faded. "No," she said. "Your questions?"

"Why don't we eat first? Might go better."

Devine ordered kotosoupa and pastitsada with beef, while Alex had gigantes beans to start and grilled vegetables with warm pita for her dinner.

Devine took one spoonful of his soup and looked at her. "Wow."

"I know, right?"

The main meals were just as savory.

"Okay," said Devine. "I'm definitely coming back here. Thanks for the introduction to Putnam's finest Greek food."

"You're welcome. Now, your questions?"

He set his knife and fork down, took the last sip of

his beer, and said, "You ever have any interactions with Benjamin Bing?"

Her eyes narrowed. "What a strange question. Why do you ask?"

"He was the police chief back when you were attacked. I was just wondering what you thought of him, how he handled things."

"I don't remember dealing with him directly. Chief Harper was a sergeant then, I believe, and they had other officers, too, but my family mostly dealt with Harper."

"How about before you were attacked? Anything with Bing?"

"I'd see him in the little Christmas parade we have every year. My father knew him quite well. It was a political friendship, I gathered. I do recall that one of the boys I went to high school with stole a car for a joyride and wrecked it while Bing was chasing him. The story was Bing pulled the boy out of the car and . . ."

"And what?" prompted Devine.

"Well, beat him up."

"How did his parents take that?"

"They sided with the chief. They thought Tim deserved to be taught a lesson. It was so unfair. He only stole that car to take a girl for a ride. And if Bing hadn't been chasing him, none of that would have happened."

"How do you know *Tim* wanted to take a girl for a ride?"

Alex blushed and rubbed the condensation off her glass. "We were sort of seeing each other then. Nothing serious. We were only fifteen. Well, he was sixteen. I was always the youngest in the class."

"Because of your late birthday and the fact that you skipped a grade." She looked at him in surprise. "Your mother told me, with a lot of pride in her voice. She said something like 'not even Jenny managed to do that.'"

Alex looked down and didn't comment.

"Did Bing know you and Tim were . . . dating?"

"It's a small town, Travis. Everyone knows your business. But why is this important?"

"Benjamin Bing hasn't been seen in Florida in about two weeks."

"So?" she said.

"So that means he could be up here."

"Why would he be in Maine as opposed to Florida? In the winter?"

"He could have been up here when Jenny was killed, when I was shot at, and when Earl was killed."

"Wait, you think Bing did those things?"

"It's possible."

"But what would be his motive? Why would he want to kill Jenny?"

"Jenny was up here on unfinished business."

"But that was about what happened to me, so . . ." She paused, her eyes becoming rigid, her gaze fixed.

For one awful moment Devine thought she was going to have another episode. *And part of me hopes she does and names Benjamin Bing as her rapist.*

"You actually think Benjamin Bing attacked me?" said Alex incredulously.

Devine looked around at the other patrons and said, "Let's keep it between us, okay? No need to let others in on this."

"I'm . . . I'm sorry. I just can't comprehend what you're saying."

"Look, it wouldn't be the first time a cop went bad. And he chases down and beats up your boyfriend? What are the odds? And then your rape kit goes missing? He would have had unfettered access to that. And then the Palmers? What if they saw him fleeing a minute before they found you?"

"There's no proof of that."

"Actually, there is. Or at least the Palmers seeing someone that night." He went on to explain to Alex about Jenny having pulled the satellite footage showing the car, and Steve and Valerie Palmer crossing paths with another car right around the time of the attack on her.

"But then why didn't they report it?" she said, looking distraught.

"They were having money problems. Maybe they were putting the squeeze on him. Frederic Bing Sr. was an early disciple of Warren Buffett. They could afford to pay so their good name would not be dragged through the mud. And Benjamin was the police chief. The Palmers might have been afraid to go up against him. And they had no real proof. But then Jenny comes up here looking for the truth and he gets wind of it? He has to nip that in the bud."

"That sounds very far-fetched. And what about Earl? You said someone killed him. What possible reason would Benjamin Bing have to kill Earl?"

"Because he got Earl to pretend to find your sister's body, and was probably afraid he would have a change of heart."

She looked gobsmacked. "How would he get Earl to lie about finding Jenny's body?"

"That one I haven't figured out yet," Devine conceded. "But you remember nothing else with Bing? Nothing that would show he might have been infatuated with you?"

"No, that's gross. He's my father's age."

"He was only forty-five when you were attacked."

"I wasn't even sixteen!" she said heatedly, drawing stares from some of the customers.

"I don't want to believe he was interested in you that way." He gripped her hand. "But if he was, Alex, it was his issue, not yours."

"But *I'm* the one suffering."

"Yes, you are," said Devine. "But I will help you in any way I can, to get through this."

64

He drove her back to Jocelyn Point. They went out to the art studio where Alex had told him she needed to work on a painting for a client that was due to be shipped out soon. He watched her work away as the night fell more deeply around them. Her movements were fluid, her concentration complete. Devine had seen that level of intensity before.

Me, in combat.

"What's that look for?"

He came out of his musings to find her staring at him as she cleaned off a brush.

"Admiration for your obvious skills," he said.

"You're such a sweet talker," she cracked.

"It's sincere, Alex."

She put down the brush and wiped off her hands. "I know, Travis. My bullshit meter is pretty sophisticated and it hasn't made a peep while you're around."

"But, like all women, you have so much more practice at it than men."

"You really are far more evolved than many of your brethren," she said, smiling.

"I try to see people for who they really are."

She drew a step closer. "And who am I, really?"

He could tell, despite the flippant and flirty content and tone of their conversation, Alex was now quite serious. "I see a young woman maybe at a crossroads."

Her features tensed. "Go on."

"There's a military term for being in the wrong place at the wrong time, though it's now used throughout popular culture: *No Man's Land*. But if you dig deeper, it gets more complicated."

"How so?" she said quickly.

"Typically, to get to No Man's Land, you had to take action. You had to move from where you were. So now you're in a bad place, a place where you don't think you should be and maybe your own survival is at stake."

Here Devine paused and contemplated stopping. He wasn't sure why he had chosen to bring up this topic, and now that he was here, he, ironically, felt like *he* was in No Man's Land. Yet the look on Alex's face told him there was only one path to take with this conversation.

"So, you have three choices: stay where you are, go back, or go forward."

"And how do you know which is the right one?" she said, a tremble in her voice.

"I wish I could tell you that there's a foolproof way to figure that out, but there's not. Sometimes it's trial and error."

She slumped and looked beaten.

"But sometimes there is a sign to tell you which way to go."

"What?" she said eagerly.

He leaned against a table and said, "When I was pulling a tour of combat duty in Iraq I would rotate through this same large village, looking for enemy combatants, informants, people who just needed help or wanted to escape certain situations. I'd go there regularly and felt like I'd gotten to know some of the villagers pretty well. Established a rapport, to the extent you can during a war. One of my jobs was to memorize every detail I could during each visit so that on future trips I could see if anything looked off. It was critical because my life and my colleagues' lives depended on it."

"I can understand that," she said in a tone that was equal parts hollow and anticipatory.

"It was sort of what you helped me do at Bertie's art studio. I never would have seen that pulley without your help, but you had been there many times before and noticed it right off. Anyway, one morning we reached the village. I did my scope of the village as we were walking through it, looking for anything that looked out of the ordinary."

"Did you see anything?"

"No, *I* didn't. But PFC Laura Diaz did."

"What did she see?"

"A female villager came out of one of the huts. She seemed fine. Calm, ordinary. She walked toward us. We had seen her before, many times. But as she grew closer,

Diaz called out, 'Bomb.' We instinctively all scattered and took cover. A second later the bomb that was secreted on the woman detonated. If Diaz hadn't warned us, we'd all be dead."

"What did she see that made her believe the woman had a bomb?"

"I asked her that very thing. Diaz told me her mother worked at a hair salon back in a small town in Texas. As a child Diaz would often go to work with her mother. Her mom did hair, makeup, nails, the whole shebang. Her mother told Diaz that women wanted to look their best in important moments. Weddings, parties, funerals. At critical times, they wanted to get their hair, makeup, and nails done. So Diaz noticed that the villager was not wearing her dusty burqa or usual hijab. She had on a beautiful robe with intricate embroidery. Her hair had been immaculately braided and done up in a fancy style. And her nails had been filed, shaped, and painted when they never had before. The woman was sacrificing her life for her cause and she wanted to look her best. That observation by Diaz saved my life and those of a lot of others because I never would have seen it.

"Now, you're probably wondering what the hell that has to do with your situation, but here it is, for what it's worth. I've sort of been Laura Diaz up here, observing you and others. Seeing things that maybe people in Putnam are too close to everything to see clearly. Your mother and others think you can be world-famous or rich or both, somewhere else. And you probably could. But I don't think those things are important to you."

"So you're saying I should stay here, in Putnam?"

"No, I'm not. I'm actually saying that you have gifts that you need to share with the *world*. Something terrible happened to you here, Alex. Most people would want to get as far away from that as they could. Now, you didn't. But I think you didn't because you were too traumatized to embrace any *part* of the world. You became fearful of going out, of being around other people." He looked out the window in the direction of the main house. "You go out but then you run back here, where you feel reasonably safe. But the thing is, your fear is no longer out there." He tapped his head. "It's in here. So you can't outrun it. You can't really hide from it, not even here."

"Then what do I do?" she said pleadingly. "How do I get out of No Man's Land?"

"You master it. You take back control of your life. *You* dictate the terms of how you will live and where you will live, not anyone else. And certainly not the person who hurt you."

"But what if he's still out there?"

"I'm sure he *is* still out there," Devine said. "It's my job to stop him. And I'm really good at my job, Alex."

He put his arms around her and held her tightly.

"Do you really think I can . . . master this?"

"I would not have suggested it if I didn't believe you could. You're a lot stronger than you think you are."

"I'm not as strong as Jenny was," she replied.

He moved her to arm's length so he could stare into her eyes. "You don't need to compare yourself to Jenny, not ever again. She loved you. She came up here to help you, to end this misery you were trapped in. And it cost your sister her life. The best way to honor that sacrifice is to cast off the devil that's in you right now and move on with your life. It's what Jenny would have wanted. And it's what *you* should want, which is what really matters."

Alex, who had begun quietly sobbing, stopped, and her expression firmed. She looked up at him. "I do want that. And I want something else, Travis."

She kissed him.

And Devine, hesitant at first, kissed her back.

The two were so focused on one another that they never saw the person who had been watching them move slowly away from the window.

65

Hours later Devine let himself out the front door of Jocelyn Point and made sure it securely locked behind him. A light drizzle had started, which the wind kicked around him as he walked to the truck.

He looked for Dak's motorcycle but didn't see it. He hadn't heard anyone come into the house when he'd been up in Alex's bedroom.

He sat in the truck and stared out the windshield at the house. His first night here he had seen Alex standing naked in her bedroom window. He had seen it as an act of defiance, or at least her feeling of sanctity in her old family home.

He had just seen her naked again, in the most intimate situation two people could experience.

Being with Alex at that moment in time had been the right thing to do, the thing he had *wanted* to do. They had taken it slow, with physical and emotional revelations by degrees, rather than all of a sudden. Their lovemaking had been assured but controlled. It was as though they somehow already knew the contours and rhythms of each other's bodies and desires, the instinctual sensations that had delivered them to an ending point that had persisted long beyond the sexual climaxes. They had lain in each other's arms talking quietly between kisses and caresses, for far longer than their physical lovemaking had endured.

Devine hadn't known the woman a full week, and yet he felt like he understood her better than he did his own brother and sister. Quantity of time together meant nothing if the desire wasn't there to learn and relate to someone, the need to *understand* them. It had been there between him and Alex like nothing he'd really experienced before.

As he fired up the truck his phone buzzed. It wasn't a call.

His surveillance monitor on the outbuilding had just gone off.

Someone was there.

He drove toward the outbuildings and then parked behind a stand of evergreen bushes, making sure his truck was out of sight. He was going to make the rest of the way to the building on foot. The noise of the waves crashing against the burly Maine substrata followed him with each footfall.

He kept his exposure over open ground to a minimum, just like the Army had trained him. And then he'd gotten a PhD in that same subject out in the field of combat, where mistakes didn't mean a failing grade but rather a burial plot and white grave marker at Arlington National.

He surveyed all compass points in front of him. It didn't take long to reach the vicinity of the building.

Devine took up position behind a bulky overgrown hedge. Peering around it he observed a Toyota pickup parked in front of the building, its lights and motor on. The door to the building was open and a light was on inside. This gave Devine a clear sight line into the space, which he enhanced using his optics.

A man was standing just inside the doorway with his back to Devine. Over his shoulder Devine could see large green plastic tubs set on tables, and he heard once more the hum of machinery, this time more distinctly with the door open.

He crouched down when he heard another vehicle approaching. He recognized the throaty purr of the Harley before he saw it. Dak pulled up next to the truck, and climbed off his bike after shutting it down.

Devine turned on the video recording feature on his phone and started filming.

Dak said, "Hey, Hal."

The man turned around, and Devine could see he was in his thirties with a trim beard and glasses. He had on jean overalls and a ski cap pulled down over his ears. Their comingled breaths rose above them in the frigid air.

"I thought you'd be here ahead of me," said Hal.

"I got tied up."

"Really? What gal did the tying?"

They both laughed at this comment, and Dak slapped the man on the shoulder.

"How's it looking in there?" Dak said, inclining his head toward the tubs.

"All systems go. I swear these critters could survive an atom bomb falling on them."

"Let's hope one doesn't hit, don't think *we* could survive it," said Dak with a chuckle.

"How long you reckon?" asked Hal.

"Two days they'll be here. But we got the shipment to pick up tonight. And the more they grow, the more they weigh. And . . ." Dak rubbed his thumb and forefinger together.

They locked up the building, climbed into the pickup, and set off.

Devine ran back to his truck and followed.

66

As soon as they were on the main road, Devine knew where they were going. The same spot along the shore. He was driving with his lights off, which wasn't a problem even with the poor visibility. He just followed the taillights ahead of him to see the contours of the road.

The truck pulled off and Devine did the same, albeit a couple of hundred yards short and behind a stand of trees growing near the road.

He flitted along until he reached a good surveillance point in time to watch through his optics as Hal carried large plastic containers toward the water. Dak was hefting some other apparatus that Devine could not really make out.

Devine headed forward and then cut toward the beach. He looked out to the water and, though it was foggy and gloomy, he could see a solitary boat's running lights slicing through the darkness out on the Gulf of Maine.

Devine crouched along a ledge of rocky shore, took out his optics, and surveyed the field in front of him. Once more, a smaller boat was lowered from the larger boat. It then traveled swiftly toward shore, breached the breakers, and came to a stop bow up in the sand. He could now see that the vessel was actually an RIB, or rigid inflatable boat, much like the kind he had used in the Army. There were two men on board. They jumped off the bow onto the sand, and greeted Dak and Hal with handshakes and backslaps. Then the four of them proceeded to unload the cargo; it was placed in the containers Hal had brought to the beach. Dak bent down and inserted the devices he had brought with him into each container.

Dak handed one of the men an envelope, and they parted ways. Dak and Hal hefted the first container. It must have been heavy, since both men struggled with the weight of it. They reached the truck, loaded it in the back, and then went back twice more to get the other containers. They drove off as the RIB was swiftly making its way back to the larger boat.

Devine had already gotten into his vehicle and was waiting. As they passed him Devine pulled out behind them. They drove straight back to Jocelyn Point, and to the same outbuilding.

They carried the containers into the building and had set down the last one when Devine appeared in the doorway.

"Hey, guys, nice gloomy night for some smuggling."

Both men whirled around and Hal's hand went to a pocket on his coat but then he was staring down the barrel of Devine's Glock. He let his hand drop to his side.

Dak barked, "You're trespassing, Devine. You have no business or right to be here."

"I saw a suspicious act take place in a public area, and the fruits of that act are right behind you in those containers."

"There's nothing illegal with what we're doing," exclaimed Dak.

"As though all legal business is done in the middle of the night on deserted beaches and involving boats coming into shore with a payoff for whatever's in those containers?" He pointed at one with his Glock's muzzle. "What is it? Drugs?"

"We're not drug dealers, for God's sake," blurted out a surprised Hal.

"What, then?"

Dak looked at Hal and then back at Devine. "It's unagi."

"Come again?"

"Unagi. It's made from elvers."

Devine cocked his head. "Elvers? Sounds like something from *The Hobbit*."

"We're buying and selling glass eels," said Hal. He pointed behind him at dozens of large tubs set up on low tables. Devine could now see that they were all hooked up to aeration equipment. He assumed that was what Dak had been carrying on the beach.

"Is it illegal?" asked Devine.

"Not if you have a license," said Dak.

"And do you?" asked Devine.

"Um, yeah. I do," said Dak nervously.

"Bullshit. Then why the middle-of-the-night shipment? Why hide your operation here?"

"Do I need a lawyer?" said Dak.

"I didn't come up here to bust illegal 'elvers.' I came up here to find out who killed your sister. So, did Jenny know about all this?" said Devine, pointing his gun around the room.

"I don't think so."

"You don't *think* so?" Devine shook his head. Had he been focusing on completely the wrong thing this whole time? He looked at Dak. "Tell me how this all operates. You tell me the truth and I'm not going to come down on you like a ton of bricks. But you lie to me, you're done and your ass is going to jail. And his, too," said Devine, indicating Hal, who seemed to be attempting to shrink into the floorboards.

Dak started talking fast. "Elvers are a huge market. The Japanese eat tons of eels. But overfishing depleted the Japanese populations. And there was an earthquake there about a decade or so ago that wiped out most of their aquaculture operations. So they turned elsewhere."

"To Europe and America," chimed in Hal, who now also seemed eager to explain things to Devine. "But the European elver population nosedived, and the eel was listed as an endangered species and exports from the EU were banned. So that left us and a few other countries in the Caribbean as the primary sources. And the prices skyrocketed. And that made for a big black market. Then that all came crashing down because the feds and the states stepped in. Most states banned the fishing. Here in Maine they started issuing licenses and imposing quotas and arresting and fining people."

"Eels don't breed in captivity," explained Dak. "So all farm-raised eels have to be first caught in the wild. And there are lots of them in Maine." He pointed behind him. "It takes up to two years to grow an eel to harvestable size. That's normally done in an eel fishery."

"How'd you two hook up?"

"Hal and I were in the Army together. He moved up here from South Carolina and told me about the eels. I researched it and we put a business plan together."

"Where was the boat tonight coming in from?"

"New Brunswick," said Dak. "Canada also has a lot of elvers."

"So are you running an eel *fishery*?"

"We don't have a license for that. And who wants to wait two years to get your money?"

"So how *do* you make your money?" asked Devine.

Dak looked at Hal. "Look, I think we need a lawyer. We've said too much already."

"What if this is connected to Jenny's murder?" pointed out Devine.

"It's not."

"She was a fed. She came up here for some reason. She was murdered. Are there bad people involved in this eel business? Is it enough money to kill over?"

Dak looked once more at Hal and closed his eyes for a moment before saying, "The price for elvers really sank during COVID, but now it's back up to around $2,300 a pound. What you see in all those tubs are worth about $250,000."

Devine stared in disbelief at the tubs. "You're shitting me."

"Nope. And you can make a lot more money off elvers than you ever can off lobster. And you don't need a boat and all that other equipment. If you have a license you set big fyke or dip nets in a stream and you wake up in the middle of the night and go down there with five-gallon buckets and load up your catch, and then go buy a house or a fishing boat. It's like Maine's version of the California Gold Rush."

"Okay. Who buys them from *you*?" asked Devine.

"Guys who come into town on a regular basis."

"What kind of guys?" asked Devine.

"Mostly Asian," said Hal. "Well, they're all Asian, really."

"How do they pay?"

"Cash. Bank wires and checks don't really work in our business."

"A quarter million in cash? What, do they bring it in suitcases?"

"Yeah, they actually do," admitted Hal. "And they put the elvers in other suitcases. They typically put a legal export fish in refrigerated bags over them, like mussels. So long as they have an oxygen supply elvers are fine. They breathe through their skin."

Devine walked over and looked in one of the tubs. He recoiled at the sight of what looked like hundreds of strands of bright white and yellow spaghetti—albeit with pairs of inky black eyes—flitting spasmodically through the water in massive hordes.

"So it is illegal the way you're doing it?"

"Well, it's not exactly legal, no," said Dak.

"Why not just set up a licensed eel fishery? Or get a fishing license?"

"The fishing licenses are given out in a lottery and capped at around four hundred or so. Believe me, there are a lot more folks than that who want to do this."

"And it ain't fair," interjected Hal. "They say it's a lottery, but I say with that much money at stake some palms are getting greased, for damn sure."

Dak said, "And as an elver farmer, it takes years to make your money back. And you have to have the capital to build a facility and buy the equipment and then you need to hire a bunch of people. And there's a limit on how many pounds you can legally process each year. We can make far more money faster this way."

"So *this* is how you get your capital to invest," Devine said to Dak. "Not partners in Boston."

"Yeah," conceded Dak. "But I'm using that money to invest in local businesses that employ lots of people, and are bringing some pride and dignity back to Putnam," he added in a defiant tone.

"Don't go all altruistic on me. You're doing it to get rich."

"Well, that too," admitted Dak.

"You got Coop Phillips and two other knuckleheads

to come after me the night we first met in the bar, didn't you?"

"I—"

"You believed I was really up here investigating you, right?"

"The thought had crossed my mind," replied Dak.

"So this elver stuff is a big business?"

"Globally, it's billions of dollars a year," said Hal in a reverential tone. "And I've been to China and Japan. Once the elvers get there, man, they are dumped into this supply chain that is full of corrupt assholes, smugglers, killers. Chinese mafia has their fingers all over unagi."

"And maybe some of them came over here because your sister was getting ready to expose them, and so they killed her?" said Devine.

Dak shook his head. "No way. I can't believe that's what happened."

"Did she ever say anything that made you suspect she knew you were involved in this?"

"Never, not once. I swear."

"Okay, so you get your supply from Canada? Why not here?"

Hal replied, "We also deal with people here, but Maine has gotten pretty good about ferreting out folks like us. And Nova Scotia is right across the Gulf and New Brunswick is just a little bit north."

"Lock this place up," ordered Devine.

Dak said, "Please, Devine, do not shut us down. I've got big plans for Putnam."

"I could give a shit about that. And you said you were going to make millions off selling this property."

"Hopefully, yeah, but that could take a year or two to complete."

"Again, I don't care. Now lock it up."

Dak was about to respond, but he didn't. Or rather couldn't.

The bullet zoomed through the open doorway and hit Dak in the arm. He slumped to the floor bleeding, and screaming in pain.

Devine already had his Glock out and fired multiple rounds in the direction of where the shot had come before taking cover behind the wall.

Then, silence. Until he heard a vehicle start up. Devine was about to run to his truck and take up pursuit when Dak screamed, "Hal!"

Devine looked over to see Hal on the floor, blood pouring from his chest. He knelt beside the stricken man.

Only one shot had been fired, so it must have ricocheted off Dak and hit Hal, concluded Devine. He didn't have time to even locate the wound before Hal gave a long rattling breath that Devine had heard before on fields of combat.

"Is Hal . . . is he going to be okay?" said a sobbing Dak, holding his bloodied arm, and crawling over to them. "Is he breathing?"

"No, he's not," said Devine curtly. "He's dead."

67

"It's been raining so much any trace from the vehicle is gone," said Sergeant Fuss. She and Devine were standing in front of the outbuilding where Hal had been killed and Dak wounded. Dak had been taken to a trauma hospital in Bangor. Hal's body had been transported to Augusta via helicopter for a high-priority postmortem. Guillaume had accompanied the flight.

Dawn was breaking, and Devine was so tired he felt he was back in Ranger School.

"Did you find a casing?" asked Devine.

"Yep."

"NATO or polymer?"

"The latter. Looks to be the same shooter as with Jenny."

"But NATO was the one that almost killed me," said Devine, really to himself.

Fuss eyed the outbuilding. "So, elvers, huh?"

"Apparently so."

"Always wondered where he got his money."

"To his mind he's reinvesting it in the town, and I guess he is."

"So what are you going to do about it?"

Devine said, "Nothing. It's not my jurisdiction. So what are *you* going to do about it?"

"I'll have to confer with the chief."

"I expect you would."

"But if we do nothing . . . ?"

"No skin off my teeth. Unless what Dak was doing is connected to his sister's murder."

"You think?"

"I don't know one way or another. I certainly have no proof."

"Okay, we'll let you know what we find."

"I'm heading over to Jocelyn Point to make sure Alex is okay. I already filled her in on what happened, but I wanted to give her an update."

"Right."

Alex answered at his first knock. She must have been watching from the front window.

"Thank God," she whispered, weeping quietly into his shoulder after he gave her a positive update on her brother. "I . . . I can't lose Dak, too."

She led Devine to the kitchen and made him coffee. "You must be exhausted," she said, watching him closely.

"I'll catch some sleep later."

"When can I see Dak?"

"He's having his surgery now. We can drive up after he's out of recovery. Bullet went in and out. If it had hit an artery he wouldn't have made it."

She paled at this stark description and he said, "I'm sorry. I shouldn't have been so blunt. I guess I just got used to doing that in the Army."

"No, I'm fine. Thank you for telling me."

"So, did you know Dak's friend, Hal?" he asked her. "I didn't get his last name."

"Hal Brockman. I knew he worked with Dak, but I didn't know how or with what. He's come by quite a few times. He seemed very nice. He was from the south, I think." She rubbed her eyes. "Who could've done this, Travis?"

Devine didn't provide an answer because he had none.

He left there with a promise to pick her up at eleven and drive her to Bangor.

Halfway down the road his phone buzzed. It was Françoise Guillaume. She sounded exhausted. She told him the post on Hal Brockman had just been completed.

"It was a .300 Norma Magnum round," she confirmed. "Pretty much intact despite it having careened through one body and entered another."

"Fuss already found the polymer casing, so I was pretty sure it would be the Norma. So maybe one shooter for Jenny *and* the shot taken at Dak?"

Guillaume said, "Out of my professional jurisdiction, but personally I would agree with that assessment."

But I had the NATO round fired at me. So was it connected to the people who kidnapped me? And then chased me the other night? That seems logical.

"Anything else?" he asked.

"Um, could you come to dinner at my house tonight? I . . . I sense things have gotten off the rails between us, and I'd like to talk to you. And . . . I might be able to share some things with you. Insights."

"Okay, sure."

She told him a time and he clicked off.

I wonder if you know where your uncle is? Maybe around a certain elver-smuggling operation early this morning shooting a .300 Norma Magnum round into two people?

He didn't have time to think about that right now. He had another mission to complete before driving Alex to Bangor.

He had to find a secret in Earl Palmer's past bad enough to blackmail the man.

68

"You want to look through my grandfather's things?" asked Annie Palmer.

Devine was sitting at the counter in Maine Brew, and she was standing across from him restocking the refrigerated cabinets.

"Yeah."

"Why?"

"To see if I can find a reason for what happened."

"He was depressed, Travis. Depressed people sometimes kill themselves."

"Granted. But I'm not sure he took his own life."

"You mentioned that before, when we were up on the roof at Jocelyn Point with Alex, but you never bothered to explain to me *why* you thought that," she said. Her face twisted in anger. "Even though you *told* me you would. And we both saw him fucking hanging there."

"Okay, it's time for me to lay out my theory for you. Better yet, I'll *show* you." Devine stood, walked over to one of the tables, grabbed a chair, and brought it back behind the counter.

"What are you doing?" she said, staring at the chair.

The place was still relatively empty at this hour, although the cook in back and two waitresses were readying the place for the morning crowd that would be arriving soon.

"Proving a point," he replied.

He climbed onto the chair and then stood on his tippy-toes while she stared goggle-eyed at him. He reached up and gripped a metal pipe that was attached to the ceiling.

"What the hell are you doing?" exclaimed Palmer.

Next, Devine tried to kick the chair away while still standing on it. To do so he had to partially lift himself off it and kick at the chair back and seat. He made several spirited attempts, flailing some, before finally managing it on his fourth try.

He dropped to the floor, a little out of breath with the exertion, and righted the chair.

"Now, I'm thirty-two, a former Army Ranger, I work out all the time."

She stared at the chair and then back at him.

He continued, "Now what if I had a fused spine, bad knees, a pair of wrecked hips, oh, and I'm about fifty years older. And one more thing: I didn't have a noose around my neck choking me to death at the time. And the noose that was used? *I'd* have a hard time fashioning it and I don't have arthritis in my fingers."

Palmer stared at Devine for a few moments before she plopped into the chair and drew a long breath. Tears shimmered in her eyes. "Shit. Someone killed him."

"I believe they did, yes."

She stood, marched over to the counter, opened a drawer, pulled out a set of keys, and tossed them to Devine.

"These are to my grandfather's place. Find the son of a bitch who did this," she said.

"I plan to," replied Devine.

69

Does it ever stop raining in this damn town? thought Devine as he ran from the truck to the front door of Earl Palmer's cottage. He'd done deployments in tropical climates where it was drier.

He unlocked the door and went inside. Devine was about to undertake a methodical search that would require several hours. What he was looking at were the remains of a life, of a family that had once lived here, cried here, and died here.

The place was neat, on the surface, but when Devine opened drawers, he found the clutter of decades that oftentimes folks just gave up on. And rather than tossing it all, they stuck it away in places that could not be seen. And as the years piled on so did the detritus.

Out of sight, out of mind.

The closet in the main floor bedroom still held Alberta Palmer's clothes and shoes, and a large assortment of women's hats. The latter were well used, billowy, some touched by the sweat and grime that came with hard work—but Earl, he was sure, would never have gotten rid of any of these things. He could imagine him opening this door every day to see the material reminders of the woman he loved.

There were lotions and a glass bottle of perfume on the bathroom sink. Two toothbrushes were still hanging from the holder built onto the wall.

In a drawer in the small den he found piles of notes that Alberta had written to her husband; most also had drawings of some kind that clearly showed the skill and talent of the artist who had created them. She had signed all of them with "Love, Your Bertie."

Devine sat down in the only chair in the room and found his eyes watering as he read one note after another. "Have a good lobster day." "Don't forget, sunscreen. This ain't the seventies anymore!" He lingered the longest over a drawing of what was clearly Earl and his missus walking hand in hand down the rocky shore. The accompanying note read simply: "Happy Retirement to Us, My Love."

He carefully folded the notes and replaced them in the drawer.

As he looked out the window the rain picked up, and there was even a slash of lightning and an accompanying crack of thunder to go along with it.

He went back into the front room and looked over a shelf of tattered VHS tapes and DVDs. Some were commercial movies but others looked to be of family and other personal events. He looked at the labels on the cases: birthday parties, weddings, anniversaries. Then his gaze held on one. The label read: WILBUR KINGMAN'S FUNERAL.

He pulled out the DVD case and looked around. Under the TV was a DVD player. He popped the disc in and turned on the TV. He sat back in a chair and started the DVD.

The scene opened in what looked to be a church. The coffin was brought in and set up near the altar. The place was packed, and Devine paused the movie so he could see who was there.

In the front row was Patricia Kingman surrounded by what was probably her family. Her black dress hung off her, as though the woman had suddenly shed weight after losing her husband.

He saw a years-younger Fred Bing up near the coffin directing the black-clad funeral home crew. Then he saw two older, tall men standing together off to the side. They looked so much like Bing that he reckoned they were his father and uncle, who had inherited the business from *their* father, before passing it on to Fred and Françoise.

And there was Françoise Guillaume near the door greeting people as they entered.

In another row were Dak, Jenny, and Alex Silkwell. This was the first time Devine had seen Jenny other than in a still picture or as a corpse on a table. She was sitting between her brother and sister and seemed to be consoling Dak, while Alex stared straight ahead with the look of a woman who wasn't really sure where she was. Clare Robards and Senator Silkwell sat next to their adult children.

Harper was in the back row, dressed in a sergeant's uniform. Devine didn't see Wendy Fuss anywhere.

There was a whole group of burly, tough-looking men in ill-fitting or ancient suits. He figured they were Kingman's fellow lobstermen, there to pay their respects to one of their own who had fallen. Their eyes were red, their faces puffy, and, to a man, they looked stricken.

A fresh-faced Annie Palmer sat next to her grandparents. She must have still been in college, Devine thought. Alberta was holding Earl's hand and looking anxiously at him. Devine could imagine the words of support she was probably saying to him. Earl's face was bandaged, and his neck was in a support brace, as was his left knee. His right arm was in a cast. A cane leaned against his chair. He sat very stiffly, and Devine knew the man would soon undergo unsuccessful surgeries to try and repair the damage.

On the other side of Earl was a tall man in a police chief's uniform. He had a face as granitelike as the bluffs that formed the extreme edge of the town's shoreline. His physique was impressive, his chest and shoulders filling out his uniform. Devine knew from the photo he'd seen at the police station, and the one that Fred Bing had texted him, that this was Benjamin Bing, the third and youngest son of the founder of Bing and Sons.

As Devine looked closer, he saw something on Bing's chest that was stunning.

Damn, so he was *a soldier?*

Devine let the film run again and he watched as Bing

leaned in next to Earl and started talking in earnest. There was so much background noise on the film that Devine could not make out what the man was saying. However, Earl's reaction was one of surprise, even shock.

Later, as the service ended, Fred Bing directed the pallbearers out with the coffin. The grieving attendees filed out after them. As Benjamin Bing and Earl left, Bing had one arm around the older, injured man as he limped along with his cane. And all the while Bing was talking and each word seemed to be like a body blow to Palmer.

Devine's attention now turned to Alex, who had hung back from the others. She seemed to be staring at the backs of Bing and Palmer. Then she visibly shuddered and put a hand on a pew to steady herself. Jenny hurried up, put an arm around her sister's waist, and helped her out. They were followed by Dak and their parents.

Next, Françoise Guillaume came back into the picture. She looked first in the direction that her uncle had gone with Earl. And then she turned her attention to the Silkwell sisters as they exited the space. Then, alone, Guillaume left, too.

The film ended and Devine popped the DVD out and pocketed it.

Though he hadn't been able to hear anything, what he had seen was telling, very telling.

As was Alex's reaction to being close to Bing.

He had to find the former policeman. And fast.

Before someone else died a violent death.

70

Devine phoned Campbell and told him about the video.

"Benjamin Bing had a Purple Heart pinned to his chest. Presumably, he was in the military at some point and was wounded. I need you to find out all you can about his service record."

"On it," said Campbell before clicking off.

Devine locked up the house and walked back to the truck fingering his West Point graduation ring. The United States Military Academy had been the first school to issue class rings. They were awarded to cadets right after the start of their senior year at the Point. After that ceremony was the "hop," a formal dinner and dance for cadets and their guests during "Ring Weekend." Devine had invited his family, but none of them had shown up. He had hung out with a fellow cadet and his parents and siblings. Not the way he had envisioned this career milestone playing out, but life was always taking swings at you, he had found. And you couldn't always duck in time. But Bing didn't have a ring on. And a man who wore a Purple Heart around certainly would have worn his West Point or other service academy ring.

So he presumably hadn't gone through West Point. But he still might have been an officer since there were other paths of commissioning in the Army.

Devine pulled off the road while the rain poured down, turning the roads a muddy brown from all the runoff. Off the coast the Atlantic thundered against the rocky shore with all it had, and still the Maine coast stood firm against every punch.

He looked down at his ring. It was more than an accessory or a prize to show off. It represented a connection to the Long Gray Line and the cadets' opportunity to join that esteemed group on graduation day. He remembered one of his instructors telling him that while Devine continued to work toward his commissioning as an officer in the world's most powerful military, his past, present, and future were all wrapped up, at least symbolically, by this thin band on his finger. It was an eternal bond to the Corps, to the Long Gray Line, allegiance to Duty, Honor, and Country.

Well, my "eternity" turned out to be a lot shorter than most.

There was an annual ring melt ceremony held at Eisenhower Hall Theatre. Rings from Army officers were donated and placed into a crucible. There were photos and information about the donors. Every donor, or their family, received a handwritten letter from a cadet in appreciation. The rings were then taken to Bartlett Hall Science Center, where they were melted into a gold ingot.

Devine had dreamed about his ring being donated one

day, either as the last full measure given by him on the battlefield, or many decades into the future as he died of old age. Technically, he could still donate it, he supposed. But he no longer thought he had the right to do so. And it wasn't like his family cared one way or another.

Okay, that's enough self-pity for one day.

So Bing was former military. Devine wondered why no one had mentioned that to him. He wasn't sure how it exactly figured into all of this. But someone with military ties could presumably get access to an experimental Norma round easier than most.

He checked his watch and pulled back onto the road. When he drove up to Jocelyn Point, Alex was waiting for him out front with a small bag.

She settled next to him and they headed to Bangor.

"Thanks for driving me," she said.

"No problem. Do you even drive? I've just seen you on your bike."

She looked out the windshield. "I never saw the point," she replied.

He snatched a glance at her at the same moment she looked at him.

She then said, "Last night was wonderful."

"Yes, it was."

"I haven't, that is to say, I . . ."

"I . . . I really wanted to be with you that night. I had to be with you. But, I'm afraid I might have taken advantage. You were in a vulnerable position."

"If anything I took advantage of *you*, Travis. And so

what? We're human beings. Sometimes . . . sometimes, you just can't help yourself."

She turned away and they drove for a bit in silence as they headed inland.

He finally said, "I was watching a video of Wilbur Kingman's funeral."

She turned to him. "A video?"

"It was at Earl's place. I don't know where it came from. You were in it, along with pretty much everyone else in town."

"It was all very sad. Wilbur was a good man."

"Who wrecked his boat on a shoal he should never have hit?"

"What is that supposed to mean?"

"Does anyone really know what happened out there?"

"Of course. Earl told us."

"And now Earl's dead."

"Wilbur's death was years ago. That can't be connected to anything happening now."

"I wish I was as sure of that as you are. Benjamin Bing was in the film. He was seated next to Earl. Bing was talking and Earl was listening, and he didn't seem too happy about what was being said. They went off together. You know anything about that?"

"No, how could I?"

"I thought you might have seen or heard something. You walked out right after they did." He paused to see if she might annotate his statement with what she might have been feeling that day, while in the vicinity of Benjamin Bing.

Like terror.

But she said nothing.

"Bing was in the military," he said.

"Wait, he was?"

"You didn't know that about him?"

"Um . . . maybe, I . . . I don't remember. I just remember him as the police chief."

"You remember nothing else about him?"

"Didn't you ask me that before?" she said, a bite to her words.

"Sometimes you get new information when you keep asking the same question over and over, because people recall more."

"I don't want to talk about *him*. What you said before gave me the creeps."

The rest of the drive went by in silence.

71

The surgery had gone well, they were told, and Dak was awake and alert when they came into his room.

Alex sat next to him and gripped his hand while Devine stood behind her.

"Are you in much pain?" she asked.

"Probably, but the morphine, or whatever it is, is doing the job." He looked at Devine. "I can't believe this happened. I can't believe Hal is dead. Do they know any more? Have they found whoever shot us?"

"No, but it was the same type casing that was discovered near where your sister's body was found."

"Harper told me the bullet that hit me then struck Hal and killed him."

"That's right."

"Shit." Dak shook his head and his eyes glimmered.

"Harper tell you anything else?" asked Devine. He was not in Alex's line of sight so he added raised eyebrows to the question to let Dak know what he was referring to.

"Uh, yeah, he said he'd get back to me on what he decides."

"What are you two talking about?" said Alex.

"Nothing important," said Dak quickly. "How are you doing, Alex? Hanging in okay?"

"Not if stuff like this keeps happening," she said with a glare. It was clear that she did not like being left out of whatever was going on between her brother and Devine.

"How well do you know Benjamin Bing?" asked Devine.

"Benjamin Bing?" said Dak curiously. "What's he got to do with anything?"

"I think he has a great deal to do with everything that's been happening."

Alex turned to scowl at him. "I'm going to get some crappy hospital coffee, which will still be preferable to listening to this."

She rose and left.

"What is going on?" exclaimed Dak.

Devine sat in the chair Alex had vacated and said, "Let me postulate a theory for you."

"Okay," said Dak nervously.

Devine proceeded to tell Dak his ideas about Benjamin Bing being the one who had attacked Alex all those years ago, and then how he believed the Palmers had seen him leaving the area, so they had to die, too.

"The Palmers were in tough financial straits back then, Annie told me. So I think they saw Bing, and after they found Alex they put it all together. They tried to blackmail him. The family is rolling in money. Only Bing doesn't play that game. So their house goes up in flames."

Devine didn't mention that Françoise Guillaume had

performed the autopsies on the Palmers, because he wasn't sure whether she had any culpability. Bing could have poisoned them or otherwise incapacitated them, and Devine now knew that Maine did not do full autopsies on people who died in fires that looked purely accidental. Whether that was the procedure fifteen years ago, though, he didn't know.

"Your sister told your mother that she came up here to take care of some unfinished business." He explained about her use of the satellite footage. "She figured out that it was Bing."

"But he's retired and living in Florida."

"No, I spoke with Fred Bing and asked him to check on that. His father told him that he hadn't seen his brother in at least two weeks."

"How would Bing know that Jenny had fingered him to be the one who attacked Alex?"

"That part I haven't figured out yet. But if he did, it gives the man a motive to kill her. Look, I've Venn-diagrammed this thing from every angle I can think of. I don't believe this had to do with what Jenny did for the government. This stems from what happened to Alex all those years ago. And Benjamin Bing was in the military. He was wearing a Purple Heart on his police uniform in a video I saw. He could probably get access to a still-in-testing .300 Norma round with a polymer casing easier than most." He looked directly at Dak. "Do you remember Bing being around your sister, showing her more attention than he should?"

Dak looked troubled. "Look, Ben Bing thought way too much of himself, okay? He was built like a stud and thought he was the handsomest, coolest guy in town. And yeah, he wore his Purple Heart and some other medals on his cop uniform, although that's against military regs and probably the police regs, not that he cared. He always bragged to the guys about the heroic shit he did in the Army, and how he nearly died in combat, but he was always short on specifics."

"So it *was* the Army and not another service branch?"

"Yeah. But I can't recall him acting inappropriate around Alex. They wouldn't have had much direct contact, actually."

"But you were away in the Army during that time."

"That's true."

"Alex told me that he personally busted her boyfriend for a traffic infraction. Beat the kid up. I don't think that was a coincidence."

"What's Alex's take on all this?"

"She doesn't want to believe it or talk about it. It's why she walked out just now. I was actually hoping that my raising it with her would cause her memory to come back and we would finally have Alex being able to ID her attacker. But it didn't happen."

"You think he took a shot at you because you're trying to find out the truth?"

"Makes the most sense so far."

"But why would he shoot *me*? Because what you're saying is he had to be the shooter from last night."

"He might have been aiming at me. But I don't really believe that."

"So why me then?"

"You're thinking of selling Jocelyn Point. So Alex would be leaving there. Maybe he got wind of that."

"But Bing lives in Florida. What does he care where Alex lives?"

"It's hard to get inside the head of someone like him. Maybe he's afraid if she leaves here her memory will come back and the truth will come out."

"Maybe," said Dak doubtfully. "And how does this tie into Earl?"

"I think Bing put Earl up to finding the body. For myriad reasons I didn't believe his account of finding Jenny. Now, I saw a video of Wilbur Kingman's funeral. In that video Bing was sitting right next to Earl. And whatever he was saying Earl was not happy about. I think he had something over Earl and he used it all these years later to make him pretend to find Jenny's body."

"And then what, Earl killed himself from the guilt?"

"No. There is no way that Earl could have hanged himself."

"Holy shit, you think Bing killed him, too?"

"Not only that, I'm pretty sure he killed Alberta, as well."

With that statement Dak sat up in bed so fast he nearly ripped out a fluid line. "What!"

Devine gently pushed him back down and explained. "Your sister had an episode in front of Bertie just days before she was killed. Now, she had one of those episodes with me and one with Annie. And in the one with me and the event with Annie she was clearly fighting someone. I think she was fighting her attacker fifteen years ago. She didn't say his name but Annie told me that Alex called the person a *friend*. But I think with Bertie Alex *named* her attacker. Bertie might have told someone and word got back to Bing. So he comes up here and takes care of that problem. And Alex's rape kit disappeared from the department's evidence room years ago. And Bing, as the chief, could easily have done that."

"But isn't there a statute of limitations on rape? And if you can't prove he killed anyone, so what if the truth comes out about Alex? The law couldn't touch him."

"I did some quick research this morning after remembering something Alex told me."

"What?"

"That she wasn't sixteen yet when she was raped. Now in Maine, if the victim is under sixteen when the act occurs, there is *no* statute of limitation for rape. So Bing can still go to prison, for a long time, maybe the rest of his life."

"My God," said Dak, putting a hand to his face. "This is a nightmare." He looked at Devine. "So what are you going to do?"

"Nail the guy."

Dak looked terrified. "But, Devine, Alex could remember the truth any minute. And Bing knows that. And so if he did kill all those people, what's one more?"

72

As Devine and Alex were driving back to Putnam through the rain Devine said, "I think I should come and stay with you, at least for a while."

"Why?"

"It's a big house, and with Dak not being there and all . . ." He didn't want to come out and tell her that he believed her life was in danger, but Dak was right: Benjamin Bing had every incentive to kill her.

"Are you going to tell me what my brother and his friend were doing at that outbuilding when they were shot? And what were *you* doing there?"

"The source of the money your brother has been using to invest in the town? It's not partners from Boston."

"What, then?"

"He's been dealing illegally."

"Oh please God, not drugs."

"No. In elvers."

"In what?" she said, her brow furrowing.

"Glass eels, which are apparently worth a ton of money."

"He's been selling *eels*? You're joking, right?"

"I take it you know nothing about the illicit eel trade?"

"I didn't even know there was such a thing."

"Well, it *is* a thing. And I've left it up to the local police to sort it out. But if I were a betting man, I don't think Harper will give him too tough a time. Dak broke the law and I can't condone that. But his intentions were good, mostly."

"Do you think that's why he was shot? Are there, I don't know, rival gangs in the eel business?"

"No, I don't think that was it."

"What, then?"

"I don't know for sure, and until I do, I really don't want to say."

She sighed. "Well, thanks for telling me about Dak."

"And what about me staying at Jocelyn Point?"

"If you want to, that's fine." She hesitated. "But I'm not sure we can . . . you know?"

He touched her arm. "That is *not* why I want to stay at Jocelyn Point. Your brother was just shot, and for all I know someone has a beef against your family. So I'd like to be close by in case they come back."

"Do you really think someone is so mad at my family that they'd do *that*?"

"It's amazing what people are capable of given the right motivation." He paused and studied her. "Do you know how to shoot a gun?"

She leaned away from him at this blunt segue. "No! Why?"

"I can teach you. I have a spare pistol."

"No, I don't want that. I hate guns."

He nodded slowly. "Okay, but I want you to have something to defend yourself with." He glanced at her. "As an artist and sculptress you must have excellent hand strength, as well as good hand-eye coordination and finger dexterity."

"So? Do you want me to gouge an attacker in the eye with a paintbrush?"

"Not a paintbrush." From under the sun visor he slipped out a knife in a leather sheath.

She looked at the weapon. "I don't like—"

"You don't have to *like* it, Alex. You just have to use it, if necessary."

He pulled off the road, unsheathed the knife, and then made a straight stabbing motion with it. "Into the belly, two inches above the navel, up to the hilt." At the end of the thrust he twisted the knife to the left and right, and then upward. "They won't hurt you after that."

"I can't possibly—"

He sheathed the knife and made her take it. "You have no idea what you're capable of until you need to be capable of it. You have one life, Alex—don't let anyone take it away from you without a fight."

He drove back to Jocelyn Point.

"Can I catch a few hours' sleep here before I head out?" he said.

"Of course. I have some things to do around the house. You can sleep in my bed. It's a lot cleaner than Dak's."

★

Three hours later his phone alarm went off. Devine rose and found Alex in the kitchen.

He said, "I've been invited to dinner tonight. I don't like leaving you, I really don't. But my instincts are telling me it's important. Now, keep the knife with you at all times, lock all the doors, and do not go to your studio. I'll be back as soon as I can. Anything looks or feels weird, and I mean anything, call the cops and then call me. I'll be here in a flash."

On his way back to the inn, Campbell phoned him.

"Benjamin Bing was in the Army for eleven years. Enlisted. Topped out an E6."

"He was still a staff sergeant after eleven years?"

"His career plateaued. He was not going to move higher than that. Disciplinary problems. Hotheaded. Unmanageable. Those were some terms I found in his file."

"Why'd he leave?"

"I had to dig deep to find it. He was stalking a woman who lived near the base where he was deployed. There were some communications, written, that went way, way over the line. There was also some vandalism at the woman's apartment, and a man that she was seeing was attacked and severely beaten. But he couldn't identify his attacker."

"How young was the woman?"

"A freshman in college."

"So the Army cut him loose to go stalking and beating up other boyfriends?"

"They didn't want the headache. You know how that works."

"So Mister Angry and Perverted comes back here to become police chief. Great. How'd he get the Purple?"

"He was shot in the ass. Seems to have been friendly fire. It was just a graze. He was in and out of the hospital in a day or two."

"And he wears it for everyone to see, the son of a bitch. Anything else?"

"Yes, and it might be the most important. While an E6, he successfully completed the Army Sniper School course."

"How the hell did a guy with his record and temperament qualify for Sniper School?"

"Apparently the dings on his record came *after* his acceptance there. And there's something else."

"What?" said Devine sharply.

"I found a recommendation letter in his file from a VIP. It might have helped carry the day on his acceptance into Sniper School."

"Who from?" asked Devine, even though he had a pretty good idea.

"Then congressman and military hero Curtis Silkwell."

"Okay," said Devine.

"So what are you going to do now?"

"I'm going to dinner."

"Dinner?" said a surprised Campbell. "Where? And with whom?"

"With Françoise Guillaume. At the *Bing* mansion. At Françoise's invitation."

"Devine, you might be walking into a trap."

"I'm sort of counting on it."

73

Devine pulled off the road and sat there for a while in Earl Palmer's truck with the engine running and the rain falling. He had a lot to think about, and this was as good a place as any to do so. The raindrops pitter-pattered on the roof in synchronicity with his cascading thoughts.

He knew that the Army Sniper School was a seven-week course at Fort Moore, formerly Fort Benning, where infantry and armor trained together at the Maneuver Center of Excellence. In going through the course Bing would have learned a number of critical skills, including fieldcraft application, concealed movement, target detection, sniper tactics, and, of course, advanced marksmanship. He'd had colleagues who had gone through it, and Devine had been impressed at the far better soldier that had come out the other end of the process. He had to take that into account when sizing up Bing as an opponent.

He also wondered if Bing was still in the area, if Devine was reading this whole thing right, that is. Despite all the "evidence" he had compiled, it was mostly circumstantial in nature, with a bit of conjecture and speculation thrown into the mix.

He texted Campbell to check on airline, train, and bus reservations to see if Bing had used one of those ways to get up here. He could have driven from Florida, but that was one long ride, pretty much the whole eastern seaboard.

However, a few things puzzled Devine, knowing what he now knew about Bing and his past training. Maybe events to come would shed light on them.

He drove to the inn and took a shower while the rain continued to pour down outside. Then he dressed in his last set of clean clothes and hurried out to the truck. As he got in, a car pulled up next to him. It was Chief Harper in a police cruiser.

Harper rolled down his window, and Devine leaned over and hand-rolled the passenger's side window down.

"What's up, Chief? You decide about Dak?"

"I've been up to talk to him at the hospital. I think we've worked things out."

"I don't think I want to ask how."

"Thing is, it *doesn't* seem fair how these elver fishing permits are handed out. They say by lottery, but who the hell really knows?"

"I can see that Dak's argument won you over."

"Well, I don't know about that, but I do know that this town needs all the help it can get. But I want to know if you're going to get involved in this because it might make me think differently if the federals will be looking over my shoulder."

"Not my job. You can have Dak and the eels all to yourself."

"Thank you for that. Now, where you heading out tonight?"

"I've been invited to dinner at the Bings."

"Well, aren't you lucky? I hear Françoise is really good in the kitchen. But did she give a reason for wanting to have you over?"

"Just said she wanted to talk."

"You still up in arms about Chief Bing?"

"I haven't ruled anyone out."

"He's in Florida."

Devine decided not to volunteer the information about Bing being AWOL. "For all I know he'll show up at dinner."

"Well, if he does, tell him I said hello."

"I will, unless he tries to kill me."

Harper waved this off. "But I do think you're right about something."

"What's that?"

"I've been giving it a lot of thought, everything you said. Hell, I even went over there myself and tried it. Well, to the extent I could. Not as easy as it looks. And I don't have the physical problems he did. And then there were the knots you talked about and all." Harper sighed. "I don't see how Earl could've hung himself. I think you're right."

"Yeah, Annie Palmer agreed with me, too, after I laid out the evidence. Only Guillaume concluded that it was suicide despite all the contradictory evidence."

"Well, sometimes the ME is wrong. I've seen that before."

Wrong or just covering up, thought Devine. He said, "How about Earl not actually finding Jenny's body? You ready to agree with me on that, too?"

"I'm not there but I'm still thinking. Now that I know someone killed him, it does give a motive. So, how's Alex?"

"Hanging in there. I took her to see Dak. It went okay. She's tougher than she knows."

"If she could just remember who attacked her, it would save us a lot of trouble."

"It's not that simple, Chief."

"I know, I know. Wishful thinking. Any luck on tracing the Norma rounds?"

"We know the manufacturer. We just don't know how those rounds came to be up here."

"Has to be the same person. Even with the NATO round shot at you. I mean, it's all sniper stuff, right?"

Devine was about to agree, but then what he had thought about before came back to him.

But they weren't all the same sniper stuff, were they? Am I wrong about it being Benjamin Bing? Or I am wrong thinking he's the only one? If my theory is correct on how Earl was murdered, a second *person is probably involved.*

He came out of these musings and said, "After I convinced her that her grandfather was murdered, Annie Palmer gave me permission to search Earl's cottage."

Harper perked up at this. "Find anything?"

Devine told him about the video of Wilbur Kingman's funeral service.

"Ben Bing was sitting right next to Earl. And he was talking to him about something. And Earl did not seem pleased."

"He wasn't *pleased* about anything that day," retorted Harper. "The man he'd worked with every day for decades was dead! And—"

Devine cut in. "Did you know Bing was in the Army?"

"Sure, he didn't hide his light under a bushel."

"But did you also know he trained as a sniper in the Army?"

Harper flinched. "No, I didn't know that."

"Well, now you do."

A troubled-looking Harper said, "Um, well, you have a good night." He added, "And please don't get shot at, or kill anybody. I want to go to sleep at a decent time tonight and not wake up until morning."

He rolled his window back up, and Devine started to do the same with his window. But he caught himself staring at the side panel of the police cruiser. A few moments later the cruiser pulled away, but not before Devine quickly took a picture of it with his phone.

On his phone he pulled up one of the satellite photos that Jenny Silkwell had obtained. The small pyramid shape that the satellite had captured had puzzled Devine to no end. But not anymore.

Unless he was much mistaken, Devine believed it was the end of the arrow point that the eagle was clutching in its claws—the symbol of the Putnam, Maine, police department.

The car that the Palmers saw driving away from where Alex had been attacked was a cop car.

And Devine was pretty sure he knew who had been driving it.

74

The gates to the Bing mansion opened as Devine approached them. He slid past in the old truck and geared down as he went up a slight rise to the house. He could hear the ocean roaring in the rear of the property as the tide pushed closer. He looked up and saw another cluster of black clouds heading in.

He parked and got out, and used a lull in the rain to make it to the front door without getting drenched.

Guillaume answered his knock. She wore a navy blue pantsuit with tiny white pinstripes, and a white open-collared blouse. She seemed cheery and relaxed, which put Devine even more on alert.

"I thought a place this big would have a butler," he said.

She smiled at his quip. "We run a lean operation, but we do have a maid service three times a week and someone to look after the grounds. But I like to cook. However, if I don't, we go out or just do leftovers."

" 'We'? You mean you and Fred?"

"Yes. Please, come in."

She led Devine through a spacious foyer into a substantial great room with ceilings that seemed nearly high enough for him to parachute from. A roaring fire blazed away in a fireplace nearly as tall as he was. The furnishings were unique enough to suggest they had been custom-built. There seemed to have been no expense spared in both building and furnishing the place.

Devine wondered why Guillaume's father had bothered dropping so much money on such a grand residence in a place like Putnam, Maine.

Guillaume seemed to be reading his mind because she said, "He wanted to rub their faces in it, of course."

Devine nodded. "Okay. And what do you think about that?"

"I wouldn't have done it. But then I didn't have a say in the matter. Would you like a drink? I opened a nice red."

"I'm more partial to beer if you have it."

She got their drinks and they settled into seats in front of the fire.

"Dinner won't be long. It's a crockpot stew. Hearty fare on a cold, rainy night."

"Sounds good. Will Fred will be joining us?"

"He had some things to finish up. He should be here shortly."

"He works hard, I take it."

"Yes, he does. Running a small business is more than a full-time job."

"But you juggle lots of balls, too."

"I suppose it runs in the family."

Okay, chitchat done. Let's get to it, thought Devine. He wanted to get back to Alex as quickly as possible.

"You wanted to talk about something?" he said. "Insights?"

She lowered her wineglass and looked alarmed that her turn on the stage had come perhaps sooner than she had expected or wanted.

"Yes, that's right," she began.

"Well, I'm happy to listen to whatever you can tell me that might be helpful."

"I take it you don't believe that Earl took his own life?"

"No, I don't," he said bluntly.

"Because he couldn't have managed the chair and all?"

"You've been talking to Harper."

"Actually, Wendy Fuss filled me in on your theory."

"Harper agrees with me now. But you still think he killed himself?"

"I admit I did not take into account his physical 'challenges' in making my conclusion. I was looking strictly at the forensic evidence."

"But not *all* the forensic evidence, because you didn't run blood or tox screens. You just chalked it up to 'adrenaline.' "

"I explained that to you. When suicide appears to be obvious there is no need. If he'd been fifty years younger and wasn't found hanging, then, yes, I would have done a full postmortem."

"So we'll never know if he was rendered unconscious so they could string him up."

"I'm sorry. I wish I could take it back, but I can't," she said firmly.

"So . . . insights?" prompted Devine, who had a feeling now that this evening was going to be a waste of time.

She set her wineglass down and seemed to steel herself. "Putnam, like many small towns, has secrets."

"The big one is who raped Alex Silkwell."

"I'm not talking about that, though it does involve the Silkwell family."

An intrigued Devine took a swig of beer. "I'm listening."

"Curtis Silkwell."

"What about him?"

"What would you say if I told you that many here believe he is Annie Palmer's father?"

"I'd say tell me more."

"Curt and Valerie Palmer were attracted to each other; everyone here knew it. He was twenty years older than she at least. But she was beautiful—Annie took after her—and she caught Curt's eye. He was quite the philanderer. But I'm sure you knew that."

"No, I didn't. Is there proof?"

"DNA? No. No one ever talked about doing that. But I can tell you that Curt paid for Annie's college education out of state before she came back here. And I understand that Dak helped with the financing of her café. But when Annie was born, Curt was a congressman with plans to one day run for the Senate, which he eventually did and won."

"So it was all hushed up?"

"Of course it was," she said. "Those sorts of affairs always are."

"And did Clare know?"

"She would have been blind not to. And Clare was never blind."

"And you're telling me this why?" asked Devine.

"I know you're interested in Steve and Valerie Palmer's deaths around the time that Alex was attacked."

"And they were the ones who discovered Alex after she was raped."

Guillaume held up four fingers. "Steve and Valerie Palmer, and Earl and Bertie Palmer. All dead. Fire, a hit-and-run, and lastly a hanging."

"You did the autopsies on Steve and Valerie."

"I did. And they died of smoke inhalation. That was as far as the postmortem went."

"Meaning what?"

"Like with Earl, I did not do blood and tox screens."

"Because it was believed to be an accident?" said Devine.

She rose and stood in front of the fire. Her tall, trim figure seemed right now to hold all sharp angles, Devine noted.

"Because I was *encouraged* to do the test for smoke inhalation and that was all."

Devine rose and stood next to her, letting the heat from the fire warm his chilled bones. And he wanted to be right next to the woman when he asked his next, obvious question.

"*Who* encouraged you to stop at the smoke inhalation test?"

"Do I really need to spell it out for you?"

"Senator Silkwell? Why? Why would he care?"

She didn't respond so Devine filled in the answer. "Because you're saying *he* killed the Palmers? What would be his motive?"

She gave him a patronizing look. "Like I just said, Agent Devine, fifteen years ago he was running for the Senate for the first time. Any hint of scandal would have derailed his campaign. Such things as adultery still counted with voters back then."

"So someone threatened to expose his secret? Who? I suppose the Palmers, if you think he had them killed and then encouraged you to do short shrift with the post-mortem. But that would have been a scandal for the Palmers too. I can't believe Steve Palmer would have wanted his wife's adultery known to the world. So where's the motive for the Palmers to spill the truth to such an extent that Silkwell would feel he needed to kill them?"

"Money. Steve Palmer was a lousy businessman and a gambler to boot. He'd lose more money than he had at the Foxwoods and Mohegan Sun casinos in Connecticut."

"So he was blackmailing Silkwell? But by then the family didn't have any money."

"Oh, they had some. How else could they keep paying the taxes on Jocelyn Point and keep it running? It's not cheap. And Curt Silkwell had invested what money he did have well. Indeed, he invested in some of the industries he oversaw as a member of certain congressional committees. As luck would have it his timing was amazing in getting into investments and then out of them in the nick of time before the bottom fell out."

"So he was trading on insider information?"

"Apparently many of them do, to this day."

"And how did you come to know all of this?"

"I made it my business to know. And I had firsthand knowledge of part of it."

"Right. You let someone encourage you *not* to do your job."

"I'm not proud of that. But I was just starting out and these were people I looked up to. I was afraid not to do as I was asked."

"And of course Senator Silkwell is in no position to defend himself against these accusations," he replied.

She took the poker and nudged some embers until they flamed up. "I'm not surprised you don't believe me. No one wants to think a war hero, a great man, could do bad things. But if I am telling the truth, does that qualify as a motive for murder, to your thinking?"

"You also mentioned Earl and Bertie Palmer?"

"Bertie spent a lot of time with Alex after she was attacked."

"So?"

"Bertie and Earl both knew about the affair."

"Bertie started spending time with Alex after she was attacked fifteen years ago. But Bertie was killed a few weeks ago, and Earl just days ago," pointed out Devine. "So why wait that long? And Curt Silkwell couldn't have been involved in either of their deaths. He's been in a hospital for a long time."

"But Clare hasn't, has she? And I understand she married a very wealthy man. A man who might be able to hire certain people to do a certain job."

"You're very well informed."

"I find that's far better than being ignorant," she retorted.

"But I'm not sure how much sense it all makes. Why would Clare, after all these years, care about an affair of her husband's from nearly thirty years ago coming out? Particularly if he had other such trysts and now she's remarried and put all that behind her?"

"Curt being Annie's biological father may not be the *only* secret the Silkwells are covering up."

"What else?"

She retook her seat while Devine continued to stand. "People around here have long wondered where Dak got the capital to invest in all these local businesses."

Devine leaned against the mantel, his mind racing ahead.

Dak's smuggling might come out after all. "You have any theories?" he asked.

"Bertie was over at Jocelyn Point a lot over the years. What if she stumbled onto his source of capital?"

"So Dak ran her over? And then killed Earl in case she had told him?"

"I'm not saying it's true, but you have to admit, it's a plausible theory."

"So who shot Jenny? And then Dak? The polymer casing links them. If it was in retaliation somehow for him killing Bertie and Earl, how does Jenny tie in?"

Devine had an advantage here. He knew about the satellite images that Jenny had found showing that the Palmers had seen what Devine believed to be a cop car racing past right before they found Alex. But for that, Guillaume's line of reasoning would be far more compelling.

"I guess it's your job to find that out," she replied curtly.

"Assuming there *is* a connection."

"Do *you* have a theory tying them all together?"

Devine had known that query was coming and it confirmed for him what this whole dinner invitation was partly about. The first part had been shifting potential guilt onto the Silkwells. And the second?

A fishing expedition. Ironic in a coastal town that makes its living off lobster. And eels.

"I've got lots of theories, but I need proof."

"Like you said before, I'm listening. And I can give you my expert opinion."

I bet you can, and then you'll run off and tell your uncle, wherever he's hiding, which might be right here.

The front door opened and closed and Fred Bing walked in, his hair and coat wet.

She looked at him. "Why didn't you pull into the garage, Fred?"

"My damn remote didn't work again." He looked at

Devine. "Hey, sorry I'm late for dinner. I hope you two went ahead and ate."

"No, we waited for you," said Guillaume. "And I've been having an interesting discussion with Mr. Devine."

Fred took a long sniff. "Well, your beef stew is calling me."

They all went in to eat.

Guillaume only had eyes for Devine. And for his part, he was surreptitiously watching her every step of the way at the same time he was on the lookout for the hulking Benjamin Bing to jump out with a gun.

75

The stew was excellent, and Devine watched in some amusement as Bing sopped up every drop of it with his bread before pushing back from the table. The tall man was as thin as a rail but had eaten three helpings.

The burial business must burn lots of calories.

But then he recalled that the man was also an outdoor enthusiast.

Guillaume rose and started clearing dishes, brushing off both men's offers to help. "You two just sit here and chat. I'll make some coffee." She disappeared into the kitchen.

A couple of minutes of silence ensued. Bing finished his water and wiped his mouth with his napkin before running his own amused gaze around the dining room table that could easily have sat twenty.

"A little much?" offered up Devine after watching him.

"There are plenty of rooms in this house I've never actually been in," replied Bing.

Devine grinned. "I'm sure." His expression turned serious. "Hey, what else can you tell me about your uncle Ben?"

"Like what?" asked Bing.

"Just your overall impression."

Bing sat back and played with his napkin. "Well, for starters, my grandfather was a brute. Ruthless and greedy. There, I said it and I'm not ashamed." He smiled briefly. "The three sons were the recipients of all that. My father, Ted, and my uncle, John, were all about doing what my grandfather wanted. He wanted them to follow him into the business, so they did."

"And Ben?"

"Wanted no part of the funeral home world or my grandfather for that matter. He joined the Army and then came back here and became a policeman. And he loved to throw that in his father's and brothers' faces."

"Do you remember Wilbur Kingman's funeral?"

"Sure. The whole town came out for it."

"I watched a video of the service. Earl had a DVD."

"Yes, we film the service if the family requests it and then make copies available to whoever wants one."

"Doesn't it make people uncomfortable having a camera at a funeral? And I'm surprised a church would allow it."

"No, the service was at our *chapel*, not a church. I believe Pat was raised Catholic, but the Kingmans weren't churchgoers. And folks never see the camera equipment, it's built into the wall of the chapel. It was my father's idea. He actually charged for it. But we give them out for free now. Not a video or DVD, of course. Now it's just a downloadable copy."

"Anyway, in the video I saw your uncle Ben talking to Earl."

"What about?"

"I couldn't hear. But whatever your uncle was saying to him, Earl looked like he wanted no part of it. After the service they left together. Do you know where they went?"

Bing shook his head. "No. My duties would have involved organizing the coffin into the hearse, arranging the procession, and getting the family and attendees to the cemetery. That was my focus. You take your eye off the ball and things can get out of hand quickly."

"I'm sure. Look, when I asked you about your uncle and Alex you seemed . . . flustered."

"No, I mean, I just didn't have anything to say. I don't *know* anything . . . about . . . that, not that there was anything."

"Stop talking, Fred, you're making a fool of yourself."

Devine turned to see Guillaume standing in the doorway of the dining room holding a tray with coffee and cups.

Bing glanced at his sister and then looked down at his lap.

Guillaume sat down across from Devine and handed out the coffees. "Mr. Devine, I leave you for a few minutes and I find you in here making allegations against our family."

"I don't remember making any allegations," replied Devine as he took the offered cup.

"Latent, not patent, to use a forensic term."

"Alex was attacked and raped. And I believe Jenny knew who had done it. And that's why she was killed."

"How could Jenny have known?" said Guillaume. "A stranger attacked Alex."

"No, I think it was someone she knew. Maybe knew very well."

Guillaume seemed taken aback. "What proof do you have of that?"

"I didn't say I had proof. Yet. And don't go cremating Hal Brockman's remains without checking with me first."

Guillaume's face twisted for a moment in anger. She shot her brother a glance and then put her palms on the table, as though to steady herself. "I'll ignore that remark, because it was spoken in ignorance."

"No, I really mean it, Dr. Guillaume," said Devine.

"What exactly are you suggesting? That I would do something *improperly*?"

"Everyone in this town is close to what happened, both years ago and today. I just think we need more objectivity inserted into the process."

"That's not unreasonable, sis," interjected Bing.

"Particularly in light of your admission that in the past you might not have carried out your professional duties to the fullest," noted Devine.

"I'll take your request under advisement," she said coldly while her brother stared at her in bewilderment.

"It's actually not a request. I'll make the formal ask to the OCME."

Guillaume barked, "And what would Jenny know

about anything? She wasn't there when Alex was attacked. And it's been fifteen years. I don't see how it's possible."

"Jenny could figure complex things out on behalf of her country. So why not this?"

Guillaume shook her head. "I think you're sniffing up the wrong tree."

"Don't you want that?" said Devine. "The truth to come out?"

"I provided you with what I believe to be the truth. A very detailed account," she added.

Bing again glanced sharply at his sister.

"And I listened," said Devine. "And I'll follow the evidence where it takes me."

Guillaume simply glowered at him.

"Anything for dessert?" asked Bing with a hopeful expression.

"No!" said his sister.

Bing rose and said, "Well, I've got some work to do."

He eyed Guillaume and Devine glaring at one another and fled the room.

76

After finishing up at the Bing mansion, and after once more instructing Guillaume to do nothing with Brockman's remains, Devine drove to Jocelyn Point. Or tried to. Halfway there the truck sputtered once, twice, and then died. He tried to restart it, but it wouldn't catch. He looked at the fuel level. It was below empty.

"Shit."

He had checked the fuel earlier. It was half full. He leaped out and ran to the rear of the truck.

The smell of gas was intense and the underside of the truck was coated in fuel. He used his flashlight to check. A hole had been punched in the tank. He looked back toward the Bing mansion.

Benjamin Bing?

He grabbed his bag and set out at a steady jog to Jocelyn Point.

He phoned Alex on the way over but she didn't answer. He looked at his watch. She might be asleep.

He finally reached Jocelyn Point and knocked on the front door. Alex didn't answer. Slightly worried now, he phoned her again. Again she did not pick up. He pounded on the front door, to no avail. He tried to open it, but it was locked.

He stepped back and looked up at her bedroom window. He tossed some loose gravel up there, where it clattered against the panes of glass. He waited, but the light didn't come on and Alex did not appear at the window.

He hustled back to the front door and used his pick gun to get inside. He dropped his bag and, Glock out, ran up the stairs calling her name. He reached her bedroom and opened the door, dreading what he might find. The room was empty. Her bed was unmade, and it appeared as though it hadn't been slept in recently. He searched every room in the house and the widow's walk and came up empty.

He raced outside to the studio. The door was not locked. Devine stepped in, turned on the lights, and looked around. Just like the house, it was empty. Just like the house, there were no signs of a struggle. No blood, thank God. But still nothing.

He was about to leave when he noticed something.

He walked over to the canvas set on an easel. This was apparently a new work in progress done in charcoal.

The outline was of a man's face. The interior was mostly blank, but there were some elements that had been drawn in. An eyebrow, the beginnings of a top lip. The lower curve of the left eye. But that was all and not enough for Devine to recognize the person. It was like the hazy remains of a dream after you woke up.

He ran his gaze over the canvas. He bent forward to

read the word that had been written near the bottom in pencil.

Him.

Devine called Harper. The man answered on the third ring.

"Please, Devine, do not tell me that—"

He cut in. "Alex is missing."

"What?"

"I arranged to stay with her at the house while Dak was recovering in the hospital. She's not here. I've looked everywhere. And she's not answering her phone. And someone sabotaged my ride."

"Any signs of a struggle? Forced entry?"

"No, nothing like that."

"When did you see her last?"

"About four hours ago. Can you get out an APB on her?"

"Yes. And I'll phone the state police. Any idea what might have happened to her?"

Devine was about to accuse the entire Bing family including Guillaume, but didn't think that would elicit extra effort from Harper to find Alex. "No. Call me if you hear or see anything."

"What will you do?" asked Harper, but Devine had already ended the call.

Devine took a photo on his phone of the partially done picture and ran back to the main house. He had noted that various keys hung from a key holder in the kitchen. He found the key to Dak's Harley and ran back out. Harper had had the motorcycle brought back here after Dak was shot. Devine pulled off the cover, fired up the bike, and first drove to the outbuildings on the possibility that Alex might have gone there for some reason, but they were all empty, except for the skittish gold-plated elvers in their tubs.

He tried calling her phone again, without luck. Then he phoned Campbell and told him what was happening. He gave his boss Alex's phone number.

"See if you can track it and let me know," he said. "As fast as you can!"

He drove aimlessly on the Harley for a few minutes while trying to get a handle on what had happened.

Shit. Diversion?

In combat the forces Devine was fighting against would often use diversionary tactics to achieve their tactical goals. The classic example was detonating a small bomb to draw in first responders and then setting off a second, larger explosive to kill as many Americans as possible.

The dinner invitation was a diversion. While I was filling my face and listening to bullshit from Guillaume, her uncle was snatching Alex.

But then Devine thought some more. *Did I say or do anything that could have prompted their taking Alex?*

Because it was a risk, a big one, to do so when they probably knew that Devine had no proof of anything that would harm them.

He went back over everything he'd said. Until he arrived at the answer and groaned.

You told her that you believed it wasn't a stranger that attacked Alex. That it was someone she knew, and maybe knew well. And Guillaume figured the only way you could have known that was if Alex told you. So they know she's starting to remember.

He turned the Harley around and hit the throttle.

77

The gates to the Bing mansion did not open this time, so he nimbly scaled the fence and dropped down to the other side. The rain had lessened, but the black clouds and the approaching growls of thunder and flashes of lightning in the distance promised a hell of a storm in a short while.

The house was dark, the only illumination the landscape lights.

He looked in one of the windows but saw nothing helpful. He ran around to the side and found a wall encircling the entire rear of the property. He quickly scaled it and dropped to the grass. The rear grounds were impressive, with a pool, now winterized, a large fire pit, a putting green, tiered landscaping as the ground sloped toward the bluffs overlooking the ocean, and what looked to be a guesthouse that resembled the main house but in miniature.

He checked the guesthouse first. The door was locked but he quickly picked it. He found the place empty.

He tried to pick the back door of the main house, but the lock wouldn't open. He went around to the front and tried to do the same thing, with the same result. Devine eyed the window next to the door. He tried to remember something. Yes, there had been an alarm pad next to the front door. He looked in the window and in the reflection of a mirror on the opposite wall he saw that the alarm was not on. He put his elbow through the window, reached in, and unlocked the door.

Breaking and entering, for a good cause. I doubt Harper will see it that way.

He stopped just past the foyer. He was waiting for Guillaume or maybe her brother to rush in, see him and the shattered glass, and call the police.

But no one came. He heard nothing except his own breathing.

This place would take a long time to search thoroughly. And he didn't have time. He eyed stairs going up and stairs going down. He doubted they would have hidden Alex on the main level.

So up or down. Heaven was up, Hell was down.

So Devine went down to Hell. Sometimes it was as simple as that.

Alex blinked once, twice, and then managed to keep her eyes open. She rubbed at her arm where it hurt and felt the slender mattress under her. She didn't remember much. Lying in her bed trying to sleep and then waking up and being surprised to find a masked person looming over her. She had dressed hastily, at the intruder's instructions.

Then, at some point, it all went blank.

Like when she had woken up in that field near the woods. After having been . . .

Alex felt around the darkened space with one of her hands, but feeling clumsy and slow; her fingers weren't really registering what they were touching. She shivered because it was cold. She clearly sensed this was not a safe place, but seemed to lack the energy to do anything about it.

She strained to hear any noise, someone else's breathing, movement, a car, or plane, or even the smell of the ocean. Alex understood she should be afraid, fearful for her life. Deep inside her fuzzy thoughts she had concluded that this was connected to what had happened to her fifteen years before.

She lay back on the mattress. In her mind she saw the image she had started to sketch. The man who had attacked her, robbed her of much of her life, made her afraid to do the things that anyone would want to do: travel, get a job, make friends, find romantic companionship. She had decided that her art might lead her mind to pluck the memory out of her, freeing it and her at last. Alex had finally concluded that the limbo she was in could only be broken by remembering who had done this to her. Then, and only then, could she move on with her life.

She hadn't gotten far on it, but she had commenced the painful journey, letting her mind guide her hand, going back over familiar, and yet unfamiliar, ground. A line here, a shadow there. She felt it coming together, she really did. This represented progress when she had been at a standstill for so long.

And now?

Will I not get a chance to finish? Will I not get a chance to keep on living?

She covered her face with her arm where the needle had gone in, to deepen the darkness even more. Alex felt herself shrinking away, to nothing.

Then she heard someone coming.

78

The stairs to the lower level emptied into a large room set up with an old-fashioned bar, and billiard and ping-pong tables. Behind a set of leather-covered double doors Devine found an elaborate home movie theater. There was also a lavish bathroom, and a well-equipped gym and sauna. Next to these spaces was a wine cellar with a glass door that allowed Devine to see that it was empty of anything except wine.

He reached one end of the basement, found nothing useful, and turned to go the other way.

He searched quickly but comprehensively, calling out Alex's name periodically. At the opposite end of the basement was a large ceramic wall with each block about two feet square. Set at one end of the wall was a large hanging clock. On the other end was a floor-to-ceiling mirror. In the middle of the wall recessed shelves held vases and knickknacks, and another section contained rows of photographs of what looked to be the Maine coastline.

Shit, was I completely wrong about all of this, thought Devine. But then he still had the upstairs to search.

Heaven. Is Alex in heaven?

Depressed, he put one hand against the wall, dropped

his head, and noted his muddy feet. He had tracked dirt in on the highly polished marble floors.

Forensic evidence to nail me on a felony.

And then his gaze drifted to the set of footprints that were situated right in front of the wall, where the recessed shelves were. Those were not his. They weren't muddy, and they were bigger than his. And there was another, even more critical, difference.

They are heading out *of the wall.*

Devine instantly started running his fingers along the ceramic blocks, grabbing every crevice that he could find. He did the same with the knickknacks but found them secured to their spots on the shelves. And then he found the pictures were fastened in place as well.

He looked at the clock. The hands were set at six and twelve. He put his ear to the clock. He heard nothing. Thinking quickly, he took the hand on the six and moved it to twelve to match the other hand.

There was an audible click, and a door-size section of the wall opened up on stainless steel pivot pins.

Devine held his gun in front of him and peered around the doorway. He couldn't see much because there was little light. He did a silent count to three and plunged in, his Glock making wide arcs as his gaze swept for threats.

Devine had imagined many things this space might contain, some outlandish, others quite possible. He had never thought of anything like this.

A hospital bed was tucked against one corner. It was empty. Next to the bed was an IV stand with empty bags on hooks. An automated medication dispenser was also attached to the IV stand. It had been turned off.

Bed covers were on the floor along with a pillow. It seemed like someone had made a quick exit.

He looked around the room some more. Under the bed he saw some lengths of rope. He examined them and then set them back down. He next spotted something else that might or might not be important.

Blood.

A few drops by one of the bed's wheels.

The upstairs search took longer than he wanted it to, especially after he found nothing.

He opened a door off the kitchen and found himself in the garage. There were four bays. Two were occupied. He walked around the four-door Chevy Equinox and then eyed the Massachusetts plates.

He opened the driver's side door and sat in the seat. He checked the glove box, found the Hertz rental agreement, and confirmed that Benjamin Bing had leased the vehicle at Logan Airport. Under the passenger seat he found a fully loaded Sig Sauer nine-mill with an extended mag. And a pair of brass knuckles. He would have had to check those in his baggage if he had indeed flown up here. He got out and popped the trunk, and in there he found zip ties, duct tape, and a serrated knife that had Bing's name stenciled on the handle.

Standard abduction tool kit. But no sniper rifle.

He leaned against the car and wondered if any of these things had been used on Jenny. Had they taken her here, strapped her to the bed, fed her a truth-drug concoction to make her talk, and then killed her here before dropping her onto the rocks?

He turned to where a white van was parked in the fourth bay. He noted the painting equipment and metal-working supplies that were positioned next to it.

He opened the van's door and checked the glove box. He found the registration and saw the name.

BING AND SONS.

He shone his light around the van, noting that the right front fender and bumper and the headlight frame were in the process of being repaired.

He knelt down and hit the underside of the van with his light. Next, he got on his back for a closer examination. That looked like blood on the underside of the bumper. And was that human hair and bits of clothing? Yeah, it probably was.

He now knew who had hit and killed Alberta Palmer.

He called Campbell, who answered on the first ring, and filled him in.

"Add Benjamin Bing to your BOLO," Devine said.

He next called Chief Harper and told him what he'd found.

"Holy shit! No sign of Fred or Françoise?"

"None," said Devine.

"You think their uncle has them?"

"I'm far more concerned about Alex."

"I've got the state police out looking. I'll tell them about this."

Devine hung up and called Dak's cell phone. The man miraculously picked up.

In succinct sentences, Devine filled Dak in about everything.

"Motherfucker," exclaimed Dak before Devine even finished. "You hang in there, Devine. I'm coming. Let me get dressed. I'll be—Aw shit, I'm bleeding. Fuck!"

"You're not going anywhere, Dak. It's not why I called you. Ring for the nurse to fix your dressings. While you're waiting, can you think of any place they might have taken Alex?"

Dak was breathing hard, and Devine could even hear some sobs from the man.

"Come on, Dak, I know this is hard. But just focus. I need some help here. Time is not on our side."

"Okay, okay."

He could hear Dak draw in one long breath and then let it go.

"Look, if Benjamin Bing is behind all this, do you think Harper is involved, too?"

"I hope not, but I don't know for sure. I told him that your sister is missing. He said he has the state police looking."

"What about Françoise and Fred? Where are they?"

"They might be dead. Ben's rental car was in the garage, so they had to know he was there. I have no idea what the secret room was originally designed for, but someone was clearly being kept in there against their will."

"Alex?" said Dak, his voice breaking.

"Maybe," Devine said cautiously. "Or Jenny. But they wouldn't have held her there long. She was seen leaving the Putnam Inn close to eight, and her death was only a few hours later."

"So are Françoise and Fred helping him do all this?"

"I think their uncle might have them under his power, at least Françoise. He seems like the sort to threaten and intimidate and then carry out those threats. And he had an infatuation with Alex. If he attacked her way back then he would know there was no statute of limitations. So Jenny comes snooping around up here and he gets wind of it. He travels here, kills her, somehow frames Earl into 'finding' the body, then kills him as a loose end."

"You really think he killed Bertie, too?"

"Maybe. But someone is fixing up the van and I doubt it was him. He could have flown up here to do that and then returned to Florida before coming back to Putnam. My people checked the airline database, but he could have used a fake identity. So, any places come to mind?"

"Would he have taken her to the funeral home?" asked Dak. "It's the only other place up here with a connection to the man. He could hardly take her to the police station."

"Good idea. Thanks."

"Devine, please find her."

"I will."

Only Devine didn't know if she would be dead or breathing.

79

Devine didn't make it to the funeral home. Not at first.

On the way he looked to his right and saw something blowing around in a field on the side of the road.

He parked the Harley, jumped off, and snagged the item. He recognized it instantly. It was the jacket Guillaume had been wearing at dinner. He looked around and saw a path through a stand of woods. He hustled down it. Then his training kicked in and he stopped. Devine listened as he crouched there in the pitch-dark Maine woods. He kept his target silhouette as narrow as possible and his viable sight lines the opposite of that. He checked his breathing and willed his heart rate to ratchet down to a level where he could do what might need to be done.

He moved forward, clearing every square inch in front of him, and not forgetting to sweep his rear flank every few seconds. He could hear nothing and he could see no one. And that was not making Devine feel good about anything.

He made it to the edge of the bluff without encountering anyone, then steeled himself and looked down. His heart sank as he saw the body splayed against the rocks.

He slowly took his optics out of his pocket and drew a magnified bead on the body.

It was Françoise Guillaume.

He pulled his gaze from her and closed his eyes for a moment.

You need to slow down for a minute and think. Running around like this and being solely reactive is what they want. You need to get ahead of them, not stay behind.

From the jumble of facts and theories and suppositions swirling in his head, Devine forced himself to focus on finding some concrete conclusions. He thought back to his theory that the sniper scenarios had been different. Jenny and the attempt on his life had been undoubtedly done by a pro, someone who knew what he was doing. The person who had shot Dak? Not a pro, not even close. Then and only then did all the puzzle pieces fall into place for Devine.

Why would the Palmers have been *surprised* to see Benjamin Bing in a police cruiser *before* they found Alex? Answer: They wouldn't. He was a cop. What other car would he be in?

No, they were surprised because it wasn't *Benjamin Bing driving the police cruiser.*

Benjamin Bing didn't rape Alex. He was just the cleanup guy.

He took out his phone and called Harper and told him about finding Guillaume.

"Oh my God!" said the police chief. "You think it was Ben who killed her?"

"I don't know. But I think he was the person who shot at me and killed Jenny."

"And Dak?"

"Another Bing. And that same Bing raped Alex."

"But there's only one—"

"I know."

"I'll be there in five minutes with a retrieval team."

"I won't be here."

"Wait, why not?"

"My job is to find Alex. I haven't finished that job yet."

"Devine, wait—"

Devine had already ended the call and was running for the Harley.

Ten minutes later he pulled into the parking lot of the funeral home and saw two cars there. One was Guillaume's big Bimmer. The other was a tan Jeep. The Jeep's driver's side door was unlocked. He checked the registration.

Fred Bing. Of course.

I've been looking at this whole case upside down and sideways.

The funeral home was, of course, dark at this hour. He could see or hear no one else in the vicinity. He tried the front door but it was securely locked.

He jogged around to the back and noted several outbuildings. Two were large garages where he assumed the hearses and other vehicles used by the funeral home were housed. And then there was the large crematorium facility at the very rear.

That's when he heard a scream and then a gunshot and another scream. A cluster of more shots followed. All from the main building.

Devine started to combat-breathe as he ran back there.

He hoped it wouldn't come to that.

But in his world it almost always did.

A moment later he got a text from Harper.

Guillaume strangled. Where the hell are you?

Devine put his phone away and kept right on walking.

There was a window that yielded to his ministrations with the Swiss Army knife he always carried. Fred Bing was in there. He hoped at least two other people were in there too. And that one of them was still alive.

Alex.

He slid inside and knelt on the floor, then surveyed each end of the hallway he was in.

People had been born with all the necessary tools for survival in most situations. Senses of sight, smell, taste, hearing, and touch. And amygdala glands that would stimulate your body to do amazing physical feats when threatened. And a brain that could figure out most things in order to keep you upright and breathing.

And he was using every one of those senses now plus his brain, all the while keeping his amygdala at bay, because he didn't need it, at least not right now.

He moved forward in a crouch, his breathing slow and even, his heart beating around sixty pops a minute, his brain as focused as it was possible for human gray matter to be.

Devine knew very little of the interior setup of the funeral home. He'd seen the front reception area, the chapel on the video, Guillaume's office, and the room they had used to show him Jenny's and Earl Palmer's bodies, plus the embalming space. But that left a lot that was completely unknown to him. And unknown terrain was always a problem. But there was no alternative, at least that Devine knew of.

The muzzle of his gun poked into the first room on the right. He flicked on the light. It was empty. So were the next three spaces behind doors. He turned right and one of his senses picked up something. A foul odor. Not so unlikely in a funeral home, but there was something about this one that was giving him pause.

Next, he heard a groan. It was male, guttural and prolonged. Devine had heard such sounds before. They all had the same cause: pain, and closer to life-threatening than not.

He edged forward and eyed the closed door. The moan came again. On the floor he saw the source of the foul odor. A pool of vomit was next to the door. And mixed with it was blood.

He eyed the pool of sick and the blood and tried to calculate how much blood had actually been lost. From the sounds of the groan it was more than a little.

He stood to one side and slowly reached out and touched the doorknob. He turned it quickly and then pulled his hand away, right before multiple bullets tore through the wood.

The voice screamed, "I will fucking kill you. Just give me the chance, you little prick."

Devine didn't recognize the voice, but he knew who it was anyway.

80

"I think you have the wrong prick in mind," Devine called through the wood.

There was no reply for a count of five. Then—

"Shit. Travis Devine, is that you?"

"Yes, it is, Mr. Bing. You don't sound very good."

He grunted in pain. "That's because I took one in the belly and I'm bleeding to death. Threw up and shit my pants."

"Anything I can do?"

"Yeah, stand in the doorway so I can blow your ass away."

"How about I call an ambulance instead?"

"So I can spend the rest of my life in prison? No thanks."

Devine pulled out his phone, moved through some screens, and then set the phone on the floor against the wall.

"Your niece is dead. Somebody strangled her and threw her off a bluff. That would have been you?"

"Poor little thing. What a way to go." There was mirth, not sadness, behind his words.

"Fred drove here in his Jeep. You got here in your

niece's Bimmer. Your rental is still at the house. I guess you didn't want any of her trace in your vehicle. And you killed Jenny and tried to kill me. But your nephew tried to kill Dak."

"How do you know Freddy tried to kill Dak, Sherlock?"

"You went to sniper school. He screwed the shot on Dak even though it would have been a piece of cake to a shooter who knew what they were doing. And you had no reason to kill Dak. What did you care if Dak was selling out and Alex might leave here? But your nephew cared. And I was the one who told him about Dak's plan to sell Jocelyn Point."

"Freddy had it really bad for gorgeous Alex, like she'd look at him twice."

"He tried to appear helpful and friendly to me, but he also tried to subtly convince me that *you* were the one interested in Alex."

"Hell, I wouldn't have minded getting in her pants, too."

"How did you know Jenny was close to figuring things out?" asked a disgusted Devine.

"Got a phone call from Freddy. 'Please, big, strong Uncle Ben, come up here and save my skinny ass.'"

"So you came up here, assessed the situation, got Jenny alone, and shot her. Then dropped the .300 Norma to implicate, what, foreign enemies from her CIA job?"

"Oh, so you're not so smart after all. You got the first part right, sure. Jenny went to meet with Françoise, because she didn't know the little bitch was in on it. But there I was instead. She had figured out it was a cop car the rapist was in and suspected it was me or Harper. I brought Freddy along for the ride so the little shit could see how it's done properly. Jenny always was a tough little gal. Took the round like a true warrior. She actually flipped me off. Then we took her to the bluff and threw her off."

"And the part I got wrong?"

"I never chambered the fuckin' Norma polymer, Devine. I was an early investor in Warwick Arsenal, and that would have been a red flag. However, this was known to certain family members, including Freddy. I'd even given them some of the fired polymer casings as souvenirs. I used the good old NATO round to shoot Jenny, and when I shot at you."

"Why dump the body at the same spot where Alex was attacked?"

"Just to confuse the shit out of everybody. We were making this stuff up as we went along. It's not like we had months to prep this sucker."

Devine tensed. "And her laptop and cell phone?"

"Chucked them in the ocean. Figured they had classified shit on them. I'm an asshole, but not a traitor."

Devine breathed a sigh of relief and jumped ahead because time was growing short. "*You* policed your brass with Jenny, but Freddy dropped the polymer casing where Jenny was found to make it look like a long-range shot, but he didn't know enough to get it right on the shot angle. But Françoise said the round fired at Dak was a .300 Norma Magnum."

"I gave the family some live rounds along with the

polymer casings as well. I thought I was going to make a killing. And then I ended up being the one killed." He laughed and then groaned. "I would have policed my brass when I shot you, too, but you ducked just in time. I had to get the hell out of there."

"And Françoise? Did she know her brother raped Alex?"

"The whole family knew. We circled the wagons. It's what we Bings do."

"I can understand why your brothers would go along with it, but why would Françoise?"

"She didn't want to labor all her good years in the mortuary business. My brother Ted is a stingy jerk, and he tied up the money his kids would eventually inherit the same way our old man did with him and my brother John. But now, with all that's happened, Françoise cut a new deal with her father. She helps get the family through this crisis, little Franny gets an *after-tax* eighty-million-dollar payout right now. Enough money to live like a queen while she's still young." He coughed up some more of his dwindling blood. "Only she didn't expect to die," he added grimly. "But you try and fuck with me you get dead."

"Fred lied and said he'd agreed to give her half the inheritance even if she didn't stay at Bing and Sons."

"Screwing people runs in the family, I guess."

"I saw you and Earl on film at Wilbur Kingman's funeral service. Were you telling him that you knew *he* was the reason the boat sank and Kingman died?"

"Damn, Devine, you are good," Bing said.

"It was actually the only logical explanation."

"Wilbur let Earl pilot the boat while he was fixing some gear. The idiot got mixed up in the fog, hit the throttle, and ran 'em right into that shoal."

"But how did you find out?"

Bing coughed up more blood, and the pace of his conversation started to noticeably slow. "The day before the funeral Earl went to Bing and Sons after the viewing was over and confessed his guilt to a corpse. The recorders were on for some reason, so my family got his confession on tape and told me about it. At the funeral I told him we knew, just in case I ever needed something from him. And boy, did I."

"Fred also killed Bertie Palmer in a hit-and-run. He's repairing the vehicle in the garage back at the house."

"They told me that Alex had some sort of fit while she was with Bertie, and named Freddy as her rapist. Bertie went straight to Françoise to see if this was possible. I mean, she had no proof, only what Alex said during the seizure."

"So Françoise tells her brother what happened with Alex, and Fred takes care of Bertie?"

"Yep. Then they waited to see if another shoe dropped, but it didn't happen. Freddy didn't want to kill Alex. He was still head over heels for the chick."

"But fifteen years ago *you* killed Steve and Valerie."

"They tried to blackmail the Bings. So I took care of that, too, and got Franny to look the other way on the autopsies. And now here I am bleeding out. No more beach, no more golf. Life sucks."

"And Earl?"

"Dude was going to crack and tell all. We gave Earl a beddy-bye shot beforehand. Françoise made sure no tests would be run that might have detected it." Bing belly-laughed and then ended up whimpering from the resulting pain.

"Then you found out about the polymer casings showing up? That was when the little band of killers fell out."

"Harper texted me. He had no idea I was up here, of course. Then I knew the little shits were setting me up to take the fall."

"So you confronted your niece and nephew and . . . ?"

"And the ungrateful little assholes got the drop on me."

"And they tied you up in the secret room, put you on the drip to sedate you, and were probably deciding how best to dispose of you?"

"But they didn't factor in that I've taken a lot of painkillers in my time and built up resistance, and I'm still strong as shit. Françoise came in to give me another dose of happy juice. I played dead but I'd gotten my hands free and turned the tables on her. She cut me with a knife but I got the upper hand. She told me what I needed to know and then I wrung her little neck, drove her to a secluded spot, dragged her there, and pitched her on the rocks. Then I headed here. Freddy came out of nowhere and shot me when I was searching the place for him. Hell, he was probably aiming at something else and hit me." He coughed for another stretch and said in a rattling, hollow voice, "Now, I've answered a lot of your questions. Answer one of mine. How did Jenny figure things out?"

"Satellite imagery Jenny dialed up from back then. Only she figured *you* for it because of the police car in the picture. I thought that initially, but then I realized there was no way a careful guy like you would take a police car to rape someone. And Alex lived. You would have made sure she was dead. And there was an image of the Palmers looking surprised as they passed the cruiser. They wouldn't have been if you were driving. They hadn't found Alex yet, you see. But they saw *Fred* driving it, not you, *that's* what surprised them."

"The little asswipe went joyriding in it like some big shot, saw the gal of his dreams all alone, and did what he did. Then he didn't have the balls to finish the job."

"Where are Fred and Alex?"

"If I were you, I'd check the crematorium. He probably wants to get rid of the evidence. And blame it on me." He hacked one more time, at the absolute limits of the human body. "Fuck, this hurts."

The next instant, Bing came up with his own painkiller solution of all solutions.

When the shot was fired, Devine snatched up his phone, kicked open the door, and saw the big man sitting against the far wall with most of his face missing.

Next instant Devine was running for the crematorium.

81

Alex awoke suddenly and slowly looked around, feeling groggy and out of sorts.

The room was large and filled with specialized equipment. The smells were bitter and unpleasant, and the sounds both erratic and ominous. She tried to sit up but something was holding her down. She saw the ropes around her. She tugged against them but they were too tight. She laid her head back and turned to the side.

And saw him hard at work.

"Fred, what are you doing?" she said in a weak voice.

He didn't appear to hear her.

"Fred!"

He turned and walked over to her. "How are you feeling?"

"Why are you doing this?"

He touched her arm gently with one hand and adjusted his glasses with the other. "I'm sorry but there's no other way."

As soon as he touched her Alex flinched, as though burned by his grip. She closed her eyes, her head pounded, and she suddenly started to gyrate, as though she were having a seizure.

Bing didn't react to this at all. He just stood there in silent acknowledgment of what was happening. She finally stopped moving, her breathing moderating. She opened her eyes and turned her head to stare at him. And this time she remembered all. And from her look, Bing understood this as well.

"I never meant to hurt you back then, Alex."

"You *raped* me and then tried to kill me."

"Things got out of hand and I didn't know what to do. I hope you can believe that."

"You were my friend. You knew my sister. You taught me in high school."

"And I loved you. From the first time I saw you, I loved you. And I never stopped."

"Then how could you do that to me?"

"I saw you on your bike riding along. You were so beautiful. And I was in the police car. I felt . . . wonderful. So free. I wanted to take you for a ride. But you didn't want to go. I believed you loved me too, so I insisted. You slapped me. That made me angry, very angry, because all I wanted to do was take you for a ride."

"So then you raped me!"

"I really thought you wanted to, Alex. But afterward you were so furious that—"

"—that you tried to kill me. You left me for dead!"

"I love you."

"If you love me, you'll let me go. Now."

He drew nearer. "I can't do that. Deep down you know that."

"You killed my sister!" she screamed.

He said hurriedly, "No, no, I didn't. My uncle—"

"Fuck you and your uncle!"

He took a step back and looked down. "I know that you're upset."

"Yes, I'm upset," she cried out. "Because now you're going to kill me."

"I wasn't going to, even if you did remember."

"What are you talking about?"

"But then you betrayed me."

"What!?"

He drew closer and studied her. "You were going to let your idiot brother sell your home. You were going to move away. Well, I took care of that, or I tried to. But that wasn't your worst betrayal."

"What do you mean?"

"I saw you in your art studio with . . . him."

"Who?" she said defiantly.

"Travis Devine. I saw how you both were looking at each other. You kissed him! You went to the house together. I know what you did. I know." He shook his head in disappointment. "I thought you would have known better."

"Just stop it. Stop it and let me go."

Bing just kept shaking his head. "I would have kept the faith, Alex, if you had."

"Just stop it. Stop it!"

"If there was any other way—"

"There is a way. You let me go and turn yourself in."

"But I'd go to prison."

"Where exactly do you think *I've* been all these years?" she screamed at him.

"I know this has been so hard for you, so hard."

"Then do the right thing. Let me go and call the police and tell them what you did."

He shook his head. "I've worked too hard to lose all this."

"All what? A funeral home? You spend all your time with dead people. Maybe that's the problem."

He grimaced. "People have always made fun of what I do, but it's a necessary service—"

"I don't care!" she shouted. "I don't give a fuck about you or what you do, okay? Just do what you're going to do to me and go on with your pathetic life." She closed her eyes, and the tears curved over her quivering cheeks.

"You won't feel a thing. I'm going to sedate you before, of course. It'll be over soon, okay? I promise. I wish things could have turned out differently, okay?"

She didn't bother to answer him.

He returned to the equipment and started to key in information in front of a screen that was attached to the cremation system. A few minutes later he looked over at her. "It's all computerized now. Input the weight and other necessary factors, and algorithms determine the temperature and time."

Alex's eyes were still closed and she was now mumbling something under her breath.

He continued, turning back to his work. "Anyway, the body is 65 percent water, and it requires a large amount of thermal energy to vaporize it, which must be done first, in the primary chamber. That chamber vaporizes the water, and the secondary chamber takes care of any leftover organic matter. Then the cremulator reduces whatever is left over to ash. That's what we put in the urns to give to the families. I thought I would scatter your ashes over Jocelyn Point. Is that okay? You always loved it there, right?"

He paused and looked at her again. She was still mumbling but only in a louder voice.

"What's that you're saying?" he said.

A minute later he walked over and leaned in closer. "What are you saying?"

She didn't answer.

He put his arms under her, lifted her up, and carried her over to a long cardboard box set on a conveyor belt. He laid her inside it.

He put a hand on her shoulder. "I'll sedate you first, of course. Then it'll all be over in about an hour."

He went back over to the control panel and worked away. A minute later Alex lifted her head slightly and looked around. Her gaze held on where the conveyor belt led—a large metal chamber. "They'll know. They'll find out the truth, Fred."

Bing looked over at her. "They'll only find out what I

want them to, which is my uncle was obsessed with you. He kidnapped you and took you somewhere. And no one will ever find out where. Then he came here and tried to kill me because I had tried to stop him. But I shot him instead. I'll be a hero." He next looked at the chamber into which he would be sending Alex on the conveyor belt. "And you can't get DNA or anything else from ashes. It will be like you never existed."

"You're sick!" she cried out.

"No, I'm just very careful."

Alex closed her eyes and started mumbling loudly, rocking from side to side, banging into the sides of the cardboard box.

Bing glanced over and saw this. "Alex, please stop."

He hurried over to a table, snatched a syringe off it, and uncapped the needle. "Just a little pinch, then you won't feel anything else." But when he tried to administer it she was gyrating so fiercely he couldn't do it.

"Stop it, stop it, Alex." He set the syringe down and gripped her shoulders. "What are you doing?" he barked. "Are you having another seizure?"

Her eyes popped open and her right hand broke free of the cut ropes as she sat up and plunged the knife Devine had given her into Bing's shoulder. Then with a long scream she twisted it in the gaping wound and jerked it upward.

Bing cried out in pain, looked at the blade quivering in his flesh, and struck Alex so hard she toppled out of the box and fell to the floor, where she lay stunned.

"Omigod, omigod," panted Bing. "Why did you do that? It hurts. Oh God, it hurts."

Alex slowly tried to stand but couldn't manage it. She fell back onto her knees.

Bing staggered around the conveyor belt and kicked her in the stomach. She cried out, and then her expression turned dark and violent. She jumped up, lunged at him, and pulled the knife free from his shoulder. Blood started to shoot out of the wound, spilling over the both of them.

Bing let out a shriek and punched her. She fell against the conveyor belt and slumped to the floor.

"It's . . . an artery. You . . . you cut my artery."

"I hope to hell I did," she gasped, wincing in pain.

Bing grabbed a heavy wrench lying on a table. He raised it to strike her.

The shot struck him cleanly in the head and the round stayed there after destroying an irreparable amount of Fred Bing's soft brain tissue.

The dead man stood wobbling over Alex, but only for a moment. He fell against the conveyor belt, bounced off it, and fell to the floor.

A battered and bloody Alex looked over at the doorway, where Devine was just now lowering his gun.

82

Dak was in a shoulder harness. Alex's physical wounds had mostly healed but her mental injuries still needed attention.

They had driven Devine to the airport in Bangor for his flight back to DC.

Devine had held meetings with both Harper and Fuss, and the federal agents Mann and Saxon, going through multiple briefings. He had done the same via Zoom with Emerson Campbell. Everyone had been complimentary of his work. They considered the investigation a success on every level, and everyone was relieved that Jenny's phone and laptop had ended up in the ocean. He'd even gotten Benjamin Bing's confession recorded on his iPhone.

Campbell had saluted him on the computer screen and said, "Thank you, Devine. Job well done. And it meant a lot to me personally."

"Yes sir."

"Clare has been briefed. She sent her thanks and gratitude to you. And I . . . I told Curt. I know he didn't understand but it made me feel better."

"Maybe he understood more than you think, sir."

However, Devine didn't agree with their assessment of a successful mission, because of the long line of dead people associated with it. If he had lost this many soldiers during an op, it would have been an abject failure in his mind, despite their achieving the mission goals.

The town had been informed, by both formal and gossip channels, about most of what had happened. To say that the citizens of Putnam were shocked to their core did not even come close to describing it accurately.

Dak shook Devine's hand with his good one. "Thanks, man. You did right by the Silkwells, I can tell you that. And you saved Alex's life."

"You're welcome. And the elver business?" asked Devine, while glancing at Alex.

"I've applied for a proper permit but we may not need it."

"Really, why not?"

"Because we've got lawyers and they've filed a wrongful death action against the whole damn Bing family. They were all in on it, or at least knew about it, as your recording of that dick Benjamin helped prove. His brothers have already offered tens of millions to settle. But I'm going to squeeze them for every last penny." He looked at Alex and his happy expression faded. "And it still won't be enough. It won't bring Jenny back."

"No, it won't," said Devine.

Dak glanced awkwardly at his sister and said, "Well, I'll give you two some alone time."

He walked off and Devine drew closer to Alex.

"How are you?" he asked. "Really?"

"I don't know," she said. "One minute I think I'm healing and the next . . . I don't know."

"It all takes time."

"Yeah, that's what everyone keeps telling me," she replied in a dismissive tone. "I'm sure by the time I'm eighty, I'll be just fine."

"You really didn't need me to save you. You took care of Fred all by yourself."

"With the help of your Army knife. When he came to the house and kidnapped me, I made sure I put on the coat that had the knife in the pocket. He was an idiot not to search me, but he probably figured I was still that same little scared teenager. I didn't manage to stab him in the gut like you showed me, but after I cut the ropes and freed myself, I did remember to twist the knife in the wound. That did the trick." She slowly shook her head in amazement. "I can't believe I just said that. It was like I was watching someone else do all of it. I'm not a violent person."

"Everyone can be violent when violence is the only way to survive."

She touched his arm. "I guess your life has been full of that."

"More than I would like, yeah." He paused. "I saw the drawing you had started. Will you finish it now?"

"I already did. Up here." She tapped her head. "You know, Fred said he loved me, as he was methodically preparing to kill me."

"Love and murder are not mutually exclusive. In fact, more murders are committed over love than hatred or jealousy or anything else."

"God, what a world we live in."

"What will you do now?"

"Grieve for my sister. Grieve for my father when the time comes. And I plan to visit him."

"I'll go with you, if you'd like me to."

She took his hand in hers. "Yes, I would. I'm not sure I could face that alone."

"I think you can face anything with or without me, Alex."

"I was planning on seeing my mother, too."

"I think that's a good idea," he said.

She looked at him curiously. "You do? Why?"

"Because as time goes on, and you start to lose people dear to you, you realize nothing should prevent you from being with them while you still can."

"Easier said than done."

Devine thought of his estrangement from his family. "Yes, it is. But people can at least try. So, will you stay in Putnam?"

"No. We're selling the property. There's nothing there for me. And I'm going to Italy, Rome, and Florence, the cities of great artists. I'd like to see some of the paintings and sculptures for real instead of in a book or on a screen. That's just to start. Like you said, it's a big world and I have a lot of catching up to do." She hesitated, looking anxious.

"What?"

"I'm sure you've been all over the world. And I was wondering—any desire to maybe go with me to some of these places?"

"I *have* been all over the world, but not with you. Let me see if I can make that work."

"I don't want you to go to any trouble."

"I don't do things I don't want to do, Alex."

She leaned against him. "Neither do I."

They lingered with each other until the very last possible second. Then Devine sprinted to his gate to make his flight.

A couple hours later he was back in DC. Devine grabbed his bags and headed to the taxi stand after weaving his way through large crowds of people in the airport.

He got into the cab and gave the driver his address. When it came time to pay he reached for his wallet in his jacket pocket. In pulling it out a slip of paper came along with it.

He unfolded it and looked down at the elegant handwriting on the sheet.

Nice bumping into you in the airport, former Captain Devine. We missed getting you twice before. But you know what they say, the third time is usually the charm. At least one can hope. See you soon. I promise.

XOXO

The Girl on the Train

Acknowledgments

To Michelle, I know how much you love Maine, so this one's for you. Enjoy the views!

To Michael Pietsch, Ben Sevier, Kirsiah Depp, Jonathan Valuckas, Matthew Ballast, Beth de Guzman, Ana Maria Allessi, Rena Kornbluh, Karen Kosztolnyik, Albert Tang, Andy Dodds, Ivy Cheng, Joseph Benincase, Alexis Gilbert, Andrew Duncan, Janine Perez, Lauren Sum, Bob Castillo, Rebecca Holland, Briana Kuchta, Mark Steven Long, Marie Mundaca, Lisa Cahn, John Colucci, Nita Basu, Alison Lazarus, Barry Broadhead, Martha Bucci, Ali Cutrone, Raylan Davis, Tracy Dowd, Melanie Freedman, Elizabeth Blue Guess, John Leary, John Lefler, Rachel Hairston, Tishana Knight, Jennifer Kosek, Suzanne Marx, Derek Meehan, Donna Nopper, Rob Philpott, Barbara Slavin, Karen Torres, Rich Tullis, Mary Urban, Avi Molder, Fantasia Brown, Julie Hernandez, Laura Shepherd, Maritza Lumpris, Dominic Stones, Leah Collins Lipsett, Jeff Shay, Carla Stockalper, Ky'ron Fitzgerald, and everyone at Grand Central Publishing. We're set for another eight books and I can't wait. You all rock.

To Aaron and Arleen Priest, Lucy Childs, Lisa Erbach Vance, Frances Jalet-Miller, Kristen Pini, and Natalie Rosselli. Love the new digs. And by the way, you all are the best in the business.

To Mitch Hoffman, for continuing to distinguish yourself as one hell of an editor.

To Joanna Prior, Jeremy Trevathan, Lucy Hale, Francesca Pathak, Stuart Dwyer, Leanne Williams, Kinza Azira, Sara Lloyd, Claire Evans, Jamie Forrest, Laura Sherlock, Jonathan Atkins, Christine Jones, Andy Joannou, Charlotte Williams, Rebecca Kellaway, Charlotte Cross, Lucy Grainger, Holly Martin, Becky Lloyd, and Neil Lang at Pan Macmillan, for keeping me right at the top. It's not easy and you all do it flawlessly.

To Praveen Naidoo and the wonderful team at Pan Macmillan in Australia, for growing my audience by leaps and bounds. See you soon!

To Caspian Dennis and Sandy Violette, who are like siblings to me, although I'm much older!

To Chuck Betack, for his expert advice on military matters.

To Tom DePont, for all things financial.

To the charity auction winners, Françoise Guillaume (The Mark Twain House & Museum), Wendy Fuss (Amelia Island Book Festival), and the family of the late Richard Wayne Harper (Homes for Our Troops), I hope you enjoyed your characters, the good and the bad!

The Edge

To my good friend Harvey Watkins, I hope you enjoyed reading about your namesake. Thanks for all you've done for us over the years.

And to Kristen White and Michelle Butler, the engines on the train.

Don't miss the thrilling first instalment in the Travis Devine series . . .

The 6:20 Man

It's time to catch a killer . . .

A decorated survivor of Afghanistan and Iraq, Travis Devine leaves the army under a cloud of suspicion. Now he's facing a different kind of danger in the cut-throat world of high finance.

On his daily commute on the 6:20 a.m. train into New York, he sees something that sounds alarm bells he cannot ignore. The mysterious death of a close friend compels Devine to investigate further. As the deaths pile up, he will need to question who he can trust and who he must fight.

1

Travis Devine took a shallow breath, ignored the heat and humidity that was rising fast along with the sun, and rushed to board the 6:20 train, like it was the last flight out of Saigon. He was wearing an off-the-rack pearl-gray suit, a wrinkled white shirt that needed laundering, and a muted dark tie. He would rather be in jeans and a T-shirt, or cammies and Army jump boots. But that couldn't happen, not on this ride.

He was freshly showered although already starting to perspire; his thick hodgepodge of hair was as neatly combed as he could manage it. His face was shaved and mildly scented with a nondescript cologne. He wore cheap tasseled loafers shined fore and aft. The imitation leather briefcase held his company-issued laptop with special encryption and no personal use permitted thereon, along with breath mints and a packet of Pepcid AC. He no longer took the neat little power pills he'd popped when suited up to fight for his country. The Army used to give them out like gummy bears so the grunts would battle longer and harder on less sleep and less to eat.

Now they cost money.

His primary weapons, instead of the Army-issued M4 carbine and M9 sidearm of yesteryear, were twin Apple Mac twenty-seven-inch screens, connected by digital tethers to mighty, encrypted clouds seeded with all the data he would ever need. It was all bullshit, really, and, strangely enough, more important to him than anything else on earth right now.

What they taught you in the world of high finance was simple really: win or lose. Eat or starve. It was a binary choice. No Taliban or Afghan soldier pretending to be your ally before banging a round into the back of your head. Here, his chief concerns were quarterly earnings projections, liquidity, free and closed markets, monopolies and oligarchies, in-house lawyers who wanted you to stick to the rules, and bosses who insisted that you didn't. And most significant of all, the persons sitting right next to Devine at the office. They were mortal foes. It was him or them in Wall Street's version of mixed martial arts.

Devine was commuting south to the big city on Metro North's Harlem Line. At age thirty-two, his entire life had changed. And he wasn't sure how he felt about it. No, he was sure. He hated it. That meant things were working according to plan.

He sat where he always did when commuting into the city—third row, window seat on the starboard side. He switched to the port side on the way back. The train puttered along with no real ambition, unlike the humans it carried. Sleek trains ran like cheetahs in Europe and Asia, but here they were snails. Yet they were faster than the cars stuck in the murderous traffic that piled in and out of the city morning, noon, and night.

Generations before him had ridden this very same route to make their living in the sweatshop spires of Manhattan. Many had died along the way from the usual suspects: widowmaker heart attacks, strokes, aneurysms, the slow death of neurological disorders and cancers, a liver painfully scuttled by too much alcohol, or self-inflicted deaths among those who could take the strain no longer.

Devine lived in Mount Kisco in a saggy town house shared with three twentysomethings trying to forge their futures in various ways. He had left them all asleep as he tried to shape his future day by day. The train would continue to fill as it wended its way along to Manhattan. It was summer, the sun was well on its way up, and the heat was building. He could have lived in the city, and paid a lot more money for the easier commute. But he liked trees and open spaces, and being surrounded by skyscrapers and concrete at all times was not his preference. He had actually been mulling over where to live when a Realtor who knew a friend of his had called out of the blue and told him she had found him a room at the town house. It was cheap enough that he was able to save a bit. And lots of people commuted into the city, even though it made for long days and nights. But that philosophy had been beaten into his psyche for most of his life.

"You work till you drop, Travis," his father had told him over and over. "Nobody in this world gives you a damn thing. You have to take it, and you take it by working harder than anybody else. Look at your sister and brother. You think they had it easy?"

Yes, his older brother and sister, Danny and Claire. Board-certified neurosurgeon at the Mayo Clinic, and CFO of a Fortune 100, respectively. They were eight and nine years older than he was, and already minted superstars. They had reached heights he never would. He had been told this so often, nothing could persuade him not to believe it.

Devine's birth had clearly been a mistake. Whether his father forgot the condom or his mother didn't realize she was ovulating and failed to keep her lustful man at bay, out he had popped and pissed off everybody in his family. His mother went back to work immediately at his father's thriving dental practice in Connecticut, where she was a hygienist. He'd learned this later, of course, but maybe he'd also sensed his parents' indifference to him as an infant. That indifference had turned to fury when Devine was a senior in high school.

That was when he'd been accepted into West Point.

His father had roared, "Playing soldier instead of going out into the world and earning a living? Well, boy, you are off the family payroll starting now. Your mother and I don't deserve this crap."

However, he'd found his place in the world of the military. After graduating from West Point he'd gone through the arduous Ranger School, passing the crawl, walk, and run tests, which was how the three phases were described. By far the hardest part had been sleep deprivation. He and his comrades had literally fallen unconscious while standing up. He'd later qualified to become a member of the elite Seventy-Fifth Ranger Regiment. That had even been tougher than Ranger School, but he had loved the special forces and the dangerous and demanding quick-strike missions that came with being a member.

These were serious accomplishments and he had written to his parents about them, hoping for some praise. He had never heard back from his mother. His father had sent an email asking him what national park he would be assigned to now that he was a *ranger*. He had signed the email, "Proud father of Smokey the Bear." He might have assumed his dad was utilizing his sense of humor, only he knew his father didn't have one.

Devine had earned twin Purples, a Silver Star, and a slew of other bits of metal and ribbons. In the world of the Army, he was known as a combat stud. He would only term himself a *survivor*.

He had gone into uniform as a boy and come out as a war machine. Six foot one and one-quarter inches, as the Army had precisely measured him, he had entered West Point a lanky 180 pounds of average physique.

Then the Army, and his own determination, had transformed him into 225 pounds of bone, muscle, and gristle. His grip was like the jaws of a croc; his stamina was off the charts; his skills at killing and not being killed placed him at the top of the food chain with orcas and great whites.

He'd risen to Captain right on schedule and had worn the twin silver bars proudly, but then Devine had called it quits because he had to. It had torn him up back then. It still tore him up. He was an Army man through and through, until he could be one no longer. Yet it was a decision he had to make.

After that he had sat in an apartment for a month wondering what to do, while old comrades phoned, emailed, and texted, asking him what the hell was he doing leaving the uniform. He had not gotten back to any of them. He had nothing he could say to them. A leader who had never had an issue giving orders and being in command, he couldn't find the words to explain what he had done.

He did have the Post-9/11 GI Bill to help him. It paid for a full ride to an in-state public university. It seemed a fair trade-off for nearly dying for his country. He'd gotten his MBA that way.

He was the oldest person in his class at Cowl and Comely, the minted powerhouse investment firm where he worked at an entry-level analyst position. When he'd applied at Cowl, he knew they had looked upon him with suspicion because of his age and unusual background. They had outwardly thanked him for his military service, because that was always automatic. But they probably had to fill a veterans quota, and he was it. He didn't care why they had picked him so long as he got a shot to make himself as miserable as possible.

Yes, he thought, as he stared out the window. *As miserable as possible.*

He had tried later trains into the city, but there were too many suits on board just like him, heading to work, heading to war. He needed to get there first, because whoever got there first, with the most, often was victorious. The military had also taught him that.

And so he stepped onto the 6:20 train every morning, and traveled to the city as punishment. And as much as he hated the work and the life that came with it, that penance would never manage to match his crime.

2

The 6:20 train passed through bucolic countryside lurking outside a metropolis of unequaled breadth and complexity. Along the way, it picked up people at stations set in affluent small towns that existed mostly to serve the hungry beast due south. It finally chugged past an enclave of homes that were some of the most expensive in the country. It seemed unfair to call them mere homes. A place nearly as large as a shopping center should have a grander name, even *mansion* or *estate* didn't cut it, Devine thought. *Palace*, maybe, yeah, *palace* seemed to work.

He lifted his gaze from his laptop, as he did every morning when passing by this area. Every time he looked out, another structure was going up, or an existing one was being made even more lavish. The cement trucks drove in with wet loads for larger and more elaborate pools, the houses went higher or wider, or a guesthouse was being built or a putting green added. It kept the working class employed, so there was some good in the greed and pretentiousness, he supposed.

The train slowed as it approached a bend and lazily

snaked upward over a lumpy knoll. It slowed some more, coming nearly to a stop. There was a signal-switching hitch here that the train people either couldn't or wouldn't do anything about. To say they had a monopoly was to say the earth revolved around the sun, so why would they give a damn?

And as they came to a complete halt, Devine *saw* her. He had seen her only a few times before, and only when the weather turned warm. He had no idea why she was up so early, but he was glad she was.

The privacy wall was high, but not high enough to block the sight line of those on the train at this point on the knoll. He knew who the owner of this particular palace was, and he also knew that there were height limits on perimeter walls and fences here. The owner had planted trees along the rear wall to compensate for this, but because of the space between the bottom of the tree canopy and the top of the wall, there was a fairly large gap that one could see through.

It was an oversight, he knew, that the owner would no doubt rectify one day, though Devine hoped not, at least while he was riding the 6:20. He felt a bit like Jimmy Stewart in *Rear Window*, the champion voyeur movie of all time. But he wasn't looking out the window because his leg was broken and he was bored, as was the case with Stewart's character. He was looking out the window because of *her*.

The woman had sauntered out from the rear door of the largest palace in this enclave. *Sauntered* was the only word that worked for how she moved. It was a smooth, leisurely pace, like a panther just getting warmed up before breaking into a sprint. The hips and glutes and thighs and shoulders all moved in the most gloriously primal choreography.

The place looming behind her was all modernistic, with glass and metal and concrete whipped into odd geometric shapes. Only the mind of an architectural savant snorting nostrils of coke could have conceived it.

She had on a short, white terry cloth robe that clung to her tanned thighs. When she took it off, revealed was an emerald-green string bikini and a body that seemed too flawless to be genuine. Her hair was all blonde highlights with intricate cuts and waves that had probably cost more than his suit.

Devine looked around to see who else was watching. All the guys were, of course. One of the women had glanced up from her computer, seen the lady in question, looked at the gents with their faces burned to the glass, and turned back to her screen in disgust. Two other women, one in her forties and dressed like a hippie, and one in her seventies, didn't look up. The former was on her phone. The latter was diligently reading her Bible, which had plenty of warnings about sins of the flesh.

The bikini lady placed her painted toenails in the water, shivered slightly, and then in she dove. She did a graceful arc under the water, pushed off the other side, and came back up to where she had started. She hoisted herself out and sat on the pool surround facing his way. She didn't seem to notice the train or anyone staring from inside it. Devine could imagine at this distance all she might see was the train's glass reflecting the sunlight.

With her body wet, the tiny bikini seemed to have shrunk, and her breasts hung heavy and firm in the twin pockets of the swimsuit top. She looked to the left and right and then behind her at the house. Next, she slipped off her top and then her bottom. She sat there for a long moment totally naked; Devine could glimpse comingled white and tanned skin. Then she jumped once more into the water and vanished.

It was about this time that the train started up again, and the next palace in the enclave appeared, only it didn't have a beautiful woman skinny-dipping in its pool. In fact, this homeowner had planted not trees but tall, thick Leyland cypresses that left no gaps through which one could peer.

Pretty much every other man on the train car groaned under his breath and slumped back with a mix of ecstasy and disappointment. Devine eyed some of them. They looked back at him, smiled, shook their heads, and mouthed things that sounded basically like, *Dude, WTF was* that*?*

Devine had never seen her strip down before. He wondered what had caused her to do it beyond some sort of playful impulse. He wondered about many things in that particular palace. It was fascinating to him what people did with all that money. Some were philanthropic; others just kept buying bigger toys. Devine told himself that if he ever got to be that rich, he would not buy the toys. He would give it all away.

Yeah, sure you would.

At the next station more people got on. And then at the next station still more.

As he looked around at the mostly twentysomethings on the train, who were already on their fired-up laptops and yanking down data clouds, and scanning documents and fine-tuning presentations and excelling at Excel, Devine knew that the enemy was everywhere. He was completely surrounded. And that should have panicked the former soldier.

And yet this morning, all Devine could think about was the naked woman in the water. And it wasn't for the obvious reasons.

To the former Ranger and Army scout, something about the lovely woman just seemed off.

Discover David Baldacci's latest thrilling standalone

Simply Lies

The truth can be deadly . . .

Former Jersey City detective, Mickey Gibson, now works for global investigation company ProEye. One day she gets a call from a colleague, Arlene Robinson, asking her to visit the home of a notorious arms dealer. Mickey arrives to discover a body hidden in a secret room – the arms dealer doesn't exist, and nobody at ProEye knows of Arlene Robinson.

So begins a cat-and-mouse showdown between Mickey and a woman with no name. For Mickey to stop her, she must first discover her true identity – and the reason why she selected Micky as her nemesis . . .

REMEMBER MY NAME

Amos Decker is the Memory Man

Once read.
Never forgotten.

Discover David Baldacci's bestselling series featuring the Memory Man, Amos Decker, an extraordinary detective who – because of a life-changing brain injury – remembers everything, including painful things he would give anything to forget.